"A Sudden Trip Home in the Spring"
by Alice Walker

The award-winning author of *The Color Purple* writes a moving story of a gifted young woman back in her Georgia hometown for her father's funeral . . . and some finally faced truths.

"Amazing Grace"
by William Hoffman

Novelist/playwright Hoffman writes a funny, down-home tale about Grandma Sharp, Uncle Henry (the son who got rich and married a steel magnolia), and the process of getting "saved."

"State Champions"
by Bobbie Ann Mason

When the Cuba, Kentucky, Cubs become state champs, a high school girl's experience becomes an *American Graffiti*-like tale . . . done in pure Southern hill-country style.

"Thomas Vincent Sullivan"
by Ernest Gaines

In this excerpt from *A Gathering of Old Men*, the author of *The Autobiography of Miss Jane Pittman* writes an explosive account of black-white relations when a football hero learns of his brother's murder.

AND 21 OTHER SELECTIONS EVOKING
SOUTHERN PLACES AND VOICES,
FAMILIES AND COMMUNITIES

SUZANNE W. JONES is Assistant Professor of English and Coordinator of Women's Studies at the University of Richmond. She is the editor of *Writing the Woman Artist* and the author of a number of essays on Southern fiction. This collection grew out of a grant she received from the Virginia Center for the Humanities to design a Southern literature curriculum for students in Virginia's schools.

GROWING UP IN THE SOUTH

AN ANTHOLOGY OF MODERN SOUTHERN LITERATURE

Edited and Introduced by
Suzanne W. Jones

A MENTOR BOOK

MENTOR
Published by the Penguin Group
Penguin Books USA Inc., 375 Hudson Street,
New York, New York 10014, U.S.A.
Penguin Books Ltd, 27 Wrights Lane, London W8 5TZ, England
Penguin Books Australia Ltd, Ringwood, Victoria, Australia
Penguin Books Canada Ltd, 2801 John Street, Markham, Ontario,
Canada L3R 1B4
Penguin Books (N.Z.) Ltd, 182-190 Wairau Road, Auckland 10, New Zealand

Penguin Books Ltd, Registered Offices:
Harmondsworth, Middlesex, England

First published by Mentor, an imprint of New American Library,
a division of Penguin Books USA Inc.

First Printing, June, 1991
10 9 8 7 6 5 4 3 2 1

ACKNOWLEDGMENTS

From *A Childhood: The Biography of a Place* by Harry Crews. Copyright © 1978 by Harry Crews. Reprinted by permission of Harper & Row, Publishers, Inc.

"A Southern Landscape" copyright © 1960 by Elizabeth Spencer. From *The Stories of Elizabeth Spencer* by Elizabeth Spencer. Used by permission of Doubleday, a division of Bantam, Doubleday, Dell Publishing Group, Inc.

"State Champions" from *Love Life* by Bobbie Ann Mason. Copyright © 1989 by Bobbie Ann Mason. Reprinted by permission of Harper & Row, Publishers, Inc. Originally appeared in *Harper's Magazine.*

"A Sudden Trip Home in the Spring" from *You Can't Keep a Good Woman Down,* copyright © 1971 by Alice Walker, reprinted by permission of Harcourt Brace Jovanovich, Inc.

"Children of Strikers" from *Moments of Light* by Fred Chappell. Copyright © 1980 by Fred Chappell. Reprinted by permission of The New South Company.

From "Listening" reprinted by permission of the publishers from *One Writer's Beginnings* by Eudora Welty, Cambridge, Mass.: Harvard University Press, Copyright, © 1983, 1984 by Eudora Welty.

"Fast Love" by Michael Malone. First appeared in *Mademoiselle,* published by Conde Nast. Copyright © 1981 by Michael Malone. Reprinted by permission of Sterling Lord Literistic, Inc.

"Artists" reprinted by permission of The Putman Publishing Group from *Cakewalk* by Lee Smith. Copyright © 1981 by Lee Smith.

"Homecoming" from *Wind Shifting West,* by Shirley Anne Grau. Copyright © 1973 by Shirley Anne Grau. Reprinted by permission of Brandt & Brandt Literary Agents, Inc.

"The President of the Louisiana Live Oak Society" from *In the Land of Dreamy Dreams* by Ellen Gilchrist. © 1981 by Ellen Gilchrist. First appeared in *Prairie Schooner.* By permission of Little, Brown and Company.

"How Far She Went" from *How Far She Went* by Mary Hood. Copyright © 1984 by Mary Hood. Reprinted by permission of the University of Georgia Press.

(The following page constitutes an extension of the copyright page.)

Ⓜ REGISTERED TRADEMARK—MARCA REGISTRADA

Library of Congress Cataloging Card Number: 91-060968

LIBRARY OF CONGRESS CATALOGING-IN-PUBLICATION DATA

Growing up in the South : an anthology of modern southern literature / edited and introduced by Suzanne W. Jones.

    p.   cm.

    ISBN 0-451-62833-0

    1. American fiction—Southern States. 2. Children—Southern States—Fiction. 3. Youth—Southern States—/Fiction. 4. American fiction—20th century. 5. Southern States Fiction. I. Jones. Suzanne Whitmore.

PS551.G76 1991

813'.0108975—dc20

                                    90-27255

                                      CIP

Without limiting the rights under copyright reserved above, no part of this publication may be reproduced, stored in or introduced into a retrieval system, or transmitted, in any form, or by any means (electronic, mechanical, photocopying, recording, or otherwise), without the prior written permission of both the copyright owner and the above publisher of this book.

Printed in the United States of America

For my family and the friends
I grew up with in Surry, Virginia.

Acknowledgments

I am indebted to the Virginia Center for the Humanities for a fellowship that gave me the time and a place to read and select these stories about growing up in the South. I owe a special thanks to my colleague Ephraim Rubenstein for the use of his painting "Abandoned House, Edwardsville, Virginia." I would also like to thank a number of readers, whose opinions have helped shape this collection: Virginia public schoolteachers Susan Hull, Alan Seaman, and Susan Hawkes; students in my southern fiction classes at the University of Richmond; graduate student research assistants, Bruce Smith and Kate Cooke; my husband, Frank Papovich, who teaches southern literature at the University of Virginia; and my stepdaughter, Sasha Papovich, who is growing up in a South very different from the one I grew up in.

Contents

Introduction   *xiii*

I. Identifying Southern Places and Voices

Harry Crews,
    from *A Childhood: The Biography of a Place*   3

Elizabeth Spencer, *A Southern Landscape*   20

Bobbie Ann Mason, *State Champions*   35

Alice Walker,
    A Sudden Trip Home in the Spring   51

Fred Chappell, *Children of Strikers*   65

Eudora Welty, from *Listening*   70

Michael Malone, *Fast Love*   78

II. Remembering Southern Families

Lee Smith, *Artists* in *Cakewalk*   93

Shirley Ann Grau, *Homecoming*   116

Ellen Gilchrist,
    The President of the Louisiana Live Oak Society   130

Mary Hood, *How Far She Went*   146

Carson McCullers, *Sucker*   157

Alice Walker, *Everyday Use*   169

William Hoffman, *Amazing Grace*   181

III. Experiencing Southern Communities

Maya Angelou,
    from *I Know Why the Caged Bird Sings*   205

Flannery O'Connor,
    Everything That Rises Must Converge   221

Gail Godwin, *The Angry Year*   240

Peter Taylor, *The Old Forest*   259

IV. Breaking Southern Stereotypes

Anne Moody, from *Coming of Age in Mississippi*   325

Joan Williams, *Spring Is Now*   353

William Faulkner, *An Odor of Verbena*   369

Ernest Gaines, *Sully*   404

Richard Wright,
    The Man Who Was Almost a Man   436

Mary Mebane, from *Mary*   451

Katherine Anne Porter, *Old Mortality*   467

Introduction

When I think of my high school English classes in rural Surry, Virginia, in the 1960s, I vividly remember reading William Faulkner's *Go Down, Moses* in my American literature class. I had always loved reading, but the experience I had with Faulkner touched me more deeply than any other. I was moved by his provocative prose, by his sense of the past, by his passion for place, and by his intense dramas of southern race relations. Faulkner spoke to me in a way that other writers I had liked that year—Hawthorne, Dickinson, Fitzgerald—did not. In reading Faulkner's work, I found myself, my family, and my community as well as the rich, complex social history of my region. That much Faulkner was not in the standard-issue literature book for eleventh grade. I was lucky to have a teacher who believed in supplemental reading, who was trying to keep us attentive on those long hot days right before summer vacation. Her strategy worked for me.

Although Faulkner may not work for all students, I would like for more students to have the opportunity to experience the challenges and rewards of southern literature, which is why I collected these stories. Southern writers, such as William Faulkner, Eudora Welty, Peter Taylor, and Ernest Gaines, rank among the best American authors of the twentieth century. Such literature can help relate art to life, as it did for me twenty years ago, by exploring issues relevant to the South, and it can also make students more sensitive to each other as they become more aware of different viewpoints. In her autobiography, *I Know Why the Caged Bird Sings*, Maya Angelou reflects on the importance of place:

What sets one Southern town apart from another, or from a Northern town or hamlet, or city high-rise? The answer must be the experience shared between the unknowing majority (it) and the knowing minority (you). All of childhood's unanswered questions must finally be passed back to the town and answered there. Heroes and bogey men, values and dislikes, are first encountered and labeled in that early environment. In later years they change faces, places and maybe races, tactics, intensities and goals, but beneath those impenetrable masks they wear forever the stocking-capped faces of childhood.[1]

Some people might wonder if the South as a region still exists. Southern novelist Walker Percy claimed that the regions of the United States are becoming homogenized because of the mass media, and he bemoaned the loss of regional and personal identity that would result. Perhaps Walker Percy's fears are reasons enough to read regional literature. However, not everyone agrees that the regions of this country have lost their distinctions. As I lecture on southern literature around Virginia, hold workshops for English teachers in our public schools, and teach southern fiction at the University of Richmond, I have noticed that students, both young and old, both native and nonnative to the South, still perceive regional differences. The older people sense that the differences have to do with a southern preoccupation with history, both familial and regional; the younger people think the differences have a great deal to do with manners, not just etiquette, but customs and values—ways of being in the world. Southern literary critic Louis D. Rubin, Jr., in his introduction to *The History of Southern Literature*, defended that book's existence by saying:

. . . there existed in the past, and there continues to exist today, an entity within American society

[1]Maya Angelou, *I Know Why the Caged Bird Sings* (New York: Random House, 1969), pp. 15–16.

known as the South, and that for better or for worse the habit of viewing one's experience in terms of one's relationship to that entity is still a meaningful characteristic of both writers and readers who are or have been part of it. The historical circumstances that gave rise to that way of thinking and feeling have been greatly modified. Yet . . . to consider writers and their writings as Southern still involves considerably more than merely a geographical grouping. History, as a mode for viewing one's experience and one's identity, remains a striking characteristic of the Southern literary imagination, black and white.[2]

The following stories, set in the South and a part of its still distinctive literary imagination, are about childhood, adolescence, and young adulthood. They treat concerns of growing up common to all regions: loss of innocence, sexual awakening, family relationships, social adjustment, schools and teachers, religions and values, initiation and identity, emotional development and growing responsibility. But the stories I have collected also explore regional concerns that have been specific to the South: a love of storytelling; a preoccupation with family and with manners; the support and suffocation occasioned by a close-knit community; a concern with race relations, social classes, and gender roles; and a passion for place that is tied up with the past and with rural life. Some of the interests and techniques of southern writers emanate from what was once a predominantly rural way of life; others come from the remnants of a traditional code of honor that has lasted longer in the South than in other regions of the country. Several of these threads run through the historical and imaginative fabric of other sections of this country, but their particular weave in the South makes it unique.

The stories in Part I reflect the sights and sounds of

[2]Louis D. Rubin, Jr., et al, *The History of Southern Literature* (Baton Rouge: Louisiana State University Press, 1985), pp. 5–6.

many different southern places and voices. Harry Crews's autobiography, *A Childhood: The Biography of a Place*, bears the cadences of his impoverished childhood among sharecroppers in rural Bacon County, Georgia. In striking contrast is the voice of Elizabeth Spencer's mannered, genteel narrator of "A Southern Landscape," who reminisces about Mississippi summer nights and decayed colonial mansions. Yet the two narrators share the same feelings of being securely anchored by their memories of childhood places, even if those places exist "nowhere but in memory" as Crews writes. Although Crews and Spencer suggest that you do not fully know a place until you have experienced it with all of your senses and nourished it in your memory, Bobbie Ann Mason's narrator in "State Champions" wonders if you can know a place at all before you have put time and distance between you and your hometown. Her narrator's memories of junior high school coalesce around the gym in Cuba, Kentucky, home of the phenomenal Cuba Cubs basketball team, but she realizes how differently she sees that time and place twenty years later and many miles away. Alice Walker's protagonist in "A Sudden Trip Home in the Spring" reveals the sense of place that people carry with them wherever they live, and she speculates about the effect place has on identity. The black narrator of Walker's story is an art student at a predominantly white women's college in New York who thinks she feels more at home there than in her native Georgia. Yet when she returns home for her father's funeral, she understands the doubts she has had in New York about the choices she has made, and she realizes that her artistic inspiration comes from the South. But Southern places themselves are changing as the rural economy becomes more industrial, and no one documents this change better than Fred Chappell with his portrait of industrial pollution in a mountain mill town. Southern literary critic Cleanth Brooks believes that if the Southern agrarians were alive today, they would be environmentalists. Fred Chappell's work exhibits a similar concern with nature. The last two stories in this section show that even as the Southern landscape changes, some southern customs remain the same, such as southern writers' interests in creating distinctive voices for their fiction. Eudora Welty explains why she thinks she often wrote "in the form of a monologue that takes possession of the speaker," and Michael Malone's story is evidence that the practice of creating a conversational narrative voice continues among the latest generation of southern storytellers.

The stories in Part II evoke the power of the southern family to impose roles, to provide support, to cause pain, and to celebrate life. For Lee Smith family relationships become the locus for exploring the paradox of southern manners, the way polite and decorous behavior can disguise truth and extinguish vitality. In "Artists" she examines how the revelation of family secrets can change our perception, not only of our families but ourselves. In "Homecoming" Shirley Ann Grau juxtaposes a teenage girl's reaction to a casual boyfriend's death in Vietnam with her mother's memories of her husband's death in the Korean War. The story centers upon generational conflicts over proper behavior and the correct thoughts and feelings about death and war. Focusing on new patterns of family behavior rather than old, Ellen Gilchrist evokes the contemporary urban South in "The President of the Louisiana Live Oak Society," a story of streetwise boys from New Orleans, who find themselves doing drugs and lying to their parents, who are in turn finding their own means of escape from the strains of contemporary life. The next two stories, by Mary Hood and Carson McCullers, are about the strong yet fragile bonds between family members and about the illusion of independence that occurs when people have family to depend on. In Mary Hood's "How Far She Went" the tension mounts as a grandmother must do battle with two tough motorcyclists for her teenage granddaughter's loyalty. Carson McCullers's "Sucker" is a poignant account of how we take our closest relatives for granted and of the family love that can be fostered or destroyed more easily than we ever know. Alice Walker's "Everyday Use" plays the themes of sibling rivalry and parental preference against the question of racial identity, when a worldly daughter returns to her provincial family for a visit. Another family reunion is the backdrop for William Hoffman's amusing story "Amazing Grace." Here country and city cousins clash, and the grandmother refuses to bake bread until her grown son, who has moved to the city, is properly baptized in the river back home.

The stories in Part III illustrate the power of a community for good and ill, and the tensions created within southern communities by race and class differences, indeed by difference of any kind. In her autobiography *I Know Why the Caged Bird Sings*, Maya Angelou's remembrance of her 1940 grade school graduation shows both the power whites possessed to discriminate against blacks and the strength blacks gained as they united as a community against this discrimination. Flannery O'Connor's "Everything That Rises Must Converge" reveals the de facto segregation that continued even after segregation was outlawed in the South. In this story a white college graduate chastises his mother for her prejudice against blacks. What essentially exists as a conflict between generations is painful, but powerful to listen to. Gail Godwin's "The Angry Year" explores class divisions among whites and a young woman's struggle for identity. In Godwin's story a middle-class college junior finds herself attracted by the mystique of wealthy fraternity men and sorority women, but repelled by their superficiality and conformity. She expresses her ambivalence in her weekly campus newspaper column as well as through the two men she dates—the handsome rich president of the Dekes and the intellectual coal miner's son whose ticket to law school is the GI Bill. Another portrait of a similar dilemma, but from the upper-class white male perspective, is seen in Peter Taylor's "The Old Forest." The protagonist finds himself torn between his desire for the companionship of a bright young woman of questionable family background and his need to remain firmly ensconced in the country-club set by marrying into a prominent local family. Both Godwin's and Taylor's protagonists discover that the security of conformity is often stronger than the desire for rebellion.

In her autobiography *Proud Shoes*, Pauli Murray writes of the southern difficulty of dealing with difference, "Always the same tune, played like a broken record, robbing one of personal identity. . . . Folks were never just folks. They were white folks! Black folks! Poor white crackers! No-count niggers! Rednecks! Darkies! Peckerwoods! Coons!"[3] The characters in the stories in Part IV wrestle with these labels as they try to move beyond them. The first two selections are set during the 1960s civil rights movement and are told first from a black perspective, then from a white perspective. The excerpt from Anne Moody's autobiography, *Coming of Age in Mississippi*, reveals that working for the civil rights movement sometimes meant rebelling against family prohibitions even when you were black. Although Anne Moody worried that whites would retaliate against her family because of her political activism, she defied her mother's demands that she drop out of the movement, and she braved white violence to fight for equal rights. Joan Williams's "Spring Is Now" is about integrating the public schools. The only blacks whom white teenager Sandra knows are field hands, maids, and janitors. Although her family and friends often speculate about what blacks are really like, only when Sandra gets to know a new black classmate, Jack Lawrence, does she begin to find out. Both William Faulkner and Ernest Gaines show their fascination with how individuals can break long-established southern traditions. They focus on male roles and the southern code of honor, which historian Bertram Wyatt-Brown argues made nineteenth-century Southerners put reputation above conscience. In Faulkner's "An Odor of Verbena" Bayard Sartoris is pressured by his community to avenge his father's death. This incident serves as a test of his character for he must choose between his personal code of right and wrong and his community's code of honor. In Gaines's *A Gathering of Old Men*, set a century later, Cajun Gil Boutan is

[3]Pauli Murray, *Proud Shoes* (New York: Harper and Brothers, 1956), p. 270.

similarly put in a position of feeling forced to uphold family honor. His brother has been killed by a black man, and his family expects him to join the vigilante group they are forming. Having become close friends with a black teammate on his college football team, Gil is embarrassed by his family's reputation for harassing blacks, and he would like to leave justice to the authorities. In each story, the protagonist's masculinity is called into question because he refuses to fight. The behavior demanded by gender roles is something that also concerns Michael Malone in "Fast Love," a story in Part I. The narrator whose favorite pastimes are chess, debating, and bicycling knows that his father would have preferred a son who was less intellectual and more interested in sports and cars. In Richard Wright's "The Man Who Was Almost a Man," race and gender stereotypes create a no-win situation for Dave, who tries to increase his stature with a gun. Wright examines the paradoxical situation of a black youth growing up in a region that for so long did not allow a black man the dignity and respect of adulthood, a region that kept him a "boy." Whereas Mary Mebane must struggle against low expectations for black women in the selection from her autobiography *Mary*, Katherine Anne Porter's Miranda tries to mediate between two confining choices for the southern white woman: her vivacious Aunt Amy destined for star-crossed love and her more serious but less attractive Cousin Eva fated for a lonely career.

Although the South of Mary Mebane, Ellen Gilchrist, and Ernest Gaines is not the South of Katherine Anne Porter, Eudora Welty, and William Faulkner, these stories reveal what it means and what it meant to grow up in the South—what southern literary critic Carol Manning has called "that interesting middle ground between the universality of the process of growing up and the particularity of each individual's experience."

PART I

Identifying Southern Places and Voices

Harry Crews

Born in 1935, Harry Crews, the son of a poor tenant farmer, never lived in one place very long so he did not have the anchor of a family *"home place,"* which he, like many other southerners defines as "that single house where you were born, where you lived out your childhood, where you grew into young manhood." In his autobiography, *A Childhood: The Biography of a Place*, from which the following selection is taken, he writes, "But because we were driven from pillar to post when I was a child, there is nowhere I can think of as the home place. Bacon County is my home place, and I've had to make do with it. If I think of where I come from, I think of the entire county. I think of all its people and its customs and all its loveliness and all its ugliness." In Bacon County Crews learned that "Nothing is allowed to die in a society of storytelling people. It is all—the good and the bad—carted up and brought along from one generation to the next. And everything that is brought along is colored and shaped by those who bring it." Harry Crews acquired the rural Georgia gift for storytelling and has written many novels, all in the tradition of southern gothic, transformed by his own unique humor. Among them are *The Gospel Singer* (1968), *A Feast of Snakes* (1976), *A Grit's Triumph* (1983), *The Knockout Artist* (1988), and most recently *Body* (1990). Author of of the column "Grits" for *Esquire*, Crews is a frequent contributor to *Sewanee Review, Georgia Review*, and *Playboy*. After enlisting in the U.S. Marines at age 17, he graduated from the University of Florida. Currently he is a professor of English at the University of Florida in Gainesville.

from A Childhood:
The Biography of a Place

It has always seemed to me that I was not so much born into this life as I awakened to it. I remember very distinctly the awakening and the morning it happened. It was my first glimpse of myself, and all that I know now—the stories, and everything conjured up by them, that I have been writing about thus far—I obviously knew none of then, particularly anything about my real daddy, whom I was not to hear of until I was nearly six years old, not his name, not even that he was my daddy. Or if I did hear of him, I have no memory of it.

I awoke in the middle of the morning in early summer from the place I'd been sleeping in the curving roots of a giant oak tree in front of a large white house. Off to the right, beyond the dirt road, my goats were trailing along in the ditch, grazing in the tough wire grass that grew there. Their constant bleating shook the warm summer air. I always thought of them as my goats although my brother usually took care of them. Before he went to the field that morning to work, he had let them out of the old tobacco barn where they slept at night. At my feet was a white dog whose name was Sam. I looked at the dog and at the house and at the red gown with little pearl-colored buttons I was wearing, and I knew that the gown had been made for me by my Grandma Hazelton and that the dog belonged to me. He went everywhere I went, and he always took precious care of me.

Precious. That was my mama's word for how it was between Sam and me, even though Sam caused her some inconvenience from time to time. If she wanted to whip me, she had to take me in the house, where Sam was

4

never allowed to go. She could never touch me when I was crying if Sam could help it. He would move quietly— he was a dog not given to barking very much—between the two of us and show her his teeth. Unless she took me somewhere Sam couldn't go, there'd be no punishment for me.

The house there just behind me, partially under the arching limbs of the oak tree, was called the Williams place. It was where I lived with my mama and my brother, Hoyet, and my daddy, whose name was Pascal. I knew when I opened my eyes that morning that the house was empty because everybody had gone to the field to work. I also knew, even though I couldn't remember doing it, that I had awakened sometime in midmorning and come out onto the porch and down the steps and across the clean-swept dirt yard through the gate weighted with broken plow points so it would swing shut behind me, that I had come out under the oak tree and lain down against the curving roots with my dog, Sam, and gone to sleep. It was a thing I had done before. If I ever woke up and the house was empty and the weather was warm—which was the only time I would ever awaken to an empty house—I always went out under the oak tree to finish my nap. It wasn't fear or loneliness that drove me outside; it was just something I did for reasons I would never be able to discover.

I stood up and stretched and looked down at my bare feet at the hem of the gown and said: "I'm almost five and already a great big boy." It was my way of reassuring myself, but it was also something my daddy said about me and it made me feel good because in his mouth it seemed to mean I was almost a man.

Sam immediately stood up too, stretched, reproducing, as he always did, every move I made, watching me carefully to see which way I might go. I knew I ought not to be outside lying in the rough curve of root in my cotton gown. Mama didn't mind me being out there under the tree, but I was supposed to get dressed first. Sometimes I did; often I forgot.

So I turned and went back through the gate, Sam at

my heels, and across the yard and up the steps onto the
porch to the front door. When I opened the door, Sam
stopped and lay down to wait. He would be there when
I came out, no matter which door I used. If I went out
the back door, he would somehow magically know it and
he would be there. If I came out the side door by the
little pantry, he would know that, too, and he would be
there. Sam always knew where I was, and he made it his
business to be there, waiting.

I went into the long, dim, cool hallway that ran down
the center of the house. Briefly I stopped at the bedroom
where my parents slept and looked in at the neatly made
bed and all the parts of the room, clean, with everything
where it was supposed to be, just the way mama always
kept it. And I thought of daddy, as I so often did because
I loved him so much. If he was sitting down, I was usually
on his lap. If he was standing up, I was usually holding
his hand. He always said soft funny things to me and
told me stories that never had an end but always continued when we met again.

He was tall and lean with flat high cheekbones and
deep eyes and black thick hair which he combed straight
back on his head. And under the eye on his left cheek
was the scarred print of a perfect set of teeth. I knew he
had taken the scar in a fight, but I never asked him about
it and the teeth marks in his cheek only made him seem
more powerful and stronger and special to me.

He shaved every morning at the water shelf on the
back porch with a straight razor and always smelled of
soap and whiskey. I knew mama did not like the whiskey,
but to me it smelled sweet, better even than the soap.
And I could never understand why she resisted it so,
complained of it so, and kept telling him over and over
again that he would kill himself and ruin everything if he
continued with the whiskey. I did not understand about
killing himself and I did not understand about ruining
everything, but I knew the whiskey somehow caused the
shouting and screaming and the ugly sound of breaking
things in the night. The stronger the smell of whiskey on

him, though, the kinder and gentler he was with me and my brother.

I went on down the hallway and out onto the back porch and finally into the kitchen that was built at the very rear of the house. The entire room was dominated by a huge black cast-iron stove with six eyes on its cooking surface. Directly across the room from the stove was the safe, a tall square cabinet with wide doors covered with screen wire that was used to keep biscuits and fried meat and rice or almost any other kind of food that had been recently cooked. Between the stove and the safe sat the table we ate off of, a table almost ten feet long, with benches on each side instead of chairs, so that when we put in tobacco, there would be enough room for the hired hands to eat.

I opened the safe, took a biscuit off a plate, and pushed a hole in it with my finger. Then with a jar of cane syrup, I poured the hole full, waited for it to soak in good, and then poured again. When the biscuit had all the syrup it would take, I got two pieces of fried pork off another plate and went out and sat on the back steps, where Sam was already lying in the warm sun, his ears struck forward on his head. I ate the bread and pork slowly, chewing for a long time and sharing it all with Sam.

When we had finished, I went back into the house, took off my gown, and put on a cotton undershirt, my overalls with twin galluses that buckled on my chest, and my straw hat, which was rimmed on the edges with a border of green cloth and had a piece of green cellophane sewn into the brim to act as an eyeshade. I was barefoot, but I wished very much I had a pair of brogans because brogans were what men wore and I very much wanted to be a man. In fact, I was pretty sure I already was a man, but the only one who seemed to know it was my daddy. Everybody else treated me like I was still a baby.

I went out the side door, and Sam fell into step behind me as we walked out beyond the mule barn where four mules stood in the lot and on past the cotton house and down the dim road past a little leaning shack where our

tenant farmers lived, a black family in which there was
a boy just a year older than I was. His name was Willalee
Bookatee. I went on past their house because I knew
they would be in the field, too, so there was no use to
stop.

I went through a sapling thicket and over a shallow
ditch and finally climbed a wire fence into the field, being
very careful of my overalls on the barbed wire. I could
see them all, my family and the black tenant family, far
off there in the shimmering heat of the tobacco field.
They were pulling cutworms off the tobacco. I wished I
could have been out there with them pulling worms
because when you found one, you had to break it in half,
which seemed great good fun to me. But you could also
carry an empty Prince Albert tobacco can in your back
pocket and fill it up with worms to play with later.

Mama wouldn't let me pull worms because she said I
was too little and might damage the plants. If I was alone
in the field with daddy, though, he would let me hunt
all the worms I wanted to. He let me do pretty much
anything I wanted to, which included sitting in his lap to
guide his old pickup truck down dirt roads all over the
county.

I went down to the end of the row and sat under a
persimmon tree in the shade with Sam and watched as
daddy and mama and brother and Willalee Bookatee,
who was—I could see even from this distance—putting
worms in Prince Albert cans, and his mama, whose name
was Katie, and his daddy, whose name was Will, I
watched them all as they came toward me, turning the
leaves and searching for worms as they came.

The moment I sat down in the shade, I was already
wondering how long it would be before they quit to go
to the house for dinner because I was already beginning
to wish I'd taken two biscuits instead of one and maybe
another piece of meat, or else that I hadn't shared with
Sam.

Bored, I looked down at Sam and said: "Sam, if you
don't quit eatin my biscuit and meat, I'm gone have to
cut you like a shoat hog."

A black cloud of gnats swarmed around his heavy muzzle, but I clearly heard him say that he didn't think I was man enough to do it. Sam and I talked a lot together, had long involved conversations, mostly about which one of us had done the other one wrong and, if not about that, about which one of us was the better man. It would be a good long time before I started thinking of Sam as a dog instead of a person. But I always came out on top when we talked because Sam could only say what I said he said, think what I thought he thought.

"If you was any kind of man atall, you wouldn't snap at them gnats and eat them flies the way you do," I said.

"It ain't a thing in the world the matter with eatin gnats and flies," he said.

"It's how come people treat you like a dog," I said. "You could probably come on in the house like other folks if it weren't for eatin flies and gnats like you do."

That's the way the talk went until daddy and the rest of them finally came down to where Sam and I were sitting in the shade. They stopped beside us to wipe their faces and necks with sweat rags. Mama asked if I had got something to eat when I woke up. I told her I had.

"You all gone stop for dinner now?"

"I reckon we'll work awhile longer," daddy said.

I said: "Well then, can Willalee and me go up to his house and play till dinnertime?"

Daddy looked at the sun to see what time it was. He could come within five or ten minutes by the position of the sun. Most of the farmers I knew could.

Daddy was standing almost dead center in his own shadow. "I reckon so," he said.

Then the whole thing had to be done over again. Willalee asked his daddy the same question. Because my daddy had said it was all right didn't mean Willalee's daddy would agree. He usually did, but not always. So it was necessary to ask.

We climbed the fence and went across the ditch and back through the sapling thicket to the three-track road that led up to the shack, and while we walked, Willalee showed me the two Prince Albert tobacco cans he had in his back pockets. They were both filled with cutworms. The worms had lots of legs and two little things on their heads that looked like horns. They were about an inch long, sometimes as long as two inches, and round and fat and made wonderful things to play with. There was no fence around the yard where Willalee lived and the whole house leaned toward the north at about a ten-degree tilt. Before we even got up the steps, we could smell the food already cooking on the wood stove at the back of the house where his grandma was banging metal pots around over the cast-iron stove. Her name was Annie, but everybody called her Auntie. She was too old to work in the field anymore, but she was handy about the house with ironing and cooking and scrubbing floors and canning vegetables out of the field and berries out of the woods.

She also was full of stories, which, when she had the time—and she usually did—she told to me and Willalee and his little sister, whose name was Lottie Mae. Willalee and my brother and I called her Snottie Mae, but she didn't seem to mind. She came out of the front door when she heard us coming up on the porch and right away wanted to know if she could play in the book with us. She was the same age as I and sometimes we let her play with us, but most of the time we did not.

"Naw," Willalee said, "git on back in there and help Auntie. We ain't studying you."

"Bring us the book," I said.

"I git it for you," she said, "if you give me five of them worms."

"I ain't studying you," said Willalee.

She had already seen the two Prince Albert cans full of green worms because Willalee was sitting on the floor now, the lids of the cans open and the worms crawling out. He was lining two of them up for a race from one crack in the floor to the next crack, and he was arranging the rest of the worms in little designs of diamonds and triangles in some game he had not yet discovered the rules for.

"You bring the book," I said, "and you can have two of them worms."

Willalee almost never argued with what I decided to do, up to and including giving away the worms he had spent all morning collecting in the fierce summer heat, which is probably why I liked him so much. Lottie Mae went back into the house, and got the Sears, Roebuck catalogue and brought it out onto the porch. He handed her the two worms and told her to go on back in the house, told her it weren't fitting for her to be out here playing with worms while Auntie was back in the kitchen working.

"Ain't nothing left for me to do but put them plates on the table," she said.

"See to them plates then," Willalee said. As young as she was, Lottie Mae had things to do about the place. Whatever she could manage. We all did.

Willalee and I stayed there on the floor with the Sears, Roebuck catalogue and the open Prince Albert cans, out of which deliciously fat worms crawled. Then we opened the catalogue at random as we always did, to see what magic was waiting for us there.

In the minds of most people, the Sears, Roebuck catalogue is a kind of low joke associated with outhouses. God knows the catalogue sometimes ended up in the outhouse, but more often it did not. All the farmers, black and white, kept dried corncobs beside their double-seated thrones, and the cobs served the purpose for which they were put there with all possible efficiency and comfort.

The Sears, Roebuck catalogue was much better used as a Wish Book, which it was called by the people out in the country, who would never be able to order anything out of it, but could at their leisure spend hours dreaming over.

Willalee Bookatee and I used it for another reason. We made up stories out of it, used it to spin a web of fantasy about us. Without that catalogue our childhood would have been radically different. The federal government ought to strike a medal for the Sears, Roebuck company for sending all those catalogues to farming families, for bringing all that color and all that mystery and all that beauty into the lives of country people.

I first became fascinated with the Sears catalogue because all the people in its pages were perfect. Nearly everybody I knew had something missing, a finger cut off, a toe split, an ear half-chewed away, an eye clouded with blindness from a glancing fence staple. And if they didn't have something missing, they were carrying scars from barbed wire, or knives, or fishhooks. But the people in the catalogue had no such hurts. They were not only whole, had all their arms and legs and eyes on their unscarred bodies, but they were also beautiful. Their legs were straight and their heads were never bald and on their faces were looks of happiness, even joy, looks that I never saw much of in the faces of the people around me.

Young as I was, though, I had known for a long time that it was all a lie. I knew that under those fancy clothes there had to be scars, there had to be swellings and boils of one kind or another because there was no other way to live in the world. And more than that, at some previous, unremembered moment, I had decided that all the people in the catalogue were related, not necessarily blood kin, but knew one another, and because they knew one another there had to be hard feelings, trouble between them off and on, violence, and hate between them as well as love. And it was out of this knowledge that I first began to make up stories about the people I found in the book.

Once I began to make up stories about them, Willalee and Lottie Mae began to make up stories, too. The stories they made up were every bit as good as mine. Sometimes better. More than once we had spent whole rainy afternoons when it was too wet to go to the field turning the pages of the catalogue, forcing the beautiful people to give up the secrets of their lives: how they felt about one another, what kind of sicknesses they may have had, what kind of scars they carried in their flesh under all those bright and fancy clothes.

Willalee had his pocketknife out and was about to operate on one of the green cutworms because he liked to pretend he was a doctor. It was I who first put the notion in his head that he might in fact be a doctor, and since we almost never saw a doctor and because they were mysterious and always drove cars or else fine buggies behind high-stepping mares, quickly healing people with their secret medicines, the notion stuck in Willalee's head, and he became very good at taking cutworms and other things apart with his pocketknife.

The Sears catalogue that we had opened at random found a man in his middle years but still strong and healthy with a head full of hair and clear, direct eyes looking out at us, dressed in a red hunting jacket and wading boots, with a rack of shotguns behind him. We used our fingers to mark the spot and turned the Wish Book again, and this time it opened to ladies standing in their underwear, lovely as none we had ever seen, all perfect in their unstained clothes. Every last one of them had the same direct and steady eyes of the man in the red hunting jacket.

I said: "What do you think, Willalee?"

Without hesitation, Willalee said: "This lady here in her step-ins is his chile."

We kept the spot marked with the lady in the step-ins and the man in the hunting jacket and turned the book again, and there was a young man in a suit, the creases sharp enough to shave with, posed with his foot casually propped on a box, every strand of his beautiful hair in place.

"See, what it is," I said. "This boy right here is seeing that girl back there, the one in her step-ins, and she is the youngun of him back there, and them shotguns behind'm belong to him, and he ain't happy."

"Why he ain't happy?"

"Cause this feller standing here in this suit looking so nice, he ain't nice at all. He's mean, but he don't look mean. That gal is the only youngun the feller in the jacket's got, and he loves her cause she is a sweet child. He don't want her fooling with that sorry man in that suit.

He's so sorry he done got hisself in trouble with the law. The high sheriff is looking for him right now. Him in the suit will fool around on you."

"How it is he fool around?"

"He'll steal anything he can put his hand to," I said. "He'll steal your hog, or he'll steal your cow out of your field. He's so sorry he'll take that cow if it's the only cow you got. It's just the kind of feller he is."

Willalee said: "Then how come it is she mess around with him?"

"That suit," I said, "done turned that young girl's head. Daddy always says if you give a man a white shirt and a tie and a suit of clothes, you can find out real quick how sorry he is. Daddy says it's the quickest way to find out."

"Do her daddy know she's messing round with him?"

"Shore he knows. A man allus knows what his young-un is doing. Special if she's a girl." I flipped back to the man in the red hunting jacket and the wading boots. "You see them shotguns behind him there on the wall? Them his guns. That second one right there, see that one, the double barrel? That gun is loaded with double-ought buckshot. You know how come it loaded?"

"He gone stop that fooling around," said Willalee.

And so we sat there on the porch with the pots and pans banging back in the house over the iron stove and Lottie Mae there in the door where she had come to stand and listen to us as we talked even though we would not let her help with the story. And before it was over, we had discovered all the connections possible between the girl in the step-ins and the young man in the knife-creased suit and the older man in the red hunting jacket with the shotguns on the wall behind him. And more than that we also discovered that the man's kin people, when they had found out about the trouble he was having with his daughter and the young man, had plans of their own to fix it so the high sheriff wouldn't even have to know about it. They were going to set up and wait on him to take a shoat hog out of another field, and when he did, they'd be waiting with their own guns and knives (which we stumbled upon in another part of the catalogue) and they was gonna throw down on him and see if they couldn't make two pieces out of him instead of one. We had in the story what they thought and what they said and what they felt and why they didn't think that the young man, as good as he looked and as well as he stood in his fancy clothes, would ever straighten out and become the man the daddy wanted for his only daughter.

Before it was over, we even had the girl in the step-ins fixing it so that the boy in the suit could be shot. And by the time my family and Willalee's family came walking down the road from the tobacco field toward the house, the entire Wish Book was filled with feuds of every kind and violence, maimings, and all the other vicious happenings of the world.

Since where we lived and how we lived was almost hermetically sealed from everything and everybody else, fabrication became a way of life. Making up stories, it seems to me now, was not only a way for us to understand the way we lived but also a defense against it. It was no doubt the first step in a life devoted primarily to men and women and children who never lived anywhere but in my imagination. I have found in them infinitely more order and beauty and satisfaction than I ever have in the people who move about me in the real world. And Willalee Bookatee and his family were always there with me in those first tentative steps. God knows what it would have been like if it had not been for Willalee and his people, with whom I spent nearly as much time as I did with my own family.

There was a part of me in which it did not matter at all that they were black, but there was another part of me in which it had to matter because it mattered to the world I lived in. It mattered to my blood. It is easy to remember the morning I found out Willalee was a nigger.

It was not very important at the time. I do not know why I have remembered it so vividly and so long. It was the tiniest of moments that slipped by without anybody marking it or thinking about it.

It was later in the same summer I awoke to a knowledge of myself in the enormous, curving oak roots. It was Sunday, bright and hot, and we were on the way to church. Everybody except daddy, who was sick from whiskey. But he would not have gone even if he were well. The few times he ever did go he could never stand more than five or ten minutes of the sermon before he quietly went out a side door to stand beside the pickup truck smoking hand-rolled Prince Albert cigarettes until it was all over.

An aunt, her husband, and their children had come by to take us to the meeting in their car. My aunt was a lovely, gentle lady whom I loved nearly as much as mama. I was out on the porch waiting for my brother to get ready. My aunt stood beside me, pulling on the thin black gloves she wore to church winter and summer. I was talking nonstop, which I did even as a child, telling her a story—largely made up—about what happened to me and my brother the last time he went to town.

Robert Jones figured in the story. Robert Jones was a black man who lived in Bacon County. Unlike any other black man I knew of, though, he owned a big farm with a great shining house on it. He had two sons who were nearly seven feet tall. They were all known as very hard workers. I had never heard anybody speak of Robert Jones and his family with anything but admiration.

". . . so me and Hoyet was passing the cotton gin and Mr. Jones was standing there with his wife and. . . ."

My aunt leaned down and put her arm around my shoulders. Her great soft breast pressed warmly at my ear. She said: "No, son. Robert Jones is a nigger. You don't say 'mister' when you speak of a nigger. You don't say 'Mr. Jones,' you say 'nigger Jones'."

I never missed a stroke in my story. ". . . so me and him was passing the cotton gin and nigger Jones was standing there with his wife. . . ."

We were all dutiful children in Bacon County, Georgia.

I don't know what difference it ever made that I found out Willalee Bookatee was a nigger. But no doubt it made a difference. Willalee was our friend, my brother's and mine, but we sometimes used him like a toy. He was always a surefire cure for boredom because among other things he could be counted on to be scared witless at the mention of a bull. How many afternoons would have been endless if we couldn't have said to one another: "Let's go get Willalee Bookatee and scare the shit out of him."

It didn't take much encouragement or deception to get Willalee out in the cornfield with us just after noon, when it was hot as only a day can be hot in the middle of an airless field in Georgia.

Hoyet turned to Willalee Bookatee and said: "You ever seen this here bull?"

"Which air bull?" Willalee rolled his eyes and shuffled his feet and looked off down the long heat-distorted rows of corn, the corn so green it seemed almost purple in the sun.

"The bull that stays in this field," I said.

My brother said: "To hook little boys that won't tote a citron."

Willalee was out in the middle of a twenty-acre field of corn, equidistant from all fences, brought there by design by Hoyet and me to see if we could make him carry a heavy citron to the gate. A citron is a vine that grows wild in the field, and it puts out a fruit which is also called a citron and looks in every way like a watermelon except it's slightly smaller. Its rind was sometimes pickled and used in fruitcakes, but by and large, it was a worthless plant and farmers did everything they could think of to get rid of them, but they somehow always managed to survive.

"Hook little boys," said Willalee.

It wasn't a question; it was only repeated into the quiet dust-laden air. There had been no rain in almost two weeks, and when you stepped between the corn rows, the dust rose and hung, not falling or blowing in the windless day, but simply hanging interminably between the purple shucks of corn.

"No siree, it's got to be bigger than that one," I said when Willalee rushed to snatch a grapefruit-sized citron off the ground. "That old bull wants you to tote one bigger'n that."

Willalee was scared to death of bulls. He had been trampled and caught on the horns of one when he was about three years old, and he never got over it. At the mention of a bull, Willalee would go gray and his eyes would get a little wild and sometimes he would get out of control with his fear. Willalee was struggling with an enormous citron, staggering in the soft dirt between the corn rows.

"That's better," I said. "That's a lot better. That old bull will never touch you with that in your arms."

Willalee couldn't have weighed more than about sixty-five pounds, and the citron he caught against his skinny chest must have weighed twenty pounds.

"How come it is you ain't got no citron?" said Willalee.

My brother and I walked on either side of him. He could hardly see over the citron he was carrying.

"We already carried ourn," I said. "That bull doesn't make you tote but one. After you tote one citron, you can take and come out here in the field anytime you want to and that bull don't pay no more mind than if you was a goat."

Willalee was a long way from the gate, and he had already started crying, soundlessly, tears tracking down through the dust on his cheeks. That citron was hurting him a lot.

"But you ain't toted your citron yet," I said, "and that big bull looking to hook into your ass if you put it down, that bull looking to hook him some ass, some good tender little-boy ass, cause that the kind he likes the best."

"I know," whispered Willalee through his tears. "I know he do."

And so Willalee made it to the fence with his citron and felt himself forever safe from the bull. He didn't hesitate at the fence but went right over it, still carrying his citron in case the bull was watching, and once over it, he didn't say anything but took off in a wild run down the road.

But Willalee was not entirely helpless, and he gave back about as good as he got. He once took a crabapple and cut the core out of it, put some cow plop down in the bottom of the hole, and then covered it over all around the top with some blackberry jam his mama had canned.

"Jam in a apple?" I said.

"Bes thing *you* ever put in your mouth," he said.

My brother, who had seen him fix the apple, stood there and watched him offer it to me, did in fact encourage me to take it.

"Had one myself," he said. "That thing is some gooooood eatin."

"I ain't had nair one with jam in it," I said.

"Take you a great big bite," said Willalee.

I not only took a great big bite, I took *two* great big bites, getting right down to the bottom. Anybody else would have known what he was eating after the first bite. It took me two. Even then, I did not so much as taste it as I smelled it.

"I believe this thing is ruint," I said.

"Nawwwww," said Willalee.

"Nawwwww," said my brother.

"It smells just like . . . like . . ." And then I knew what he had fed me.

Willalee was laughing when he should have been running. I got him around the neck and we both went into the dust, where we wallowed around for a while before my brother got tired of watching it and pulled us apart. No matter what we did to one another, though, Willalee and I never stayed angry at each other for more than an hour or two, and I always felt welcome at his family's house. Whatever I am, they had a large part in making.

Elizabeth Spencer

Elizabeth Spencer was born in 1921 in Carrollton, Mississippi. Her early memories are of small-town life in an agrarian society and of a large extended family in which books were a staple of conversation. She attended Belhaven College in Jackson, Mississippi, and became friends with Eudora Welty, who later wrote the foreword to Spencer's collected stories, *The Stories of Elizabeth Spencer* (1981). Spencer received her M.A. at Vanderbilt and went on to teach at the University of Mississippi. She received an award from the National Institute of Arts and Letters for her second novel, *This Crooked Way* (1952), and an award from the American Academy of Arts and Letters for her next novel, *The Voice at the Back Door* (1956). Her greatest commercial success was a novella set in Italy, *The Light in the Piazza* (1960), which was made into a movie by M-G-M. After setting a couple of other works in Italy, she returned to the South for *The Snare* (1972), *Marilee* (1981), and *The Salt Line* (1984). Her stories have won O. Henry prizes and a medal from the American Academy and Institute for Arts and Letters, which elected her as a member in 1985. Her most recent work is a collection of short fiction, *Jack of Diamonds* (1988). Elizabeth Spencer has lived in Italy and in Montreal, where she taught creative writing at Concordia University from 1976 to 1986, but in 1986 she moved to Chapel Hill to teach at the University of North Carolina. Her fiction reveals her mastery of idiomatic speech and her love of the landscape of her youth.

A Southern Landscape

If you're like me and sometimes turn through the paper reading anything and everything because you're too lazy to get up and do what you ought to be doing, then you already know about my home town. There's a church there that has a gilded hand on the steeple, with the finger pointing to Heaven. The hand looks normal size, but it's really as big as a Ford car. At least, that's what they used to say in those little cartoon squares in the newspaper, full of sketches and exclamation points—"Strange As It Seems," "This Curious World," or Ripley's "Believe It or Not." Along with carnivorous tropical flowers, the Rosetta stone, and the cheerful information that the entire human race could be packed into a box a mile square and dumped into Grand Canyon, there it would be every so often, that old Presbyterian hand the size of a Ford car. It made me feel right in touch with the universe to see it in the paper—something it never did accomplish all by itself. I haven't seen anything about it recently, but then, Ford cars have got bigger, and, come to think of it, maybe they don't even print those cartoons any more. The name of the town, in case you're trying your best to remember and can't, is Port Claiborne, Mississippi. Not that I'm *from* there; I'm from *near* there.

Coming down the highway from Vicksburg, you come to Port Claiborne, and then to get to our house you turn off to the right on State Highway No. 202 and follow along the prettiest road. It's just about the way it always was—worn deep down like a tunnel and thick with shade in summer. In spring, it's so full of sweet heavy odors, they make you drunk, you can't think of anything—you feel you will faint or go right out of yourself. In fall, there is the rustle of leaves under your tires and the smell of them, all sad and Indian-like. Then in the winter, there are only dust and bare limbs, and mud when it rains, and everything is like an old dirt-dauber's nest up in the corner. Well, any season, you go twisting along this tunnel for a mile or so, then the road breaks down into a flat open run toward a wooden bridge that spans a swampy creek bottom. Tall trees grow up out of the bottom—willow and cypress, gum and sycamore—and there is a jungle of brush and vines—kudzu, Jackson vine, Spanish moss, grapevine, Virginia creeper, and honeysuckle—looping, climbing, and festooning the trees, and harboring every sort of snake and varmint underneath. The wooden bridge clatters when you cross, and down far below you can see water, lying still, not a good step wide. One bank is grassy and the other is a slant of ribbed white sand.

Then you're going to have to stop and ask somebody. Just say, "Can you tell me where to turn to get to the Summerall place?" Everybody knows us. Not that we *are* anybody—I don't mean that. It's just that we've been there forever. When you find the right road, you go right on up through a little wood of oaks, then across a field, across a cattle gap, and you're there. The house is nothing special, just a one-gable affair with a bay window and a front porch—the kind they built back around fifty or sixty years ago. The shrubs around the porch and the privet hedge around the bay window were all grown up too high the last time I was there. They ought to be kept trimmed down. The yard is a nice flat one, not much for growing grass but wonderful for shooting marbles. There were always two or three marble holes out near the pecan trees where I used to play with the colored children.

Benjy Hamilton swore he twisted his ankle in one of those same marble holes once when he came to pick me up for something my senior year in high school. For all I know, they're still there, but Benjy was more than likely drunk and so would hardly have needed a marble hole for an excuse to fall down. Once, before we got the cattle gap, he couldn't open the gate, and fell on the barbed wire trying to cross the fence. I had to pick him out, thread at a time, he was so tangled up. Mama said, "What were you two doing out at the gate so long last night?" "Oh, nothing, just talking," I said. She thought for the longest time that Benjy Hamilton was the nicest boy that ever walked the earth. No matter how drunk he was, the presence of an innocent lady like Mama, who said *"Drinking?"* in the same tone of voice she would have said *"Murder?"* would bring him around faster than any number of needle showers, massages, ice packs, prairie oysters, or quick dips in December off the northern bank of Lake Ontario. He would straighten up and smile and say, "You made any more peach pickle lately, Miss Sadie?" (He could even say "peach pickle.") And she'd say no, but that there was always some of the old for him whenever he wanted any. And he'd say that was just the sweetest thing he'd ever heard of, but she didn't know what she was promising—anything as good as her peach pickle ought to be guarded like gold. And she'd say, well, for most anybody else she'd think twice before she offered any. And he'd say, if only everybody was as sweet to him as she was. . . . And they'd go on together like that till you'd think that all creation had ground and wound itself down through the vistas of eternity to bring the two of them face to face for exchanging compliments over peach pickle. Then I would put my arm in his so it would look like he was helping me down the porch steps out of the reflexes of his gentlemanly upbringing, and off we'd go.

It didn't happen all the time, like I've made it sound. In fact, it was only a few times when I was in school that I went anywhere with Benjy Hamilton. Benjy isn't his name, either; it's Foster. I sometimes call him "Benjy" to myself, after a big overgrown thirty-three-year-old idiot in *The Sound and the Fury*, by William Faulkner. Not that Foster was so big or overgrown, or even thirty-three years old, back then; but he certainly did behave like an idiot.

I won this prize, see, for writing a paper on the siege of Vicksburg. It was for the United Daughters of the Confederacy's annual contest, and mine was judged the best in the state. So Foster Hamilton came all the way over to the schoolhouse and got me out of class—I felt terribly important—just to "interview" me. He had just graduated from the university and had a job on the paper in Port Claiborne—that was before he started work for the *Times-Picayune* in New Orleans. We went into an empty classroom and sat down.

He leaned over some blank sheets of coarse-grained paper and scribbled things down with a thick-leaded pencil. I was sitting in the next seat; it was a long bench divided by a number of writing arms, which was why they said that cheating was so prevalent in our school— you could just cheat without meaning to. They kept trying to raise the money for regular desks in every classroom, so as to improve morals. Anyway, I couldn't help seeing what he was writing down, so I said, " 'Marilee' is all one word, and with an 'i,' not a 'y.' 'Summerall' is spelled just like it sounds." "Are you a senior?" he asked. "Just a junior," I said. He wore horn-rimmed glasses; that was back before everybody wore them. I thought they looked unusual and very distinguished. Also, I had noticed his shoulders when he went over to let the window down. I thought they were distinguished, too, if a little bit bony. "What is your ambition?" he asked me. "I hope to go to college year after next," I said. "I intend to wait until my junior year in college to choose a career."

He kept looking down at his paper while he wrote, and when he finally looked up at me I was disappointed to see why he hadn't done it before. The reason was, he couldn't keep a straight face. It had happened before that people broke out laughing just when I was being my most earnest and sincere. It must have been what I said, because I don't think I *look* funny. I guess I don't look like much of any one thing. When I see myself in the mirror, no adjective springs right to mind, unless it's "average." I am medium height, I am average weight, I buy "natural"-colored face powder and "medium"-colored lipstick. But I must say for myself, before this goes too far, that every once in a great while I look Just Right. I've never found the combination for making this happen, and no amount of reading the make-up articles in the magazines they have at the beauty parlor will do any good. But sometimes it happens anyway, with no more than soap and water, powder, lipstick, and a damp hairbrush.

My interview took place in the spring, when we were practicing for the senior play every night. Though a junior, I was in it because they always got me, after the eighth grade, to take parts in things. Those of us that lived out in the country Mrs. Arrington would take back home in her car after rehearsal. One night, we went over from the school to get a Coca-Cola before the drugstore closed, and there was Foster Hamilton. He had done a real nice article—what Mama called a "write-up." It was when he was about to walk out that he noticed me and said, "Hey." I said "Hey" back, and since he just stood there, I said, "Thank you for the write-up in the paper."

"Oh, that's all right," he said, not really listening. He wasn't laughing this time. "Are you going home?" he said.

"We are after 'while," I said. "Mrs. Arrington takes us home in her car."

"Why don't you let me take you home?" he said. "It might—it might save Mrs. Arrington an extra trip."

"Well," I said, "I guess I could ask her."

So I went to Mrs. Arrington and said, "Mrs. Arrington, Foster Hamilton said he would be glad to drive me home." She hesitated so long that I put in, "He says it might save you an extra trip." So finally she said, "Well, all right, Marilee." She told Foster to drive carefully. I could tell she was uneasy, but then, my family were known as real good people, very strict, and of course she didn't want them to feel she hadn't done the right thing.

That was the most wonderful night. I'll never forget it. It was full of spring, all restlessness and sweet smells. It was radiant, it was warm, it was serene. It was all the things you want to call it, but no word would ever be the right one, nor any ten words, either. When we got close to our turnoff, after the bridge, I said, "The next road is ours," but Foster drove right on past. I knew where he was going. He was going to Windsor.

Windsor is this big colonial mansion built back before the Civil War. It burned down during the 1890s sometime, but there were still twenty-five or more Corinthian columns, standing on a big open space of ground that is a pasture now, with cows and mules and calves grazing in it. The columns are enormously high and you can see some of the iron grillwork railing for the second-story gallery clinging halfway up. Vines cling to the fluted white plaster surfaces, and in some places the plaster has crumbled away, showing the brick underneath. Little trees grow up out of the tops of columns, and chickens have their dust holes among the rubble. Just down the fall of the ground beyond the ruin, there are some Negro houses. A path goes down to them.

It is this ignorant way that the hand of Nature creeps back over Windsor that makes me afraid. I'd rather there'd be ghosts there, but there aren't. Just some old story about lost jewelry that every once in a while sends somebody poking around in all the trash. Still it is magnificent, and people have compared it to the Parthenon and so on and so on, and even if it makes me feel this undertone of horror, I'm always ready to go and look at it again. When all of it was standing, back in the old days, it was higher even than the columns, and had a cupola, too. You could see the cupola from the river, they say, and the story went that Mark Twain used it to steer by. I've read that book since, *Life on the Mississippi*, and it seems he used everything else to steer by, too—crawfish mounds, old rowboats stuck in the mud, the tassels on somebody's corn patch, and every stump and stob from New Orleans to Cairo, Illinois. But it does kind of connect you up with something to know that Windsor was there, too, like seeing the Presbyterian hand in the newspaper. Some people would say at this point, "Small world," but it isn't a small world. It's an enormous world, bigger than you can imagine, but it's all connected up. What Nature does to Windsor it does to everything, including you and me—there's the horror.

But that night with Foster Hamilton, I wasn't thinking any such doleful thoughts, and though Windsor can be a pretty scary-looking sight by moonlight, it didn't scare me then. I could have got right out of the car, alone, and walked all around among the columns, and whatever I heard walking away through the weeds would not have scared me, either. We sat there, Foster and I, and never said a word. Then, after some time, he turned the car around and took the road back. Before we got to my house, though, he stopped the car by the roadside and kissed me. He held my face up to his, but outside that he didn't touch me. I had never been kissed in any deliberate and accomplished way before, and driving out to Windsor in that accidental way, the whole sweetness of the spring night, the innocence and mystery of the two of us, made me think how simple life was and how easy it was to step into happiness, like walking into your own rightful house.

This frame of mind persisted for two whole days—enough to make a nuisance of itself. I kept thinking that Foster Hamilton would come sooner or later and tell me that he loved me, and I couldn't sleep for thinking about him in various ways, and I had no appetite, and nobody could get me to answer them. I half expected him at play practice or to come to the schoolhouse, and I began to wish he would hurry up and get it over with, when, after play practice on the second night, I saw him uptown, on the corner, with this blonde.

Mrs. Arrington was driving us home, and he and the blonde were standing on the street corner, just about to get in his car. I never saw that blonde before or since, but she is printed eternally on my mind, and to this good day if I'd run into her across the counter from me in the ten-cent store, whichever one of us is selling lipstick to the other one, I'd know her for sure because I saw her for one half of a second in the street light in Port Claiborne with Foster Hamilton. She wasn't any ordinary blonde, either—dyed hair was in it. I didn't know the term "feather-bed blond" in those days, or I guess I would have thought it. As it was, I didn't really think anything, or say anything, either, but whatever had been galloping along inside me for two solid days and nights came to a screeching halt. Somebody in the car said, being real funny, "Foster Hamilton's got him another girl friend." I just laughed. "Sure has," I said. "Oh, Marileee!" they all said, teasing me. I laughed and laughed.

I asked Foster once, a long time later, "Why didn't you come back after that night you drove me out to Windsor?"

He shook his head. "We'd have been married in two weeks," he said. "It scared me half to death."

"Then it's a mercy you didn't," I said. "It scares *me* half to death right now."

Things had changed between us, you realize, between that kiss and that conversation. What happened was—at least, the main thing that happened was—Foster asked me the next year to go to the high school senior dance with him, so I said all right.

I knew about Foster by then, and that his reputation was not of the best—that it was, in fact, about the worst our county had to offer. I knew he had an uncommon thirst and that on weekends he went helling about the countryside with a fellow that owned the local picture show and worked at a garage in the daytime. His name was A. P. Fortenberry, and he owned a new convertible in a sickening shade of bright maroon. The convertible was always dusty—though you could see A.P. in the garage every afternoon, during the slack hour, hosing it down on the wash rack—because he and Foster were out in it almost every night, harassing the countryside. They knew every bootlegger in a radius of forty miles. They knew girls that lived on the outskirts of towns and girls that didn't. I guess "uninhibited" was the word for A.P. Fortenberry, but whatever it was, I couldn't stand him. He called me into the garage one day—to have a word with me about Foster, he said—but when I got inside he backed me into the corner and started trying it on. "Funny little old girl," he kept saying. He rattled his words out real fast. "Funny little old girl." I slapped him as hard as I could, which was pretty hard, but that only seemed to stimulate him. I thought I'd never get away from him—I can't smell the inside of a garage to this good day without thinking about A.P. Fortenberry.

When Foster drove all the way out to see me one day soon after that—we didn't have a telephone in those days—I thought he'd come to apologize for A.P., and I'm not sure yet he didn't intend for me to understand that without saying anything about it. He certainly put himself out. He sat down and swapped a lot of Port Claiborne talk with Mama—just pleased her to death—and then he went out back with Daddy and looked at the chickens and the peach trees. He even had an opinion on growing peaches, though I reckon he'd given more thought to peach brandy than he'd ever given to orchards. He said when we were walking out to his car that he'd like to take me to the senior dance, so I said O.K. I was pleased; I had to admit it.

Even knowing everything I knew by then (I didn't tell Mama and Daddy), there was something kind of glamorous about Foster Hamilton. He came of a real good family, known for being aristocratic and smart; he had uncles who were college professors and big lawyers and doctors and things. His father had died when he was a babe in arms (tragedy), and he had perfect manners. He had perfect manners, that is, when he was sober, and it was not that he departed from them in any intentional way when he was drunk. Still, you couldn't exactly blame me for being disgusted when, after ten minutes of the dance, I discovered that his face was slightly green around the temples and that whereas he could dance fairly well, he could not stand up by himself at all. He teetered like a baby that has caught on to what walking is, and knows that now is the time to do it, but hasn't had quite enough practice.

"Foster," I whispered, "have you been drinking?"

"Been *drinking*?" he repeated. He looked at me with a sort of wonder, like the national president of the W.C.T.U. might if asked the same question. "It's so close in here," he complained.

It really wasn't that close yet, but it was going to be. The gym doors were open, so that people could walk outside in the night air whenever they wanted to. "Let's go outside," I said. Well, in my many anticipations I had foreseen Foster and me strolling about on the walks outside, me in my glimmering white sheer dress with the blue underskirt (Mama and I had worked for two weeks on that dress), and Foster with his nice broad aristocratic shoulders. Then, lo and behold, he had worn a white dinner jacket! There was never anybody in creation as proud as I was when I first walked into the senior dance that night with Foster Hamilton.

Pride goeth before a fall. The fall must be the one Foster took down the gully back of the boys' privy at the schoolhouse. I still don't know quite how he did it. When we went outside, he put me carefully in his car, helped to tuck in my skirts, and closed the door in the most polite way, and then I saw him heading toward the privy in his white jacket that was swaying like a lantern through the dark, and then he just wasn't there any more. After a while, I got worried that somebody would come out, like us, for air, so I got out and went to the outside wall of the privy and said, "Foster, are you all right?" I didn't get any answer, so I knocked politely on the wall and said, "Foster?" Then I looked around behind and all around, for I was standing very close to the edge of the gully that had eroded right up to the borders of the campus (somebody was always threatening that the whole schoolhouse was going to cave off into it before another school year went by), and there at the bottom of the gully Foster Hamilton was lying face down, like the slain in battle.

What I should have done, I should have walked right off and left him there till doomsday, or till somebody came along who would use him for a model in a statue to our glorious dead in the defense of Port Claiborne against Gen. Ulysses S. Grant in 1863. The battle was over in about ten minutes, too. But I had to consider how things would look—I had my pride, after all. So I took a look around, hiked up my skirts, and went down into the gully. When I shook Foster, he grunted and rolled over, but I couldn't get him up. I wasn't strong enough. Finally, I said, "Foster, Mama's here!" and he soared up like a Roman candle. I never saw anything like it. He walked straight up the side of the gully and gave me a hand up, too. Then I guided him over toward the car and he sat in the door and lighted a cigarette.

"Where is she?" he said.

"Who?" I said.

"Your mother," he said.

"Oh, I just said that, Foster. I had to get you up someway."

At that, his shoulders slumped down and he looked terribly depressed. "I didn't mean to do this, Marilee," he said. "I didn't have any idea it would hit me this way. I'm sure I'll be all right in a minute."

I don't think he ever did fully realize that he had fallen in the gully. "Get inside," I said, and shoved him over. There were one or two couples beginning to come outside and walk around. I squeezed in beside Foster and closed the door. Inside the gym, where the hot lights were, the music was blaring and beating away. We had got a real orchestra especially for that evening, all the way down from Vicksburg, and a brass-voiced girl was singing a 1930s' song. I would have given anything to be in there with it rather than out in the dark with Foster Hamilton.

I got quite a frisky reputation out of that evening. Disappearing after ten minutes of the dance, seen snuggling out in the car, and gone completely by intermission. I drove us away. Foster wouldn't be convinced that anybody would think it at all peculiar if he reappeared inside the gym with red mud smeared all over his dinner jacket. I didn't know how to drive, but I did anyway. I'm convinced you can do anything when you have to—speak French, do a double back flip off a low diving board, play Rachmaninoff on the piano, or fly an airplane. Well, maybe not fly an airplane; it's too technical. Anyway, that's how I learned to drive a car, riding up and down the highway, holding off Foster with my elbow, marking time till midnight came and I could go home without anybody thinking anything out of the ordinary had happened.

When I got out of the car, I said, "Foster Hamilton, I never want to see you again as long as I live. And I hope you have a wreck on the way home."

Mama was awake, of course. She called out in the dark, "Did you have a good time, Marilee?"

"Oh yes, ma'am," I said.

Then I went back to my shed-ceilinged room in the back wing, and cried and cried. And cried.

There was a good bit of traffic coming and going out to our house after that. A. P. Fortenberry came, all pallid and sober, with a tie on and a straw hat in his hand. Then A.P. and Foster came together. Then Foster came by himself.

The story went that Foster had stopped in the garage with A.P. for a drink before the dance, and instead of water in the drink, A.P. had filled it up with grain alcohol. I was asked to believe that he did this because, seeing Foster all dressed up, he got the idea that Foster was going to some family do, and he couldn't stand Foster's family, they were all so stuck-up. While Foster was draining the first glass, A.P. had got called out front to put some gas in a car, and while he was gone Foster took just a little tap more whiskey with another glassful of grain alcohol. A.P. wanted me to understand that Foster's condition that night had been all his fault, that instead of three or four ounces of whiskey, Foster had innocently put down eighteen ounces of sheer dynamite, and it was a miracle only to be surpassed by the resurrection of Jesus Christ that he had managed to drive out and get me, converse with Mama about peach pickle, and dance those famous ten minutes at all.

Well, I said I didn't know. I thought to myself I never

heard of Foster Hamilton touching anything he even mistook for water.

All these conferences took place at the front gate. "I never saw a girl like you," Mama said. "Why don't you invite the boys to sit on the porch?"

"I'm not too crazy about A. P. Fortenberry," I said. "I don't think he's a very nice boy."

"Uh-*huh*," Mama said, and couldn't imagine what Foster Hamilton was doing running around with him, if he wasn't a nice boy. Mama, to this day, will not hear a word against Foster Hamilton.

I was still giving some thought to the whole matter that summer, sitting now on the front steps, now on the back steps, and now on the side steps, whichever was most in the shade, chewing on pieces of grass and thinking, when one day the mailman stopped in for a glass of Mama's cold buttermilk (it's famous) and told me that Foster and A.P. had had the most awful wreck. They had been up to Vicksburg, and coming home had collided with a whole carload of Negroes. The carnage was awful—so much blood on everybody you couldn't tell black from white. They were both going to live, though. Being so drunk, which in a way had caused the wreck, had also kept them relaxed enough to come out of it alive. I warned the mailman to leave out the drinking part when he told Mama, she thought Foster was such a nice boy.

The next time I saw Foster, he was out of the hospital and had a deep scar on his cheekbone like a sunken star. He looked handsomer and more distinguished than ever. I had gotten a scholarship to Millsaps College in Jackson, and was just about to leave. We had a couple of dates before I left, but things were not the same. We would go to the picture show and ride around afterward, having a conversation that went something like this:

"Marilee, why are you such a nice girl? You're about the only nice girl I know."

"I guess I never learned any different, so I can't help it. Will you teach me how to stop being a nice girl?"

"I certainly will not!" He looked to see how I meant

it, and for a minute I thought the world was going to turn over, but it didn't.

"Why won't you, Foster?"

"You're too young. And your mama's a real sweet lady. And your daddy's too good a shot."

"Foster, why do you drink so much?"

"Marilee, I'm going to tell you the honest truth. I drink because I like to drink." He spoke with real conviction.

So I went on up to college in Jackson, where I went in for serious studies and made very good grades. Foster, in time, got a job on the paper in New Orleans, where, during off hours, or so I understood, he continued his investigation of the lower things in life and of the effects of alcohol upon the human system.

It is twenty years later now, and Foster Hamilton is down there yet.

Millions of things have happened; the war has come and gone. I live far away, and everything changes, almost every day. You can't even be sure the moon and stars are going to be the same the day after tomorrow night. So it has become more and more important to me to know that Windsor is still right where it always was, standing pure in its decay, and that the gilded hand on the Presbyterian church in Port Claiborne is still pointing to Heaven and not to Outer Space; and I earnestly feel, too, that Foster Hamilton should go right on drinking. There have got to be some things you can count on, would be an ordinary way to put it. I'd rather say that I feel the need of a land, of a sure terrain, of a sort of permanent landscape of the heart.

Bobbie Ann Mason

Bobbie Ann Mason was born in Mayfield, Kentucky, in 1940, the daughter of a dairy farmer. After she graduated from the University of Kentucky, she moved to New York City to write for television and movie fan magazines. Later she received an M.A. from the State University of New York at Binghamton and a Ph.D. from the University of Connecticut. Her prize-winning stories appear in such journals as *The New Yorker, Atlantic,* and *Redbook.* Her characters typically are farmers and working-class people who inhabit a contemporary rural southern landscape that is rapidly changing. Bobbie Ann Mason has said, "I think the culture I write about is very distinctly Southern. I don't think the people I write about are obsessed with the Past. I don't think they know anything about the Civil War, and I don't think they care. They're kind of naive and optimistic for the most part: they think better times are coming." Although she lives in Pennsylvania, her work captures the colloquial speech of the place where she grew up. She has written two story collections, *Shiloh and Other Stories* (1982) and *Love Life* (1989), and two novels, *Spence & Lila* (1988) and *In Country* (1985), which won the PEN/Hemingway award. She is also the author of two works of criticism, *Nabokov's Garden: A Nature Guide to Ada* (1974) and *The Girl Sleuth: A Feminist Guide to the Bobbsey Twins, Nancy Drew, and Their Sisters* (1975). She has written that her interest in childhood "extends all the way from Nancy Drew to Nabokov, whose magnificent childhood permeates all his works. . . . He read Pushkin as a child, whereas I read Nancy Drew. I am interested in that contrast as a literary theme, and in the culture shock one can experience because of geographical and economic isolation."

State Champions

In 1952, when I was in the seventh grade in Cuba, Kentucky, the Cuba Cubs were the state champions in high school basketball. When the Cubs returned from the tournament in Lexington, a crowd greeted them at Eggner's Ferry bridge over Kentucky Lake, and a convoy fourteen miles long escorted them to Mayfield, the county seat. It was a cold day in March as twelve thousand people watched the Cubs ride around the courthouse square in convertibles. The mayor and other dignitaries made speeches. Willie Foster, the president of the Merit Clothing Company, gave the players and Coach Jack Story free suits from his factory. The coach, a chunky guy in a trench coat like a character in a forties movie, told the crowd, "I'm mighty glad we could bring back the big trophy." And All-Stater Howie Crittenden, the razzle-dazzle dribbler, said, "There are two things I'm proud of today. First, we won the tournament, and second, Mr. Story said we made him feel like a young mule."

The cheerleaders then climbed up onto the concrete seat sections of the Confederate monument and led a final fight yell.

Chick-a-lacka, chick-a-lacka chow, chow, chow
Boom-a-lacka, boom-a-lacka bow, wow, wow
Chick-a-lacka, boom-a-lacka, who are we?
Cuba High School, can't you see?

The next day the Cubs took off in the convertibles again, leading a motorcade around western Kentucky, visiting the schools in Sedalia, Mayfield, Farmington, Murray, Hardin, Benton, Sharpe, Reidland, Paducah, Kevil, La Center, Barlow, Wickliffe, Bardwell, Arlington, Clinton, Fulton, and Pilot Oak.

I remember the hoopla at the square that day, but at the time I felt a strange sort of distance, knowing that in another year another community would have its champions. I was twelve years old and going through a crisis, so I thought I had a wise understanding of the evanescence of victory.

But years later, in the seventies, in upstate New York, I met a man who surprised me by actually remembering the Cuba Cubs' championship. He was a Kentuckian, and although he was from the other side of the state, he had lasting memories of Howie Crittenden and Doodle Floyd. Howie was a great dribbler, he said. And Doodle had a windmill hook shot that had to be seen to be believed. The Cubs were inspired by the Harlem Globetrotters—Marcus Haynes's ball handling influenced Howie and Goose Tatum was Doodle's model. The Cuba Cubs, I was told, were, in fact, the most incredible success story in the history of Kentucky high school basketball, and the reason was that they were such unlikely champions.

"Why, they were just a handful of country boys who could barely afford basketball shoes," the man told me in upstate New York.

"They were?" This was news to me.

"Yes. They were known as the Cinderella Cubs. One afternoon during the tournament they were at Memorial Coliseum watching the Kentucky Wildcats practice. The Cubs weren't in uniform, but one of them called for a ball and dribbled it a few times and then canned a two-hand set shot from midcourt. Adolph Rupp happened to be watching. He's another Kentucky basketball legend—don't you know anything about Kentucky basketball? He rushed to the player at midcourt and demanded, 'How did you do that?' The boy just smiled. 'It was easy, Mr. Rupp,' he said. 'Ain't no wind in here.' "

Of course that was not my image of the Cuba Cubs at all. I hadn't realized they were just a bunch of farm boys who got together behind the barn after school and shot baskets in the dirt, while the farmers around complained that the boys would never amount to anything. I hadn't known how Coach Jack Story had started them off in the seventh grade, coaching the daylights out of those kids until he made them believe they could be champions. To me, just entering junior high the year they won the tournament, the Cuba Cubs were the essence of glamour. Seeing them in the gym—standing tall in those glossy green satin uniforms, or racing down the court, leaping like deer—took my breath away. They had crew cuts and wore real basketball shoes. And the cheerleaders dressed smartly in Crayola-green corduroy circle skirts, saddle oxfords, and rolled-down socks. They had green corduroy jackets as well as green sweaters, with a C cutting through the symbol of a megaphone. They clapped their hands in rhythm and orchestrated their elbows in a little dance that in some way mimicked the Cubs as they herded the ball down the court. "Go, Cubs, Go!" "Fight, Cubs, Fight!" They did "Locomotive, locomotive, steam, steam, steam," and "Strawberry shortcake, huckleberry pie." We had pep rallies that were like revival services in tone and intent. The cheerleaders pirouetted and zoomed skyward in unison, their legs straight and clean like jump shots. They whirled in their circle skirts, showing off their green tights underneath.

I never questioned the words of the yells, any more than I questioned the name Cuba Cubs. I didn't know what kind of cubs they were supposed to be—bear cubs or wildcats or foxes—but I never thought about it. I doubt if anyone did. It was the sound of the words that mattered, not the meaning. They were the Cubs. And that was it. Cuba was a tiny community with a couple of general stores, and its name is of doubtful origin, but local historians say that when the Cuba post office opened, in the late 1850s, the Ostend Manifesto had been in the news. This was a plan the United States had for getting control of the island of Cuba in order to expand the slave trade. The United States demanded that Spain either sell us Cuba at a fair price or surrender it outright.

Perhaps the founding fathers of Cuba, Kentucky (old-time pronunciation: Cubie), were swayed by the fuss with Spain. Or maybe they just had romantic imaginations. In the Jackson Purchase, the western region of Kentucky and Tennessee that Andrew Jackson purchased from the Chickasaw Indians in 1818, there are other towns with faraway names: Moscow, Dublin, Kansas, Cadiz, Beulah, Paris, and Dresden.

The gymnasium where the Cuba Cubs practiced was the hub of the school. Their trophies gleamed in a glass display case near the entrance of the school, between the principal's office and the gymnasium, and the enormous coal furnace that heated the gym hunched in a corner next to the bleachers. Several classrooms opened onto the gym floor, with the study hall at one end. The lower grades occupied a separate building, and in those grades we used an outhouse. But in junior high we had the privilege of using the indoor restrooms, which also opened onto the gym. (The boys' room included a locker room for the team, but like the outhouses, the girls' room didn't even have private compartments.) The route from the study hall to the girls' room was dangerous. We had to walk through the gym, along the sidelines, under some basketball hoops. There were several baskets, so many players could practice their shots simultaneously. At recess and lunch, in addition to the Cuba Cubs, all the junior high boys used the gym too, in frantic emulation of their heroes. On the way to the restroom you had to calculate quickly and carefully when you could run beneath a basket. The players pretended that they were oblivious to you, but just when you thought you were safe and could dash under the basket, they would hurl a ball out of nowhere and the ball would fall on your head as you streaked by. Even though I was sort of a tomboy and liked to run—back in the fifth grade I could run as fast as most of the boys—I had no desire to play basketball. It was too violent.

Doodle Floyd himself bopped me on the head once, but I doubt if he remembers it.

The year of the championship was the year I got in trouble for running in the study hall. At lunch hour one day, Judy Howell and I decided to run the length of the gym as fast as we could, daring ourselves to run through the hailstorm of basketballs flying at us. We raced through the gym and kept on running, unable to slow down, finally skidding to a stop in the study hall. We were giggling because we had caught a glimpse of what one of the senior players was wearing under his green practice shorts (different from the satin show shorts they wore at the games), when Mr. Gilhorn, the history teacher, big as a buffalo, appeared before us and growled, "What do you young ladies think you're doing?"

I had on the tightest Levi's I owned. When they were newly washed and ironed, they fit snug. My mother had ironed a crease in them. I had on a cowboy shirt and a bandanna.

Mr. Gilhorn went on, "Now girls, do we run in our own living rooms? Does your mama let you run in the house?"

"Yes," I said, staring at him confidently. "My mama always lets me run in the house." It was a lie, of course, but it was my habit to contradict whatever anybody assumed. If I was supposed to be a lady, then I would be a cowboy. The truth in this instance was that it had never occurred to me to run in our house. It was too small, and the floorboards were shaky. Therefore, I reasoned, my mother had never laid down the law about not running in the house.

Judy said, "We won't do it again." But I wouldn't promise.

"I know what would be good for you girls," said Mr. Gilhorn in a kindly, thoughtful tone, as if he had just had a great idea.

That meant the duckwalk. As punishment, Judy and I had to squat, grabbing our ankles, and duckwalk around the gym. We waddled, humiliated, with the basketballs beating on our heads and the players following our progress with loud quacks of derision.

"This was your fault," Judy claimed. She stopped

speaking to me, which disappointed me because we had been playmates since the second grade. I admired her short blond curls and color-coordinated outfits. She had been to Detroit one summer.

During study-hall periods, we could hear the basketballs pounding the floor. We could tell when a player made a basket—that pause after the ball hit the backboard and sank luxuriously into the net before hitting the floor. I visited the library more often than necessary just to get a glimpse of the Cubs practicing as I passed the door to the gym. The library was a shelf at one end of study hall, and it had a couple of hundred old books— mostly hand-me-downs from the Graves County Library, including outdated textbooks and even annuals from Kentucky colleges. That year I read some old American histories, and a biography of Benjamin Franklin, and the "Junior Miss" books. On the wainscoted walls of the study hall were gigantic framed pictures, four feet high, each composed of inset portraits of all the faculty members and the seniors of a specific year. They gazed down at us like kings and queens on playing cards. There was a year for each frame, and they dated all the way back to the early forties.

In junior high, we shared the study hall with the high school students. The big room was drafty, and in the winter it was very cold. The boys were responsible for keeping the potbelly stove filled with coal from the coal pile outside, near where the school buses were parked. In grade school during the winter, I had worn long pants under my dresses—little starched print dresses with gathered skirts and puffed sleeves. But in junior high, the girls wore blue jeans, like the boys, except that we rolled them up almost to our knees. The Cuba Cubs wore Levi's and green basketball jackets, and the other high school boys—the Future Farmers of America—wore bright blue FFA jackets. Although the FFA jackets didn't have the status of the basketball jackets, they were beautiful. They were royal-blue corduroy and on the back was an enormous gold eagle, embraced by the words "KENTUCKY" and "GRAVES" (for Graves County).

I had a crush on a freshman named Glenn in an FFA jacket. He helped manage the coal bucket in the study hall. Glenn didn't ride my bus. He lived in Dukedom, down across the Tennessee line. Glenn was one of the Cuba Cubs, but he wasn't one of the major Cubs—he was on the B team and didn't yet have a green jacket. But I admired his dribble, and his long legs could travel that floor like a bicycle. When I waited at the edge of the gym for my chance to bolt to the girls' room, I sometimes stood and watched him dribble. Then one day as I ran pell-mell to the restroom, his basketball hit me on the head and he called to me flirtatiously. "I got a claim on her," he yelled out to the world. If a boy had a claim on a girl, it meant she was his girlfriend. The next day in study hall he showed me an "eight-page novel." It was a Li'l Abner comic strip. In the eight-page novel, Li'l Abner peed on Daisy Mae. It was disgusting, but I was thrilled that he showed me the booklet.

"Hey, let me show you these hand signals," Glenn said a couple of days later, out on the playground. "In case you ever need them." He stuck his middle finger straight up and folded the others down. "That's single *F*," he said. Then he turned down his two middle fingers, leaving the forefinger and the little finger upright, like horns. "That's double *F*," he said confidently.

"Oh," I said. At first I thought he meant hand signals used in driving. Cars didn't have automatic turn signals then.

There were other hand signals. In basketball, the coach and the players exchanged finger gestures. The cheerleaders clapped us on to victory. And with lovers, lightly scraping the index finger on the other's palm meant "Do you want to?" and responding the same way meant "Yes." If you didn't know this and you held hands with a boy, you might inadvertently agree to do something that you had no intention of doing.

Seventh grade was the year we had a different teacher for each subject. Arithmetic became mathematics. The English teacher paddled Frances High and me for stealing Jack Reed's Milky Way from his desk. Jack Reed had even told us he didn't mind that we stole it, that he wanted us to have it. "The paddling didn't hurt," I said to him proudly. He was cute, but not as cute as Glenn, who had a crooked grin I thought was fascinating and later found reincarnated in Elvis. In the study hall I stood in front of the stove until my backside was soaked with heat. I slid my hands down the back of my legs and felt the sharp crease of my Levi's. I was in a perpetual state of excitement. It was 1952 and the Cuba Cubs were on their way to the championship.

Judy was still mad at me, but Glenn's sister Willow-dean was in my class, and I contrived to go home with her one evening, riding her unfamiliar school bus along gravel roads far back into the country. Country kids didn't socialize much. To go home with someone and spend the night was a big event, strange and unpredict-able. Glenn and Willowdean lived with three brothers and sisters in a small house surrounded by bare, stubbled tobacco fields. It was a wintry day, but Willowdean and I played outdoors, and I watched for Glenn to arrive.

He had stayed late at school, practicing ball, and the coach brought him home. Then he had his chores to do. At suppertime, when he came in with his father from milking, his mother handed him a tray of food. "Come on and go with me," he said to me. His Levi's were smudged with cow manure.

His mother said, "Make sure she's got her teeth."

"Have you got your teeth?" Glenn asked me with a grin.

His mother swatted at him crossly. "I meant Bluma. You know who I meant."

Glenn motioned with a nod of his head for me to fol-low him, and we went to a tiny back room where Glenn's grandmother sat in a wheelchair in a corner with a heater at her feet. She had dark hair and lips painted bright orange and a growth on her neck.

"She don't talk," Glenn said. "But she can hear."

The strange woman jerked her body in a spasm of acknowledgment as Glenn set the supper tray in her lap.

He fished her teeth out of a glass of water and poked them in her mouth. She squeaked like a mouse.

"Are you hungry?" Glenn asked me as we left the room. "We've got chicken and dumplings tonight. That's my favorite."

That night I slept with Willowdean on a fold-out coach in the living room, with newspaper-wrapped hot bricks at our feet. We huddled under four quilts and whispered. I worked the conversation around to Glenn.

"He told me he liked you," Willowdean said.

I could feel myself blush. At supper, Glenn had tickled me under the table.

"I'll tell you a secret if you promise not to tell," she said.

"What?" I loved secrets and usually didn't tell them.

"Betty Jean's going to have a baby."

Willowdean's sister Betty Jean was a sophomore. On the school bus her boyfriend Roy Matthews had kept his arm around her during the whole journey, while she cracked gum and looked pleased with herself. That evening at the supper table, Glenn and his brothers had teased her about Roy's big feet.

Willowdean whispered now, "Did you see the way she ate supper? Like a pig. That's because she has to eat for two. She's got a baby in her stomach."

"What will she do?" I asked, scared. The warmth of the bricks was fading, and I knew it would be a freezing night.

"Her and Roy will live with us," said Willowdean. "That's what my sister May Lou did at first. But then she got mad and took the baby off and went to live with her husband's folks. She said they treated her better."

The high school classes were small because kids dropped out, to have babies and farm. They seemed to disappear, like our calves going off to the slaughterhouse in the fall, and it was creepy.

"I don't want to have a baby and have to quit school," I said.

"You don't?" Willowdean was surprised. "What do you want to go to school for?"

I didn't answer. I didn't have the words handy. But she didn't seem to notice. She turned over and pulled the quilts with her. In the darkness, I could hear a mouse squeaking. But it wasn't a mouse. It was Willowdean's grandmother, in her cold room at the back of the house.

That winter, while basketball fever raged, a student teacher from Murray State College taught Kentucky history. She was very pretty and resembled a picture of Pocahontas in one of the library books. One time when she sat down, flipping her large gathered skirt up, I saw her panties. They were pink. She was so soft-spoken she didn't know how to make us behave well enough to accomplish any classwork. Daniel Boone's exploits were nothing, compared to Doodle Floyd's. During the week the Cubs were at the tournament Pocahontas couldn't keep us quiet. The school was raising money for next year's basketball uniforms, and each class sold candy and cookies our mothers had made. Frequently there was a knock at the door, and some kids from another grade would be there selling Rice Krispies squares wrapped in waxed paper, or brownies, or sometimes divinity fudge. One day, while Pocahontas was reading to us about Daniel Boone and the Indians, and we were throwing paper wads, there was a sudden pounding on the door. I was hoping for divinity, and I had a nickel with me, but the door burst open and Judy Howell's sister Georgia was there, crying, "Judy Bee! Mama's had a wreck and Linda Faye's killed."

Judy flew out of the room. For one moment the class was quiet, and then it went into an uproar. Pocahontas didn't know what to do, so she gave us a pop quiz. The next day we learned that Judy's little sister Linda Faye, who was three years old, had been thrown into a ditch when her mother slammed into a truck that had pulled out in front of her. The seventh-grade class took up a collection for flowers. I was stunned by the news of death, for I had never known a child to die. I couldn't sleep, and my mind went over and over the accident, imagining the truck plowing into the car and Linda Faye pitching out the door or through the window. I created various scenes, ways it might have happened. I kept seeing her stretched out stiff on her side, like the dead animals I had seen on our farm. At school I was sleepy, and I escaped into daydreams about Glenn, imagining that I had gone to Lexington too, to watch him in triumph as he was called in from the sidelines to replace Doodle Floyd, who had turned his ankle.

It was a sober, long walk from the study hall to the restroom. The gymnasium seemed desolate, without the Cubs practicing. I walked safely down the gym, remembering the time in the fourth grade when I was a flower girl in the court of the basketball queen. I had carried an Easter basket filled with flower petals down the center of the gym, scattering rose petals so the queen could step on them as she minced slowly toward her throne.

I was too scared to go to the funeral, and my parents didn't want me to go. My father had been traumatized by funerals in his childhood and he didn't think they were a good idea. "The Howells live so far away," Mama said. "And it looks like snow."

That weekend, the tournament was on the radio, and I listened carefully, hoping to hear Glenn's name. The final game was crazy. In the background, the cheerleaders chanted:

> Warren, Warren, he's our man
> If he can't do it—
> Floyd can
> Floyd, Floyd, he's our man
> If he can't do it
> Crittenden can—

The announcer was saying, "Crittenden's dribbling has the crowd on its feet. It's a thrilling game! The Cubs were beaten twice by this same Louisville Manual squad during the season, but now they've just inched ahead. The Cubs pulled even at 39–39 when Floyd converted a charity flip, and then Warren sent them ahead for the

first time with a short one-hander on Crittenden's pass.
The crowd is going wild!"

Toward the end of the game the whole Coliseum—
except for a small Manual cheering section—was yelling,
"Hey, hey, what do you say? It looks like Cuba all the
way!"

As I listened to the excited announcer chatter about
huddles and timeouts and driving jumps and hook shots,
I forgot about Judy, but then on Sunday, when I went
to the courthouse square to welcome the Cubs home, her
sister's death struck me again like fresh news. Seeing so
many people celebrating made me feel uncomfortable, as
if the death of a child always went unnoticed, like a dead
dog by the side of the road. It was a cold day, and I had
to wear a dress because it was Sunday. I wanted to see
Glenn. I had an audacious plan. I had been thinking
about it all night. I wanted to give him a hug, of congratulations. I would plant a big wet kiss on his cheek. I had
seen a cheerleader do this to one of the players once
after he made an unusual number of free throws. It was
at a home game, one of the few I attended. I wanted to
hug Glenn because it would be my answer to his
announcement that he had a claim on me. It would be
silent, without explanation, but he would know what it
meant.

I managed to lose my parents in the throng and I
headed for the east side of the square, where the dime
store was. Suddenly I saw Judy, with her mother, in front
of a shoe store. I knew the funeral had been the day
before, but here they were at the square, in the middle
of a celebration. Judy and her mother were still in their
Sunday church clothes. Judy saw me. She looked straight
at me, then turned away. I pretended I hadn't seen her
and I hurried to the center of the square, looking for
Glenn.

But when I finally saw him up ahead, I stopped. He
looked different. The Cubs, I learned later, had all gone
to an Army surplus store and bought themselves pairs
of Army fatigue pants and porkpie hats. Glenn looked
unfamiliar in his basketball jacket—now he had one—

and the baggy Army fatigues instead of his Levi's. The hat looked silly. I thought about Judy, and how her sister's death had occurred while Glenn was away playing basketball and buying new clothes. I wanted to tell him what it was like to be at home when such a terrible thing happened, but I couldn't, even though I saw him not thirty feet from me. As I hesitated, I saw his parents and Willowdean and one of his brothers crowd around him. Playfully Willowdean knocked his hat off.

The tournament was over, but we were still wild with our victory. Senior play practice started then, and we never had classes in the afternoon because all the teachers were busy coaching the seniors on their lines in the play. Maybe they had dreams of Broadway. If the Cubs could go to the tournament, anything was possible. Judy returned to school, but everyone was afraid to speak to her. They whispered behind her back. And Judy began acting aloof, as though she had some secret knowledge that lifted her above us.

On one last cool day in early spring we had cleanup day, and there were no classes all day. Everyone was supposed to help clean the school grounds, picking up all the discarded candy wrappers and drink bottles. There was a bonfire, and instead of a plate lunch in the lunchroom—too much like the plain farm food we had to eat at home—we had hot dogs, boiled outside in a kettle over the fire. The fat hot dogs in the cold air tasted heavenly. They steamed like breath.

Just as I finished my hot dog and drank the last of my RC (we had a choice between RC Cola and Orange Crush and I liked to notice which people chose which—it seemed to divide people into categories), Judy came up behind me and whispered, "Come out there with me." She pointed toward the graveyard across the road.

I followed her, and as we walked between solemn rows of Wilcoxes and Ingrahams and Morrisons and Crittendens, the noise of the playground receded. Judy located a spot of earth, a little brown heap that was not grassed over, even though the dandelions had already come up and turned to fluff. She knelt beside the dirt pile, like a child in a sandbox, and fussed with a pot of artificial flowers. She straightened them and poked them down into the pot, as if they were real. As she worked tenderly but firmly with the flowers, she said, "Mama says Linda Faye will be waiting for us in heaven. That's her true home. The preacher said we should feel special, to think we have a member of our family all the way up in heaven."

That was sort of how I had felt about Glenn, going to Lexington to the basketball tournament, and I didn't know what to say. I couldn't say anything, for we weren't raised to say things that were heartfelt and gracious. Country kids didn't learn manners. Manners were too embarrassing. Learning not to run in the house was about the extent of what we knew about how to act. We didn't learn to congratulate people; we didn't wish people happy birthday. We didn't even address each other by name. And we didn't jump up and spontaneously hug someone for joy. Only cheerleaders claimed that talent. We didn't say we were sorry. We hid from view, in case we might be called on to make appropriate remarks, the way certain old folks in church were sometimes called on to pray. At Cuba School, there was one teacher who, for punishment, made her students write "I love you" five hundred times on the blackboard. "Love" was a dirty word, and I had seen it on the walls of the girls' restroom—blazing there in ugly red lipstick. In the eight-page novel Glenn showed me, Li'l Abner said "I love you" to Daisy Mae.

Alice Walker

Alice Walker was born in Eatonton, Georgia, in 1944, the daughter of a man who was a sharecropper and a woman whose creativity she celebrated in her influential essay, "In Search of Our Mothers' Gardens." Walker attended Spelman College and received a B.A. from Sarah Lawrence. She worked in the voter registration drive in Georgia in the 1960s, in a Head Start Program in Mississippi, and for the New York City welfare department. She has taught at Jackson State, Tougaloo, Wellesley, the University of Massachusetts, Berkeley, and Brandeis. A frequent contributor to such periodicals as *Negro Digest, Ms., Southern Voices*, and *Essence*, she has written five volumes of poetry and two collections of essays. Her collections of stories are *In Love and Trouble* (1973) and *You Can't Keep a Good Woman Down* (1981), and her novels are *The Third Life of Grange Copeland* (1970), *Meridian* (1976), *The Temple of My Familiar* (1989), and *The Color Purple* (1982), which won a Pulitzer Prize and the American Book Award and was made into a major motion picture. While Alice Walker's writing is often about the racism and sexism black women experience, writer Gloria Steinem finds a universality in her work: "She speaks the female experience more powerfully for being able to pursue it across boundaries of race and class." At the same time that Walker writes of the tragedies in black women's lives, her vision tends toward affirmation, reconciliation, and transformation. Although she lives in San Francisco, she has said that her roots as a writer go back to the tradition of oral storytelling that has been "respected" in the South.

A Sudden Trip Home
in the Spring

For the Wellesley Class

Sarah walked slowly off the tennis court, fingering the back of her head, feeling the sturdy dark hair that grew there. She was popular. As she walked along the path toward Talfinger Hall her friends fell into place around her. They formed a warm jostling group of six. Sarah, because she was taller than the rest, saw the messenger first.

"Miss Davis," he said, standing still until the group came abreast of him, "I've got a telegram for ye." Brian was Irish and always quite respectful. He stood with his cap in his hand until Sarah took the telegram. Then he gave a nod that included all the young ladies before he turned away. He was young and good-looking, though annoyingly servile, and Sarah's friends twittered.

"Well, open it!" someone cried, for Sarah stood staring at the yellow envelope, turning it over and over in her hand.

"Look at her," said one of the girls, "isn't she beautiful! Such eyes, and hair, and *skin*!"

Sarah's tall, caplike hair framed a face of soft brown angles, high cheekbones and large dark eyes. Her eyes enchanted her friends because they always seemed to know more, and to find more of life amusing, or sad, than Sarah cared to tell.

Her friends often teased Sarah about her beauty; they loved dragging her out of her room so that their boyfriends, naive and worldly young men from Princeton and Yale, could see her. They never guessed she found this distasteful. She was gentle with her friends, and her outrage at their tactlessness did not show. She was most often inclined to pity them, though embarrassment sometimes drove her to fradulent expressions. Now she smiled and raised eyes and arms to heaven. She acknowledged their unearned curiosity as a mother endures the prying impatience of a child. Her friends beamed love and envy upon her as she tore open the telegram.

"He's dead," she said.

Her friends reached out for the telegram, their eyes on Sarah.

"It's her father," one of them said softly. "He died yesterday. Oh, Sarah," the girl whimpered, "I'm so sorry!"

"Me too." "So am I." "Is there anything we can do?" But Sarah had walked away, head high and neck stiff.

"So graceful!" one of her friends said.

"Like a proud gazelle" said another. Then they all trooped to their dormitories to change for supper.

Talfinger Hall was a pleasant dorm. The common room just off the entrance had been made into a small modern art gallery with some very good original paintings, lithographs and collages. Pieces were constantly being stolen. Some of the girls could not resist an honest-to-God Chagall, signed (in the plate) by his own hand, though they could have afforded to purchase one from the gallery in town. Sarah Davis's room was next door to the gallery, but her walls were covered with inexpensive Gauguin reproductions, a Rubens ("The Head of a Negro"), a Modigliani and a Picasso. There was a full wall of her own drawings, all of black women. She found black men impossible to draw or to paint; she could not bear to trace defeat onto blank pages. Her women figures were matronly, massive of arm, with a weary victory showing in their eyes. Surrounded by Sarah's drawings was a red SNCC poster of a man holding a small girl whose face nestled in his shoulder. Sarah often felt she was the little girl whose face no one could see.

To leave Talfinger even for a few days filled Sarah with fear. Talfinger was her home now; it suited her better than any home she'd ever known. Perhaps she loved it because in winter there was a fragrant fireplace and snow outside her window. When hadn't she dreamed of fireplaces that really warmed, snow that almost pleasantly froze? Georgia seemed far away as she packed; she did not want to leave New York, where, her grandfather had liked to say, "the devil hung out and caught young gals by the front of their dresses." He had always believed the South the best place to live on earth (never mind that certain people invariably marred the landscape), and swore he expected to die no more than a few miles from where he had been born. There was tenacity even in the gray frame house he lived in, and in scrawny animals on his farm who regularly reproduced. He was the first person Sarah wanted to see when she got home.

There was knock on the door of the adjoining bathroom, and Sarah's suite mate entered, a loud Bach concerto just finishing behind her. At first she stuck just her head into the room, but seeing Sarah fully dressed she trudged in and plopped down on the bed. She was a heavy blonde girl with large milk-white legs. Her eyes were small and her neck usually gray with grime.

"My, don't you look gorgeous," she said.

"Ah, Pam," said Sarah, waving her hand in disgust. In Georgia she knew that even to Pam she would be just another ordinarily attractive *colored* girl. In Georgia there were a million girls better looking. Pam wouldn't know that, of course; she'd never been to Georgia; she'd never even seen a black person to speak to, that is, before she met Sarah. One of her first poetic observations about Sarah was that she was "a poppy in a field of winter roses." She had found it weird that Sarah did not own more than one coat.

"Say listen, Sarah," said Pam, "I heard about your father. I'm sorry. I really am."

"Thanks," said Sarah.

"Is there anything we can do? I thought, well, maybe

you'd want my father to get somebody to fly you down. He'd go himself but he's taking Mother to Madeira this week. You wouldn't have to worry about trains and things."

Pamela's father was one of the richest men in the world, though no one ever mentioned it. Pam only alluded to it at times of crisis, when a friend might benefit from the use of a private plane, train, or ship; or, if someone wanted to study the characteristics of a totally secluded village, island or mountain, she might offer one of theirs. Sarah could not comprehend such wealth, and was always annoyed because Pam didn't look more like a billionaire's daughter. A billionaire's daughter, Sarah thought, should really be less horsey and brush her teeth more often.

"Gonna tell me what you're brooding about?" asked Pam.

Sarah stood in front of the radiator, her fingers resting on the window seat. Down below girls were coming up the hill from supper.

"I'm thinking," she said, "of the child's duty to his parents after they are dead."

"Is that all?"

"Do you know," asked Sarah, "about Richard Wright and his father?"

Pamela frowned. Sarah looked down at her.

"Oh, I forgot," she said with a sigh, "they don't teach Wright here. The poshest school in the U.S., and the girls come out ignorant." She looked at her watch, saw she had twenty minutes before her train. "Really," she said almost inaudibly, "why Tears Eliot, Ezratic Pound, and even Sara Teacake, and no Wright?" She and Pamela thought e.e. cummings very clever with his perceptive spelling of great literary names.

"Is he a poet then?" asked Pam. She adored poetry, all poetry. Half of America's poetry she had, of course, not read, for the simple reason that she had never heard of it.

"No," said Sarah, "he wasn't a poet." She felt weary. "He was a man who wrote, a man who had trouble with his father." She began to walk about the room, and came to stand below the picture of the old man and the little girl.

"When he was a child," she continued, "his father ran off with another woman, and one day when Richard and his mother went to ask him for money to buy food he laughingly rejected them. Richard, being very young, thought his father Godlike. Big, omnipotent, unpredictable, undependable and cruel. Entirely in control of his universe. Just like a god. But, many years later, after Wright had become a famous writer, he went down to Mississippi to visit his father. He found, instead of God, just an old watery-eyed field hand, bent from plowing, his teeth gone, smelling of manure. Richard realized that the most daring thing his 'God' had done was run off with that other woman."

"So?" asked Pam. "What 'duty' did he feel he owed the old man?"

"So," said Sarah, "that's what Wright wondered as he peered into that old shifty-eyed Mississippi Negro face. What was the duty of the son of a destroyed man? The son of a man whose vision had stopped at the edge of fields that weren't even his. Who was Wright without his father? Was he Wright the great writer? Wright the Communist? Wright the French farmer? Wright whose white wife could never accompany him to Mississippi? Was he, in fact, still his father's son? Or was he freed by his father's desertion to be nobody's son, to be his own father? Could he disavow his father and live? And if so, live as what? As whom? And for what purpose?"

"Well," said Pam, swinging her hair over her shoulders and squinting her small eyes, "if his father rejected him I don't see why Wright even bothered to go see him again. From what you've said, Wright earned the freedom to be whoever he wanted to be. To be a strong man a father is not essential."

"Maybe not," said Sarah, "but Wright's father was one faulty door in a house of many ancient rooms. Was that one faulty door to shut him off forever from the rest of

the house? That was the question. And though he answered this question eloquently in his work, where it
really counted, one can only wonder if he was able to
answer it satisfactorily—or at all—in his life."

"You're thinking of his father more as a symbol of
something, aren't you?" asked Pam.

"I suppose," said Sarah, taking a last look around her
room. "I see him as a door that refused to open, a hand
that was always closed. A fist."

Pamela walked with her to one of the college limou-
sines, and in a few minutes she was at the station. The
train to the city was just arriving.

"Have a nice trip," said the middle-aged driver courte-
ously, as she took her suitcase from him. But for about
the thousandth time since she'd seen him, he winked at
her.

Once away from her friends she did not miss them.
The school was all they had in common. How could they
ever know her if they were not allowed to know Wright,
she wondered. She was interesting, "beautiful," only
because they had no idea what made her, charming only
because they had no idea from where she came. And
where they came from, though she glimpsed it—in themselves and in F. Scott Fitzgerald—she was never to enter.
She hadn't the inclination or the proper ticket.

2

Her father's body was in Sarah's old room. The bed had
been taken down to make room for the flowers and
chairs and casket. Sarah looked for a long time into the
face, as if to find some answer to her questions written
there. It was the same face, a dark Shakespearean head
framed by gray, woolly hair and split almost in half by a
short, gray mustache. It was a completely silent face, a
shut face. But her father's face also looked fat, stuffed,
and ready to burst. He wore a navy-blue suit, white shirt
and black tie. Sarah bent and loosened the tie. Tears
started behind her shoulder blades but did not reach her
eyes.

"There's a rat here under the casket," she called to her brother, who apparently did not hear her, for he did not come in. She was alone with her father, as she had rarely been when he was alive. When he was alive she had avoided him.

"Where's that girl at?" her father would ask. "Done closed herself up in her room again," he would answer himself.

For Sarah's mother had died in her sleep one night. Just gone to bed tired and never got up. And Sarah had blamed her father.

Stare the rat down, thought Sarah, surely that will help. *Perhaps it doesn't matter whether I misunderstood or never understood.*

"We moved so much looking for crops, a place to *live*," her father had moaned, accompanied by Sarah's stony silence. "The moving killed her. And now we have a real house, with *four* rooms, and a mailbox on the *porch*, and it's too late. She gone. *She* ain't here to see it." On very bad days her father would not eat at all. At night he did not sleep.

Whatever had made her think she knew what love was or was not?

Here she was, Sarah Davis, immersed in Camusian philosophy, versed in many languages, a poppy, of all things, among winter roses. But before she became a poppy she was a native Georgian sunflower, but still had not spoken the language they both knew. Not to him.

Stare the rat down, she thought, and did. The rascal dropped his bold eyes and slunk away. Sarah felt she had, at least, accomplished something.

Why did she have to see the picture of her mother, the one on the mantel among all the religious doodads, come to life? Her mother had stood stout against the years, clean gray braids shining across the top of her head, her eyes snapping, protective. Talking to her father.

"He called you out your name, we'll leave this place today. Not tomorrow. That be too late. Today!" Her mother was magnificent in her quick decisions.

"But what about your garden, the children, the change of schools?" Her father would be holding, most likely, the wide brim of his hat in nervously twisting fingers.

"He called you out your name, we go!"

And go they would. Who knew exactly where, before they moved? Another soundless place, walls falling down, roofing gone; another face to please without leaving too much of her father's pride at his feet. But to Sarah then, no matter with what alacrity her father moved, foot-dragging alone was visible.

The moving killed her, her father had said, *but the moving was also love*.

Did it matter now that often he had threatened their lives with the rage of his despair? That once he had spanked the crying baby violently, who later died of something else altogether . . . and that the next day they moved?

"No," said Sarah aloud, "I don't think it does."

"Huh?" It was her brother, tall, wiry, black, deceptively calm. As a child he'd had an irrepressible temper. As a grown man he was tensely smooth, like a river that any day will overflow its bed.

He had chosen a dull gray casket. Sarah wished for red. Was it Dylan Thomas who had said something grand about the dead offering "deep, dark defiance"? It didn't matter; there were more ways to offer defiance than with a red casket.

"I was just thinking," said Sarah, "that with us Mama and Daddy were saying NO with capital letters."

"I don't follow you," said her brother. He had always been the activist in the family. He simply directed his calm rage against any obstacle that might exist, and awaited the consequences with the same serenity he awaited his sister's answer. Not for him the philosophical confusions and poetic observations that hung his sister up.

"That's because you're a radical preacher," said Sarah, smiling up at him. "You deliver your messages in person with your own body." It excited her that her brother had at last imbued their childhood Sunday sermons with the

reality of fighting for change. And saddened her that no
matter how she looked at it this seemed more important
than Medieval Art, Course 201.

3

"Yes, Grandma," Sarah replied. "Cresselton is for girls
only, and *no*, Grandma, I am not pregnant."

Her grandmother stood clutching the broad wooden
handle of her black bag, which she held, with elbows
bent, in front of her stomach. Her eyes glinted through
round wire-framed glasses. She spat into the grass outside the privy. She had insisted that Sarah accompany
her to the toilet while the body was being taken into the
church. She had leaned heavily on Sarah's arm, her own
arm thin and the flesh like crepe.

"I guess they teach you how to really handle the
world," she said. "And who knows, the Lord is everywhere. I would like a whole lot to see a Great-Grand.
You don't specially have to be married, you know. That's
why I felt free to ask." She reached into her bag and
took out a Three Sixes bottle, which she proceeded to
drink from, taking deep swift swallows with her head
thrown back.

"There are very few black boys near Cresselton,"
Sarah explained, watching the corn liquor leave the bottle in spurts and bubbles. "Besides, I'm really caught up
now in my painting and sculpting. . . ." Should she mention how much she admired Giacometti's work? No, she
decided. Even if her grandmother had heard of him, and
Sarah was positive she had not, she would surely think
his statues much too thin. This made Sarah smile and
remember how difficult it had been to convince her
grandmother that even if Cresselton had not given her a
scholarship she would have managed to go there anyway.
Why? Because she wanted somebody to teach her to
paint and to sculpt, and Cresselton had the best teachers.
Her grandmother's notion of a successful granddaughter
was a married one, pregnant the first year.

"Well," said her grandmother, placing the bottle with

dignity back into her purse and gazing pleadingly into Sarah's face, "I sure would 'preshate a Great-Grand." Seeing her granddaughter's smile, she heaved a great sigh, and, walking rather haughtily over the stones and grass, made her way to the church steps.

As they walked down the aisle, Sarah's eyes rested on the back of her grandfather's head. He was sitting on the front middle bench in front of the casket, his hair extravagantly long and white and softly kinked. When she sat down beside him, her grandmother sitting next to him on the other side, he turned toward her and gently took her hand in his. Sarah briefly leaned her cheek against his shoulder and felt like a child again.

4

They had come twenty miles from town, on a dirt road, and the hot spring sun had drawn a steady rich scent from the honeysuckle vines along the way. The church was a bare, weather-beaten ghost of a building with hollow windows and a sagging door. Arsonists had once burned it to the ground, lighting the dry wood of the walls with the flames from the crosses they carried. The tall spreading red oak tree under which Sarah had played as a child still dominated the churchyard, stretching its branches widely from the roof of the church to the other side of the road.

After a short and eminently dignified service, during which Sarah and her grandfather alone did not cry, her father's casket was slid into the waiting hearse and taken the short distance to the cemetery, an overgrown wilderness whose stark white stones appeared to be the small ruins of an ancient civilization. There Sarah watched her grandfather from the corner of her eye. He did not seem to bend under the grief of burying a son. His back was straight, his eyes dry and clear. He was simply and solemnly heroic; a man who kept with pride his family's trust and his own grief. *It is strange*, Sarah thought, *that I never thought to paint him like this, simply as he stands; without anonymous meaningless people hovering beyond*

*his profile; his face turned proud and brownly against the
light.* The defeat that had frightened her in the faces of
black men was the defeat of black forever defined by
white. But that defeat was nowhere on her grandfather's
face. He stood like a rock, outwardly calm, the comfort
and support of the Davis family. The family alone
defined him, and he was not about to let them down.

"One day I will paint you, Grandpa," she said, as they
turned to go. "Just as you stand here now, with just"—
she moved closer and touched his face with her hand—
"just the right stubborn tenseness of your cheek. Just
that look of Yes and No in your eyes."

"You wouldn't want to paint an old man like me," he
said, looking deep into her eyes from wherever his mind
had been. "If you want to make me, make me up in
stone."

The completed grave was plump and red. The wreaths
of flowers were arranged all on one side so that from the
road there appeared to be only a large mass of flowers.
But already the wind was tugging at the rose petals and
the rain was making dabs of faded color all over the
green foam frames. In a week the displaced honeysuckle
vines, the wild roses, the grapevines, the grass, would be
back. Nothing would seem to have changed.

5

"What do you mean, come *home*?" Her brother seemed
genuinely amused. "We're all proud of you. How many
black girls are at that school? Just *you*? Well, just one
more besides you, and she's from the North. That's really
something!"

"I'm glad you're pleased," said Sarah.

"Pleased! Why, it's what Mama would have wanted, a
good education for little Sarah; and what Dad would
have wanted too, if he could have wanted anything after
Mama died. You were always smart. When you were two
and I was five you showed me how to eat ice cream
without getting it all over me. First, you said, nip off the
bottom of the cone with your teeth, and suck the ice

cream down. I never knew *how* you were supposed to eat the stuff once it began to melt."

"I don't know," she said, "sometimes you can want something a whole lot, only to find out later that it wasn't what you *needed* at all."

Sarah shook her head, a frown coming between her eyes. "I sometimes spend *weeks*," she said, "trying to sketch or paint a face that is unlike every other face around me, except, vaguely, for one. Can I help but wonder if I'm in the right place?"

Her brother smiled. "You mean to tell me you spend *weeks* trying to draw one face, and you still wonder whether you're in the right place? You must be kidding!" He chucked her under the chin and laughed out loud. "You learn how to draw the face," he said, "then you learn how to paint me and how to make Grandpa up in stone. Then you can come home or go live in Paris, France. It'll be the same thing."

It was the unpreacherlike gaiety of his affection that made her cry. She leaned peacefully into her brother's arms. She wondered if Richard Wright had had a brother.

"You are my door to all the rooms," she said. "Don't ever close."

And he said, "I won't," as if he understood what she meant.

6

"When will we see you again, young woman?" he asked later, as he drove her to the bus stop.

"I'll sneak up one day and surprise you," she said.

At the bus stop, in front of a tiny service station, Sarah hugged her brother with all her strength. The white station attendant stopped his work to leer at them, his eyes bold and careless.

"Did you ever think," said Sarah, "that we are a very old people in a very young place?"

She watched her brother from a window of the bus; her eyes did not leave his face until the little station

was out of sight and the big Greyhound lurched on
its way toward Atlanta. She would fly from there to
New York.

7

She took the train to the campus.

"My," said one of her friends, "you look wonderful!
Home sure must agree with you!"

"Sarah was home?" Someone who didn't know asked.
"Oh, *great*, how was it?"

"Well, how was it?" went an echo in Sarah's head.
The noise of the echo almost made her dizzy.

"How was it?" she asked aloud, searching for, and
regaining, her balance.

"How was it?" She watched her reflection in a pair of
smiling hazel eyes.

"It was fine," she said slowly, returning the smile,
thinking of her grandfather. "Just fine."

The girl's smile deepened. Sarah watched her swinging
along toward the back tennis courts, hair blowing in the
wind.

Stare the rat down, thought Sarah; *and whether it disappears or not, I am a woman in the world. I have buried my father, and shall soon know how to make my grandpa up in stone.*

Fred Chappell

Born in 1936 in Canton, North Carolina, a small industrial town in the mountains, Fred Chappell often writes about his rural roots. He is particularly interested in personality disintegration in the wake of cultural change in the new South. He is the author of five novels—*It Is Time, Lord* (1963), *The Inkling* (1965), *Dagon* (1968), *The Gaudy Place* (1973), and *I Am One of You Forever* (1985)—and a collection of stories, *Moments of Light* (1980). His most recent work is a collection of poems, *First and Last Words* (1989). In *Midquest: A Poem* (1981) he brought together four individually published volumes based on images of the four elements: *River* (1975), *Bloodfire* (1978), *Wind Mountain* (1979), and *Earthsleep* (1980). A contributor to *Sewanee Review, Saturday Evening Post, American Review,* and other periodicals, he has won numerous awards and grants for his writing. A graduate of Duke University, he lives in Greensboro, North Carolina.

Children of Strikers

They were walking, the twelve-year-old girl and the younger bleached-looking boy, by the edge of the black chemical river. A dreadful stink rose off the waters but they scarcely noticed it, scuffling along in the hard sawgrass among the stones. It was a dim day, rain-threatening, and the girl's dun face and dark eyes looked even darker than usual. The boy trailed some little distance behind her and would stop now and again and shade his eyes and look upstream and down. But there was no more reason for him to look about than there was for him to shade his eyes.

Occasionally the girl would bend down and look at something which caught her eye. A scrap of tin, a bit of drowned dirty cloth, jetsam thrown up from the river that poured through the paper factory above and then by the mill settlement behind them. This, "Fiberville," was a quadruple row of dingy little bungalows, and it was where the two of them lived. In the girl's dark face was something harsh and tired, as if she had foretold all her life and found it joyless.

Now she reached down and plucked something off a blackened wale of sand. She glanced at it briefly and thrust it into the pocket of her thin green sweater.

The boy had seen. He caught up with her and demanded to have a look.

"Look at what?" she asked.

"What you found, let me see it."

"It ain't nothing you'd care about."

"How do you know what I care? Let me have a look."

She turned to face him, gazed directly into his sallow

annoying face, those milky blue eyes. "I ain't going to let you," she said.

He gave her a stare, then turned aside and spat. "Well, hell then, it ain't nothing."

"That's right." She walked on and he kept behind. But she knew he was gauging his chances, considering when to run and snatch it out of her pocket. When she heard his footsteps coming sneaky-fast, she wheeled and, without taking aim, delivered him such a ringing slap that his eyes watered and his face flushed.

"God damn you," he said, but he didn't cry.

"I've told you to keep your hands away from me. I told you I wouldn't say it again."

"You ain't so much," he said. "I seen better." But his voice, though resentful, was not bitter.

They walked on a space and she began to relent. "It's a foot," she said.

"What you mean? What kind of foot?"

"It's a baby's foot."

"No!" He glared at her. "I ain't believing that."

"You can believe just whatever little thing you want to."

"I ain't believing you found no baby's foot. Let me see it."

"No."

"Well then, you ain't got nothing . . . How big is it?"

"It's real tiny."

"Gaw," he said. It had seized his imagination. "Somebody probably kilt it."

"Might be."

"They must of kilt it and cut it up in little bits and throwed it in the river." He was wild with the thought of it. "It was some girl got knocked up and her boy friend made her do it."

She shrugged.

"Ain't that awful to think about? A poor little baby . . . Come on and show it to me. I got to see that baby foot."

"What'll you give me?"

They marched along, and he struck a mournful air. "Nothing," he said at last. "I ain't got nothing to give."

She stopped and looked at him, surveyed him head to toe with a weary satisfaction. "No, I guess you ain't," she said. "You ain't got a thing."

"Well then, what you got? Nothing but a poor little dead baby's foot which I don't believe you've got anyhow."

Slowly she reached into her pocket and produced it, held it toward him in her open palm, and he leaned forward, breathless, peering. He shivered, almost imperceptibly. Then his face darkened and his eyes grew brighter and he slapped her hand. The foot jumped out of her hand and fell among the grasses.

"That ain't nothing. It's a doll, it's just a doll-baby's foot."

She could tell that he was disappointed but feeling smug too because, after all, he had caught her in the expectable lie. "I never told you it was real." She stooped and retrieved it. It lay pink and soiled in her soiled palm. Bulbous foot and ankle, little toes like beads of water. It looked too small and too separate from the rest of the world to be anything at all.

He took it from her. "I knowed it wasn't no real baby." Became thoughtful, turning it in his fingers. "Hey, look at this."

"I don't see nothing."

He held the tubular stub of it toward her. "Look how smooth it's cut off. It's been cut with a knife."

She touched it and the amputation was as smooth as the mouth of a soft drink bottle. "What's that got to do with anything?"

It had got darker now, drawing on toward the supper hour. Fiberville grew gloomier behind them, though most of the lights were on in the kitchens of the houses.

"Means that somebody went and cut it on purpose . . ." Another flushed fantasy overcame him. "Say, what if it was a Crazy Man? What if it was a man practicing up before he went and kilt a real baby?"

"It's just some little kid messing around," she said.

"Ain't no kid would have a knife like that." He ran his thumb over the edge of the cut. "Had to be a real *sharp* knife. Or an axe. Maybe it was a meat chopper!"

"Kid might get a knife anywhere."

He shook his head firmly. "No. Look how even it is and ain't hacked up. Kid would rag it up. A man went and done it, being real careful."

At last she nodded assent. Now at the same moment they turned and looked up the river bank into Fiberville, the squat darkening houses where the fathers and mothers and older sons now wore strained strange faces. The men didn't shave everyday now and the women cried sometimes. They had all turned into strangers, and among them at night in the houses were real strangers from far-off places saying hard wild sentences and often shouting and banging tabletops. In the overheated rooms both the light and the shadows loomed with an unguessable violence.

Eudora Welty

Eudora Welty was born in Jackson, Mississippi, in 1909 and still lives in her childhood home. She graduated from the University of Wisconsin and attended Columbia University School of Advertising. During the Depression she worked in Mississippi for newspaper and radio stations and as a publicity agent for the Works Progress Administration from 1933–1936, a job that took her all over the state. She wrote feature stories, took photographs, and talked and listened to people—thereby gathering material for the stories she would write, becoming interested in the importance of place in fiction, and attuning her ear to the rhythms of southern speech. A member of the National Institute of Arts and Letters, she has received numerous grants and awards for her fiction. Among them are two O. Henry awards for her short stories, the Howell medal of the American Academy of Arts and Letters for *The Ponder Heart* (1954), a National Book Award nomination for *Losing Battles* (1970), and a Pulitzer Prize for *The Optimist's Daughter* (1972). She has published a collection of her stories, *The Collected Stories of Eudora Welty* (1980), and her photographs, *Eudora Welty: Photographs* (1989). Although she has lectured and taught at a number of colleges and universities in the United States and in England, she has always returned to Jackson. Welty thinks that affinity with place gives southerners a "narrative sense of human destiny." In a 1972 interview, she explained, "There's someone to remember a man's whole life, every bit of the way along. I think that's a marvelous thing, and I'm glad I got to know something of it. In New York you may have the greatest and most congenial friends, but it's extraordinary if you ever know anything about them except that little wedge of their life that you meet with the little wedge of your life. You don't get that sense of a continuous narrative line. You never see the full circle. But in the South, where people don't move about as much, even now, and where they once hardly ever moved at all, the pattern of life was always right there." Welty's first novel, *Delta Wedding* (1946), was inspired by her memories of growing up. More recently she completed an autobiographical work about her development as a writer, *One Writer's Beginnings* (1984). The following excerpts from the "Listening" section of this work are meditations on the development of her distinctive fictional voices.

from One Writer's Beginnings

Evangelists visited Jackson then; along with the Redpath Chautauqua and political speakings, they seemed to be part of August. Gypsy Smith was a great local favorite. He was an evangelist, but the term meant nothing like what it stands for today. He had no "team," no organization, no big business, no public address system; he wasn't a showman. Billy Sunday, a little later on, who preached with the athletics of a baseball player, threw off his coat when he got going, and in his shirtsleeves and red suspenders, he wound up and pitched his punchlines into the audience.

Gypsy Smith was a real Gypsy; in this may have lain part of his magnetism, though he spoke with sincerity too. He was so persuasive that, as night after night went by, he saved "everybody in Jackson," saved all the well-known businessmen on Capitol Street. They might well have been churchgoers already, but they never had been saved by Gypsy Smith. While amalgamated Jackson church choirs sang "Softly and Tenderly Jesus Is Calling" and "Just as I Am," Gypsy Smith called, and being saved—standing up and coming forward—swept Jackson like an epidemic. Most spectacular of all, the firebrand editor of the evening newspaper rose up and came forward one night. It made him lastingly righteous so that he knew just what to say in the *Jackson Daily News* when one of our fellow Mississippians had the unmitigated gall to publish, and expect other Mississippians to read, a book like *Sanctuary*.

Gypsy Smith may have been a Methodist; I don't know. At any rate, our Sunday school class was expected to attend, but I did not go up to be saved. Though all my life susceptible to anyone on a stage, I never would have been able to hold up my hand in front of the crowd at the City Auditorium and "come forward" while the choir leaned out singing "Come home! Come home! All God's children, come home, come home!" And I never felt anything like the pang of secular longing that I'd felt as a much younger child to go up onto the stage at the Century Theatre when the magician dazzlingly called for the valuable assistance of a child from the audience in the performance of his next feat of magic.

Neither was my father among the businessmen who were saved. As if the whole town were simply going through a temperamental meteorological disturbance, he remained calm and at home on Congress Street.

My mother did too. She liked reading her Bible in her own rocking chair, and while she rocked. She considered herself something of a student. "Run get me my Concordance," she'd say, referring to a little book bound in thin leather, falling apart. She liked to correct herself. Then from time to time her lips would twitch in the stern books of the Bible, such as Romans, providing her as they did with memories of her Grandfather Carden who had been a Baptist preacher in the days when she grew up in West Virginia. She liked to try in retrospect to correct Grandpa too.

I painlessly came to realize that the reverence I felt for the holiness of life is not ever likely to be entirely at home in organized religion. It was later, when I was able to travel farther, that the presence of holiness and mystery seemed, as far as my vision was able to see, to descend into the windows of Chartres, the stone peasant figures in the capitals of Autun, the tall sheets of gold on the walls of Torcello that reflected the light of the sea; in the frescoes of Piero, of Giotto; in the shell of a church wall in Ireland still standing on a floor of sheep-cropped grass with no ceiling other than the changing sky.

I'm grateful that, from my mother's example, I had found the base for this worship—that I had found a love of sitting and reading the Bible for myself and looking up things in it.

How many of us, the South's writers-to-be of my generation, were blessed in one way or another, if not blessed alike, in not having gone deprived of the King James Version of the Bible. Its cadence entered into our ears and our memories for good. The evidence, or the ghost of it, lingers in all our books.

"In the beginning was the Word."

In that vanished time in small-town Jackson, most of the ladies I was familiar with, the mothers of my friends in the neighborhood, were busiest when they were sociable. In the afternoons there was regular visiting up and down the little grid of residential streets. Everybody had calling cards, even certain children; and newborn babies themselves were properly announced by sending out their tiny engraved calling cards attached with a pink or blue bow to those of their parents. Graduation presents to high-school pupils were often "card cases." On the hall table in every house the first thing you saw was a silver tray waiting to receive more calling cards on top of the stack already piled up like jackstraws; they were never thrown away.

My mother let none of this idling, as she saw it, pertain to her; she went her own way with or without her calling cards, and though she was fond of her friends and they were fond of her, she had little time for small talk. At first, I hadn't known what I'd missed.

When we at length bought our first automobile, one of our neighbors was often invited to go with us on the family Sunday afternoon ride. In Jackson it was counted an affront to the neighbors to start out for anywhere with an empty seat in the car. My mother sat in the back with her friend, and I'm told that as a small child I would ask to sit in the middle, and say as we started off, "Now *talk*."

There was dialogue throughout the lady's accounts to my mother. "I said" . . . "He said" . . . "And I'm told she very plainly said" . . . "It was midnight before they finally heard, and what do you think it *was*?"

What I loved about her stories was that everything happened in *scenes*. I might not catch on to what the root of the trouble was in all that happened, but my ear told me it was dramatic. Often she said, "The crisis had come!"

This same lady was one of Mother's callers on the telephone who always talked a long time. I knew who it was when my mother would only reply, now and then, "Well, I declare," or "You don't say so," or "Surely not." She'd be standing at the wall telephone, listening against her will, and I'd sit on the stairs close by her. Our telephone had a little bar set into the handle which had to be pressed and held down to keep the connection open, and when her friend had said goodbye, my mother needed me to prize her fingers loose from the little bar; her grip had become paralyzed. "What did she say?" I asked.

"She wasn't *saying* a thing in this world," sighed my mother. "She was just ready to talk, that's all."

My mother was right. Years later, beginning with my story "Why I Live at the P.O.," I wrote reasonably often in the form of a monologue that takes possession of the speaker. How much more gets told besides!

This lady told everything in her sweet, marveling voice, and meant every word of it kindly. She enjoyed my company perhaps even more than my mother's. She invited me to catch her doodlebugs; under the trees in her backyard were dozens of their holes. When you stuck a broom straw down one and called, "Doodlebug, doodlebug, your house is on fire and all your children are burning up," she believed this is why the doodlebug came running out of the hole. This was why I loved to call up her doodlebugs instead of ours.

My mother could never have told me her stories, and I think I knew why even then: my mother didn't believe them. But I could listen to this murmuring lady all day. She believed everything she heard, like the doodlebug. And so did I.

This was a day when ladies' and children's clothes were

very often made at home. My mother cut out all the dresses and her little boys' rompers, and a sewing woman would come and spend the day upstairs in the sewing room fitting and stitching them all. This was Fannie. This old black sewing woman, along with her speed and dexterity, brought along a great provision of up-to-the-minute news. She spent her life going from family to family in town and worked right in its bosom, and nothing could stop her. My mother would try, while I stood being pinned up. "Fannie, I'd rather Eudora didn't hear that." "That" would be just what I was longing to hear, whatever it was. "I don't want her exposed to gossip"— as if gossip were measles and I could catch it. I did catch some of it but not enough. "Mrs. O'Neil's oldest daughter she had her wedding dress *tried on*, and all her fine underclothes featherstitched and ribbon run in and then— " "I think that will do, Fannie," said my mother. It was tantalizing never to be exposed long enough to hear the end.

Fannie was the worldliest old woman to be imagined. She could do whatever her hands were doing without having to stop talking; and she could speak in a wonderfully derogatory way with any number of pins stuck in her mouth. Her hands steadied me like claws as she stumped on her knees around me, tacking me together. The gist of her tale would be lost on me, but Fannie didn't bother about the ear she was telling it to; she just liked telling. She was like an author. In fact, for a good deal of what she said, I daresay she *was* the author.

Long before I wrote stories, I listened for stories. Listening *for* them is something more acute than listening *to* them. I suppose it's an early form of participation in what goes on. Listening children know stories are *there*. When their elders sit and begin, children are just waiting and hoping for one to come out, like a mouse from its hole.

It was taken entirely for granted that there wasn't any lying in our family, and I was advanced in adolescence before I realized that in plenty of homes where I played with schoolmates and went to their parties, children lied to their parents and parents lied to their children and to each other. It took me a long time to realize that these very same everyday lies, and the strategems and jokes and tricks and dares that went with them, were in fact the basis of the *scenes* I so well loved to hear about and hoped for and treasured in the conversation of adults.

My instinct—the dramatic instinct—was to lead me, eventually, on the right track for a storyteller: the *scene* was full of hints, pointers, suggestions, and promises of things to find out and know about human beings. I had to grow up and learn to listen for the unspoken as well as the spoken—and to know a truth, I also had to recognize a lie.

Michael Malone

Michael Malone was born in North Carolina in 1942 and was educated at the University of North Carolina at Chapel Hill and at Harvard. He is the author of a play, several nonfiction books, and five novels—*Painting the Roses Red* (1975), *The Delectable Mountains* (1977), *Dingley Falls* (1980), *Uncivil Seasons* (1983), and *Time's Witness* (1989). He has taught creative writing at several colleges and now makes his home in Clinton, Connecticut.

Fast Love

It was love at first sight out of the corner of my eye as she flew past the showroom window where I stood eating a double cheeseburger and trying not to hear Merle Longfielder bore our only customer with exaggerations about his racing a 560 horsepower Mustang down in South Carolina last Sunday. It was love in a blur, too. At first I thought maybe something rabid or mentally defective was after her. I didn't think of muggers; we don't have crime in Toomis. (As our billboard for some reason brags, "Toomis is the Smallest Industrial Town in Piedmont, North Carolina." The industries are the state mental hospital and a snuff factory. If you live here, you don't notice the smell.)

So she ran by, and when nothing else followed her, I did. Destiny can't be ignored, no matter how unlikely it may look at first sight—as my grandmother told me when she bought her bus ticket to go march with Martin Luther King, and my father caught her and put her in the (mental) Hospital. This running object of my sudden affection looked unlikely because the women of Toomis walked, on the few occasions when they weren't driving their cars, and in mid-October—whether it was forty degrees or eighty degrees—they wore wool plaid skirts with cardigan sweaters looped over their shoulders. *She* had on white shorts with red stripes and red shoes with white stripes and a sleeveless T-shirt with a picture of Margaret Mead the anthropologist on it. Her red hair in its ponytail leapt all over the place like a fire chasing her down the street.

She wasn't wearing a bra either; I don't mind mentioning that I noticed, because I'd already decided to marry her. We Wintrip males have a long family tradition of choosing a bride in the twinkling of an eye, though I believe I was the first to spot one on the run. My grandfather saw his future wife threatening a bully with a pitchfork as she stood atop a hayrick with her skirts tucked up. My father first glimpsed my mother as she and her fiancé were winning a Tri-Delta jitterbug contest. And I fell in love in a flash with the first jogger anyone ever saw in Toomis, North Carolina. I had loved only once before—unhappily—and now as I panted towards the town limits, a stitch in my side, a throb in my back, fear tingled through me: would this girl break my heart as Betsy Creedmoor had long ago?

I lost her just on the ridge of the first long upgrade of Route 55. The double cheeseburger and knee-high Frye boots did me in. After the spasms ended, I crawled along the shoulder until I felt well enough to walk back to Wintrip Motors where Merle Longfielder, my dad's other vice-president, amused himself by hurling me to the ground on the pretense that he'd already called an ambulance to rush me off for rabies shots. He'd seen the girl, too. "Nice bod," was all the oaf could think of to say.

Merle is my sex, race, and age. So much for what we have in common. His brain is thick and porous. He sports a forty-eight-long maroon polyester blazer, a crew cut, and ought to clip the hairs in his nostrils. In the summer my father and Merle lie side by side together under cars in our driveway; their legs stick out like those of Greek soldiers making love. In their time, they say, they both crunched a lot of cartilage playing high school football. I suspect Dad wishes Merle was his son. So do I. The truth is, during my youth, team sports were never that compelling. I had a weakness for learning; chess, debating, and bicycling were also favorite pastimes—all enthusiasms that struck my dad like a collapsed lung.

My senior year, when my life was in shambles over Betsy Creedmoor, the track coach lured me into a letter sweater. As it happened, I was good. But I'd always been a runner. From childhood on, wherever I was supposed to be, I ran there fast. I ran after the schoolbus. I ran after the footballs my father was always kicking at me in the backyard. I ran like the wind out of necessity. Toughs in my neighborhood, murderous with the baffled envious rage that the stupid sometimes feel for the intelligent, would occasionally bolt out at me from behind bushes or cars and try to destroy my body. When we were twelve, Merle Longfielder chased me through the Baptist nursery school playground with a branch of poison sumac he planned to rub into my eyes. I was jumping three-year-olds as if they were hurdles.

So you might say life trained me as a sprinter; now I planned to use that training to win a wife. Sunday night I pawed my old tennis shoes out from under my bed. Wearing them Monday, I was on the watch for my future bride as soon as I had finished my "real" job and hurried over to Wintrip Motors where from five to eight weekdays and all day Saturday I worked for my dad as one of his two vice-presidents. I did it for the money and for my mother who begged me. Maybe she thought that if my dad's only child refused his offer, he'd put me in the Hospital too, like he did his mother. When he first heard about my real job—state social work—he told me I was nuts. As soon as I tried to explain (on the way home from my college graduation), he let me know *social* meant socialist and *worker* meant Red Square. Then he jack-knifed to a stop, swelled into a frenzy, and announced he was going to beat the Commie crap out of my head with his pistol butt. By the time he got the glove compartment opened, I'd done the quarter mile in four seconds less than my old coach's best hopes. Plus done it wearing an academic gown.

My father's response didn't surprise me. He was a man of the fifties, and in the fifties people all over the country were scared to death that the Communists might take over and brainwash Americans into thinking they had a right to other people's property—especially that property belonging to these people who were scared to death of the Communists. Nearly all the parents in Toomis were afraid their children were going to *catch* Communism;

they thought it was like polio, only there wasn't a vaccine. So when I was nine, I sold glitter-dusted Christmas cards door-to-door and the money went to help fight the Red Menace. From my father's point of view I obviously hadn't sold enough, for Russia had gotten me in the end and mesmerized me into preferring social services to the showroom of Wintrip Motors. And so, for my mother's sake, to allow him to hold up his gray (flattop) head in Toomis, and to help pay my apartment rent so I wouldn't have to live at home with him, I moonlighted at Wintrip Motors.

Thank God I did, and that Wintrip Motors hogged the side of Main Street where Meredith Krantzsky jogged. Meredith Krantzsky was her name, though horribly enough it was Merle Longfielder who formally introduced her to me. My own first try was interrupted. Wearing my sneakers, I was in a nonchalant crouch by the showroom door at six o'clock Monday when she flashed around the corner of Parritt's Diner and flew towards me. By the time we reached the end of the block I could see there were gold specks in the green irises of her eyes. She was altogether as beautiful as I'd suspected from my original blurred impression.

I tried to be casual. "Mind if I run along with you for a little bit?"

She turned, arching a copper brown eyebrow at my seersucker jacket and best paisley tie.

"My name's Blake Wintrip. Felt like. Little exercise. Just happen to notice . . ."

But then I tripped to avoid a baby in a stroller, and while I spiraled about to catch my balance, old Mrs. Etherege spied me from her bus stop bench. She clawed me to a standstill to tell me she'd spent the morning visiting my grandmother at the Hospital. By the time I could unclench her tiny relentless fingers, my bride-to-be was floating like a sunset through the intersection of Culloden and Main. But suddenly she turned, smiled at me; and then she ran on. My heart burst.

Mrs. Etherege pushed up my eyelids and stared. "Blake, are you all right? Heaven's sake. What's the matter? Your face is a deep plum purple. Almost heliotrope." (Mrs. Etherege has been an amateur painter since Southern primitivism became fashionable; she and my grandmother—original founders of the Ladies Art League to which Mother also belonged—used to take their canvases up into the Appalachians where the gift galleries would sell them to tourists.) "Are you sick, son?"

"I'm in love," I told her. "I'm about to propose."

"Oh well, isn't that wonderful? Your folks must be so relieved. Who's the lucky girl?"

"There she goes." I pointed with a sigh as Meredith Krantzsky bounced away towards the horizon.

Mrs. Etherege's tactless remark about my parents' relief was a reference to a sorrow from which only time and an inadvertent discovery of the truth had cured me. My high school sweetheart Betsy Creedmoor temporarily lost her mind senior year under the pressure of being forced by her mother to pretend to be stupid for popularity's sake. Betsy was brainy, and in our region the intellectual life was frowned upon for females. (For males, too, as far as that goes.) Betsy's breakdown—she would sit with her bare feet in the gutter outside Toomis High, drawing designs on her legs with lipstick—was my fall from innocence. The sight of her beautiful vacant eyes was the sword that drove me from the garden into a life of social work among children of Cain. That was almost how my grandmother put it when I went to the Hospital to ask her what I ought to do. She sat at her potter's wheel, hummed her old marching song, "We Shall Overcome," while she thought. Finally, she told me to go to the state university and study injustice. Just be warned, she added, the world felt no obligation to make sense, much less be fair. Grandma was in a position to know. Here she was, perfectly sane, locked away to weave place-mats. Here was Betsy Creedmoor deteriorating beyond repair, and her mother accused me of cruelty when I pleaded that her daughter needed medical help. "Blake, Blake, why do you persecute me and my Betsy so? Why are you trying day and night to lock our little girl away in a snake pit with old nutty trashy types, when you yourself have been so crazy about her ever since fifth grade and followed her around like a little puppy dog?''

Mrs. Creedmoor had never liked me; her feelings were requited. She had blue hair and leathery arms as brown as her golf bag. She smoked five packs of cigarettes a day; even when she was doing the dishes she would pinch her cigarette with a sudsy hand and stick it in a plastic ashtray over the sink. I told her Betsy was getting sicker. She'd sigh. "Oh Blake, darling, what makes you talk that ugly way? Manic-depressive? Why, Betsy's just worked too hard being a silly old bookworm, *like you*, and got herself a little run-down.'' And as this woman was speaking, her sixteen-year-old daughter stood weeping at her reflection in the hall mirror, then stuck her fingers in her mouth and stretched it into a grin howling pig Latin.

Betsy missed so much school because of her nervous breakdown that her grades slipped into the norm. This did, in fact, enhance her popularity. She gave up debate club and playing chess with me at lunch; instead she'd wander about the high school grounds with other girls, collecting, as she wafted by, a huddle of large retarded boyfriends—among them Merle Longfielder. With her mother's blessing, Merle escorted Betsy to the Senior Prom. There, all misty in her trance, she was elected prom queen, and by midnight she lay thrashing like a silverfish in the back seat of Merle's stripped-down Ford. A "friend" told me he saw them. At commencement Betsy was awarded the "Most Popular Girl" trophy. Eventually I began to realize that although Betsy really had lost her mind, it wasn't going to make any difference to people; the man she eventually married, a Sigma Chi pre-dental booze-hound, never even noticed.

Betsy and I both enrolled in the state university. She went, according to her mother's instructions, to work on an M.R.S. degree. I went on my grandmother's recommendation. After my arrival, my father mailed me a local editorial calling the college a "radical-infested swamp of subversives, a compost heap where budding Communist homosexuals meet by night to hide their shameful scheming from God's all-seeing eye." But the truth is we were pitiably behind the times. While everywhere else they had hippies in the sixties, we had beatniks. While the New Left was ripping the ragged social fabric into headbands, we lay on the campus green playing Pete Seeger songs on our bongos. By the time we got around to burning the Marine recruiting stand in front of the dining hall, everywhere else they were back to toga parties and panty raids. I gave up running, except to the john, and passed the time drinking beer and studying injustice.

Betsy Creedmoor said only two things to me throughout our stay. My first year I stood out in the quad listening to a speech by a famous socialist who kept running for president and insisting that somebody arrest him. He told us, "Social reform begins at home. Stand still and look around you!" He went all over the world giving this speech. A group of us were greatly under this man's influence as freshmen. We were cheering him as Betsy ambled by with a weight lifter. She said, "I kid you not. Never take life to heart." That was all. And then our final term I squeezed past her coming out of the bathroom of Slaughterhouse Five, a horribly foul college bar. This time she said, "Check and mate." But her eyes weren't focused, and she may not have even been talking to me. My sole consolation then had been that Betsy had cast off Merle Longfielder for the dentist who wore colored knit shirts with an alligator over his left nipple and who lugged a golf bag to classes.

Yet now three years later all I could wish was that Betsy and Merle were off somewhere in Arizona, upwardly mobile, celebrating their wooden anniversary. The pain might have faded, and arriving at Parritt's Diner I would have been spared the agonizing sight of that hulking body in the maroon blazer leaning across two chili dogs towards Meredith Krantzsky, the girl of my dreams, whom I recognized despite the fact that she was sitting still and wearing a dress. Merle was regaling her with the news that Richard Petty's pit crew could change two tires and fill a gas tank in 12.5 seconds flat when I reached their table. He punched me chummily in the stomach, and after I caught my breath I grabbed the table edge to keep myself from stabbing forks into his cabbage-size hands.

"Merry Krantzsky, I want you to meet Blake Wintrip for about two seconds. Then forget him. He's married with six kids, impotent, queer, and he's got V.D. Say byebye, Blake." (Merle prided himself on his witty urbanity.)

"We've sort of met," she said, and looked up from her tuna salad. "Wintrip? I've got a bone to pick with you. I know your grandmother, I spend a lot of time with her, and . . ."

"How?" My heart cramped with dread. She didn't *look* mad. But of course everyone had let poor Betsy Creedmoor run loose through life, too.

"I work at the Hospital. I'm a psychiatric social worker, and your grandmother shouldn't be in there."

"I know. But I don't think anybody else should be in there either. I'm a social work field coordinator. Nice to meet you."

Right then I could tell she'd decided there was a chance she eventually might like me.

"Merry here's a Yankee. She's been telling me about herself. Just moved down to Toomis from New Hampshire."

"Rhode Island."

"One of those little ones." Merle was holding both his chili dogs in one hand; worse, he was eating them that way as he talked. "I'm pretty sure I drove right through Rhode Island once. I wish I could remember the name of that nice place right off the highway where I ate supper. I bet you'd know it."

I found out (because Merle bragged about it) that he had simply muscled his way into her lunch booth uninvited. That evening in my old high school track shorts I was doing knee bends in front of Parritt's Diner. I'd called in sick; Merle answered the phone and I told him my V.D. was getting worse.

At last through the red and yellow leaves on the trees I saw Meredith Krantzsky jogging towards me. Saw *her*, and in a weaving line behind her, all whooping and sniffling, the eleven members of the Ladies Art League of Toomis—among them old Mrs. Etherege with a stop watch (high-stepping as an ibis), and my mother in Bermuda shorts, though she still looped the obligatory cardigan sweater over her shoulders. Crouching in the doorway, I pretended to relace my sneaker until this extraordinary procession trotted by. Later I learned from my mother that the ladies of the Art League "just loved Merry to death" and were all crazy about jogging, to which Merry had introduced them when they'd invited her to Newcomer's Day.

Reports (and there were plenty) that my mother was out every evening jogging through the streets of Toomis with a throng of elderly female marathoners hit my father like a karate chop. She was also serving broiled fish and raw vegetables for supper, and constantly talking about things like biomechanics. Dad told her succinctly, "You've gone nuts, Hattie."

"Then lucky my jogging coach is a mental health expert," replied my mother from the floor where she was doing sit-ups, her feet in their Adidas stuck under the settee.

"And I don't like the sound of that girl's name. Meredith Krantzsky. You know what kind of name that is? Krantzsky? A you-know-what, I bet. And she works in a nut house, doesn't she? Some kind of Left Wing nut, I bet."

I asked a question then. "If you don't like the nut house, why'd you put Grandma in there?"

"You're out of line, Mister." He talked as if he thought we were in a western movie.

"I think I'm going to ask Miss Krantzsky to marry me."

"Oh Blake! I love her to death." My mother looked me over. "I'm sure she'll tell you to eat less and get more exercise."

"Marry her and you're fired," my dad promised.

My curtain line I gave skipping backwards. "Hey, you

better tell old Merle Longfielder she could be a you-know-what. Because he's after her, too."

Three weeks had now passed since my first sight of my fiancée, and not only were we not engaged, we had never sat down together. But we ran. November flared the trees the bright color of Merry's hair. Indian summer did its best for me, holding back the chill, keeping the evenings crisp and slow. Good jogging weather. I trained, for love, like a fiend. I went on my mother's diet. Whenever Merry wasn't running with the Art League, she and I jogged in the twilight. We exchanged life stories along the way. Her college really had bred all those radical subversives my father itched to pistol-whip. Her version of a Betsy Creedmoor had been a hippie flautist named Matthew who took a charter pilgrimage to Katmandu, where he was arrested for smuggling mescaline. She played chess.

We ran out towards the Hospital where we saw my grandmother and Mrs. Etherege trotting about the grounds as they discussed price hikes they planned to spring on their Appalachian gift galleries. The four of us crossed paths. I said to my grandmother, "What's your advice?"

"Marry this one," she told me.

Merry laughed. I raced to heaven.

That Saturday Merle Longfielder and I walked to Parritt's Diner together for lunch. Inside, he twisted my bicep with his horrible hand. "Now hey! Isn't that that girl from New Hampshire over there? What was her name? Merry? Been saving her for a rainy day. Watch this and learn something, boy."

"Forget it. I don't want you near that girl. Now or ever." I shoved him back. "I catch you around her, I'll shove your jaw up into that cavity where your brain's supposed to be."

Merle stared at me as if I had just stepped out of a UFO. He'd bullied me for more than twenty years. First he started to laugh—it was almost a giggle—then it changed to a puffing snort, and then he swung. I ducked under his basketball of a fist and socked him twice in the gut with a lifetime of injustice behind my punch. By the time he stood back up I was at the door in a prance. Just out of his reach I teased him up that long incline on Route 55. But Merle never even made it to the top.

Meredith Krantzsky and I were married in June. Grandma has the extra bedroom. When the baby comes, we'll move to someplace bigger.

Merle was always quoting Joe Namath: "When you win, nothing hurts." He was right. I feel great.

PART II

Remembering Southern Families

Lee Smith

As soon as Lee Smith learned to write, she began writing fiction. Her first novel was published the year after she graduated from Hollins College, where southern literary critic Louis D. Rubin, Jr., was her professor. Born in Grundy, Virginia, in 1944, Lee Smith sets much of her fiction in or near the Appalachian Mountains. She has written two collections of stories, *Cakewalk* (1980) and *Me and My Baby View the Eclipse* (1990) and seven novels, including the widely acclaimed *Oral History* (1983) and *Fair and Tender Ladies* (1988). She often satirizes what she calls the "rarified world of the finer things in life," a world she depicts in the story "Artists." Her ability to capture the everyday speech of such a wide variety of characters from turn-of-the century mountain herbalists to contemporary teenage boys has caused critics to compare her with Eudora Welty and Flannery O'Connor. Lee Smith says that when she is writing, she hears "it all out loud. While I write, I write real fast, and I almost never revise. I have a sense that I'm sort of transcribing something almost." The winner of numerous prizes for her fiction, including several O. Henry awards, Lee Smith teaches English at North Carolina State University in Raleigh.

Artists

It is one of those hot Sunday afternoons that seem to stretch out, all green and gauzy and golden, over the length of my childhood; I walk in my grandmother's garden. The others are back on the porch in the curly wicker chairs, talking. Their voices come to me in little waves, musical and nonsensical like the sound of bees in the garden, across the wide green grass. I hear my mother's laugh. I cannot see her, or the others. They are cool up there on the porch, I know it; they have iced tea in the tall skinny glasses, with mint. But I want none of that. I attain the roses and halt before them, self-consciously. *I am transfixed by beauty*, I think. In fact I like the names of the roses perhaps more than I like the roses themselves—Pink Cloud, Peace, Talisman, Queen Elizabeth—the names unfurl across my mind like a silken banner, like the banner the children carry in the processional on Easter Sunday. I held a corner of that banner then. My grandmother taught me these names. I lean forward, conscious of myself leaning forward, to examine a Peace rose more closely. It is perfect: the pale velvety outer petals wide and graceful, then turning, curling and closing inward to its strange deep crimson center. The leaves are profuse, glossy, and green. There are thorns. I draw back. What I really prefer is the baby's breath along this border, the riot of pinks by the fountain, the snapdragons like a sassy little army at my feet. But my grandmother has told me that these roses are the pride of her heart. And she grows no common flowers here— no zinnias, no marigolds. This baby's breath is so fragile I can see through it and beyond, to where a lizard flashes shining across a stone and is gone in the phlox. I suck in my breath, feeling dizzy. The sun is so hot on my head and my feet hurt a lot in my patent leather pumps with the straps—because I have nearly outgrown them, I guess, just like my mother says. She says it is time for me to buy some more grown-up shoes, but I have been resisting this, finding excuses not to shop. I like these shoes; I hope that the pain will make me a better person and improve my soul.

For I am all soul these days. I have not missed Sunday School in four years, not even on the occasions when my mother hauls me off to Tucson or Florida and I have to attend strange churches where I ask pastors with funny names to sign affidavits concerning my presence. I mail these documents back to Mr. Beech at the First Methodist Church, so that nothing will mar my record. I have earned so many gold bars for good attendance and special merit that they clink when I walk and Daddy says I look like a major general. I have gone forward to the altar so many times during summer revivals that my mother, embarrassed by my zeal, refuses to let me attend them any more unless I make a solemn pledge that I will not rededicate my life.

"Religious," then, I am also prone to fears and tremblings of a more general nature, and just about anything can set me off: my father when he's in a hurry; my black-headed first cousin Scott who is up in that big old sycamore tree right now, gathering a collection of sycamore balls; anything at all about cripples, puppies, or horses. For instance I had to go to bed for three days after my aunt Dora foolishly read me "The Little Match Girl" a couple of winters ago. I am "sensitive," "artistic," and "delicate," and everybody knows this is how I am, because my grandmother has laid down the law. Rarely does she lay down the law in such definite terms, preferring that her wishes be intuited, but now she has and this is it: *Do not tease Jennifer. Do not cut her hair.*

I wear a white piqué dress in my grandmother's garden this Sunday, a dress my mother ordered from Miller and Rhoads in Richmond, and I love it because I think it makes me look even thinner than I am. I want to be Peter Pan. I also want to be a ballerina, a detective, a missionary among the savages. My pale blond hair, pulled back by a white velvet bow, hangs down to my waist. My bars for good attendance and special merit jangle ever so slightly when I walk. They are calling me now from the porch. I pretend not to hear them, crossing the grass to where the iron marker has been placed near the thicket of willow trees at the edge of the creek. This marker reads

> *The Scent of the Rose for Pardon*
> *The Song of the Birds for Mirth*
> *I am Closer to God in my Garden*
> *Than Anywhere Else on Earth.*

I stop and run my fingers over the raised iron lettering, hot from the sun. "Rose for Pardon" blazes into my palm, and in the back of my mind I see myself in fifteen years or so on a terrible gory battlefield somewhere or maybe it is a dingy tenement, pardoning a man both elegant and doomed—a *rake*. I think he has tuberculosis.

"Jennifer!" My mother stands beside the rose garden, shading her eyes with her hand. "Come on! Your father is ready to go."

My mother wears a red linen dress and black-and-white spectator shoes. She likes golf, bridge, and dancing to jazz music. She hates these Sunday dinners. I follow her back to the porch, pretending not to see Scott, who throws his sycamore balls down with great skill so that they land silently in the grass just close enough to annoy me, too far away for me to complain. Scott is one of the crosses I have to bear. It's too soon for me to tell whether Sammy, my own little brother, will turn out to be such a cross or not; sometimes he exhibits certain promise, I think. Other times he is awful. When he had a virus, for instance, he threw up all over my diary, eliminating February. Sammy is already in the car when we reach the porch. I can see his blond head bobbing up and down in the rear window. My father stands by the gate in his seersucker suit, waiting for us.

"Let's go!" he calls.

"Hurry and make your manners, now," my mother tells me in an undertone. "I can't wait to get out of this damn dress."

I ignore her vulgarity and head for the porch, as full of relatives as it is every Sunday, where I have to wait for my uncle Carl—my great-uncle, actually—to finish telling a story. The other people on the porch are my cousin Virginia, Scott's pretty older sister, whom I hate; my aunt Lucia, Scott's mother, who holds a certain interest for me because of a nervous breakdown she is rumored to have had in her twenties; Scott's boring father, Bill; my maiden aunts Dora and Fern; my grandfather, sweet and bent over in his chair, whittling; and my grandmother, of course, imperious as a queen in the glider, moving ever so slightly back and forth as if pushed by a personal breeze. My grandmother wears a pink brocade suit and a rhinestone sunburst pin, which I consider beautiful. Her hair, faintly blue, is piled into wispy curls that float above her wide white forehead, above her pale blue milky eyes, which look away from them all and across the river to the mountains where the sun goes down.

"And so I hollered, 'Well, John, start it up,' and John started his up, and I got in and started mine—" My uncle Carl is a famous storyteller even in Richmond, where he is in the Legislature, and he will not be hurried. The story he is telling now is one I've heard about a million times before, but it's one of Grandaddy's favorites, all about how Uncle Carl and Grandaddy were the first people in this county to consider automobiles, how they went to Richmond on the train and bought themselves an automobile apiece and drove them home, and then—the climax of the story—how they, the owners of the only two cars in the county at that time, went out driving with their new young wives one Sunday ("in the springtime of our lives," as my uncle Carl always put it) and had a head-on collision on the hairpin curve at the bend of the Green River.

Grandaddy claps his knees with both hands and doubles over laughing, scattering wood chips all over the porch. He is the best-humored man in town—everybody says so—and everybody loves him. He could have been in politics himself, like Uncle Carl, if he had had the ambition. But he did not. He laughs so hard he coughs, and then he can't stop coughing. The wood chips fly all over the porch.

"What a display, Mr. Morris," my grandmother says without moving her mouth.

"Daddy, are you all right?" My own father moves from his place at the gate, starts up the concrete walk. My aunt Lucia stands up by her chair.

"Sure, sure," Grandaddy wheezes and laughs. "But do you remember how those cars *looked*, Carl, how they looked all nosed into each other thataway? And old man Rob Pierce asked if we was trying to mate them."

Daddy grins, on the step below, but Grandmother leans forward to examine the undersides of the fern in the pot by her feet.

"Don't you remember that, Mother?" Daddy asks her.

My grandmother sits up very straight. "Oh yes," she says in her whispery voice. "Oh, yes. I was cast into the river," she says, her head turned away from us all. The glider moves back and forth with the slightest of motions so that in her pink brocade suit she appears to shimmer, tiny and iridescent before us, like a rainbow on the verge of disappearing.

"Now, hell, Flo, that didn't happen at all!" Grandaddy says. "We were right there on the curve where Stinson's store is now. Nobody went in the water."

"Cast into the rushing stream," my grandmother says, looking off.

Uncle Carl guffaws, Grandaddy slaps his knee, and everybody else laughs and laughs.

"Come on now, Jenny," my mother calls. She gets in the car.

"Thank you so much for dinner," I say.

"Oh, can't she stay, Roy?" My grandmother suddenly springs to life. "Can't she?"

"Well, sure, I guess so," my daddy says, with an uneasy look back at the car. "That is, if she—"

"Oh please, Daddy, please please please!" I run down the steps and cling to his hand and beg him.

"Have you met my daughter, Sarah Bernhardt?" my mother says to nobody in particular.

"Please," I beg.

"Well, I suppose so, Jenny, but—" my father says.

My mother closes her door.

"I'll bring her home in the morning," Grandaddy calls from the porch. He stands up to wave as they pull off down the long dirt driveway. Sammy sticks his thumbs in his ears and wiggles his fingers, and grins out the car's back window. They round the bend beyond the willows, almost out of sight. I know that right now inside our car, my mother and my father are lighting cigarettes; I know that they will go home and sit on wrought-iron chairs in the yard with gin and tonic, and Sammy will play with the hose. I wave. When the blue Buick has disappeared, I enter my grandmother's house where it is always cool, always fragrant with something like potpourri, where even the air is cool and dense, and the pictures of people I never knew stare out of the gloom at me from the high dark walls.

My grandmother was famous in our town, and her character was widely discussed. Her dedication to what she referred to as the "finer things of life" was admired by many people and ridiculed by others who found her affected or even laughable. I had heard Mrs. Beech, the preacher's wife, refer to her passionately as a "great lady." I had seen my mother's sister Trixie hold her sides laughing as she and my mother recalled incident after incident in which my grandmother played the role of a comic figure, "putting on airs."

In any case everyone knew her. For at least forty years she had been a fixture in the First Methodist Church, taking her place each Sunday in the third row from the front, left hand side, directly beneath a stained glass win-

dow that depicted Jesus casting the moneylenders out of
the temple in a fury of vermilion and royal blue. She had
headed the Methodist Ladies' Auxiliary and the Garden
Club until all the ladies died who had voted for her year
after year and these groups were overrun by younger
women with pantsuits and new ideas. She still wrote long,
complicated letters to local newspapers on the subjects
of town beautification, historic preservation, and the
evils of drink; she wore hats and white gloves on every
possible occasion. Her manner of dress had changed so
little over the years that even I could recognize its eccen-
tricity. She *dressed up* all the time. I never saw her in
my life without her pale voile or silk or brocade dresses,
without her stockings, without her feet crammed into elegant shoes at least two sizes too small for her, so that at
the end her feet were actually crippled. I never saw her
without her makeup or the flashing rhinestone earrings
and brooches and bracelets that finally she came to
believe—as I believed then—were real.

I never ate dinner in her kitchen, either. Meals were
served in the octagonal dining room with its dark blue
velvet draperies held back by the golden tassels, its wall-
paper featuring gods and goddesses and nymphs. Meals
there were interminable and complicated, involving courses
intended to be brought in and taken away by that long
procession of servants my grandmother hired and then
dispensed of, big hardy dough-faced country women who
could hoe all day but didn't know what to do next when
she rang that silver bell. I was present at the table when
one of them, after a fatal error that escapes me now,
threw her white apron entirely up over her head crying
out "Lord God" in a strangled voice, and fled forever
out the back door as fast as her feet would take her.
(Some people, my grandmother informed me solemnly
after this memorable meal, cannot be taught anything
and are best left down in the mire.) Of course I looked
up "mire." Of course I remember everything on that
table, to this day: the roses in the center, in a silver
bowl; the pale pink crystal water goblets, beaded with icy
drops, sitting on their cut-glass coasters; pale pink linen

napkins and mats or maybe pale green ones and on special occasions the white Irish lace tablecloth; the silver salt and peppers, shaped like swans; the little glass basket, wonderfully wrought, which held pickles or mints or nuts. My grandmother declared the round mahogany table itself to be a family heirloom, then an antique, then a priceless antique from France. In any case it was large, dark, and shining, supported by horrible clawed feet with talons three or four inches long. The knowledge of these cruel taloned feet, right there beneath the table, added greatly to my enjoyment of these meals.

One ate only at the table in that house. Sometimes, though, I let my bestial elements get the best of me and snuck down into the kitchen for a snack after I was sure she was asleep. Once I surprised my grandaddy doing the same thing. The light from the refrigerator turned him light blue in his long flannel nightshirt and he broke into a delighted cackle at the sight of me. We ate cold fried chicken and strawberry ice cream together at the kitchen table and he told me about how he had traded a pony for a bicycle one time when he was a boy and how he tried and tried to get it back after his sprocket chain broke. We laughed a lot. I washed our dishes and he dried them and put them away and kissed me goodnight. His moustache tickled my cheek and I loved him so much at that moment; yet I felt disloyal, too. I climbed up the long stairs in shame.

Grandaddy called my grandmother Flo, but everyone else called her Florence. "Flo," she said severely, "has connotations." I did not know what those were, nor did I inquire. I called her Grandmother, as instructed. Grandmother called Grandaddy "Mr. Morris" in public all her life. Yet despite her various refinements, my grandmother was a country woman herself, born right in this county. Her father had started the First Methodist Church by importing a circuit rider to preach beneath the big sycamore tree, before the house was built. Her father had been by all accounts a hard, dangerous kind of a man, too, who had made a lot of money and had carried a pistol with him at all times. He had not believed

in the education of women, so my grandmother never
went to school. Eventually he was murdered, but no one
ever mentioned this fact in front of my grandmother. She
had married my grandaddy when she was only fifteen
years old, but we didn't mention this fact either. Grandaddy was a carpenter who refused to elevate himself;
he loved his work and he worked only as much as he
had to. At least she had inherited the house.

All her ideas of refinement had come from books and
from the self-improvement courses she took by mail,
many of these deriving from a dubious institution known
as the LaGrande University of Correspondence, which
figured largely in my mother's and Trixie's glee. My
grandmother knew all about these, among other things:
Christianity, including particularly the lives of the saints;
Greek mythology; English country houses; etiquette;
Japanese flower arranging; Henry VIII and all his wives;
crewel embroidery; and the Romantic poets. She wrote
poetry herself and locked it away in a silver filigree box.
She made Japanese flower arrangements for everyone,
strange flat affairs usually involving one large dried
flower, a considerable array of sticks, and little procelain
Oriental men with huge sacks on their backs. She had
ordered dozens of these little men for her arrangements.
My grandmother had read the entire *Encyclopaedia Bri-
tannica* cover to cover, or claimed to have read it; even
my mother found this admirable, although Trixie did not.

The primary cross my grandmother had to bear was
Grandaddy, who steadfastly refused to be drawn into the
rarefied world of the finer things in life. He stayed there,
in fact, only long enough to eat. Otherwise he was whittling, smoking cigars out back, cracking jokes, drinking
coffee in the Rexall drugstore downtown, building cabi-
nets occasionally. He liked to drink bourbon and go
hunting with his friends Mr. J.O. McCorkle and Mr.
Petey Branch. My grandmother seemed to amuse him, I
would say, more than anything else: he liked to "get her
going," as he said. My father did not even like to "get
her going"; but he was her son, too, in many ways, consumed by all that ambition my grandfather lacked, a man

eaten up with the romance of making money. He made a great deal of money, luckily, since my mother was an expensive wife. Very early in their marriage she developed delicate health and terrible sinus allergies that required her removal, for months at a time, to Tucson, where Trixie lived, or to Coral Gables, Florida, where my father bought her a house. My father encouraged these illnesses, which got us all out of town, and in retrospect I can see that they broadened my horizons considerably. At the time, of course, I never wanted to go. I wanted to stay with my grandmother, and sometimes I was allowed to and sometimes not.

I am alone in the parlor while my grandmother works on a watercolor at her easel in the garden (her newest enthusiasm) and Grandaddy is off to the barber shop. I love this parlor, mine now; I love the gloom. I love the blackish gnarled voluptuous roses in the patterned carpet, the tufted velvet chairs and the horsehair sofa; I don't care how uncomfortable anything is. I love the doilies on the tables and the stiff antimacassars on the arms and the backs of the chairs, the *Leaves of Gold* book of poems on the table. I consider this the most beautiful room in the world. I move from portrait to portrait—mostly old daguerrotypes—along the walls, looking. There is stern-faced old Willie Lloyd Morris, her father, staring down his hatchet nose at me across the years. *Murdered.* A delicious chill travels from the top of my head down the length of my spine. There is my grandmother herself, a young girl with a face like a flower, seated primly in a wing chair before a painted backdrop of mountains and stormy clouds. She wears white. I see countless babies, my father among them, in stiff embroidered dresses and little caps. My aunt Lucia gazes soulfully out of her gold-leaf frame at me with strangely glistening dark eyes, like a movie star. My father stands at attention in high boots and the uniform he had to wear at military school, a wonderful uniform with at least a hundred shiny buttons on it. He looks furious. I pause before a family portrait that must have been taken just

after my father finished at the University and swept my
mother off her feet at a debutante ball in Richmond: it
includes my aunts Dora and Fern, young then; my uncle
Carl with a pipe in his mouth; my grandaddy grinning
broadly, his thumbs locked in his suspenders; my grandmother standing slightly to one side; my father, young
and impossibly dashing; and my mother with her hair all
a tangle of curls. Then it hits me: *I am not there.* I am
not anywhere at all in this picture. Looking at this picture
is like being *dead.*

"Gotcha." Scott gooses me.

I whirl around, absolutely furious, mainly because I
don't know how long he's been in this room. I don't
know how long he's been watching me. I jump on him
and we fall in a tangle onto the rose-figured carpet; I
kick him in the nose until it bleeds.

"Hey," Scott keeps saying. "Hey."

We lie on our backs breathing hard.

"What's the matter with you?" Scott says.

"You can't just come in here like this," I say. "You
can't." I start to cry.

Emboldened by my weakness, Scott sits up. "What do
you do in here all the time?" he asks. He scoots closer.
He looks like an Indian, having inherited my aunt Lucia's
dark exotic charm.

"Nothing."

"Come on, Jenny," Scott moves closer still. *He exerts
a certain fascination for her,* I think. *Jennifer succumbs
to his appeal.*

"It's just so pretty," I falter. "I like to look at
everything."

"Like what?" His black eyes shine through the shadows, close to mine.

"Well, like that table over there, like all the stuff on
it." In my confusion I indicate what is in truth my favorite piece of furniture in the room, a multi-tiered mahogany stand that holds my grandmother's figurine collection,
a wondrous array of angels, whistling boys, soldiers,
Colonial ladies, cardinals and doves, unicorns—a whole
world, in fact, topped by her "*pièce de résistance*" as she

calls it, a white porcelain replica of Michelangelo's *David* displayed alone on the top tier. She ordered it from the Metropolitan Museum of Art in New York City. I love the *David* best of all because he seems entirely noble as well as beautiful, his left leg thrust forward in pursuit of justice in some doomed and luminous cause.

"I know why you like that one," Scott sneers.

"What one?"

"That one on the top. That naked guy."

"That's not a naked guy, Scott." I am enraged. "That is Michelangelo's famous statue *David*. It's a work of Art, if you know anything about Art, which you don't, of course." I do not forget to pronounce the statue's name *Daveed*.

"You don't know anything about art either," Scott hollers. "You just like to look at him because he hasn't got any clothes on, that's all."

I stand up shakily. "I'm going to tell Grandmother," I announce.

Scott stands up too. "Go on then. Tell her," he says. "Just go on and tell her. She's even crazier than you are. She's so crazy because Grandaddy has a girlfriend, that's what my mother says. She says it's a good thing Grandmother has an outlet—"

Even in my horror I recognize a certain terrible authenticity in Scott's words; he sounds like his mother, who uses psychological terms with great aplomb—something I have, in fact, admired about my aunt Lucia in the past.

Now I hate her.

"That's a *lie*!" I scream. "Get out of here!"

Instead, Scott grabs me by the shoulders and pulls me to him and kisses me on the mouth until I get my senses together and push him away. "Yuck!" I wipe my mouth with the back of my hand.

Scott is laughing, doubled up with laughing in my grandmother's parlor. "You're crazy, Jenny," he says. "I'm the best kisser in the eighth grade. Everybody says so."

Still laughing he goes out the front door and gets on

his bike and rides off down the curving drive. I go upstairs and brush my teeth. Then I go in the bedroom, fling myself down on the bed, and wait to have a nervous breakdown. *In anguish she considers the violation of her person*, I think.

After a while I went out into the garden and asked Grandmother if I could try painting a rose. "Why yes, Jennifer," she said. Her pale blue eyes lit up. She sent me into the house for more paper, a glass of water, and the lap desk, so that my paper might remain, as she told me, absolutely stationary.

"Anything worth doing is worth doing well," she said severely. "Now then." She dipped her brush into the water and I did the same. "Not too much," she cautioned. "There now."

We painted all that afternoon, until the sun was gone. I did three and a half roses. Then we gathered up all our materials and put them away just so. I went ahead of her, carrying the lap desk and the easel into the hall. I came back out to the porch and found that Grandmother had spread my roses out on the glider. She was studying them. I thought they were pretty good, considering. We stood together and looked at them for some time as they glided ever so gently back and forth.

Grandmother turned to me and clasped me violently against her, smashing me into the spiky sunburst brooch on her bosom. "Jennifer, Jennifer," she said. She had grown little and frail by then and we were almost the same size; I couldn't see her face, but I was lost in her lavender perfume. "Jennifer, Jennifer," she was sobbing. "You must live your life, my darling. You must not get caught up in the press of circumstance; you must escape the web of fate."

I couldn't breathe and I had no idea what "web of fate" she referred to, but I felt as though I had received a solemn commission. "I *will*, Grandmother," I said. "I *will*."

"Hello, ladies!" It was my grandaddy, stumbling a bit on the steps. Mr. J.O. McCorkle stood behind him, grinning broadly. They both appeared to be in a wonderful humor.

"Oh, Mr. Morris, you gave me such a turn!" Grandmother whirled around; seeing Mr. J.O. McCorkle, her eyes narrowed. "Well, Mr. Morris!" she said with a certain significance. She swept up my three and a half roses and vanished mysteriously into the house.

"Now Flo, don't you Mr. Morris me!" Grandaddy called after her. He and Mr. McCorkle laughed. Grandaddy came up on the porch and gave me a whiskery kiss. "How about some checkers?" he asked me.

"Not right now." *Jennifer said meaningfully*, I thought. I turned and went into the house.

This was the first indication of my Talent. Spurred on by my grandmother's enthusiasm, I painted more roses and at length a morning glory. I ventured into daisies, then columbine; I mastered Swedish ivy and attempted, at last, a Still Life. This proved somewhat more difficult because Sammy kept eating the apples and spoiling my arrangement. "Never mind," Grandmother told me when I rode my bicycle over to her house to weep after one such disaster. "Never mind. Great art requires great suffering," my grandmother said.

The second indication of my Talent came from school, where I had written a sonnet, which my English teacher, Miss Hilton, praised extravagantly. This sonnet compared life to a carousel ride, in highly symbolic terms. It was named "The Ride of Life." Miss Hilton sent "The Ride of Life" to the local newspaper, which printed it on the book page. My mother drummed her fingers on the tabletop, reading it. "For heaven's sake!" she said, staring at me. My grandmother clipped it and had it framed. I was suddenly so artistic that my only problem came from trying to decide in which direction to focus my Talent. I did not forget to suffer, either, lying on my bed for a while each afternoon in order to do so.

It didn't surprise me at all, consequently, when I came down with a virus, which all turned into bronchitis, then pneumonia. For a long time I was so sick that they thought I might die. The doctor came every day for a while, and everyone tiptoed. A spirit lamp hissed night and day in my bedroom, casting out a wispy blue jet of steam that formed itself into the camphorous blue haze that still surrounds my entire memory of that illness. Grandaddy came every day, bringing little wooden animals and people carved from pine. Once he brought a little chest of drawers he had made for me. It was incredibly intricate; each drawer opened and shut. I dozed in my blue cloud holding the chest in my hand. Every now and then, when I awakened, I would open and close the drawers. Once when I woke up I saw my mother, in tears, standing beside the bed. This shocked me. I asked for Coca-Cola and drank it; then I sat up and ate some soup; and at the end of that illness it was Grandaddy, not me, who died.

He had a heart attack in the Post Office; after examining him, the hospital doctors said there was nothing they could do and sent him home, where he lived for three more days. During this time, my grandmother's house was filled with people—all our relatives, all his friends—in and out. The kitchen was full of food. My grandmother did not enter his bedroom, as she had not entered mine. Illness made her faint and she had always said so; nobody expected her to. She stayed in the Florida room, painting cardinals and doves, while my aunts sat on the divan and watched her.

From the time they brought Grandaddy home, my own father sat by his bed. I have never, before or since, seen my father as upset—*distraught*, actually, is the word—as he was then. On the morning of the second day, Grandaddy raised his head from the pillow and rolled his eyes around the room. Daddy came forward and bent over him, taking his hand. Grandaddy made a horrible gargling kind of noise in his throat; he was trying to talk. Daddy bent closer. Grandaddy made the noise again. The veins in his forehead stood out, awful and blue. Daddy listened. Then he stood up straight and cleared his own throat.

"By God, I'll do it!" my father announced in a ringing

voice, like somebody in a movie. He turned and left the room abruptly, and all of the people remaining looked at one another. My grandfather continued to stare wildly around the room, with his breath rattling down in his throat.

Twenty minutes later my father came back bringing Mollie Crews, the woman who had been my grandaddy's lover for twenty-five years. Mollie Crews was a large, heavy woman with curly and obviously dyed red hair; she was a beautician, with a shop over the Western Auto store downtown. Mollie Crews wore her white beautician's uniform, an orange cardigan sweater, and white lace-up shoes with thick crepe soles. Her hands flew up to her face when she saw Grandaddy, and her big shoulders shook. Then she rushed over to take the chair at the side of his bed, dropping her purse on the floor. "Oh, Buddy," she sobbed. *Buddy?* I was stunned. Grandaddy's eyes fastened on her and an expression like a smile came to his face. He sank back into the pillow, closing his eyes. The rattle of his breathing softened. Still firmly holding his hand, Mollie Crews took off her cardigan—awkwardly, with her free hand—and slung it over the back of the chair. She reached down and fumbled around in her purse and got a cigarette and lit it with a gold lighter. She exhaled, crossing her legs, and settled down into the chair. My father brought her an ashtray. Aunt Lucia stood up abruptly, flashing her black eyes at everyone. She started to speak and then did not. Aunt Lucia exited theatrically, jerking me from the room along with her. My cousin Virginia followed. The hall outside Grandaddy's room was full of people, and Aunt Lucia pulled me straight through them all, sailing out of the house. Scott was in the front yard. "What did I tell you?" he said. "What did I tell you?"

Aunt Lucia never returned to Grandaddy's room, nor did my uncle Bill or my cousin Virginia or my old maid aunts. Uncle Carl came back from Richmond that night and stayed with him until the end. So did my father, and my mother was in and out. The whole family had to take sides. I went in and sat dutifully with Grandmother, working at her easel in the Florida room. "This is a woodpecker," she said once, exhibiting her latest. "Note the pileations." But I couldn't stay away from Grandaddy's room either, where I was mesmerized by Mollie Crews with her generous slack mouth and her increasingly rumpled beautician's uniform. She looked like a nurse. *A fallen woman*, I told myself, and I watched her sit there hour after hour holding his hand, even when he was in coma and no longer knew she was there. *A Jezebel*, I thought, watching her. I wondered whether she would go to hell.

When my grandfather actually died, everyone left the room except Mollie Crews, and after a long while she came out too, shaking her curls and throwing her head back as she opened the door. We were crowded into the hall. She looked at all of us, and then for some reason she came back to me. "He was a fine man," Mollie Crews said. She was not crying. She looked at everyone again and then she walked out of the house as abruptly as she had come and sat on the front porch until somebody in a battered sky blue Oldsmobile picked her up, and then she was completely and finally gone.

Mollie Crews was the only person in town who did not attend the funeral. Grandmother wore her black silk suit with a hat and a veil. She came in like royalty and sat between Daddy and Aunt Lucia, never lifting her veil, and she stood straight with my mother and me under a black umbrella when they buried Grandaddy in the church cemetery afterward, in a fine gray drizzle that started then and went on for days. Everyone in town paid a call on my grandmother during the week after that, and she sat in her parlor on the tufted sofa beside the tiered table and received them. But her blue eyes had grown mistier, paler than ever, and sometimes the things she said did not connect.

I am walking by the ocean, alone, on the beach near my mother's house in Florida. It is a bright, clear morning. Sometimes I bend down to pick up a shell. Other times I pause and gaze dramatically out to sea, but this

Florida sea is not as I would have it: not tempest-tossed, not filled with drowning nobility clutching at shards of ships. This is a shiny blue Florida sea, determinedly cheerful. The waves have all been choreographed. They arch and break like clockwork at my feet, bringing me perfect shells. The weather is perfect, too. Everything in Florida is hot and easy and tropical and I hate it. My mother has yanked Sammy and me out of school and brought us down here to humor her famous allergies, but I can't even see that she has any allergies: all she does in Florida is shop and play bridge. I feel like a deserter from a beautiful sinking ship. I have deserted my grandmother, just when she needs me most.

My mother has arranged for me to have a Cuban tutor who is supposed to teach me Spanish as well as other things. This Cuban tutor is named Dominica Colindres. She is a plump, dark young woman with greasy hair and big sagging bosoms and pierced ears. She sweats under her arms. I hate Dominica Colindres. I refuse to learn anything she tries to teach me, and I refuse to have anything at all to do with any of the other children my age who try to befriend me on the beach. I walk the shoreline, picking up shells. I think about sin, art, heaven, and hell. Since my arrival in Florida I have written two poems I am rather proud of, although no one else has seen them. One is a poem about the ocean, named "The Sea of Life." The other is named "Artifacts of Existence," about shells.

The sun is hot on my back, even through my long-sleeved shirt, so I pick up one last shell and walk back up the beach to our house. I wear a hat and long pants, too, wet now below the knee: I refuse to get a tan.

My mother is entertaining our next-door neighbors, Mr. and Mrs. Donlevy from Indiana, on the patio. She wears a yellow sundress, looks up and smiles. Mr. and Mrs. Donlevy smile. I do not smile, and my mother raised her eyebrows at Mr. and Mrs. Donlevy in a significant manner. I know they've been talking about me. They are drinking bloody marys and reading the morning paper. The hibiscus around the patio is pink and gaudy in the sun.

I go into my room to work on my shell collection. I have classified my shells as to type, and arranged each type in gradations of hue. This means that every time I find a good shell, I have to move *everything*, in order to put the new shell into its proper place. I take a certain pleasure in the difficulty of this arrangement. I am hard at work when the bells begin to ring, and then, of course, it hits me. *Sunday!* Mother and the Donlevys were reading the Sunday *Times!* It's the first time I've missed Sunday school in four years; my perfect attendance record is broken.

I put my last shell, a *Tellina lineata*, carefully in place. I leave my room. Mother is telling Mr. and Mrs. Donlevy goodbye at the front door. It's already hot; the air conditioner clicks on. I cross the white carpet in the living room, the red tile kitchen floor. Once on the patio, I rush toward the round glass table with its striped umbrella and push it violently, overturning it onto the flagstone. The whole glass top shatters. The umbrella crushes the hibiscus. The frosted bloody mary glasses are flung into the grass, and one of them breaks.

I go back in the kitchen and find Sammy, who has just gotten up, eating Wheaties at the kitchen table. He has made a little mess of his own, fixing his cereal, and this gives me extra satisfaction.

"I had a funny dream," Sammy says.

"What was it about?" I sit down with Sammy at the kitchen table. My mother comes through the kitchen humming and goes out into the patio.

"It was real funny," Sammy says. Milk dribbles down his chin.

"But what was it *about*?" I ask. Out on the patio, my mother has started to shriek.

"I can't remember what it was about." Sammy looks at me with his big blue eyes. "But the name of it was 'The Secret of the Seven Arrows.' "

I get up and hug Sammy as hard as I can, laughing. He *is* cute. Maybe he won't be a cross after all. Then I start to cry. I cry for two hours as hard as I can, and then after that I feel fine and my mother takes Sammy and me out to a fancy restaurant for dinner.

My mother never said a word to me about the broken table, although I knew—in the way children know things, almost like osmosis—that she *knew*. Workmen in overalls came the next day and replaced it. The new umbrella was lime green, with a flowered lining. My mother took me shopping and we bought new bathing suits for both of us; eventually I acquired a tan. I even learned a little Spanish, and on the day before we left, Dominica Colindres pierced my ears.

The day we came back—this was in February—I went straight over to my grandmother's house, of course, riding my bicycle through the falling snow; but even though Daddy had told me how it would be there, I was not prepared. Grandmother had "failed considerably"— those were his words—in the eight weeks we had been gone. Daddy had hired two practical nurses to stay with her, one at night and one in the daytime, and he had turned the dining room into a downstairs bedroom since Grandmother could no longer manage the steps. When I arrived, Grandmother was sitting in the tufted rose velvet wing chair where she always sat in the winter, but she seemed to have shrunk by one or two feet. Or maybe I had grown. In any case Grandmother was so small that she looked lost in the chair, and her feet dangled above the floor. She was dressed as carefully as always, though, and this reassured me at first as I stood in the dark hall pulling off my gloves, my boots, my coat. Noise from the television blared out into the hall: this was very unusual, since Grandmother hated television and said that it had been invented to amuse those people who needed such amusements. The parlor looked all different somehow, lit primarily by the glow of the TV. A tall thin woman stood up from where she sat in the rocking chair. "You must be Jennifer," she said. "I'm Mrs. Page." Mrs. Page wore her hair in a bun; she was crocheting a brown and white afghan.

"It's so nice to meet you." *Jennifer said mechanically like a windup doll*, I thought as I crossed the flowered carpet to take my grandmother's hand. Her hand was little and frail, her bones like the bones of birds. She would not look at me.

"Grandmother!" I said. "Grandmother! It's me, Jennifer." Grandmother watched the TV. I noticed that she wore three of her huge rhinestone brooches in an uneven row on the front of her dress. "Grandmother," I said.

"Excuse me, miss, but she doesn't know anybody right now. She just doesn't. It takes them that way sometimes." Mrs. Page looked up from her afghan and smiled.

"Well, this is my grandmother and she will know *me*!" I snapped.

But she didn't.

The only response she made came later, in that same awful afternoon. I had been sitting on a footstool beside her while it grew darker outside and more snow fell and the bluish-white light of the television danced off the bones of her face. The program had changed again; this time it was a stock car race, and it seemed to interest her. She leaned forward and said something under her breath.

"Do you like this, Grandmother?" I asked.

"Listen," Mrs. Page said. "She just likes it all. She doesn't even know what she's watching."

This infuriated me. "What are you watching, Grandmother?" I asked. On the television screen, the cars went around and around the track, and one of them turned over and burst into flames.

"Serves him right for driving that thing," Mrs. Page remarked.

"*Grandmother*," I said.

Grandmother turned to face me, fully, for the first time. Her light blue eyes seemed to have grown larger. They shone in the pale bony planes of her face. In front of her, the numbered cars went around a track somewhere in Georgia. Grandmother opened her mouth and stared back and forth from me to the television screen.

"What are you watching, Grandmother?" I asked again.

"Art," she said. "I'm watching art, Jennifer."

The cars went around and around on the television, and after watching them for a while longer I put on all my things and rode my bike home through the snow. The road had been scraped but it was still icy in spots, and a fine mist of snow covered the asphalt. I should have been careful, riding, but I was not. I pedaled as hard as I could, gulping huge mouthfuls of cold air and falling flakes of snow. I was moving so fast that the snow seemed to rush straight at me, giving me an odd sense of weightlessness, as if I were somehow suspended between the earth and the sky.

This feeling of suspension—a kind of not belonging, a sense of marking time—hung on even after my grandmother died, which happened a few weeks after our return. Her house was bought by a young attorney. Everything in the house was parceled out among the relatives, who insisted that I should have all the art supplies and the entire figurine collection, including *David*. These things sat in two cardboard boxes in my room for a long time, while I remained suspended. Then one Saturday morning in early May, I knew exactly what I wanted to do. I hauled both boxes out to the tool shed, placing them neatly beside the garden tools. I closed the tool shed door. I went inside and took the saved-up allowance money out of my jewelry box; then I got on my bike and rode straight downtown, parking my bicycle in front of the Western Auto store. Mollie Crews cut my hair off in a page boy, which curled softly under my ears. It looked terrific. Then I rode my bike over to see Scott, who turned out to be—exactly as he had promised—a good kisser. So I grew up. And I never became an artist, although my own career has certainly had its ups and downs, like most careers. Like most lives. Now I keep my grandmother's figurine collection on a special low table for my own children, who spend long hours arranging and rearranging all the little figures in their play.

Shirley Ann Grau

Born in 1929, Shirley Ann Grau grew up in New Orleans, Louisiana, and Montgomery, Alabama. She majored in English at Sophie Newcomb College of Tulane University and went on to graduate school there. She published her first collection of stories, *The Black Prince and Other Stories* (1955), when she was only 24. She has written two other story collections, *The Wind Shifting West* (1973), and most recently *Nine Women* (1985), and five novels, one of which, *The Keepers of the House* (1964), won the Pulitzer Prize. Grau sees in her own family "the two strains—New England and Southern—that were careful to preserve a sense of family continuity," and her writing often focuses on the southern interest in family history. She also writes about people whose harsh lives are reflected in their violent behavior. Although she resists the label of southern writer as too limiting, her works exhibit a strong sense of place and recognizable southern characters. Grau divides her time between Metarie, Louisiana, and Martha's Vineyard, Massachusetts.

Homecoming

The telegram was in the middle of the dining room table. It was leaning against the cut-glass bowl that sometimes held oranges, only this week nobody had bought any. There was just the empty bowl, lightly dust coated and flecked with orange oil. And the telegram.

"Did you have to put it there?" Susan asked her mother.

"It's nothing to be ashamed of," her mother said.

"I'm not ashamed," she said, "but why did you put it there?"

"It's something to be proud of."

"It looks just like a sign."

"People will want to see it," her mother said.

"Yes," Susan said, "I guess they will."

She took her time dressing, deliberately. Twice her mother called up the stairs, "Susan, hurry. I told people any time after three o'clock."

And they were prompt, some of them anyway. (How many had her mother asked? She'd been such a long time on the phone this morning . . .) Susan heard them come, heard their voices echo in the high-ceilinged hall, heard the boards creak with unaccustomed weight. She could follow their movements in the sounds of the old boards. As clearly as if she were looking at them, she knew that the women had stayed inside and the men had moved to the porches.

Wide porches ran completely around two sides of the house, south and west. "Porches are best in old houses like this," her mother often said. "Good, useful porches."

The west porch was the morning porch. Its deep over-hang kept off the sun even in these July afternoons. There was a little fringe of moonflower vine too, across the eaves, like lace on a doily. The big white moonflowers opened each night like white stars and each morning, like squashed bugs, dropped to the ground. They were trained so carefully on little concealed wires up there that they never once littered the porch . . . The south porch was the winter porch. The slanted winter sun always reached that side, bare and clear, no vines, no planting. A porch for old people. Where the winter sun could warm their thin blood, and send it pumping through knotty blue veins. Her grandmother sat out there, sight-less in the sun, all one winter. Every good day, every afternoon until she died . . .

Susan always thought one porch was much bigger until she measured them—carefully, on hands and knees, with a tape measure. How funny, she thought; they seemed so different to be just the same.

On this particular afternoon, as Susan came down-stairs—slowly, reluctantly, hesitating at each step—she glanced toward the sound of men's voices on the south porch. Looking through the screen into the light, she saw no faces, just the glaring dazzle of white shirts. She heard the little rattle of ice in their glasses and she smelled the faint musty sweet odor of bourbon.

Like a wake, she thought. Exactly like a wake.

Her mother called: "In the dining room, dear."

There was coffee on the table, and an ice bucket and a bottle of sherry and two bottles of bourbon. "Come in, Susan," her mother said. "The girls are here to see you."

Of course, Susan thought. They had to be first, her mother's best friends, Mrs. Benson and Mrs. Watkins, each holding a sherry glass. Each kissed her, each with a puff of faint flower scent from the folds of their flowered dresses. "We are so sorry, Susan," they said one after the other.

Susan started to say thank you and then decided to say nothing.

Mrs. Benson peered over her sherry glass at the telegram propped on the table next to the good silver coffeepot. "I thought the Defense Department sent them," she said, "that's what I always heard."

Susan's mother said emphatically, her light voice straining over the words, just the way it always did: "They sent me one for my husband."

"That's right." Mrs. Watkins nodded. "I saw it just now when I came in. Right under the steps in the hall. In that little gold frame."

"When I read that telegram," Susan's mother said, "I got a pain in my heart that I never got rid of. I carried that pain in my heart from that day to this."

And Susan said, patiently explaining: "The army told Harold's parents."

"And the Carters sent word to you," her mother said firmly. Her hand with its broad wedding band flapped in the air. "There on the table, that's the word they sent."

All of a sudden Susan's black dress was too hot and too tight. She was perspiring all over it. She would ruin it, and it was her good dress.

"I'm so hot," she said. "I've got to change to something lighter."

Her mother followed her upstairs. "You're upset," she said, "but you've got to control yourself."

"The way you controlled yourself," Susan said.

"You're mocking now, but that's what I mean, I had to control myself, and I've learned."

"I've nothing to control," Susan said. She stripped off the black dress. The wet fabric stuck and she jerked it free. Close to her ear, a couple of threads gave a little screeching rip. "I've got to find something lighter. It's god-awfully hot down there."

"White," her mother said. "White would be correct."

Susan looked at her, shrugged, and took a white piqué out of the closet.

"Are you all right?"

"I'm fine," Susan said, "I'm great."

* * *

She put the white piqué dress across a chair and sat down on her bed. Its springs squeaked gently. She stretched out and stared up at the crocheted tester and felt her sweat-moistened skin turn cool in the air. She pulled her slip and her bra down to her waist and lay perfectly still.

Abruptly she thought: If there were a camera right over me, it would take a picture of five eyes: the two in my head, the one in my navel, and the two on my breasts. Five eyes staring up at the ceiling.

She rolled over on her stomach.

It was a foolish thing to think. Very foolish. She never seemed to have the proper thoughts or feelings. Her mother now, she had the right thoughts, everybody knew they were right. But Susan didn't . . .

Like now. She ought to be more upset now. She ought to be in tears over the telegram. She'd found it stuck in the crack of the door this morning. "Have been informed Harold was killed at Quang Tri last Thursday." She should have felt something. When her mother got the news of her father's death in Korea, the neighbors said you could hear her scream for a block; they found her huddled on the floor, stretched out flat and small as she could be with the bulging womb that held an almost completed baby named Susan.

Susan lifted her head and looked at the picture on her night table. It was a colored photograph of her father, the same one her mother had painted into a portrait to hang over the living room fireplace. Susan used to spend hours staring into that small frame, trying to sharpen the fuzzy colored lines into the shape of a man. She'd never been quite able to do that; the only definite thing she knew about him was the sharp white lines of his grave marker in Arlington.

"That picture looks just exactly like him," her mother would say. "I almost think he'll speak to me. I'm so glad you can know what your father looked like."

And Susan never said: I still don't know. I never will.

And this whole thing now, her mourning for Harold, it was wrong. All wrong. She hadn't even known him very well. He was just a nice boy from school, a tall thin boy who worked in the A & P on Saturdays and liked to play pool on Sundays, who had a clear light tenor and sang solo parts with her in the glee club. His father worked for the telephone company and they lived on the other side of town on Millwood Street—she knew that much. He'd finished high school a year ago and he'd asked her to his senior prom, though she hadn't expected him to. On the way home, he offered her his class ring. "You can take it," he said. She could see his long narrow head in the light from the porch. "Till I get out of the army."

"Or some other girl wants it."

"Yeah."

Because she couldn't think of anything else, she said: "Okay, I'll keep it for you. If you want it, just write and I'll send it to you."

That was how she got the ring. She never wore it, and he didn't ask for it back. She didn't even see him again. His family moved away to the north part of the state, to Laurel, and Harold went there on his leaves. He didn't come back to town and he didn't call her. He did send a chain to wear the ring on—it was far too big for her finger—from California. She wrote him a thank-you note the very same day. But he didn't answer, and the ring and the chain hung on the back of her dresser mirror. He was just a boy she knew who went in the army. He was just a boy whose ring she was keeping.

Maybe he'd told his parents something more. Why else would they wire her? And what had he told them? All of a sudden there were things she couldn't ask. The world had changed while she wasn't looking.

And Harold Carter was killed. Harold was the name of an English king, and he was killed somewhere too. Now there was another Harold dead. How many had there been in between? Thousands of Harolds, thousands of different battles . . .

Her mother opened the door so quickly it slipped from her hand and smashed into the wall. The dresser mirror shivered and the class ring swung gently on its chain. "Susan, I thought, I just thought of something . . ."

What, Susan asked silently. Did you forget the extra ice? Something like that? Will people have to have warm drinks?

"You're acting very strangely. I've never seen you act like this . . . Did something go on that shouldn't have? Tell me."

Susan tossed a hairbrush from hand to hand. "Maybe it's me," she said, "but I just don't know what people are talking about any more."

"All right," her mother said, "you make me put it this way. Are you going to have a baby?"

Susan stared at the broken edges of the bristles, and she began to giggle. "Harold left a year ago, Mother."

"Oh," her mother said, "oh oh oh." And she backed out the door.

Susan said after her, sending her words along the empty hall where there was nobody to hear them: "That was you who was pregnant. And it was another war."

She put on some more perfume; her flushed skin burned at its touch. She glanced again at the photograph of her father.

You look kind of frozen there. But then I guess you really are. Frozen at twenty-three. Smile and crooked cap and all.

And Susan remembered her grandmother sitting on the porch in the sun, eyes hooded like a bird's, fingers like birds' claws. Senility that came and went, like a shade going up and down. "He don't look nothing like the pictures," she said. She always called her dead son-in-law he, never used his name. "Never looked like that, not dead, not alive." The one hand that was not paralyzed waved at an invisible fly. "Died and went to glory, that boy. Those pictures your mother likes, they're pictures of him in glory. Nothing more nor less than glory."

The old woman was dead now too. There weren't any pictures of her. She'd gone on so long she fell apart, inch by inch of skin. All the dissolution visible outside the grave . . .

Susan breathed on the glass front of her father's picture and polished it with the hem of her slip. The young glorious dead . . . like Harold. Only she didn't have a picture of Harold. And she didn't really remember what he looked like.

She could hear the creak of cane rockers on the porch, the soft mumbling of men's talk. She stood by the screen to listen.

"I'll tell you." Harry Benson, the druggist, was sitting in the big chair, the one with the fancy scrolled back. "They called us an amphibious unit and put us ashore and they forgot about us. Two weeks with nothing to do but keep alive on that beach."

That would be Okinawa. She had heard about his Okinawa.

"And after a while some of the guys got nervous. If they found a Jap still alive they'd work him over good, shoot him seven or eight times, just to see him jump. They kind of thought it was fun, I guess."

"Hold it a minute, Harry," Ed Watkins, who was the railroad agent, said. "Here's Susan."

They both stood up. They'd never done that before.

"We were talking about our wars, honey," Mr. Benson said. "I'm afraid we were."

"That's all right," Susan said. "I don't mind."

"It was crazy, plain crazy," Mr. Watkins said. "Like that guy, must have been '51 or '52."

"Ed, look," Mr. Benson said. "Maybe we ought to stop talking about this."

"Nothing so bad . . . This guy, I don't think I ever knew his name, he was just another guy. And in those days you remember how they came down in waves from the North. You could hear them miles away, yelling and blowing horns. So this time, you could hear them like always, and this guy, the one I didn't know a name for, he puts a pistol right under his jaw and blows the top of his head off. The sergeant just looked at him, and all he can say is, 'Jesus Christ, that son of a bitch bled all over my gun.' "

"Hard to believe things like that now," Mr. Benson said.

"I believe them," Susan said. "Excuse me, I have something to do in the kitchen."

She had to pass through the dining room. Mrs. Benson still had a sherry glass in her hand, her cheeks were getting flushed and her eyes were very bright. Mrs. Watkins had switched from sherry to whiskey and was putting more ice in her highball. Susan's mother poured herself coffee.

Susan thought: Mrs. Benson's going to have an awful sherry hangover and Mrs. Watkins' ulcer is going to start hurting from the whiskey and my mother's drunk about twenty cups of coffee today and that's going to make her sick . . .

She only said, "I'm just passing through."

But she found herself stopping to look at the telegram. At the shape of the letters and the way they went on the page. At the way it was signed: "Mr. and Mrs. Carter." She thought again how strange that was. They were both big hearty people—"Call me Mike," Mr. Carter said to all the kids. "We're Mike and Ida here." Now all of a sudden they were formal.

Like a wedding invitation, Susan thought suddenly. Only just the opposite.

She reached out and touched the paper. It crackled slightly under her fingers. She went on rubbing her thumb across the almost smooth surface, watching the sweat of her skin begin to stain the yellow paper. A little stain, a little mark, but one that would grow if she kept at it.

That was the end of Harold Carter, she thought. He ended in the crisp, crunchy feel of a piece of paper. A tall thin boy who'd taken her to a dance and given her a ring that was too big for her. All that was left of him was a piece of paper.

She'd send the ring back to his parents. Maybe they'd like to have it.

Or maybe they'd rather she kept it. But keeping it would be keeping him. All of a sudden she saw the ring hanging on the side of her dresser mirror, and she looked into its blue stone and way down in its synthetic depths she saw a tiny little Harold, germ-sized and far away. As she looked he winked out.

She put the telegram down. "I really was just going to the kitchen."

"You're not wearing your ring," Mrs. Watkins said.

"No," she said, "no, I never did wear it."

"You must be so upset." Mrs. Benson sipped delicately at the edge of the yellow sherry. "Just like your poor mother."

"I wasn't married to him," Susan said, "it's different."

Her mother was standing next to her, hand on her shoulder. "You would have married him."

"No," Susan said, "no, I don't think so."

"Of course you would have." Her mother was firm. "Why else would he have given you the ring?"

Susan started to say: Because he didn't have anybody else to give it to and he couldn't give it to his mother.

Her mother went on patting her shoulder. "We should be proud of them, Susan. Harold was a fine young man."

Was he? She didn't have the heart to say that aloud either. Did he shoot people to see them squirm? Did he pull the trigger against his own head with fear?

"The young men are so heroic," her mother said. The two women murmured consent. Her mother would know; her mother had lost a husband in a war, she would know.

All the brave young men that die in their glory, Susan thought. And leave rings to girls they hardly knew, and pictures on mantels in houses where they never lived. Rings that don't fit and pictures that don't resemble them.

"Harold was an English king," she said aloud.

"Yes, dear," her mother said patiently. "That's history."

Harold Carter didn't get to sit on porches and remember, the way Watkins and Benson were doing now. He hadn't got to do anything, except go to high school and die. But then, you didn't really know that either, Susan thought. You really didn't know what he did out there, what memories he might have brought back inside his head.

Mrs. Watkins repeated, "All the young men are so brave."

"No," Susan said abruptly. "Not my father, and not Harold. They weren't brave, they just got caught."

In the silence she could hear the soft wheeze of their astonished breaths, and, as she turned, the creak of old boards under her heel. "They don't die in glory." The words came out sounding like her speech at the Senior Debating Society. "They just die dead. Anyway, I was on my way to fix a cup of tea."

Nobody followed her to the kitchen, just the little ribbon of sound from her high heels on the bare boards and the linoleum. She flipped on the fire under the kettle, decided it would take too long and began to heat some water in a pan. Her feet hurt; she kicked off her shoes. The water warmed and she poured it over the instant tea. There were no lemons in the refrigerator; she remembered suddenly that there weren't any oranges on the dining room table either, that today had been marketing day and nobody had gone.

She put sugar in the tea and tasted it. It was barely warm and nasty, salty almost. She'd forgotten to rinse the dishes again. She would drink it anyway, while she made another proper cup. She put the flame back under the kettle. She pushed open the screen door and went out on the kitchen porch.

It was very small, just wide enough for one person to pass between the railing and the garbage can that always stood there. She'd often argued with her mother over that. "Put it in the yard, it just brings flies into the house." "A clean can," her mother said, "does not attract flies." And the can stayed.

She sat down on the railing, wondering if it would leave a stripe on her white dress. She decided she didn't care. She sipped the cold tea and stared out into the back yard, at the sweet peas growing along the wire fence, at the yellow painted boards on the house next door.

She was still staring over there, not seeing anything in particular, not thinking anything at all, when Mr. Benson came around the corner of the house. He walked across the back yard and stopped, finally, one foot on the bottom step.

"You left the girls in quite a state back there," he said.

So they had rushed to the porch to tell the men . . . Susan didn't take her eyes off the sweet peas, the soft gentle colors of the sweet peas. "They get upset real easy."

"I reckon they do," he said, "and they quiet down real easy too."

She began to swing her leg slowly. I shouldn't have left my shoes in the kitchen, she thought. I'll ruin my stockings out here.

"I take it he wasn't even a very good friend of yours," Mr. Benson said.

"You'd take it right." Because that sounded rude, she added quickly: "Nobody understands that. He was just a boy I knew."

"Shouldn't be so hard to understand."

"It's like a wake in there, and that's silly."

"Well," Mr. Benson said, "he was nineteen and maybe when it's somebody that young, you don't even have to know him to mourn after him."

"He was twenty." Susan looked at Mr. Benson then, the short stocky man, with a fringe of black hair around his ears and a sweaty pink skull shining in the heat. His eyes, buried in folds of puffy skin, were small sharp points of blue. My father might have looked like that, she thought.

"Twenty's still pretty young," he said.

"This whole thing is my mother. The minute she saw the telegram all she could think of is how history is repeating itself. She's called everybody, even people she doesn't like."

"I know your mother," Mr. Benson said.

"And that dying in glory talk." Susan hopped off the railing and leaned against it, palms pressing the rough wood. "That's all I ever hear. My mother knows those stories—the ones you were telling on the porch—she knows it's awful and stupid and terrible."

"No," Mr. Benson said, "it isn't awful." He pulled a

cigarette holder from his pocket and began to suck it. "I gave up smoking and this is all I got left . . . You're wrong, child, but maybe the stories don't say it clear enough."

Susan said slowly, "You talk about it all the time, any time."

He nodded slowly and the empty cigarette holder whistled in the hot afternoon air. "Because it was the most glorious thing ever happened to us."

"Too bad you can't tell Harold," she said.

"Take Harold now." Mr. Benson's voice was dull and monotonous, singsonging in the heat. "He didn't have to join up right out of high school. Draft calls been pretty low around here lately."

"He knew he was going to have to, that's why."

"It don't happen like that." He blew through the cigarette holder again, then tapped it on his palm. "Always seemed to me like men have got to have their war. I had to have mine twenty-five years ago. When you're in it maybe it's different, but you got to go. Once you hear about it, you got to go to it."

"That doesn't make any sense to me," Susan said. "None."

"Even when you're in it, you know that if you live, you're going to remember it all the rest of your life. And you know that if there was another war and you were young enough, you'd go again."

"That's stupid," Susan said.

"Maybe. You forget places you've been and you forget women you had, but you don't forget fighting."

Behind her the tea kettle gave a shriek. He glanced up. "Sounds like your water is boiling."

"Yes," she said, "I'll see to it."

He nodded and walked away, leaving a light smell of bourbon behind him. He turned once, lifted his hands, palms up in a little shrugging gesture.

She made her tea. As if she were obeying a set of rules. Things were beginning to feel less strange to her. Even the talk about Harold didn't seem as silly as it had.

I'm beginning not to mind, she thought, but it's still

all mixed up. He was the sort of boy I could have married, but I didn't even know him. And that's lucky for me. Otherwise I might be like my mother. His being dead doesn't really change anything for me. I'll get married after a while to somebody as good as him or even better . . .

She drank her tea slowly; she was sad and happy at once. Harold was a young man who had died. He didn't leave a memory behind, he didn't leave anything. He was just gone and there wasn't even a mark at the place where he had been.

Her mother stood in the door. "Do you feel well enough to come back in, child?"

Susan chuckled, a quiet little self-contented chuckle.

"Whatever is funny, child?"

"You're having such a good time, Mother, you haven't had such a good time in ages."

"Well, really."

"You're alive and I'm alive and Harold's not alive."

"That's horrible."

"Sure."

She followed her mother across the waxed linoleum. "Wait, I've got to put my shoes on."

There just isn't anything, she thought. I'm sorry, Harold. I hope it wasn't too bad and I hope it didn't hurt too much. You and my father. I bet your parents have your picture on the mantel too.

Her shoes were on now and she straightened up.

"Good-by," she said in a very light whisper. "You poor bastard."

And she went inside to join the people.

Ellen Gilchrist

Born in Vicksburg, Mississippi, in 1935, Ellen Gilchrist received her philosophy degree from Millsaps College and later attended the University of Arkansas. She has worked as a contributing editor of the *Vieu Carre Courier* and a commentator on National Public Radio. Besides receiving awards for her poetry and several Pushcart prizes for her stories, her first collection of stories, *In the Land of Dreamy Dreams* (1981), was named an honor book of the Louisiana Library Association, and her second collection, *Victory over Japan* (1984), won an American Book Award. Her most recent collection is *I Cannot Get You Close Enough* (1990). She has also written *Light Can Be Both Wave and Particle* (1989), along with two novels, *The Annunciation* (1983) and *The Anna Papers* (1988), and a screenplay, "A Season of Dreams," which was based on Eudora Welty's short stories and which won a National Educational Television network award. *In the Land of Dreamy Dreams*, from which the following story was taken, focuses on the lives of rich adolescents, most of whom live in New Orleans. Critics have praised Gilchrist's ability to capture the speech patterns of this region. Writer Beverly Lowry has remarked that "The stories are wonderful to tell aloud," and critics have noticed that Gilchrist writes the way she talks. In an interview she said, "I like the feel of words in my mouth and the sound of them in my ears and the creation of them with my hands."

The President of the
Louisiana Live Oak Society

The spring that Robert McLaurin was fourteen he had a black friend named Gus who lived underneath a huge live oak tree in Audubon Park. It was a tree so old and imposing that people in New Orleans called it the President of the Louisiana Live Oak Society.

Gus had a regular home somewhere inside the St. Thomas Street project, with a mother and brothers and sisters, but for all practical purposes he lived underneath the two-hundred-year-old tree in front of Dr. Alton Ochsner's palatial stucco house on Exposition Boulevard.

Imagine a brilliant day in early spring. It is the middle of the afternoon and under the low-hanging branches of the oak tree the air is quiet and cool and smells of all the gardens on the boulevard; confederate jasmine, honeysuckle, sweet alyssum, magnolia, every stereotyped southern flower you can imagine has mingled its individual odor into an ardent humid soup.

In the distance traffic is going along the avenue and a snatch of music floats across the street from the conservatory at Loyola University.

There is room under the tree for twenty or thirty kids on a good day. It is a perfect office for the youngest and most successful dope pushers on the river side of St. Charles Avenue.

Those spring afternoons of 1971 Robert would cut his last-period physical education class and come riding up on his bike playing his portable radio at full volume. Station WTIX would be playing a love song by Judy Collins or "American Pie" by Don McLean, the national anthem of 1971.

Gus would be curled up asleep in the roots of the tree. From a distance he looked like an old catcher's mitt. He wore the same thing every day, a brown leather flight jacket and a pair of indefinite-colored plaid pants so worn that the lines of the plaid all ran together at the edges.

"You got any money?" Gus would ask, rubbing the sleep from his eyes with a dirty fist.

"Yeah, I got plenty. Last week they gave me twenty dollars to buy a track suit with. You want to get a mufflelata?"

"Let's smoke first."

Then Gus would open his cigar box, carefully remove a paper from its folder, pour the beautifully manicured dope onto the paper and roll it into a thin cylinder. He was careful, keeping his back to the wind if there was any so as not to spill a piece. He performed his ceremony to perfection, the rank aroma of his slept-in clothes rising to meet the spectacular smell of the marijuana as he lit the joint with dignity and passed it to Robert.

"How much stuff we got?" Robert asked.

"Not much. We got to find Uncle Clarence and hit him up. We hardly got enough for everyone that's coming today."

Roman Catholic girls in plaid uniform skirts rode by on bikes, their legs flashing in the sunlight.

"You know many of them Catholic girls?" Gus asked, making conversation.

"Yeah, I know them, but they don't talk to me. They're pretty stuck-up."

"How come?" Gus said.

"They go out with older guys. See that one over there," and he pointed out Darlene Trilling, riding by on a ten-speed; "she's really Jewish. She loves a senior in high school but her parents won't let her go out with him. She lives next door to me. She's probably going off somewhere to meet him right this minute."

"How come they won't let her?" Gus asked.

"They're probably afraid he'll give her some dope or something."

Gus started laughing his famous laugh. His face lit up like a three-tiered chandelier. He didn't hold anything back when he laughed.

"You should have seen my momma last Saturday," he said. "She outran a black cop. He couldn't catch her for anything and he knows that block as good as she does. She's fast as lightning. I'm fast like her."

"Is she a big woman?" Robert asked politely.

"Naw, she's little like me. One time when I got sick she put me in her nightgown. It just fit."

The oak tree held the boys like a spell. They rolled another joint.

"Someday I'll get a Buick and deal out of it," Gus said.

"What if they make dope legal?"

Gus looked scared. He looked like Robert had suggested they were going to drop a bomb on the park that very afternoon.

"They can't make it legal. The bars won't let them. It would run all the bars out of business."

They smoked in peace, talking about cars.

"Let's go get a mufflelata before the other kids get here," Robert said, stretching and getting up.

Gus hopped on the handlebars of Robert's bike and they rode off to Tranchina's, an Italian restaurant on Magazine Street that sells mufflelata sandwiches to go. A mufflelata is a plate-sized loaf of wop bread piled high with salami, bologna, pepperoni, mozzarella cheese, and soaked with olive salad. Gus and Robert ate out frequently that spring and this was one of their favorite meals.

"I wish we could get a cold beer to go with the mufflelata."

"There's no place will sell us one. I'll steal some out of the refrigerator for tomorrow."

"What about Darby's, the bookie?"

"Naw, he won't take a chance just to sell a couple of beers."

"Well, we can get an Icee at the Tote-Sum store."

A baby-blue Lincoln Continental turned the corner by the Chandlers' white picket fence and nearly ran over them. They were stoned, riding along looking at the red-and-pink azaleas and didn't see it coming. Gus managed to jump free and landed on his feet still holding the cigar box.

"Robert!" It was his mother. She had just come from the beauty parlor and her hair looked like a helmet for the Los Angeles Rams.

"Robert, come here to me." She pulled his head into the car window. "What are you doing with that black boy?" Robert's mother was a liberal. She never called black people niggers or Negroes even when she was mad at them.

"He's just a kid. I was giving him a ride to the Tote-Sum."

"Why aren't you at practice?" Her helmet moved up and down as she talked.

"They canceled it. The coach is sick. Listen, you almost ran over us, do you know that?" He had her on the defensive. She was very sensitive about her driving.

"Robert, I'm on my way to the grocery. You be home at six."

She drove off wearing her philosophical look. Jean-Paul Sartre couldn't have done it better.

"That was my mother."

"You scared of her?"

"God no. She's scared of me. She's afraid I'll die like my brother. He died when he was four. He had something wrong with him when he was born."

"Only person I'm scared of is my mother. She'll beat the daylights out of me if she finds out I'm dealing. My cousin just got put in jail for dealing. They put him in the House of D for a week."

"The what?"

"The House of D. The House of Detention. It's supposed to be for over eighteen and he ain't but sixteen but that's where he is and he cries every time they talk to him. Somebody stole his towel the first day he was there."

They ate the mufflelata and drank an Icee and rode back to the park and sold the rest of their stuff. Then they decided to ride down to the project and look for Uncle Clarence.

Supplies were a problem. They tried raising a crop on the back side of the levee, but the cops dug it up. They managed to bring in a small crop in Robert's grandmother's backyard while she was on a tour of Scandinavia with her bridge club, but that was a one-shot deal.

They started off for the project. They rode down Tchoupitoulas Street, which runs in a crescent along the levee lined with wharves and warehouses.

It was supposed to be dangerous to go into the project, but from Robert's elevated point of view the project just looked like a lot of old brick apartment buildings with iron balconies hanging off the sides like abandoned birds' nests and aluminum foil on half the windows to keep out the heat.

It was late afternoon and people were sitting on the stoops talking and drinking beer. Some kids were having a war with Coke bottles full of muddy water for ammunition. Robert and Gus went up a flight of stairs in one of the buildings and Gus's oldest sister met them at the door. She was taller and lighter than Gus, dressed in a ruffled white shirt and a short blue skirt.

"Where you think you been?" she demanded. Robert could smell her cool perfume.

"I been out on business," Gus said. "Where's momma?"

"She's gone to the store and you better stay here till she gets back. She sent Uncle Clarence looking for you yesterday."

She gave Robert a haughty look and settled back on the sofa where she was polishing her fingernails and watching a movie on television. She was studying to be a secretary.

The apartment was small and crowded with furniture. In one corner was a brass coatrack with ten or twelve different colored coats on it. It looked like a melted carousel. Robert kept staring at it, pulling in his pupils to make it look weirder and weirder.

"What's wrong with him?" Gus's sister demanded, pointing a newly coated nail at Robert.

"That's Robert. He does business with me uptown. There ain't nothing wrong with him some food won't fix. Where's Uncle Clarence now. You seen him?"

"He's probably still looking for you."

Gus liked to eat all the time when he was high. He made some peanut-butter sandwiches and they went off looking for his uncle.

They found Clarence sitting on the steps of a neighboring building drinking Apple Jack wine and flirting with a girlfriend. He was light-complected and wore a mustache and a carefully ironed African Mau-Mau shirt.

"Good evening," Gus smiled politely at the lady. "Uncle Clarence, you been looking for me?"

"Come here, Gus," Clarence said and pulled the boys out of earshot of the lady. "Gus, you got me in all kinds of trouble with your momma. She yelled at me for an hour yesterday. What you been doing with that stuff, smoking it yourself?"

"No, I ain't. This here is my partner, Robert. We don't do nothing but sell it to rich white kids in the park. Robert lets me keep supplies in his basement when we got anything to keep. And I got the money I owe you too." Gus produced three ten dollar bills and some crumpled ones and started counting it out to his uncle.

"Well, you ain't getting any more shit off me one way or the other." Clarence was feeling good. He had drunk just the right amount of Apple Jack. He kept his hand on the boy's shoulder as he talked. "I don't feel like having your momma after me and I'm off you for laying out so much. That's what's got her so hot."

"Uncle Clarence, you can't do me this way. I got my

partner, I got my business, I got my customers. Momma ain't gonna find out anything. I'll stay home every night. I never knew you to be so scared of her before."

Gus was pulling out all the stops. Great tears were forming in the corners of his eyes.

"Oh, for Jesus' sake," Clarence said, not wanting the lady to see him making a kid cry. "I'll give you enough for one more week and we'll see how you stay home and keep her pacified. You come over to my place after dinner and I'll fix you up."

Gus and Robert looked at each other. Their eyes lit up like someone had just dropped a quarter in a pinball machine. They were set for another week.

Robert McLaurin's father, his name was Will, thought the spring of 1971 was the worst time he had ever lived through. He was a management lawyer. All he did at work was try Equal Opportunity Employment cases, and he had lost five in a row. All he did at home was argue with Robert McLaurin's mother, her name was Lelia, about whether or not Robert was taking drugs.

They argued so much about Robert they had stopped being in love with each other. All day long at the office Will thought about the argument from the day before and used his legal mind to think up ways to make his arguments more convincing.

He would drive up in front of his house after work and sometimes it would take him three or four minutes to get ready to go inside and start arguing. He would look up at the fine house he had bought for his family and wish he was someplace else. Finally he would pick up his briefcase and go on in.

Lelia would be running around the kitchen in a tennis skirt trying to get dinner on the table so Will wouldn't know she hadn't done anything all day but play tennis. Will would say, "Did you call Robert's coach?"

"I couldn't get him on the phone."

"What do you mean, you couldn't get him on the phone? They don't have phones anymore at Horace Green School?"

"Are you accusing me of lying?"

Will McLaurin was not a big man. He was five nine with broad shoulders and curly red hair and black eyes. When he started arguing he lit up like an actor on the stage.

"Lelia, I said did you call the coach or did you not call the coach. Don't make something up. Just answer the question."

Lelia McLaurin looked like a blonde housewife on a television commercial. She had a good figure from playing tennis all the time and she had a bad temper from getting her way all the time.

"I don't have to listen to this. I don't have to hear this while I'm cooking dinner. If you keep this up I'll leave and you can cook your own dinner." She was furiously buttering French bread to go with the fried chicken the cook had left warming in the oven.

"Lelia, listen to me. All I'm asking is did you call Robert's coach or not. I'm not accusing you of anything and I'm not trying to put anything over on you. Did you call Robert's coach and ask him if Robert has been showing up for practice?"

"I left a message but he didn't call back."

"Did you go out and see if he was at practice?"

"I'm not going to spy on my own child. Stop ruining my evening. Have a drink or something. He goes to practice. He bought a new track suit just last week."

"Lelia, will you look at this for a minute. Just look at this and then we won't discuss it anymore," and Will handed her a yellow legal pad with a list printed on the first page.

"What in the hell is this?" She turned toward him fiercely, her pleated skirt twirling around her legs.

"That is a partial list of the furnishings, decorations, and trinkets in our only son's bedroom. I was hoping you might sit down and read it and think about it."

"This legal garbage. This goddamn lawyer list," and Lelia ripped the page from the legal pad and threw it at the pantry door.

The list read:

1. Black light
2. Two strobe lights for altering perception of light
3. Poster of androgynous figure on motorcycle smoking a marijuana cigarette
4. Poster of Peter Fonda smoking a marijuana cigarette
5. Package of sandwich-size baggies, often used to parcel out marijuana into what are known as "lids"
6. 36 long-playing record albums featuring artists who smoke marijuana and advocate the use of various drugs in the lyrics of their songs
7. Recipe, supposedly a joke, for the manufacture of LSD from sunflower seeds

"You have to stop spying on Robert! That's just their way of being cute. He pretends he's in the revolution. I think you hate him."

"If you call walking in his room spying. That is a list of objects that can be seen by a person of normal eyesight standing in the middle of his room."

"You hate him."

"Lelia, I don't hate him. I hate him hanging around the park all the time. I hate him barely passing at school and never reading a book anymore. Lelia, a madness is stalking this city and I don't want to lose my son to it."

They were out in the hall. Lelia was getting a raincoat out of a closet. It wasn't raining. She was getting out the raincoat because it is hard to walk out on someone wearing only a tennis skirt and a LaCoste shirt. She was crying.

Will took the raincoat away from her and tried to put his arms around her. They hadn't made love to each other for two weeks.

"Look, tomorrow is Friday. Leave Robert with your mother and we'll drive to Biloxi for the weekend. We can lie around in the sun and talk things over. Let's get out of town and try to love each other and see if we can think straight."

"All right. If you won't talk about it anymore tonight. The other day I saw him riding a little black boy around on his handlebars. You've got me so paranoid I thought there was something wrong with that."

"What time tomorrow could you leave?"

"I'm going to the beauty parlor at four. I'll pick you up at the office at five-thirty and we'll take the expressway from downtown. We can stop in Mandeville and have dinner at Begue's."

"Sure we can. Bring a shaker of martinis. We'll drink all the way to the coast like the old days."

Then the McLaurins had a peaceful meal for a change and Will and Lelia went up early to bed.

As soon as they disappeared Robert called up Gus and told him the good news that they would have the house to themselves for the weekend. He smoked a joint and drifted off to sleep listening to his radio. *"Drove my Chevy to the levee but the levee was dry, drove my Chevy to the levee but the levee was dry."*

Gus was waiting for Robert in the front yard when Robert came home the next day. Gus was excited. He loved the McLaurins' beautiful old house. He had spent the night there once before when Robert had a babysitter. Robert had sneaked him in. What Gus really liked was Robert's father's shower. It had an attachment that gave you a massage while you took a shower. Gus said it felt like little pieces of diamonds hitting your skin.

On this particular Friday Robert felt good to be walking in the front door with his friend. The McLaurin house was built around a wide central hall. At the far end of the hall a staircase five feet wide rose to the second floor. The hall was hung with an amazing assortment of paintings.

"Your momma sure does have a lot of pictures."

"She painted this one herself."

"What's it a picture of?" Gus asked.

"What does it look like to you?"

"A fire. A big field of fire."

"Well, she says it's a picture of the inside of her head when she was going to have me as a baby."

"I wouldn't have guessed it."

The boys went on in the kitchen. They decided to really have a party.

Lelia entered the Magic Slipper Beauty Salon with a sigh. She was exhausted from rushing to get there on time.

"Tim, I'm sorry I'm late. I got in school traffic on the Avenue."

"It's okay, sweetie, but we'll have to skip the manicure. I've got a date at six." He handed her a leopard-printed smock and nodded toward the dressing room. His silver hair was cut in a Prince Valiant. He was vain of his body and his clientele. He put up with a lot from Lelia because she had been named to the list of Beautiful Activists two years in a row before she had turned herself into a tennis-playing machine.

"He's driving me crazy," she said, settling into the shampoo chair. "Between the two of them I don't care if I live or die. I can't even play tennis worth a damn. I lost every important match I played last week. I'm down to six on the ladder."

"Sweetie, you can't let them do that to you. What does Arthur say?" They shared a psychiatrist. This creates a strange bond between people.

"He says I have to work through it. Will and I are going to the coast for the weekend to talk it over. We may end up sending Robert off to school. Will wants me to treat Robert the way his mother treated him, the old guilt routine. Look what it did to him. He doesn't even know he's neurotic. At least I know I'm neurotic."

"Lelia, is that you?" Danny Adler's mother came up with her hair wrapped in a turban on the way to the back for a pedicure.

"Janet, how are you?"

"Listen, thanks for asking Danny to spend the night. It really worked out beautifully because we are planning on being out late tonight."

"Janet," Lelia sat up, half-rinsed, "Janet, I didn't ask Danny to spend the night. Will and I are going out of town for the weekend. Robert is staying with Mother. Are you sure he said Robert asked him?"

"Yes, he said you-all were taking them to the movies."

Tim started laughing. "The old mom's-out-of-town game. I'll bet they're shacked up with some charmers in your bedroom right this minute."

"I'm going home," Lelia said. "Tim, get this stuff off my hair and comb me out."

"You can't go home like this."

"I don't care. Just comb out my hair. I mean it, Tim. Janet, I'll call you later."

"Sweetie, take a Valium. You want a Valium?"

"Oh, could you, thanks."

Tim fished a bottle out of his pocket. "One or two?"

"Two."

Lelia parked the car two houses away and walked across the lawn and onto her front porch. She felt like a member of the CIA. She could hear the music playing as she walked across the yard. She could hear the music before she stepped onto the porch. She could hear the music and through the floor-length windows of the living room she could see Robert draped over the beige-and-white-striped loveseat holding a cigarette in one hand and nodding dreamily with his eyes closed. She could see the mirrored cocktail table with the silver champagne bucket and the two-hundred-year-old red crystal Madeira glasses beside it. Robert got up and walked into the next room to change the record.

Lelia stepped into the hall.

Gus came walking down the stairs. He came walking down the carpeted stairs and down the wide walnut hall with its sixteen-foot ceilings. He came walking down the hall wrapped in a plush baby-blue monogrammed towel from the Lylian Shop. Pearls of water were dripping down his face from his thick soft hair. Widely grinning, hugely smiling, Gus came down the hall, down the Aubusson runner, down Lelia's schizophrenic, eclectic art gallery of a hall, past the Walter Andersons, the deCallatays, the

Leroy Morais, the Rolland Golden, the Stanford, past the portrait of Robert's grandfather in the robes of a state supreme court justice, past the Dufy. He had just passed the edge of the new Leonor Fini when Lelia stepped into the hall and they spotted each other.

Here Gus came, in the baby-blue towel, black as a walnut tree in winter, draped as a tiny emperor, carrying his empty champagne glass in one hand and using the other for an imperial robe clasp. Expansively, ecstatically pleased to be, delighted to be, charmed to be alive on this, the fourteenth day of April, nineteen hundred and seventy-one; he, Gus, man of parts, friend of white man and black man, friend of oak tree, levee, and river, citizen of New Orleans, Louisiana, dope pusher to the Audubon Park, dispenser of the new Nirvana. He, Gus, five feet one inches, one hundred and two pounds of pure D Gus, walking down the hall.

Lelia screamed. She screamed six months of unscreamed screaming. She screamed an ancestral, a territorial scream. She screamed her head off.

"What in the name of God are you doing in my house?" she screamed.

"Robert," she screamed, "what is this black child doing in my house? What is this goddamn black pusher doing in my house? Robert," she screamed, "get in here this second."

Gus's eyes met hers at a forty-degree angle. His huge black eyes met her wide aluminum ones down the long hall and held for a moment and then Gus cut and ran back up the stairs to the bedroom, trailing the towel behind him, his tiny black butt shining in the reflected light from the stained-glass window in the stairway alcove.

Robert ran past his mother's screaming and up the stairs behind Gus and the two boys ran into the master bedroom and slammed the door and threw the safety bolt and Robert stood with his back to the door breathing like a runaway mule.

"What are we gonna do now?" Robert said, his heart pushing against his fake soccer shirt.

"I'm getting out of here. That's what I'm doing," Gus said, pulling on his plaid pants and searching for his boots.

"You can't get out of here. There isn't any way out."

"There's that window," Gus said. "There's that window and that's the way I'm going out." He pointed to a double French window that opened onto a false balcony and overlooked the side yard. The top twelve feet of an old crepe myrtle tree pushed against the balcony waving its clusters of soft pink flowers in the breeze.

"You can't get out there. It's forty feet to the ground."

"I'm going down that tree."

"That's a crepe myrtle. You can't climb down a crepe myrtle."

"If it's the only tree I got, I can climb down it," Gus said, putting on his jacket and pushing open the French doors.

Lelia was beating on the door with her fists.

"Robert, if you don't open this door you will never leave this house again. If you don't open this door this minute you will be sent to Saint Stanislaus. I'll call the police. I've already called your father. He'll be here any minute. You might as well open the door. You better hurry and open this door. You better answer me this minute."

"That's the maddest woman I ever heard in my life," Gus said, throwing one leg over the balcony.

"Don't do it, Gus. Gus, don't do it," Robert said, grabbing him. "She won't really call the police. She's just saying that. It will be all right when my father gets here."

"Let go of me, Robert," Gus warned.

"Robert," she screamed, "if you don't open this door you will be the sorriest boy in New Orleans."

Robert turned to look at the door. He looked past the beautiful white-lacquered four-poster bed with Lelia's favorite sun hats hanging gaily from the bedposts.

As he turned to look at the door Gus shook his head and reached down and bit the freckled hand that held him. He bit Robert's hand as hard as he could bite it and Robert let go.

Gus jumped into the heart of the crepe myrtle tree. He dove into the tree and swayed in its branches like a cat. He steadied, grabbed for a larger branch, found a temporary footing, grabbed again, and began to fall through the upthrust branches like a bird shot in flight. As Robert watched, Gus came to rest upon the ground, his wet black hair festooned with the soft pink blossoms of the crepe myrtle.

Then, as Robert watched, Gus pushed off from the earth. He began to ascend back up through the broken branches like a movie played in reverse, like a wild kite rising to meet the sun, and Robert was amazed and enchanted by the beauty of this feat and jumped from the window high into the air to join Gus on his journey.

And far away in the loud hall Lelia beat on the door and beat on the door and beat on the door.

Mary Hood

Mary Hood was born in Brunswick, Georgia, in 1946, and educated at Georgia State University in Atlanta. Her short stories, set in rural Georgia, have been published in numerous periodicals, including *Harper's, Southern Magazine, Georgia Review, Kenyon Review,* and *Yankee Magazine.* Her first collection, *How Far She Went* (1984), won both the Flannery O'Connor award and the *Southern Review*/Louisiana State University Press award, and her second collection, *And Venus Is Blue* (1986), won the Townsend Prize. Mary Hood's characters, often isolated and lonely, have difficulty communicating with each other as this story from her first collection shows. Critic David Baker noted that Hood's South "finds its families falling apart, its women stranded yet struggling individually to grow stronger, and its very past—the history and nostalgia so important to Southern tradition—vanishing or vanished."

How Far She Went

They had quarreled all morning, squalled all summer about the incidentals: how tight the girl's cut-off jeans were, the "Every Inch a Woman" T-shirt, her choice of music and how loud she played it, her practiced inattention, her sullen look. Her granny wrung out the last boiled dishcloth, pinched it to the line, giving the basin a sling and a slap, the water flying out in a scalding arc onto the Queen Anne's lace by the path, never mind if it bloomed, that didn't make it worth anything except to chiggers, but the girl would cut it by the everlasting armload and cherish it in the old churn, going to that much trouble for a weed but not bending once—unbegged—to pick the nearest bean; she was sulking now. Bored. Displaced.

"And what do you think happens to a chigger if nobody ever walks by his weed?" her granny asked, heading for the house with that sidelong uneager unanswered glance, hoping for what? The surprise gift of a smile? Nothing. The woman shook her head and said it. "Nothing." The door slammed behind her. Let it.

"I hate it here!" the girl yelled then. She picked up a stick and broke it and threw the pieces—one from each hand—at the laundry drying in the noon. Missed. Missed.

Then she turned on her bare, haughty heel and set off high-shouldered into the heat, quick but not far, not far enough—no road was *that* long—only as far as she dared. At the gate, a rusty chain swinging between two lichened posts, she stopped, then backed up the raw drive to make a run at the barrier, lofting, clearing it clean, her long hair wild in the sun. Triumphant, she looked back at the

147

house where she caught at the dark window her granny's face in its perpetual eclipse of disappointment, old at fifty. She stepped back, but the girl saw her.

"You don't know me!" the girl shouted, chin high, and ran till her ribs ached.

As she rested in the rattling shade of the willows, the little dog found her. He could be counted on. He barked all the way, and squealed when she pulled the burr from his ear. They started back to the house for lunch. By then the mailman had long come and gone in the old ruts, leaving the one letter folded now to fit the woman's apron pocket.

If bad news darkened her granny's face, the girl ignored it. Didn't talk at all, another of her distancings, her defiances. So it was as they ate that the woman summarized, "Your daddy wants you to cash in the plane ticket and buy you something. School clothes. For here."

Pale, the girl stared, defenseless only an instant before blurting out, "You're lying."

The woman had to stretch across the table to leave her handprint on that blank cheek. She said, not caring if it stung or not, "He's been planning it since he sent you here."

"I could turn this whole house over, dump it! Leave you slobbering over that stinking jealous dog in the dust!" The girl trembled with the vision, with the strength it gave her. It made her laugh. "Scatter the Holy Bible like confetti and ravel the crochet into miles of stupid string! I could! I will! I won't stay here!" But she didn't move, not until her tears rose to meet her color, and then to escape the shame of minding so much she fled. Just headed away, blind. It didn't matter, this time, how far she went.

The woman set her thoughts against fretting over their bickering, just went on unalarmed with chores, clearing off after the uneaten meal, bringing in the laundry, scattering corn for the chickens, ladling manure tea onto the porch flowers. She listened though. She always had been a listener. It gave her a cocked look. She forgot why she had gone into the girl's empty room, that ungirlish, tenuous lodging place with its bleak order, its ready suitcases never unpacked, the narrow bed, the contested radio on the windowsill. The woman drew the cracked shade down between the radio and the August sun. There wasn't anything else to do.

It was after six when she tied on her rough oxfords and walked down the drive and dropped the gate chain and headed back to the creosoted shed where she kept her tools. She took a hoe for snakes, a rake, shears to trim the grass where it grew, and seed in her pocket to scatter where it never had grown at all. She put the tools and her gloves and the bucket in the trunk of the old Chevy, its prime and rust like an Appaloosa's spots through the chalky white finish. She left the trunk open and the tool handles sticking out. She wasn't going far.

The heat of the day had broken, but the air was thick, sultry, weighted with honeysuckle in second bloom and the Nu-Grape scent of Kudzu. The maple and poplar leaves turned over, quaking, silver. There wouldn't be any rain. She told the dog to stay, but he knew a trick. He stowed away when she turned her back, leaped right into the trunk with the tools, then gave himself away with exultant barks. Hearing him, her court jester, she stopped the car and welcomed him into the front seat beside her. Then they went on. Not a mile from her gate she turned onto the blue gravel of the cemetery lane, hauled the gearshift into reverse to whoa them, and got out to take the idle walk down to her buried hopes, bending all along to rout out a handful of weeds from between the markers of old acquaintance. She stood there and read, slow. The dog whined at her hem; she picked him up and rested her chin on his head, then he wriggled and whined to run free, contrary and restless as a child.

The crows called strong and bold MOM! MOM! A trick of the ear to hear it like that. She knew it was the crows, but still she looked around. No one called her that now. She was done with that. And what was it worth anyway? It all came to this: solitary weeding. The sinful

fumble of flesh, the fear, the listening for a return that
never came, the shamed waiting, the unanswered prayers, the perjury on the certificate—hadn't she lain there
weary of the whole lie and it only beginning? and a voice
telling her, "Here's your baby, here's your girl," and the
swaddled package meaning no more to her than an extra
anything, something store-bought, something she could
take back for a refund.

"Tie her to the fence and give her a bale of hay," she
had murmured, drugged, and they teased her, excused
her for such a welcoming, blaming the anesthesia, but it
went deeper than that; *she* knew, and the *baby* knew:
there was no love in the begetting. That was the secret,
unforgivable, that not another good thing could ever
make up for, where all the bad had come from, like a
visitation, a punishment. She knew that was why Sylvie
had been wild, had gone to earth so early, and before
dying had made this child in sudden wedlock, a child
who would be just like her, would carry the hurting on
into another generation. A matter of time. No use raising
her hand. But she *had* raised her hand. Still wore on its
palm the memory of the sting of the collision with the
girl's cheek; had she broken her jaw? Her heart? Of
course not. She said it aloud: "Takes more than that."

She went to work then, doing what she could with her
old tools. She pecked the clay on Sylvie's grave, new-
looking, unhealed after years. She tried again, scattering
seeds from her pocket, every last possible one of them.
Off in the west she could hear the pulpwood cutters sawing through another acre across the lake. Nearer, there
was the racket of motorcycles laboring cross-country,
insect-like, distracting.

She took her bucket to the well and hung it on the
pump. She had half filled it when the bikers roared up,
right down the blue gravel, straight at her. She let the
bucket overflow, staring. On the back of one of the
machines was the girl. Sylvie's girl! Her bare arms
wrapped around the shirtless man riding between her
thighs. They were first. The second biker rode alone.
She studied their strangers' faces as they circled her.

They were the enemy, all of them. Laughing. The girl was laughing too, laughing like her mama did. Out in the middle of nowhere the girl had found these two men, some moth-musk about her drawing them (too soon!) to what? She shouted it: "What in God's—" They roared off without answering her, and the bucket of water tipped over, spilling its stain blood-dark on the red dust.

The dog went wild barking, leaping after them, snapping at the tires, and there was no calling him down. The bikers made a wide circuit of the churchyard, then roared straight across the graves, leaping the ditch and landing upright on the road again, heading off toward the reservoir.

Furious, she ran to her car, past the barking dog, this time leaving him behind, driving after them, horn blowing nonstop, to get back what was not theirs. She drove after them knowing what they did not know, that all the roads beyond that point dead-ended. She surprised them, swinging the Impala across their path, cutting them off; let them hit it! They stopped. She got out, breathing hard, and said, when she could, "She's underage." Just that. And put out her claiming hand with an authority that made the girl's arms drop from the man's insolent waist and her legs tremble.

"I was just riding," the girl said, not looking up.

Behind them the sun was heading on toward down. The long shadows of the pines drifted back and forth in the same breeze that puffed the distant sails on the lake. Dead limbs creaked and clashed overhead like the antlers of locked and furious beasts.

"Sheeeut," the lone rider said. "I told you." He braced with his muddy boot and leaned out from his machine to spit. The man the girl had been riding with had the invading sort of eyes the woman had spent her lifetime bolting doors against. She met him now, face to face.

"Right there, missy," her granny said, pointing behind her to the car.

The girl slid off the motorcycle and stood halfway between her choices. She started slightly at the poosh!

as he popped another top and chugged the beer in one uptilting of his head. His eyes never left the woman's. When he was through, he tossed the can high, flipping it end over end. Before it hit the ground he had his pistol out and, firing once, winged it into the lake.

"Freaking lucky shot," the other one grudged.

"I don't need luck," he said. He sighted down the barrel of the gun at the woman's head. "POW!" he yelled, and when she recoiled, he laughed. He swung around to the girl; he kept aiming the gun, here, there, high, low, all around. "Y'all settle it," he said, with a shrug.

The girl had to understand him then, had to know him, had to know better. But still she hesitated. He kept looking at her, then away.

"She's fifteen," her granny said. "You can go to jail."

"You can go to hell," he said.

"Probably will," her granny told him. "I'll save you a seat by the fire." She took the girl by the arm and drew her to the car; she backed up, swung around, and headed out the road toward the churchyard for her tools and dog. The whole way the girl said nothing, just hunched against the far door, staring hard-eyed out at the pines going past.

The woman finished watering the seed in, and collected her tools. As she worked, she muttered, "It's your own kin buried here, you might have the decency to glance this way one time . . ." The girl was finger-tweezing her eyebrows in the side mirror. She didn't look around as the dog and the woman got in. Her granny shifted hard, sending the tools clattering in the trunk.

When they came to the main road, there were the men. Watching for them. Waiting for them. They kicked their machines into life and followed, close, bumping them, slapping the old fenders, yelling. The girl gave a wild glance around at the one by her door and said, "Gran'ma?" and as he drew his pistol, "Gran'ma!" just as the gun nosed into the open window. She frantically cranked the glass up between her and the weapon, and her granny, seeing, spat, "Fool!" She never had been one to pray for peace or rain. She stamped the accelerator right to the floor.

The motorcycles caught up. Now she braked, hard, and swerved off the road into an alley between the pines, not even wide enough for the school bus, just a fire scrape that came out a quarter mile from her own house, if she could get that far. She slewed on the pine straw, then righted, tearing along the dark tunnel through the woods. She had for the time being bested them; they were left behind. She was winning. Then she hit the wallow where the tadpoles were already five weeks old. The Chevy plowed in and stalled. When she got it cranked again, they were stuck. The tires spattered mud three feet up the near trunks as she tried to spin them out, to rock them out. Useless. "Get out and run!" she cried, but the trees were too close on the passenger side. The girl couldn't open her door. She wasted precious time having to crawl out under the steering wheel. The woman waited but the dog ran on.

They struggled through the dusky woods, their pace slowed by the thick straw and vines. Overhead, in the last light, the martins were reeling free and sure after their prey.

"Why? Why?" the girl gasped, as they lunged down the old deer trail. Behind them they could hear shots, and glass breaking as the men came to the bogged car. The woman kept on running, swatting their way clear through the shoulder-high weeds. They could see the Greer cottage, and made for it. But it was ivied-over, padlocked, the woodpile dry-rotting under its tarp, the electric meterbox empty on the pole. No help there.

The dog, excited, trotted on, yelping, his lips white-flecked. He scented the lake and headed that way, urging them on with thirsty yips. On the clay shore, treeless, deserted, at the utter limit of land, they stood defenseless, listening to the men coming on, between them and home. The woman pressed her hands to her mouth, stifling her cough. She was exhausted. She couldn't think.

"We can get under!" the girl cried suddenly, and pointed toward the Greers' dock, gap-planked, its walkway grounded on the mud. They splashed out to it, wading in, the woman grabbing up the telltale, tattletale dog in her arms. They waded out to the far end and ducked under. There was room between the foam floats for them to crouch neck-deep.

The dog wouldn't hush, even then; never had yet, and there wasn't time to teach him. When the woman realized that, she did what she had to do. She grabbed him whimpering; held him; held him under till the struggle ceased and the bubbles rose silver from his fur. They crouched there then, the two of them, submerged to the shoulders, feet unsteady on the slimed lake bed. They listened. The sky went from rose to ocher to violet in the cracks over their heads. The motorcycles had stopped now. In the silence there was the glissando of locusts, the dry crunch of boots on the flinty beach, their low man-talk drifting as they prowled back and forth. One of them struck a match.

"—they in these woods we could burn 'em out."

The wind carried their voices away into the pines. Some few words eddied back.

"—lippy old smartass do a little work on her knees besides praying—"

Laughter. It echoed off the deserted house. They were getting closer.

One of them strode directly out to the dock, walked on the planks over their heads. They could look up and see his boot soles. He was the one with the gun. He slapped a mosquito on his bare back and cursed. The carp, roused by the troubling of the waters, came nosing around the dock, guzzling and snorting. The girl and her granny held still, so still. The man fired his pistol into the shadows, and a wounded fish thrashed, dying. The man knelt and reached for it, chuffing out his beery breath. He belched. He pawed the lake for the dead fish, cursing as it floated out of reach. He shot it again, firing at it till it sank and the gun was empty. Cursed that too. He stood then and unzipped and relieved himself of some of the beer. They had to listen to that. To know that about him. To endure that, unprotesting.

Back and forth on shore the other one ranged, restless.
He lit another cigarette. He coughed. He called, "Hey!
They got away, man, that's all. Don't get your shorts in
a wad. Let's go."

"Yeah." He finished. He zipped. He stumped back
across the planks and leaped to shore, leaving the dock
tilting amid widening ripples. Underneath, they waited.

The bike cranked. The other ratcheted, ratcheted,
then coughed, caught, roared. They circled, cut deep
ruts, slung gravel, and went. Their roaring died away and
away. Crickets resumed and a near frog bic-bic-bicked.

Under the dock, they waited a little longer to be sure.
Then they ducked below the water, scraped out from
under the pontoon, and came up into free air, slogging
toward shore. It had seemed warm enough in the water.
Now they shivered. It was almost night. One streak of
light still stood reflected on the darkening lake, drew
itself thinner, narrowing into a final cancellation of day.
A plane winked its way west.

The girl was trembling. She ran her hands down her
arms and legs, shedding water like a garment. She
sighed, almost a sob. The woman held the dog in her
arms; she dropped to her knees upon the random stones
and murmured, private, haggard, "Oh, honey," three
times, maybe all three times for the dog, maybe once for
each of them. The girl waited, watching. Her granny
rocked the dog like a baby, like a dead child, rocked
slower and slower and was still.

"I'm sorry," the girl said then, avoiding the dog's
inert, empty eye.

"It was him or you," her granny said, finally, looking
up. Looking her over. "Did they mess with you? With
your britches? Did they?"

"No!" Then, quieter, "No, ma'am."

When the woman tried to stand up she staggered,
lightheaded, clumsy with the freight of the dog. "No,
ma'am," she echoed, fending off the girl's "Let me."
And she said again, "It was him or you. I know that.
I'm not going to rub your face in it." They saw each

other as well as they could in that failing light, in any light.

The woman started toward home, saying, "Around here, we bear our own burdens." She led the way along the weedy shortcuts. The twilight bleached the dead limbs of the pines to bone. Insects sang in the thickets, silencing at their oncoming.

"We'll see about the car in the morning," the woman said. She bore her armful toward her own moth-ridden dusk-to-dawn security light with that country grace she had always had when the earth was reliably progressing underfoot. The girl walked close behind her, exactly where *she* walked, matching her pace, matching her stride, close enough to put her hand forth (if the need arose) and touch her granny's back where the faded voile was clinging damp, the merest gauze between their wounds.

Carson McCullers

Carson McCullers was born in Columbus, Georgia, in 1917, and attended Columbia University and New York University. She was a member of the American Academy of Arts and Letters. Her major works of fiction, *The Heart Is a Lonely Hunter* (1940), *Reflections in a Golden Eye* (1941), "The Ballad of the Sad Cafe" (1943), and *The Member of the Wedding* (1946), were all written when she was in her twenties. Her work reflects the isolation that she felt throughout her life, a feeling she identified as the basis of most of her themes. McCullers adapted her most autobiographical novel, *The Member of the Wedding*, for the stage and won a number of awards, including the New York Drama Critics Circle Award.

Carson McCullers died in 1967 at age 50, a victim of poor health for much of her life. Her novels, *The Heart Is a Lonely Hunter*, *Reflections in a Golden Eye*, and *The Member of the Wedding* were all made into movies.

Sucker

It was always like I had a room to myself. Sucker slept in my bed with me but that didn't interfere with anything. The room was mine and I used it as I wanted to. Once I remember sawing a trap door in the floor. Last year when I was a sophomore in high school I tacked on my wall some pictures of girls from magazines and one of them was just in her underwear. My mother never bothered me because she had the younger kids to look after. And Sucker thought anything I did was always swell.

Whenever I would bring any of my friends back to my room all I had to do was just glance once at Sucker and he would get up from whatever he was busy with and maybe half smile at me, and leave without saying a word. He never brought kids back there. He's twelve, four years younger than I am, and he always knew without me even telling him that I didn't want kids that age meddling with my things.

Half the time I used to forget that Sucker isn't my brother. He's my first cousin but practically ever since I remember he's been in our family. You see his folks were killed in a wreck when he was a baby. To me and my kid sisters he was like our brother.

Sucker used to always remember and believe every word I said. That's how he got his nick-name. Once a couple of years ago I told him that if he'd jump off our garage with an umbrella it would act as a parachute and he wouldn't fall hard. He did it and busted his knee. That's just one instance. And the funny thing was that no matter how many times he got fooled he would still believe me. Not that he was dumb in other ways—it was just the way he acted with me. He would look at everything I did and quietly take it in.

There is one thing I have learned, but it makes me feel guilty and is hard to figure out. If a person admires you a lot you despise him and don't care—and it is the person who doesn't notice you that you are apt to admire. This is not easy to realize. Maybelle Watts, this senior at school, acted like she was the Queen of Sheba and even humiliated me. Yet at this same time I would have done anything in the world to get her attentions. All I could think about day and night was Maybelle until I was nearly crazy. When Sucker was a little kid and on up until the time he was twelve I guess I treated him as bad as Maybelle did me.

Now that Sucker has changed so much it is a little hard to remember him as he used to be. I never imagined anything would suddenly happen that would make us both very different. I never knew that in order to get what has happened straight in my mind I would want to think back on him as he used to be and compare and try to get things settled. If I could have seen ahead maybe I would have acted different.

I never noticed him much or thought about him and when you consider how long we have had the same room together it is funny the few things I remember. He used to talk to himself a lot when he'd think he was alone—all about him fighting gangsters and being on ranches and that sort of kids' stuff. He'd get in the bathroom and stay as long as an hour and sometimes his voice would go up high and excited and you could hear him all over the house. Usually, though, he was very quiet. He didn't have many boys in the neighborhood to buddy with and his face had the look of a kid who is watching a game and waiting to be asked to play. He didn't mind wearing the sweaters and coats that I outgrew, even if the sleeves did flop down too big and make his wrists look as thin and white as a little girl's. That is how I remember him— getting a little bigger every year but still being the same.

That was Sucker up until a few months ago when all this trouble began.

Maybelle was somehow mixed up in what happened so I guess I ought to start with her. Until I knew her I hadn't given much time to girls. Last fall she sat next to me in General Science class and that was when I first began to notice her. Her hair is the brightest yellow I ever saw and occasionally she will wear it set into curls with some sort of gluey stuff. Her fingernails are pointed and manicured and painted a shiny red. All during class I used to watch Maybelle, nearly all the time except when I thought she was going to look my way or when the teacher called on me. I couldn't keep my eyes off her hands, for one thing. They are very little and white except for that red stuff, and when she would turn the pages of her book she always licked her thumb and held out her little finger and turned very slowly. It is impossible to describe Maybelle. All the boys are crazy about her but she didn't even notice me. For one thing she's almost two years older than I am. Between periods I used to try and pass very close to her in the halls but she would hardly ever smile at me. All I could do was sit and look at her in class—and sometimes it was like the whole room could hear my heart beating and I wanted to holler or light out and run for Hell.

At night, in bed, I would imagine about Maybelle. Often this would keep me from sleeping until as late as one or two o'clock. Sometimes Sucker would wake up and ask me why I couldn't get settled and I'd tell him to hush his mouth. I suppose I was mean to him lots of times. I guess I wanted to ignore somebody like Maybelle did me. You could always tell by Sucker's face when his feelings were hurt. I don't remember all the ugly remarks I must have made because even when I was saying them my mind was on Maybelle.

That went on for nearly three months and then somehow she began to change. In the halls she would speak to me and every morning she copied my homework. At lunch time once I danced with her in the gym. One afternoon I got up nerve and went around to her house with a carton of cigarettes. I knew she smoked in the girls' basement and sometimes outside of school—and I didn't want to take her candy because I think that's been run into the ground. She was very nice and it seemed to me everything was going to change.

It was that night when this trouble really started. I had come into my room late and Sucker was already asleep. I felt too happy and keyed up to get in a comfortable position and I was awake thinking about Maybelle a long time. Then I dreamed about her and it seemed I kissed her. It was a surprise to wake up and see the dark. I lay still and a little while passed before I could come to and understand where I was. The house was quiet and it was a very dark night.

Sucker's voice was a shock to me. "Pete? . . ."

I didn't answer anything or even move.

"You do like me as much as if I was your own brother, don't you, Pete?"

I couldn't get over the surprise of everything and it was like this was the real dream instead of the other.

"You have liked me all the time like I was your own brother, haven't you?"

"Sure," I said.

Then I got up for a few minutes. It was cold and I was glad to come back to bed. Sucker hung on to my back. He felt little and warm and I could feel his warm breathing on my shoulder.

"No matter what you did I always knew you liked me."

I was wide awake and my mind seemed mixed up in a strange way. There was this happiness about Maybelle and all that—but at the same time something about Sucker and his voice when he said these things made me take notice. Anyway I guess you understand people better when you are happy than when something is worrying you. It was like I had never really thought about Sucker until then. I felt I had always been mean to him. One night a few weeks before I had heard him crying in the dark. He said he had lost a boy's beebee gun and was scared to let anybody know. He wanted me to tell him what to do. I was sleepy and tried to make him hush and when he wouldn't I kicked at him. That was just one of the things I remembered. It seemed to me he had always been a lonesome kid. I felt bad.

There is something about a dark cold night that makes you feel close to someone you're sleeping with. When you talk together it is like you are the only people awake in the town.

"You're a swell kid, Sucker," I said.

It seemed to me suddenly that I did like him more than anybody else I knew—more than any other boy, more than my sisters, more in a certain way even than Maybelle. I felt good all over and it was like when they play sad music in the movies. I wanted to show Sucker how much I really thought of him and make up for the way I had always treated him.

We talked for a good while that night. His voice was fast and it was like he had been saving up these things to tell me for a long time. He mentioned that he was going to try to build a canoe and that the kids down the block wouldn't let him in on their football team and I don't know what all. I talked some too and it was a good feeling to think of him taking in everything I said so seriously. I even spoke of Maybelle a little, only I made out like it was her who had been running after me all this time. He asked questions about high school and so forth. His voice was excited and he kept on talking fast like he could never get the words out in time. When I went to sleep he was still talking and I could still feel his breathing on my shoulder, warm and close.

During the next couple of weeks I saw a lot of Maybelle. She acted as though she really cared for me a little. Half the time I felt so good I hardly knew what to do with myself.

But I didn't forget about Sucker. There were a lot of old things in my bureau drawer I'd been saving—boxing gloves and Tom Swift books and second rate fishing tackle. All this I turned over to him. We had some more talks together and it was really like I was knowing him for the first time. When there was a long cut on his cheek I knew he had been monkeying around with this new first razor set of mine, but I didn't say anything. His face seemed different now. He used to look timid and sort of like he was afraid of a whack over the head. That expression was gone. His face, with those wide-open eyes and his ears sticking out and his mouth never quite shut, had the look of a person who is surprised and expecting something swell.

Once I started to point him out to Maybelle and tell her he was my kid brother. It was an afternoon when a murder mystery was on at the movie. I had earned a dollar working for my dad and I gave Sucker a quarter to go and get candy and so forth. With the rest I took Maybelle. We were sitting near the back and I saw Sucker come in. He began to stare at the screen the minute he stepped past the ticket man and he stumbled down the aisle without noticing where he was going. I started to punch Maybelle but couldn't quite make up my mind. Sucker looked a little silly—walking like a drunk with his eyes glued to the movie. He was wiping his reading glasses on his shirt tail and his knickers flopped down. He went on until he got to the first few rows where the kids usually sit. I never did punch Maybelle. But I got to thinking it was good to have both of them at the movie with the money I earned.

I guess things went on like this for about a month or six weeks. I felt so good I couldn't settle down to study or put my mind on anything. I wanted to be friendly with everybody. There were times when I just had to talk to some person. And usually that would be Sucker. He felt as good as I did. Once he said: "Pete, I am gladder that you are like my brother than anything else in the world."

Then something happened between Maybelle and me. I never have figured out just what it was. Girls like her are hard to understand. She began to act different toward me. At first I wouldn't let myself believe this and tried to think it was just my imagination. She didn't act glad to see me anymore. Often she went out riding with this fellow on the football team who owns this yellow roadster. The car was the color of her hair and after school she would ride off with him, laughing and looking into his face. I couldn't think of anything to do about it and she was on my mind all day and night. When I did get a chance to go out with her she was snippy and didn't seem to notice me. This made me feel like something was the matter—I would worry about my shoes clopping too loud on the floor or the fly of my pants, or the bumps on my chin. Sometimes when Maybelle was around, a devil would get into me and I'd hold my face stiff and call grown men by their last names without the Mister and say rough things. In the night I would wonder what made me do all this until I was too tired for sleep.

At first I was so worried I just forgot about Sucker. Then later he began to get on my nerves. He was always hanging around until I would get back from high school, always looking like he had something to say to me or wanted me to tell him. He made me a magazine rack in his Manual Training class and one week he saved his lunch money and bought me three packs of cigarettes. He couldn't seem to take it in that I had things on my mind and didn't want to fool with him. Every afternoon it would be the same—him in my room with this waiting expression on his face. Then I wouldn't say anything or I'd maybe answer him rough-like and he would finally go on out.

I can't divide that time up and say this happened one day and that the next. For one thing I was so mixed up the weeks just slid along into each other and I felt like Hell and didn't care. Nothing definite was said or done. Maybelle still rode around with this fellow in his yellow roadster and sometimes she would smile at me and sometimes not. Every afternoon I went from one place to another where I thought she would be. Either she would act almost nice and I would begin thinking how nice things would finally clear up and she would care for me— or else she'd behave so that if she hadn't been a girl I'd have wanted to grab her by that white little neck and choke her. The more ashamed I felt for making a fool of myself the more I ran after her.

Sucker kept getting on my nerves more and more. He would look at me as though he sort of blamed me for something, but at the same time knew that it wouldn't last long. He was growing fast and for some reason began to stutter when he talked. Sometimes he had nightmares or would throw up his breakfast. Mom got him a bottle of cod liver oil.

Then the finish came between Maybelle and me. I met her going to the drug store and asked for a date. When she said no I remarked something sarcastic. She told me she was sick and tired of my being around and that she had never cared a rap about me. She said all that. I just stood there and didn't answer anything. I walked home very slowly.

For several afternoons I stayed in my room by myself. I didn't want to go anywhere or talk to anyone. When Sucker would come in and look at me sort of funny I'd yell at him to get out. I didn't want to think of Maybelle and I sat at my desk reading *Popular Mechanics* or whittling at a toothbrush rack I was making. It seemed to me I was putting that girl out of my mind pretty well.

But you can't help what happens to you at night. That is what made things how they are now.

You see a few nights after Maybelle said those words to me I dreamed about her again. It was like that first time and I was squeezing Sucker's arm so tight I woke him up. He reached for my hand.

"Pete, what's the matter with you?"

All of a sudden I felt so mad my throat choked—at myself and the dream and Maybelle and Sucker and every single person I knew. I remembered all the times Maybelle had humiliated me and everything bad that had ever happened. It seemed to me for a second that nobody would ever like me but a sap like Sucker.

"Why is it we aren't buddies like we were before? Why—?"

"Shut your damn trap!" I threw off the cover and got up and turned on the light. He sat in the middle of the bed, his eyes blinking and scared.

There was something in me and I couldn't help myself. I don't think anybody ever gets that mad but once. Words came without me knowing what they would be.

It was only afterward that I could remember each thing I said and see it all in a clear way.

"Why aren't we buddies? Because you're the dumbest slob I ever saw! Nobody cares anything about you! And just because I felt sorry for you sometimes and tried to act decent don't think I give a damn about a dumb-bunny like you!"

If I'd talked loud or hit him it wouldn't have been so bad. But my voice was slow and like I was very calm. Sucker's mouth was part way open and he looked as though he'd knocked his funny bone. His face was white and sweat came out on his forehead. He wiped it away with the back of his hand and for a minute his arm stayed raised that way as though he was holding something away from him.

"Don't you know a single thing? Haven't you ever been around at all? Why don't you get a girl friend instead of me? What kind of a sissy do you want to grow up to be anyway?"

I didn't know what was coming next. I couldn't help myself or think.

Sucker didn't move. He had on one of my pajama jackets and his neck stuck out skinny and small. His hair was damp on his forehead.

"Why do you always hang around me? Don't you know when you're not wanted?"

Afterward I could remember the change in Sucker's face. Slowly that blank look went away and he closed his mouth. His eyes got narrow and his fists shut. There had never been such a look on him before. It was like every second he was getting older. There was a hard look to his eyes you don't see usually in a kid. A drop of sweat rolled down his chin and he didn't notice. He just sat there with those eyes on me and he didn't speak and his face was hard and didn't move.

"No you don't know when you're not wanted. You're too dumb. Just like your name—a dumb Sucker."

It was like something had busted inside me. I turned off the light and sat down in the chair by the window. My legs were shaking and I was so tired I could have bawled. The room was cold and dark. I sat there for a long time and smoked a squashed cigarette I had saved. Outside the yard was black and quiet. After a while I heard Sucker lie down.

I wasn't mad any more, only tired. It seemed awful to me that I had talked like that to a kid only twelve. I couldn't take it all in. I told myself I would go over to him and try to make it up. But I just sat there in the cold until a long time had passed. I planned how I could straighten it out in the morning. Then, trying not to squeak the springs, I got back in bed.

Sucker was gone when I woke up the next day. And later when I wanted to apologize as I had planned he looked at me in this new hard way so that I couldn't say a word.

All of that was two or three months ago. Since then Sucker has grown faster than any boy I ever saw. He's almost as tall as I am and his bones have gotten heavier and bigger. He won't wear any of my old clothes any more and has bought his first pair of long pants—with some leather suspenders to hold them up. Those are just the changes that are easy to see and put into words.

Our room isn't mine at all any more. He's gotten up this gang of kids and they have a club. When they aren't digging trenches in some vacant lot and fighting they are always in my room. On the door there is some foolishness written in Mercurochrome saying "Woe to the Outsider who Enters" and signed with crossed bones and their secret initials. They have rigged up a radio and every afternoon it blares out music. Once as I was coming in I heard a boy telling something in a loud voice about what he saw in the back of his big brother's automobile. I could guess what I didn't hear. *That's what her and my brother do. It's the truth—parked in the car.* For a minute Sucker looked surprised and his face was almost like it used to be. Then he got hard and tough again. "Sure, dumbbell. We know all that." They didn't notice me. Sucker began telling them how in two years he was planning to be a trapper in Alaska.

But most of the time Sucker stays by himself. It is

worse when we are alone together in the room. He sprawls across the bed in those long corduroy pants with the suspenders and just stares at me with that hard, half-sneering look. I fiddle around my desk and can't get settled because of those eyes of his. And the thing is I just have to study because I've gotten three bad cards this term already. If I flunk English I can't graduate next year. I don't want to be a bum and I just have to get my mind on it. I don't care a flip for Maybelle or any particular girl any more and it's only this thing between Sucker and me that is the trouble now. We never speak except when we have to before the family. I don't even want to call him Sucker any more and unless I forget I call him by his real name, Richard. At night I can't study with him in the room and I have to hang around the drug store, smoking and doing nothing, with the fellows who loaf there.

More than anything I want to be easy in my mind again. And I miss the way Sucker and I were for a while in a funny, sad way that before this I never would have believed. But everything is so different that there seems to be nothing I can do to get it right. I've sometimes thought if we could have it out in a big fight that would help. But I can't fight him because he's four years younger. And another thing—sometimes this look in his eyes makes me almost believe that if Sucker could he would kill me.

Alice Walker

Alice Walker was born in Eatonton, Georgia, in 1944, the daughter of a man who was a sharecropper and a woman whose creativity she celebrated in her influential essay, "In Search of Our Mothers' Gardens." Walker attended Spelman College and received a B.A. from Sarah Lawrence. She worked in the voter registration drive in Georgia in the 1960s, in a Head Start Program in Mississippi, and for the New York City welfare department. She has taught at Jackson State, Tougaloo, Wellesley, the University of Massachusetts, Berkeley, and Brandeis. A frequent contributor to such periodicals as *Negro Digest, Ms., Southern Voices*, and *Essence*, she has written five volumes of poetry and two collections of essays. Her collections of stories are *In Love and Trouble* (1973) and *You Can't Keep a Good Woman Down* (1981), and her novels are *The Third Life of Grange Copeland* (1970), *Meridian* (1976), *The Temple of My Familiar* (1989), and *The Color Purple* (1982), which won a Pulitzer Prize and the American Book Award and was made into a major motion picture. While Alice Walker's writing is often about the racism and sexism black women experience, writer Gloria Steinem finds a universality in her work: "She speaks the female experience more powerfully for being able to pursue it across boundaries of race and class." At the same time that Walker writes of the tragedies in black women's lives, her vision tends toward affirmation, reconciliation, and transformation. Although she lives in San Francisco, she has said that her roots as a writer go back to the tradition of oral storytelling that has been "respected" in the South.

Everyday Use

for your grandmama

I will wait for her in the yard that Maggie and I made so clean and wavy yesterday afternoon. A yard like this is more comfortable than most people know. It is not just a yard. It is like an extended living room. When the hard clay is swept clean as a floor and the fine sand around the edges lined with tiny, irregular grooves, anyone can come and sit and look up into the elm tree and wait for the breezes that never come inside the house.

Maggie will be nervous until after her sister goes: she will stand hopelessly in corners, homely and ashamed of the burn scars down her arms and legs, eying her sister with a mixture of envy and awe. She thinks her sister has held life always in the palm of one hand, that "no" is a word the world never learned to say to her.

You've no doubt seen those TV shows where the child who has "made it" is confronted, as a surprise, by her own mother and father, tottering in weakly from backstage. (A pleasant surprise, of course: What would they do if parent and child came on the show only to curse out and insult each other?) On TV mother and child embrace and smile into each other's faces. Sometimes the mother and father weep, the child wraps them in her arms and leans across the table to tell how she would not have made it without their help. I have seen these programs.

Sometimes I dream a dream in which Dee and I are suddenly brought together on a TV program of this sort.

Out of a dark and soft-seated limousine I am ushered into a bright room filled with many people. There I meet a smiling, gray, sporty man like Johnny Carson who shakes my hand and tells me what a fine girl I have. Then we are on the stage and Dee is embracing me with tears in her eyes. She pins on my dress a large orchid, even though she has told me once that she thinks orchids are tacky flowers.

In real life I am a large, big-boned woman with rough, man-working hands. In the winter I wear flannel night-gowns to bed and overalls during the day. I can kill and clean a hog as mercilessly as a man. My fat keeps me hot in zero weather. I can work outside all day, breaking ice to get water for washing; I can eat pork liver cooked over the open fire minutes after it comes steaming from the hog. One winter I knocked a bull calf straight in the brain between the eyes with a sledge hammer and had the meat hung up to chill before nightfall. But of course all this does not show on television. I am the way my daughter would want me to be: a hundred pounds lighter, my skin like an uncooked barley pancake. My hair glistens in the hot bright lights. Johnny Carson has much to do to keep up with my quick and witty tongue.

But this is a mistake. I know even before I wake up. Who ever knew a Johnson with a quick tongue? Who can even imagine me looking a strange white man in the eye? It seems to me I have talked to them always with one foot raised in flight, with my head turned in which-ever way is farthest from them. Dee, though. She would always look anyone in the eye. Hesitation was no part of her nature.

"How do I look, Mama?" Maggie says, showing just enough of her thin body enveloped in pink skirt and red blouse for me to know she's there, almost hidden by the door.

"Come out into the yard," I say.

Have you ever seen a lame animal, perhaps a dog run over by some careless person rich enough to own a car, sidle up to someone who is ignorant enough to be kind to him? That is the way my Maggie walks. She has been like this, chin on chest, eyes on ground, feet in shuffle, ever since the fire that burned the other house to the ground.

Dee is lighter than Maggie, with nicer hair and a fuller figure. She's a woman now, though sometimes I forget. How long ago was it that the other house burned? Ten, twelve years? Sometimes I can still hear the flames and feel Maggie's arms sticking to me, her hair smoking and her dress falling off her in little black papery flakes. Her eyes seemed stretched open, blazed open by the flames reflected in them. And Dee. I see her standing off under the sweet gum tree she used to dig gum out of; a look of concentration on her face as she watched the last dingy gray board of the house fall in toward the red-hot brick chimney. Why don't you do a dance around the ashes? I'd wanted to ask her. She had hated the house that much.

I used to think she hated Maggie, too. But that was before we raised the money, the church and me, to send her to Augusta to school. She used to read to us without pity; forcing words, lies, other folks' habits, whole lives upon us two, sitting trapped and ignorant underneath her voice. She washed us in a river of make-believe, burned us with a lot of knowledge we didn't necessarily need to know. Pressed us to her with the serious way she read, to shove us away at just the moment, like dimwits, we seemed about to understand.

Dee wanted nice things. A yellow organdy dress to wear to her graduation from high school; black pumps to match a green suit she'd made from an old suit somebody gave me. She was determined to stare down any disaster in her efforts. Her eyelids would not flicker for minutes at a time. Often I fought off the temptation to shake her. At sixteen she had a style of her own: and knew what style was.

I never had an education myself. After second grade the school was closed down. Don't ask me why: in 1927 colored asked fewer questions than they do now. Sometimes Maggie reads to me. She stumbles along good-naturedly but can't see well. She knows she is not bright. Like good looks and money, quickness passed her by. She will marry John Thomas (who has mossy teeth in an earnest face) and then I'll be free to sit here and I guess just sing church songs to myself. Although I never was a good singer. Never could carry a tune. I was always better at a man's job. I used to love to milk till I was hooked in the side in '49. Cows are soothing and slow and don't bother you, unless you try to milk them the wrong way.

I have deliberately turned my back on the house. It is three rooms, just like the one that burned, except the roof is tin; they don't make shingle roofs any more. There are no real windows, just some holes cut in the sides, like the portholes in a ship, but not round and not square, with rawhide holding the shutters up on the outside. This house is in a pasture, too, like the other one. No doubt when Dee sees it she will want to tear it down. She wrote me once that no matter where we "choose" to live, she will manage to come see us. But she will never bring her friends. Maggie and I thought about this and Maggie asked me, "Mama, when did Dee ever *have* any friends?"

She had a few. Furtive boys in pink shirts hanging about on washday after school. Nervous girls who never laughed. Impressed with her they worshiped the well-turned phrase, the cute shape, the scalding humor that erupted like bubbles in lye. She read to them.

When she was courting Jimmy T she didn't have much time to pay to us, but turned all her faultfinding power on him. He *flew* to marry a cheap city girl from a family of ignorant flashy people. She hardly had time to recompose herself.

When she comes I will meet—but there they are!

Maggie attempts to make a dash for the house, in her shuffling way, but I stay her with my hand. "Come back here," I say. And she stops and tries to dig a well in the sand with her toe.

It is hard to see them clearly through the strong sun. But even the first glimpse of leg out of the car tells me it is Dee. Her feet were always neat-looking, as if God himself had shaped them with a certain style. From the other side of the car comes a short, stocky man. Hair is all over his head a foot long and hanging from his chin like a kinky mule tail. I hear Maggie suck in her breath. "Uhnnnh," is what it sounds like. Like when you see the wriggling end of a snake just in front of your foot on the road. "Uhnnnh."

Dee next. A dress down to the ground, in this hot weather. A dress so loud it hurts my eyes. There are yellows and oranges enough to throw back the light of the sun. I feel my whole face warming from the heat waves it throws out. Earrings gold, too, and hanging down to her shoulders. Bracelets dangling and making noises when she moves her arm up to shake the folds of the dress out of her armpits. The dress is loose and flows, and as she walks closer, I like it. I hear Maggie go "Uhnnnh" again. It is her sister's hair. It stands straight up like the wool on a sheep. It is black as night and around the edges are two long pigtails that rope about like small lizards disappearing behind her ears.

"Wa-su-zo-Tean-o!" she says, coming on in that gliding way the dress makes her move. The short stocky fellow with the hair to his navel is all grinning and he follows up with "Asalamalakim, my mother and sister!" He moves to hug Maggie but she falls back, right up against the back of my chair. I feel her trembling there and when I look up I see the perspiration falling off her chin.

"Don't get up," says Dee. Since I am stout it takes something of a push. You can see me trying to move a second or two before I make it. She turns, showing white heels through her sandals, and goes back to the car. Out she peeks next with a Polaroid. She stoops down quickly and lines up picture after picture of me sitting there in front of the house with Maggie cowering behind me. She never takes a shot without making sure the house is included. When a cow comes nibbling around the edge of the yard she snaps it and me and Maggie *and* the house. Then she puts the Polaroid in the back seat of the car, and comes up and kisses me on the forehead.

Meanwhile Asalamalakim is going through motions with Maggie's hand. Maggie's hand is as limp as a fish, and probably as cold, despite the sweat, and she keeps trying to pull it back. It looks like Asalamalakim wants to shake hands but wants to do it fancy. Or maybe he don't know how people shake hands. Anyhow, he soon gives up on Maggie.

"Well," I say. "Dee."

"No, Mama," she says. "Not 'Dee,' Wangero Leewanika Kemanjo!"

"What happened to 'Dee'?" I wanted to know.

"She's dead," Wangero said. "I couldn't bear it any longer, being named after the people who oppress me."

"You know as well as me you was named after your aunt Dicie," I said. Dicie is my sister. She named Dee. We called her "Big Dee" after Dee was born.

"But who was *she* named after?" asked Wangero.

"I guess after Grandma Dee," I said.

"And who was she named after?" asked Wangero.

"Her mother," I said, and saw Wangero was getting tired. "That's about as far back as I can trace it," I said. Though, in fact, I probably could have carried it back beyond the Civil War through the branches.

"Well," said Asalamalakim, "there you are."

"Uhnnnh," I heard Maggie say.

"There I was not," I said, "before 'Dicie' cropped up in our family, so why should I try to trace it that far back?"

He just stood there grinning, looking down on me like somebody inspecting a Model A car. Every once in a while he and Wangero sent eye signals over my head.

"How do you pronounce this name?" I asked.

"You don't have to call me by it if you don't want to," said Wangero.

"Why shouldn't I?" I asked. "If that's what you want us to call you, we'll call you."

"I know it might sound awkward at first," said Wangero.

"I'll get used to it," I said. "Ream it out again."

Well, soon we got the name out of the way. Asalamalakim had a name twice as long and three times as hard. After I tripped over it two or three times he told me to just call him Hakim-a-barber. I wanted to ask him was he a barber, but I didn't really think he was, so I didn't ask.

"You must belong to those beef-cattle peoples down the road," I said. They said "Asalamalakim" when they met you, too, but they didn't shake hands. Always too busy: feeding the cattle, fixing the fences, putting up saltlick shelters, throwing down hay. When the white folks poisoned some of the herd the men stayed up all night with rifles in their hands. I walked a mile and a half just to see the sight.

Hakim-a-barber said, "I accept some of their doctrines, but farming and raising cattle is not my style." (They didn't tell me, and I didn't ask, whether Wangero (Dee) had really gone and married him.)

We sat down to eat and right away he said he didn't eat collards and pork was unclean. Wangero, though, went on through the chitlins and corn bread, the greens and everything else. She talked a blue streak over the sweet potatoes. Everything delighted her. Even the fact that we still used the benches her daddy made for the table when we couldn't afford to buy chairs.

"Oh, Mama!" she cried. Then turned to Hakim-a-barber. "I never knew how lovely these benches are. You can feel the rump prints," she said, running her hands underneath her and along the bench. Then she gave a sigh and her hand closed over Grandma Dee's butter dish. "That's it!" she said. "I knew there was something I wanted to ask you if I could have." She jumped up from the table and went over in the corner where the churn stood, the milk in it clabber by now. She looked at the churn and looked at it.

"This churn top is what I need," she said. "Didn't

Uncle Buddy whittle it out of a tree you all used to have?"

"Yes," I said.

"Uh huh," she said happily. "And I want the dasher, too."

"Uncle Buddy whittle that, too?" asked the barber.

Dee (Wangero) looked up at me.

"Aunt Dee's first husband whittled the dash," said Maggie so low you almost couldn't hear her. "His name was Henry, but they called him Stash."

"Maggie's brain is like an elephant's," Wangero said, laughing. "I can use the churn top as a centerpiece for the alcove table," she said, sliding a plate over the churn, "and I'll think of something artistic to do with the dasher."

When she finished wrapping the dasher the handle stuck out. I took it for a moment in my hands. You didn't even have to look close to see where hands pushing the dasher up and down to make butter had left a kind of sink in the wood. In fact, there were a lot of small sinks; you could see where thumbs and fingers had sunk into the wood. It was beautiful light yellow wood, from a tree that grew in the yard where Big Dee and Stash had lived.

After dinner Dee (Wangero) went to the trunk at the foot of my bed and started rifling through it. Maggie hung back in the kitchen over the dishpan. Out came Wangero with two quilts. They had been pieced by Grandma Dee and then Big Dee and me had hung them on the quilt frames on the front porch and quilted them. One was in the Lone Star pattern. The other was Walk Around the Mountain. In both of them were scraps of dresses Grandma Dee had worn fifty and more years ago. Bits and pieces of Grandpa Jarrell's Paisley shirts. And one teeny faded blue piece, about the size of a penny matchbox, that was from Great Grandpa Ezra's uniform that he wore in the Civil War.

"Mama," Wangero said sweet as a bird. "Can I have these old quilts?"

I heard something fall in the kitchen, and a minute later the kitchen door slammed.

"Why don't you take one or two of the others?" I asked. "These old things was just done by me and Big Dee from some tops your grandma pieced before she died."

"No," said Wangero. "I don't want those. They are stiched around the borders by machine."

"That'll make them last better," I said.

"That's not the point," said Wangero. "These are all pieces of dresses Grandma used to wear. She did all this stitching by hand. Imagine!" She held the quilts securely in her arms, stroking them.

"Some of the pieces, like those lavender ones, come from old clothes her mother handed down to her," I said, moving up to touch the quilts. Dee (Wangero) moved back just enough so that I couldn't reach the quilts. They already belonged to her.

"Imagine!" she breathed again, clutching them closely to her bosom.

"The truth is," I said, "I promised to give them quilts to Maggie, for when she marries John Thomas."

She gasped like a bee had stung her.

"Maggie can't appreciate these quilts!" she said. "She'd probably be backward enough to put them to everyday use."

"I reckon she would," I said. "God knows I been saving 'em for long enough with nobody using 'em. I hope she will!" I didn't want to bring up how I had offered Dee (Wangero) a quilt when she went away to college. Then she had told me they were old-fashioned, out of style.

"But they're *priceless*!" she was saying now, furiously; for she has a temper. "Maggie would put them on the bed and in five years they'd be in rags. Less than that!"

"She can always make some more," I said. "Maggie knows how to quilt."

Dee (Wangero) looked at me with hatred. "You just will not understand. The point is these quilts, *these* quilts!"

"Well," I said, stumped. "What would *you* do with them?"

"Hang them," she said. As if that was the only thing you *could* do with quilts.

Maggie by now was standing in the door. I could almost hear the sound her feet made as they scraped over each other

"She can have them, Mama," she said, like somebody used to never winning anything, or having anything reserved for her. "I can 'member Grandma Dee without the quilts."

I looked at her hard. She had filled her bottom lip with checkerberry snuff and it gave her face a kind of dopey, hangdog look. It was Grandma Dee and Big Dee who taught her how to quilt herself. She stood there with her scarred hands hidden in the folds of her skirt. She looked at her sister with something like fear but she wasn't mad at her. This was Maggie's portion. This was the way she knew God to work.

When I looked at her like that something hit me in the top of my head and ran down to the soles of my feet. Just like when I'm in church and the spirit of God touches me and I get happy and shout. I did something I never had done before: hugged Maggie to me, then dragged her on into the room, snatched the quilts out of Miss Wangero's hands and dumped them into Maggie's lap. Maggie just sat there on my bed with her mouth open.

"Take one or two of the others," I said to Dee.

But she turned without a word and went out to Hakim-a-barber.

"You just don't understand," she said, as Maggie and I came out to the car.

"What don't I understand?" I wanted to know.

"Your heritage," she said. And then she turned to Maggie, kissed her, and said, "You ought to try to make something of yourself, too, Maggie. It's really a new day for us. But from the way you and Mama still live you'd never know it."

She put on some sunglasses that hid everything above the tip of her nose and her chin.

Maggie smiled; maybe at the sunglasses. But a real smile, not scared. After we watched the car dust settle I asked Maggie to bring me a dip of snuff. And then the two of us sat there just enjoying, until it was time to go in the house and go to bed.

William Hoffman

William Hoffman was born in 1925 in Charleston, West Virginia, but most of his fiction is set in Virginia where he went to college and now lives. He received a B.A. from Hampden-Sydney College and began law school at Washington and Lee University. There he took a creative writing course, "just as a lark" he told a *McCall's* interviewer, but became "trapped" by writing, and decided to give up law school and attend the University of Iowa's Writers' Workshop for a year. Afterward he worked for a newspaper in Washington, D.C., and a bank in New York City, but eventually returned to Hampden-Sydney to teach English. In 1967 he was playwright-in-residence at the Barter Theatre in Abingdon, Virginia, where he wrote "The Love Touch." He is the author of several novels, including *The Trumpet Unblown* (1955), *The Dark Mountains* (1963), *A Walk to the River* (1970), *A Death of Dreams* (1973), and *Furor's Die* (1989). He has also published a collection of stories, *Virginia Reels* (1978). He makes his home in Charlotte Court House, Virginia, where he breeds horses.

Amazing Grace

The way we knew was that Nana, my grandmother, stopped making bread and instead of running the kitchen like a drill sergeant she walked out into the front yard and sat on a bench under the Indian cigar-tree.

"Maybe she's tired," my father said when he and I came in from changing the tire on the John Deere. "There's times I'd like to sit under that tree."

"That's not it," my mother said and slapped at me for reaching to get a hot corn-dodger from the stove.

My mother had to drive to the store to buy us bread. None of us remembered how sorry store-boughten tasted because Nana baked three times a week ever since I could remember—biscuits, rolls, and loaves, some of the loaves salt-rising bread which smelled up the house, and she had a cool dusky pantry with wooden shelves where she set her dough and bread, covering them with clean white cloths. Though there was a GE electric stove in the kitchen now, she still liked the old wood-burning Kalamazoo for her baking, or had until she walked out to sit under the Indian cigar-tree.

She sat and looked past the plank fence to the meadow and past the meadow to the barbed-wire fence at the road. Beyond the road the valley sloped up to a ridge, and on the other side of that ridge was Virginia, but here in the valley it was West Virginia, not the coal-mining part, but farming. The grassy hills had outcroppings of limestone, and sometimes it was hard to see the difference between the limestone and sheep grazing the slopes.

"It's Henry," my mother said to my father on Wednesday night after Nana went to bed. My mother and father were sitting in the kitchen, at the metal table that had paper towels for mats, their arms on the table, sitting not to eat or drink but to talk. My father was tall, which was unusual for us Sharps, who ran to heft, yet he had their blond hair and heaviness of jaw, like me. My mother, a Henson, was a small woman, though strong, and her hair and eyes were dark brown.

"What about Henry?" my father asked.

"He's not been to the river," my mother said. "None of his has."

My daddy's two sisters, Aunt Henrietta and Aunt Cornelia, were both older than him. They and their husbands, Albert and Asa, came the next night to the kitchen, again after Nana was in bed. It was agreed my father should speak to Henry in person since that would be more effective than just a letter or a phone call. Early Friday Daddy put on his gray suit and drove the Ford pickup to Pittsburgh.

The night he came back I was scrubbing my hair. Every Saturday night I had to wash my hair, and my mother inspected it, parted the hair to look at my scalp the way a person would search for a dime lost in the grass.

"They own a house out of town now," my father said. "Place called Sewickley, kind of in the country."

"Smoke and grit?" my mother asked.

"Not yesterday and today when I left, though Henry never minded smoke and grit," my father said. "Henry always claims smoke and grit shakes off money. You can live clean and pure in the desert where the air's perfect, Henry says, but that's all you got except sand. Where people do honest work, there's going to be some smoke and grit, Henry says."

"Dale Blue still have the same color hair?" my mother asked about Henry's wife.

"That's enough," my father said.

Uncle Henry was the member of the family who'd left. He first played football for West Virginia University, right tackle, and afterwards he became a mining engineer. His job took him to the southwest part of the state near Kentucky, and while he was driving a shaft into a seam of bituminous coal a steel company bought the seam, and he found himself in the steel business. Now he had an office in Pittsburgh overlooking the Monongahela River and barges carrying his money.

"That's not coal in those barges," he told me when he came back to the farm and showed snapshots. "Those are black lumps of money being shoved to my bank."

That's the way I thought of him, sitting up high in his shiny office watching the tugs nose his money to the bank. I guess the bank had a rear door on the river to take the money through.

During the summer Nana sat under the Indian cigartree. One afternoon she lifted her chin, and I saw the car glint a long ways off. The road was paved, but the speed of the car still raised tan dust along both shoulders. The horn started honking. It had to be.

"It's him!" I shouted, running to Nana. "It's Uncle Henry!"

"Drives too fast," she said.

I'd seen pictures of Nana when she was a girl in high school, and she'd been thin, like my daddy, and smiling, her head lowered, her dark hair parted in the middle and pulled back, her eyes raised, her feet set a little pigeon-toed. It'd been graduation time, and she'd worn a white dress and black slippers.

Over the years she'd grown shorter and thicker, not fat because she'd never stayed still long enough to gather fat, but stout the way an oak tree is stout. When I kissed her before she went to bed, I felt the strength in her. She was no puny old woman. Her forearm was as hard as my father's. I'd seen her hit a mule so hard with a hoe handle that he was cross-eyed for ten minutes.

I climbed the plank fence, ran across the meadow, and jumped the ditch to open the gate for Uncle Henry. Naturally he came in his big car. He knew I'd be disappointed if he didn't. One of the things he'd do on visits was to take me in his car and run her up to about a hundred. This time it was a gunmetal Cadillac with white sidewalls and tinted windows.

Dale Blue, his wife, was in front beside him. Like my mother would, the first thing I did was look at her hair, yellowish now, though I'd seen it both black and platinum, sometimes short, sometimes long, now piled on top of her head in a twist. It reminded me of custard on a cone at the Tastee Freeze.

She was the prettiest woman I'd ever seen. We lived in the country, but we had TV, and I'd drive in the truck with Daddy to the livestock market in Lewisburg, so I'd seen some pretty women, but she was the best yet, always licked to a gloss, her jewelry glittering, her clothes bright and fresh, herself sweet-smelling. The last time she was on the farm I walked into the bathroom while she was drying and stepping from the tub, and I saw one of her creamy bosoms. I get hot in the face even thinking about it.

After opening and shutting the gate, I rode in with them. Dale Blue gave me a wet, perfumed kiss. Uncle Henry shook hands and roughed my hair. In the back seat was Dawson, their son and my cousin. He was my age. Though built low and square like the Sharps, he had red hair. As soon as his parents weren't looking, he frogged me on the arm. That frog jumped out at least three inches.

"Oh aw!" I said.

"What's that, hon?" Dale Blue asked, turning and smiling.

"Just clearing my throat," I said.

"Got him a frog in it," Dawson said.

Uncle Henry drove to the house. He didn't wait for Dale Blue or Dawson but was out of the car and vaulting the plank fence before they opened a door. He kissed Nana, hugged her, and knelt on the ground beside her, not caring about grass stain on his peach slacks.

"How come you sitting out here and not fixing me an angel food?" Uncle Henry asked. "You always fix me my angel food cake when I come."

"You going to the river before I die?" Nana asked.

"What, you die? Listen, Momma, I don't want any talk of dying around here, and I been wetted anyhow.

I'm a bonafide deacon in the church. I have my own pew every Sunday, and I bought a big window showing Jesus with the twelve."

"You weren't wetted in our river," Nana said.

Dale Blue and Dawson had walked through the gate, and my mother was coming from the porch. My father drove his tractor toward the house. As soon as Uncle Henry was in the county, things happened. The summer air stirred, and our water ran cooler. We touched each other and laughed. No wonder the rich people in Pittsburgh liked him.

"And look here, Momma, here's Dale Blue and little Dawson," Uncle Henry said. "They all want to kiss you."

As she leaned to Nana, one of Dale Blue's diamond earrings got tangled in Nana's white hair. For a minute Dale Blue and Uncle Henry were laughing and calling out as they unsnagged the earring, but Nana wasn't laughing. She stared at Dale Blue and Dawson as if they'd stolen the church.

"None's been to the river," Nana said.

"Ah come on, Momma, forget the river a second, will you?" Uncle Henry said. He ran and jumped the plank fence to reach his Caddy. In the trunk he had presents for everybody. I got me a baseball mitt. My mother was handed a five-pound can of peanut brittle, and Daddy shouldered a big net sack of Florida grapefruits.

For Nana Uncle Henry had a clock, a grandfather clock which he and my daddy lugged in pieces across the grass and put together under the Indian cigar-tree. They leveled it and hooked on golden weights shaped like pine cones. The brass pendulum swung into a shaft of sunshine. When the clock ticked and gonged, the cows stopped grazing and lifted their heads. Two crows spiraled cawing from the corn.

"Eight days," Uncle Henry explained to Nana. "Eight whole days and you don't have to pull the chains to wind her."

Nana eyed the clock. She had an oval face, and her

hair was thin, wispy cotton. She adjusted her glasses to peer at the clock. Then she turned away.

"But don't you like it?" Dale Blue asked. "Henry went to lots of trouble to bring it."

"All that clock tells me is my days are running out, and nobody's been to the river," Nana said.

She wouldn't look at the clock again. The men carried it into the hall to set it up a second time, but she went to bed without glancing at it. Uncle Henry and Dale Blue came to the kitchen where they sat around the table with my mother and daddy as well as Aunt Henrietta and Aunt Cornelia and their husbands Albert and Asa.

"She's sure low," Aunt Cornelia said while she poured iced tea from a glass pitcher, her arms brown from helping Uncle Asa in the hayfields. "I've not seen her this far down since lightning hit the heifers."

"Spoiled is what she is," Dale Blue said.

Boy, eyes bugged at Dale Blue as if she was a snake on a rock. She was in the family but not of it. She colored, touched her frozen-custard hair, and shrugged.

"Honey, maybe you better let me do the talking here," Uncle Henry said.

"But she's pouting like a child," Dale Blue said.

"All the work she's done for this family she's got a right to pout until Moses makes sauerkraut out of little sour apples in December," Aunt Henrietta said.

Dale Blue kind of sniffed, crossed her arms, and jiggled a pretty foot in a black-and-white slipper. From time to time while the others talked she'd raise her nose as if she wasn't sure she should be breathing the same air as the rest of us. She came from West Virginia too, from Beckley, but she didn't tell anybody if she could help it.

"Give me another day anyhow," Uncle Henry said, standing. "Maybe I can fun her up tomorrow."

"I know you're tired," my mother said. "The spare room's ready."

"Oh, well, we won't be needing the spare room, thanks," Dale Blue said. "Henry made us a reservation over at White Sulphur. Allows him to combine business with pleasure. The railroad men are having a convention."

Nobody said anything, first because they couldn't imagine a member of the family not staying at the farm and second because no one in our family had ever slept at the resort before—a white hotel covering acres and acres where they had a private airport, golf courses, stables, and foreign servants who wore red jackets. To us in the county the resort and grounds were like another country.

"I don't know whether you ought to do that, Henry," my father said. "Momma might not understand."

"Blame me," Dale Blue said. "I've signed up for a bath."

"You can use the tub here," I said and thought of the time I'd seen her creamy bosom fall over the lilac towel. I again got hot in the face.

"Sh-h-h," my mother said to me, and Dawson snickered.

"What difference does it make except cause you all less trouble?" Dale Blue asked. "Henry and Dawson will come back tomorrow and spend the day."

She led them out to the car. We watched the Caddy's red taillights in the darkness. My mother made me go up to bed, but I sneaked down to hear them talking in the kitchen.

"Henry's changed," Aunt Henrietta said and sighed.

"It's not Henry," Aunt Cornelia said. "Nothing's wrong with Henry."

"I wonder Dale Blue don't make him wear a bib at the table," my daddy said.

I sank to sleep hearing the ticking and gonging of the grandfather clock downstairs, and then I woke because I wasn't hearing it. I peeked over the railing. Nana was at the clock. She held her flashlight, and her hand had stilled the pendulum. She shuffled to her bedroom.

"Can't sleep with all that clanging," she said.

The next morning I was mowing as soon as the sun dried the orchard grass. I drove the small tractor, the Ford, running her in second gear and keeping the swaths neat as the clattering blade felled the grass. My father drove the big tractor, the John Deere, and was pulling the bailer over windrows in a seven-acre field we'd cut three days earlier. My uncles loaded bales on the wagon.

When Uncle Henry came, he too threw bales on the wagon. He showed off his strength by tossing the bales like basketballs. He laughed and joked with his brothers. He wasn't dressed for work but wore a red shirt, apricot pants, and what he called shag chukkas, which my daddy asked him to spell. Uncle Henry worked until he was sweat shiny.

He tried everything to cheer up Nana. He tuned the banjo, his old one from the hall closet, and sang "Rye Whiskey," "The Possum's Lament," and "The Coal Miner's Daughter." He stomped as he played, and later, sitting on the bench beside Nana, he told her stories about Pittsburgh and his new house which had doors that opened and closed when he pushed buttons. It had a sauna and a putting green.

"That house'll do everything for you except pick your teeth," he said.

"Will it bake bread?" I asked.

"Sh-h-h," my mother said.

Nana listened and watched. She kept her bluish-gray eyes on him every second, but she never smiled or put out her hand to him, though she loved him so much she'd set his picture on the center of the mantel in her bedroom. She had other pictures, but his was the place of honor, and she sometimes draped a rose or shasta daisy over the frame.

We ate lunch on the grass around the Indian cigartree, a picnic in the yard for all the hands—cold chicken, melons, and lemonade. Nana swallowed a bite or two, but not as if she enjoyed it. Mostly she nibbled and looked at the sheep on the sunny slope. She seemed to forget she was eating.

That afternoon Preacher Arbogast came. He drove a Chevy which he parked beside Uncle Henry's Caddy. Preacher Arbogast was a small pop-eyed man always washed to a waxy finish. When he walked, he did it like a person measuring every step. He shook hands around.

There was chicken for him, but he wouldn't sit on the grass to eat it the way the rest of the men did. He let my daddy bring him a chair from the house.

"I was hoping to meet your wife this time, Henry," Preacher Arbogast said.

"She's in the bathtub all day," I said.

"Sh-h-h," my mother said, and Dawson again snickered.

After the picnic it was time to go back to haying. Nana, Uncle Henry, and Preacher Arbogast stayed in the yard. I was now driving Uncle Asa's International and pulling the wagon. Dawson rode behind me on the drawbar. He wanted to steer.

"If a hick-freak like you can do it, anybody can," he said.

"Everybody in Pennsylvania got mouths as big as yours?" I asked.

He punched me in the ribs. I almost fell off the seat. My daddy saw us and hollered. Dawson jumped from the drawbar and walked to Daddy who listened to him. Daddy waved to stop me, came over to the tractor, and told me to teach Dawson to drive.

The thing that made me maddest was that after a few minutes Dawson drove the International almost as good as I could, that and the fact he got to sit up there in his new jeans and act like a king while I had to throw bales on the wagon. Those bales weighed fifty or sixty pounds. I was strong for my age, eleven, but it was man's work, and the next time we unloaded at the barn, I snuck to the house to see if I could find some of that picnic lemonade.

Nana, Preacher Arbogast, and Uncle Henry were still in the yard. I tiptoed through the front bedroom to listen at a window screen that flies buzzed around and bumped against.

"But, Momma, I got here an affidavit," Uncle Henry said. "It's signed and sworn to by my pastor in Sewickley. It's duly notarized. It proves I'm a baptized member of the church."

"You've not been baptized like a Sharp in our river," Nana said.

"But it's not required," Uncle Henry said. "Ask the

Reverend Arbogast here about it, and he'll tell you I'm genuinely saved."

"Technically I have to agree," Preacher Arbogast said.

"What do you mean 'technically'?" Uncle Henry asked, and he was angry.

"Outside the denomination you've been," Preacher Arbogast said. "We don't know for sure what they're doing up in Pennsylvania."

"You telling me only you and the Greenbrier River Baptists around here can save me?" Uncle Henry asked, flapping his arms.

"All the Sharps has been to our river," Nana said. "You escaped because you were a sickly boy, and for a time we went without a preacher. Then you slipped away from the county before anybody remembered you'd not been in the river."

It's all I was able to hear. My mother came tiptoeing into the same bedroom. She almost jumped out of her shoes when she pulled back the curtain and saw me standing there looking at her. She yelped and chased me off by shoving me on the back. I went, but I knew she stayed and listened.

In the hayfield Dawson was wheeling around on the International. My daddy stared at me and spat because I'd been gone. I again threw bales on the wagon. Each time I lifted I grunted, and sweat stung my eyes. Chaff made me sneeze. Dawson was driving the tractor so fast I had to hurry with the bales. I fell, but he didn't wait. He grinned at me.

When we finally got the field cleared and the bales stacked in the barn, I lay down in the shade of a syca-more tree. I rested and wondered if Uncle Henry was going to be too worried to take me for a fast ride in the gunmetal Caddy. Dawson walked by. He was still clean in his T-shirt, pressed jeans, and white tennis shoes.

"What's the matter, Cousin Willie Hick-freak?" he asked.

"You going to make me get up out of this shade to whip you?" I asked.

"You'd commit suicide just because I called you Willie

Hick-freak?" he asked. "Your name's Willie, isn't it, and you got to admit you're a hick. At least that's what my momma says. Tell me this: you ever been on a jet plane or an escalator?"

"No," I admitted.

"You ever eaten in a French restaurant or swum in an Olympic-size pool?"

"No," I said.

"You ever seen the ocean?" he asked.

"No," I said.

"Then how can you claim you're not a hick-freak?" he asked.

"This is how," I said. I stood and punched him in the mouth.

He came back at me. He might be a city boy, but he was strong like Uncle Henry and knew more about boxing than I did. He was hitting me two or three times for every one I got him. I had to rush him, trip him, and close the scissors on him. I also put the stranglehold on him. He was gasping in the grass.

"Tell me how sorry you are," I said.

"Sorry you're a hick-freak," he said.

I tightened up. He flopped around and became sick. I let go fast. My nose was bleeding. I crawled away, lay on my back, and looked at the yellowish sky.

"You don't fight fair," Dawson said, his head hung like a whipped dog. "We were supposed to be boxing."

"You want to fight about what we were supposed to be doing?" I asked.

"At my school you don't rassle and box at the same time," he said.

"At your school the boys probably wear their hair like girls too," I said.

"Yeah, some of them do," he said. "And I've been to a stylist."

He touched his hair like a girl would, and that got me laughing. He started laughing. My nose had stopped bleeding. We walked to the barn to wash ourselves at the spigot. We bowed our heads under the water and blew into it. As to the bruise on my cheek, I told my mother I'd slipped against the hay wagon. She glanced at Dawson and would've questioned him about his torn T-shirt except she was too excited with news of Uncle Henry.

"He's going to do it," she told my daddy. "Him and Dale Blue and little Dawson."

"Little Dawson," I snickered.

"Has Dale Blue been told yet?" my daddy asked.

"Tonight," my mother said. "Give thanks."

"She ought to be clean enough," I said. "All day in a bath."

Dawson kicked me in the leg. Nobody saw him. I hopped around and hollered.

"Sh-h-h," my mother said.

Next morning when I woke, I heard a sound, something more than the birds, the cattle, and the creaking of the tin roof heating under the sun. I walked to the hallway. My mother and daddy were already standing there, she wearing her white nightgown, Daddy in his undershorts. They were smiling, and I smiled too because downstairs Nana was humming a hymn in her bedroom.

Still everybody was nervous Uncle Henry wouldn't be able to persuade Dale Blue. We watched the road from White Sulphur. Daddy looked at his watch. Uncle Asa spat tobacco juice into the geraniums, and Aunt Cornelia fussed at him for it.

When the Caddy came, it raised a whirling rooster-tail of dust. I ran to the gate. Dale Blue was sitting in the car with Uncle Henry and Dawson. Nana had walked out onto the porch. Uncle Henry hurried to her and hugged her.

"It's okay, Momma," he said. "Tell that old river to get itself set because a bunch of sharp Sharps is coming."

Nana held onto him and laughed. I saw how lively and pretty she must've been as a girl. Dale Blue wore a pink scarf and a pink pantsuit. Though Nana didn't like women in breeches, she kept herself from complaining and even offered her face to Dale Blue for a kiss. Dawson, while nobody was watching, tried to frog me. I was ready and elbowed him in the stomach. He moved around bent over. Uncle Asa drove off in his pickup to see if Preacher Arbogast could do the baptizing that afternoon.

"I don't understand how Henry swung it," Daddy whispered to my mother. "Dale Blue's acting almost pleased about going to the water."

I found out about that. Dawson and I ran to the barn to check the tractors and throw clods at the Hereford bull in the lot. We also punched each other a couple of times. Dawson was excited about the river.

"Will they let me swim?" he asked. "I never swam in anything except an Olympic-size pool and the ocean."

"No, you poor city-freak, Preacher Arbogast won't let you swim," I said. "He'll dunk you three times, but maybe you and me can slip back afterwards."

"If Momma doesn't get too worried about her hair," Dawson said. "I wish they didn't have to wet that."

"They do unless she can take it off first," I said.

"Well she shouldn't holler too loud since Dad's promised her a green Mercedes and a trip to Italy," Dawson said.

We ate lunch on the lawn. Daddy and my uncles carried out tables, and my mother and aunts covered them with Nana's linen cloths. Family arrived not only from Pocahontas County, but also from the other side of the mountain. They were served ham, snaps, deviled eggs, and seven kinds of pie people brought with them, including brown sugar, sweet potato, and lemon chess. Dawson and I gorged until we couldn't breathe except through our mouths. We were too bloated to punch each other. We stretched out on the grass and let flies walk over us.

"But what does one wear to the river?" Dale Blue asked, lifting her palms. "I simply don't have a thing with me."

"We'll supply you with a clean sheet," Aunt Henrietta said. "Everybody wears a sheet, man, woman, or child."

"Is there anything special I should dress in underneath?" Dale Blue asked and giggled.

"You wear underneath what you would to church," Aunt Cornelia said, disapproving.

The time for the baptism was four o'clock, and at three-thirty we filled up cars and started for the Greenbrier. Dale Blue, Dawson, and Uncle Henry had wrapped themselves in their sheets. The river was seven miles from the farm. We left the highway and wound on an unmarked black-top road through a state forest and into a gorge which was already partly shaded by the west slope of the wooded mountain.

The green river was shallow and fast, no mud in it because the bottom was all stones that had been shaped by the current until they were rounded like Nana's loaves of Jesus bread. On the rocky beach cars were parked.

"If anybody had ever told me I'd be doing a crazy thing like this," Dale Blue said.

"Salvation's not crazy," Nana said.

"What if I get water up my nose?" Dale Blue asked.

"Just breathe out when you go under," Uncle Henry said.

"If I get water up my nose, I might need a trip to Greece too," she said.

She didn't like the crowd, not only kin, but also a good many of the congregation as well as some fishermen and a group of sightseers. The thing that made her buck, though, was the photographers from Lewisburg who'd come because of Uncle Henry's reputation.

"No!" Dale Blue said, refusing to leave the Caddy. "He's not taking my picture! Suppose they see it in Sewickley. I couldn't show my face."

"Please, Dale Blue, for Momma," Uncle Henry pleaded.

"Not for anybody, not Dawson either, and not you if you remember who you are. They'll laugh you out of the Iron and Coal Club!"

She pulled the door shut, rolled up the window, and drew the sheet tight around herself. Uncle Henry circled the car begging her. Dawson was mad because he wanted to get into the river. The skinny photographer angled with his camera. He tried to take a picture of Dale Blue through the tinted windshield. She covered her face with her sheet. Uncle Henry, growing redder every second, ran him off, tripped on his sheet, and fell, showing for an instant his purple-and-white striped drawers, pale legs and wine garters.

"That's enough," Nana, between Uncle Asa and Albert, said. "We'll leave."

"They can do it to me," Uncle Henry said. "I'm ready to go to the water."

"Me too," Dawson said.

"We'll go home," Nana said.

We moved among gawking people to get back into the cars, and like a funeral procession we drove to the farm, all except Uncle Henry who tore off in the Caddy with Dale Blue and Dawson. Nana again sat on the bench under the Indian cigar-tree. Family milled around, picked at the ham, and dribbled away home.

"What'll Henry do to Dale Blue?" my mother asked my daddy that night.

"What'd Henry ever do but turn it so she'd have an easy time kicking it?" my daddy asked.

"Turn what?" I asked.

"Sh-h-h," my mother said. "Go to bed."

Barking dogs woke me. Daddy carried his flashlight and shotgun outside to see about it. He thought a fox or coon was after our chickens, but the henhouse was quiet. Finally the dogs stopped barking, though they whined a while.

I thought Uncle Henry, Dale Blue, and Dawson were gone to Pittsburgh, but the next morning they drove to the farm. They kissed Nana and pretended nothing had happened. Uncle Henry joked with her. She sat under the tree without moving.

Dale Blue hummed and prissed about. She had on earrings shaped like sunflowers, and she wore a yellow shirt, yellow shorts, and yellow tennis shoes. Her legs were the prettiest I'd ever seen, all the hair smoothed off, the skin tan and satiny, like a dancing girl instead of a married woman. I got caught looking at her legs. She smiled at me, and there I was hot in the face again.

"We thought you'd left," my mother said.

"Oh, we're going after while," Uncle Henry said. He

was dressed like Dale Blue, yellow shorts, yellow shirt, though his tennis shoes were white. His lumpy muscled legs were funny with hair curled man-thick over them. "I want to show Dale Blue around. She hasn't had much chance to see the farm, especially the view."

"The view?" my daddy asked.

"From the silo," Uncle Henry said. "I told her you can see a lot of the valley from the silo."

My mother looked at my daddy who looked at her as I looked at them, and they looked at me. Not many people would climb our silo. I'd do it, yet the first time and the second time too I'd been scared because the silo, made of reinforced concrete slabs, was a hundred and twenty feet high.

You ducked into a vertical hatch and went up an iron ladder covered by a wooden canopy to protect climbers from wind and weather. It was like rising in a dim upright tunnel, and at the top was a sliding metal door not to see the view from but to blow in silage and for ventilation. Beams and boards had been laid across the slabs just under the galvanized dome. My mother would never climb the silo, and it'd been a long time since my daddy had.

"At least she's got nerve," my daddy said as Uncle Henry, Dawson, and Dale Blue crossed the pasture toward the barn. Uncle Henry slowed to swing a hand down and pick up a pebble. He fingered the pebble.

I ran after them. The hatch on the silo was inside the barn. Dawson, acting brave, claimed he wanted to be the first to go up, but Uncle Henry told him ladies first. Dale Blue was afraid she'd dirty her yellow shirt or shorts. She didn't like putting her hands on the rusty rungs. She made a face.

"I don't think I want to," she said.

"You'll love it," Uncle Henry said. "You can see so far your eyes get tired from the distance."

"Go on without me," she said.

"Hon, you know I like to share everything with you," he said.

Still making a face, she started up. Uncle Henry went

after her, and me after Dawson. Since we were inside the wooden tunnel, we couldn't tell how high we'd climbed. Light came in only from cracks and from the opening at the top. We must've gone up a couple of minutes before Dale Blue got nervous.

"How far now?" she asked.

"We're close," Uncle Henry said, which was a lie.

"I'm tired," Dale Blue said after we climbed a while farther.

"Too much invested to stop now," Uncle Henry said. "Rest at the top."

"I don't think I like this," Dale Blue said. "We must be pretty high."

"You're pretty, high or low," Uncle Henry said. "And you'll forget the climb when you see the view."

Old Dawson wasn't talking much. Earlier he'd bragged about how he'd shinnied a rope up to the steel rafters of his school gym, but now all I heard was his breathing. I accidentally bumped against his leg and felt him trembling.

"Making it all right, city-freak?" I asked.

"Whew!" was the only thing he said.

At the top Dale Blue was really nervous. Her voice quivered.

"I'll help you up on the boards," Uncle Henry said.

"I don't like any of this," she said.

"Just ease on over," Uncle Henry said.

"Don't push!" she said.

He got her up on the boards, but he stayed on the ladder.

"Occurs to me they probably haven't replaced these boards and beams in years," Uncle Henry said. "Have they, Willie?"

"Not that I know about," I said.

"Hope they're not rotten," Uncle Henry said.

"Rotten!" Dale Blue said.

"Just look at that view, will you?" Uncle Henry said.

"The hell with the view!" Dale Blue said.

"You can see the old gristmill," Uncle Henry said.

"The hell with the old gristmill too," she said. "Am I on rotten boards?"

"Just don't move around a whole lot," Uncle Henry said. "It's higher than I remembered up here. Stick your head out the hole and look down, but be careful of the boards."

"No!" Dale Blue said.

"There's another way we can tell how high we are," Uncle Henry said. "I'll drop this pebble, and we'll see how long it takes to hit bottom."

He held out his hand and let go the pebble. I don't know, even for me who was used to the height, the pebble seemed to take about half an hour to hit. It caused a little plunk in the sour silage-mash, the plunk echoing in the hollowness of the dark silo.

"Get me down from here!" Dale Blue said.

"If you don't like the view, we can leave, but be careful of those boards," Uncle Henry said. "Don't move too much on those boards."

"Give me your hand!" Dale Blue said. "Henry?"

"You sound scared," he said.

"My teeth are clicking," she said.

"Momma, don't be afraid," Dawson said, but he was shivering on the ladder.

"Well I guess I'll help you down then," Uncle Henry said. "I forgot about those boards being up here so long they'd rot. Don't move fast now. And there is one thing before I give you my hand. You have to go to the river with me and Dawson."

"Damn you, Henry, don't you fool around with me up here!" she said.

"Who's fooling?" he asked. "Just tell me you'll go, and I'll give you my hand and help you down off those rotten boards which might give under you any second if you move too much."

"Henry, you bastard, you get me down or I'll make you so sorry you'll wish you lived under a rock!"

"I don't think you ought to talk to me like that, Dale Blue, not in the situation you're in."

"The situation you're in is if you don't get me down off here in a hurry I'll bust your ass!" she said.

"Let's climb down, boys," Uncle Henry said.

"You can't just leave her!" Dawson said.

"Henry, goddamn you, I'll go to the lawyers," Dale Blue said. "They'll take you tonsils to toenails."

"Your last opportunity," Uncle Henry said. "I'll help you off the boards and down the ladder if you promise to go to the river with Dawson and me. If you don't, you can come down by yourself. Now I wouldn't start yelling too loud on those boards."

I was already backing when she screamed words at him I never knew a woman could use. She didn't sound like herself, not only the cussing, but her voice in the silo seemed to be coming from ten directions at the same time. Dawson began crying. Uncle Henry had to force him down.

"Go on, boy," Uncle Henry said. "Go on now."

After I reached bottom, she was still shouting. Dawson was carrying on too. My mother and father were running toward the barn. Chickens squawked, cattle stampeded, and pigeons flapped so hard they shed feathers.

"I'm going back up!" Dawson hollered and tried to get on the ladder, but Uncle Henry dragged him away.

"Those beams and boards are all right," Uncle Henry said softly to Dawson. "I climbed up last night. They'll hold."

Daddy and I looked at each other and nodded. The barking dogs were explained.

"But she might fall anyhow!" Dawson said, his face wet, his lips bubbling.

"You know I love her too much to hurt her," Uncle Henry said. "And she thinks too much of herself to fall."

Uncle Henry stayed at the barn but made the rest of us leave. My daddy had to pull Dawson. All morning and afternoon she hollered. At dark she still hadn't come down. Dawson was sent home with Aunt Henrietta and Uncle Albert. I lay in my bed hearing Dale Blue's voice carry over the pasture. She cussed, she screamed, she cried.

"Henry Sharp, you'll wish you were dead when I'm finished with you!" she hollered. "You'll wish you were in a meat grinder!"

Before sunup I was down the back steps on my bare feet and out the dining room window. I ran among cornstalks which rattled and bashed me. I snuck through mist to the barn where I hid behind bales of the new hay.

Dale Blue wasn't yelling any more. She wept and talked pitifully.

"What'd I ever do to make you treat me this way?" she asked.

"It's for your own good," Uncle Henry said. "Yours and everybody's own good."

"I bore your child and have tried to be a loving wife," she said.

"Come to the river with me, and I'll lay the world at your feet," Uncle Henry said up the silo.

"You go to hell on a Honda!" she wailed.

Daddy came to the barn, but Uncle Henry sent him back to the house. About mid-morning Uncle Henry called up to Dale Blue, who was sniffling.

"You want me to bring you your comb?" Uncle Henry called. "The photographer's going to be here after while."

"Who?" Dale Blue asked, and her voice echoed in the silo: who? who? who?

"That photographer from the Lewisburg paper," Uncle Henry said.

"No!" she sobbed.

"Can't stop the press," Uncle Henry said. "Now wouldn't it be better just to let me climb up there, bring you down so you can rest a while, and then we'll drive to the river?"

She whimpered.

"I love you," Uncle Henry called. "I'd rather die than be hurting you. Dale Blue, do this one thing for me."

"Henry, please come get me off these goddamn boards!" she cried.

He ran up that ladder after her and half carried her down. All the way she bawled. Her shorts weren't so yellow any longer, but most of her hair was still on top her head, though falling apart.

Uncle Henry kissed her a long time. He helped her

across the pasture to the house, washed her off in the bathtub, and put her to bed in the spare room with the shades drawn.

Later my mother, Aunt Henrietta, and Aunt Cornelia got Dale Blue on her feet to dress her in her sheet. She, Dawson, and Uncle Henry were dipped by the Reverend Arbogast in the Greenbrier River at four-thirty. There was to be a party at the house, but Dale Blue wouldn't leave the Caddy. Uncle Henry had to drive her to White Sulphur. She was still hugging the sheet around her, and her wet hair had toppled.

The next morning sunshine and crows woke me. Something was different in the house. Downstairs the grandfather clock ticked and chimed. I sniffed the keen, charred odor of hickory and the warm, fermented scent of buttermilk biscuits rising from the old Kalamazoo. My stomach flipflopped. Whooping, I kicked the sheet straight up and grabbed for my jeans on the run to the kitchen.

PART III

Experiencing Southern Communities

Maya Angelou

Maya Angelou was born in 1928 in St. Louis, Missouri, and grew up in Stamps, Arkansas. She is a singer and actress as well as a writer and a teacher. In 1954 and 1955 she appeared in a production of *Porgy and Bess*, which toured twenty-two countries. She then went on to act in several off-Broadway plays. During the 1960s she became a lecturer and civil rights activist, working both in America and Africa. When writer James Baldwin encouraged her to publish the stories she enjoyed telling about her childhood, she began a steady output of auto-biographical writings for which she has become well-known. The first volume, *I Know Why the Caged Bird Sings* (1970), chronicles the early years with her grand-mother in Stamps and with her mother in St. Louis and San Francisco. *The Heart of a Woman* (1981) covers the era of civil rights marches both at home and abroad, and *All God's Children Need Traveling Shoes* (1986) describes her stay in Ghana when that country won its independence. She has produced a television series on African traditions in American life, written television screenplays, including *I Know Why the Caged Bird Sings*, and authored a series of documentaries, *Maya Angelou's America*. She is also the author of five collections of poetry, including her most recent work, *I Shall Not Be Moved* (1990). A chorus of critics attributes her genius to her ability to capture the idiosyncratic language and imagery of her childhood. Annie Gottlieb writes that "the wisdom, rue and humor of her storytelling are borne on a lilting rhythm completely her own, the product of a born writer's senses nourished on black church singing and preaching, soft mother talk and salty street talk, and on literature." Maya Angelou is currently Reynolds Professor at Wake Forest University in Winston-Salem, North Carolina.

from I Know Why the Caged Bird Sings

The children in Stamps trembled visibly with anticipation. Some adults were excited too, but to be certain the whole young population had come down with graduation epidemic. Large classes were graduating from both the grammar school and the high school. Even those who were years removed from their own day of glorious release were anxious to help with preparations as a kind of dry run. The junior students who were moving into the vacating classes' chairs were tradition-bound to show their talents for leadership and management. They strutted through the school and around the campus exerting pressure on the lower grades. Their authority was so new that occasionally if they pressed a little too hard it had to be overlooked. After all, next term was coming, and it never hurt a sixth grader to have a play sister in the eighth grade, or a tenth-year student to be able to call a twelfth grader Bubba. So all was endured in a spirit of shared understanding. But the graduating classes themselves were the nobility. Like travelers with exotic destinations on their minds, the graduates were remarkably forgetful. They came to school without their books, or tablets or even pencils. Volunteers fell over themselves to secure replacements for the missing equipment. When accepted, the willing workers might or might not be thanked, and it was of no importance to the pregraduation rites. Even teachers were respectful of the now quiet and aging seniors, and tended to speak to them, if not as equals, as beings only slightly lower than themselves. After tests were returned and grades given, the student body, which acted like an extended family, knew who did well, who excelled, and what piteous ones had failed.

Unlike the white high school, Lafayette County Training School distinguished itself by having neither lawn, nor hedges, nor tennis court, nor climbing ivy. Its two buildings (main classrooms, the grade school and home economics) were set on a dirt hill with no fence to limit either its boundaries or those of bordering farms. There was a large expanse to the left of the school which was used alternately as a baseball diamond or a basketball court. Rusty hoops on the swaying poles represented the permanent recreational equipment, although bats and balls could be borrowed from the P. E. teacher if the borrower was qualified and if the diamond wasn't occupied.

Over this rocky area relieved by a few shady tall persimmon trees the graduating class walked. The girls often held hands and no longer bothered to speak to the lower students. There was a sadness about them, as if this old world was not their home and they were bound for higher ground. The boys, on the other hand, had become more friendly, more outgoing. A decided change from the closed attitude they projected while studying for finals. Now they seemed not ready to give up the old school, the familiar paths and classrooms. Only a small percentage would be continuing on to college—one of the South's A & M (agricultural and mechanical) schools, which trained Negro youths to be carpenters, farmers, handymen, masons, maids, cooks and baby nurses. Their future rode heavily on their shoulders, and blinded them to the collective joy that had pervaded the lives of the boys and girls in the grammar school graduating class.

Parents who could afford it had ordered new shoes and ready-made clothes for themselves from Sears and Roebuck or Montgomery Ward. They also engaged the best seamstresses to make the floating graduating dresses and to cut down secondhand pants which would be pressed to a military slickness for the important event.

Oh, it was important, all right. Whitefolks would attend the ceremony, and two or three would speak of

God and home, and the Southern way of life, and Mrs. Parsons, the principal's wife, would play the graduation march while the lower-grade graduates paraded down the aisles and took their seats below the platform. The high school seniors would wait in empty classrooms to make their dramatic entrance.

In the Store I was the person of the moment. The birthday girl. The center. Bailey had graduated the year before, although to do so he had had to forfeit all pleasures to make up for his time lost in Baton Rouge.

My class was wearing butter-yellow piqué dresses, and Momma launched out on mine. She smocked the yoke into tiny crisscrossing puckers, then shirred the rest of the bodice. Her dark fingers ducked in and out of the lemony cloth as she embroidered raised daisies around the hem. Before she considered herself finished she had added a crocheted cuff on the puff sleeves, and a pointy crocheted collar.

I was going to be lovely. A walking model of all the various styles of fine hand sewing and it didn't worry me that I was only twelve years old and merely graduating from the eighth grade. Besides, many teachers in Arkansas Negro schools had only that diploma and were licensed to impart wisdom.

The days had become longer and more noticeable. The faded beige of former times had been replaced with strong and sure colors. I began to see my classmates' clothes, their skin tones, and the dust that waved off pussy willows. Clouds that lazed across the sky were objects of great concern to me. Their shiftier shapes might have held a message that in my new happiness and with a little bit of time I'd soon decipher. During that period I looked at the arch of heaven so religiously my neck kept a steady ache. I had taken to smiling more often, and my jaws hurt from the unaccustomed activity. Between the two physical sore spots, I suppose I could have been uncomfortable, but that was not the case. As a member of the winning team (the graduating class of

1940) I had outdistanced unpleasant sensations by miles. I was headed for the freedom of open fields.

Youth and social approval allied themselves with me and we trammeled memories of slights and insults. The wind of our swift passage remodeled my features. Lost tears were pounded to mud and then to dust. Years of withdrawal were brushed aside and left behind, as hanging ropes of parasitic moss.

My work alone had awarded me a top place and I was going to be one of the first called in the graduating ceremonies. On the classroom blackboard, as well as on the bulletin board in the auditorium, there were blue stars and white stars and red stars. No absences, no tardinesses, and my academic work was among the best of the year. I could say the preamble to the Constitution even faster than Bailey. We timed ourselves often: "WethepeopleoftheUnitedStatesinordertoformamoreperfectunion . . ." I had memorized the Presidents of the United States from Washington to Roosevelt in chronological as well as alphabetical order.

My hair pleased me too. Gradually the black mass had lengthened and thickened, so that it kept at last to its braided pattern, and I didn't have to yank my scalp off when I tried to comb it.

Louise and I had rehearsed the exercises until we tired out ourselves. Henry Reed was class valedictorian. He was a small, very black boy with hooded eyes, a long, broad nose and an oddly shaped head. I had admired him for years because each term he and I vied for the best grades in our class. Most often he bested me, but instead of being disappointed I was pleased that we shared top places between us. Like many Southern Black children, he lived with his grandmother, who was as strict as Momma and as kind as she knew how to be. He was courteous, respectful and soft-spoken to elders, but on the playground he chose to play the roughest games. I admired him. Anyone, I reckoned, sufficiently afraid or sufficiently dull could be polite. But to be able to operate at a top level with both adults and children was admirable.

His valedictory speech was entitled "To Be or Not to

Be." The rigid tenth-grade teacher had helped him write it. He'd been working on the dramatic stresses for months.

The weeks until graduation were filled with heady activities. A group of small children were to be presented in a play about buttercups and daisies and bunny rabbits. They could be heard throughout the building practicing their hops and their little songs that sounded like silver bells. The older girls (nongraduates, of course) were assigned the task of making refreshments for the night's festivities. A tangy scent of ginger, cinnamon, nutmeg and chocolate wafted around the home economics building as the budding cooks made samples for themselves and their teachers.

In every corner of the workshop, axes and saws split fresh timber as the woodshop boys made sets and stage scenery. Only the graduates were left out of the general bustle. We were free to sit in the library at the back of the building or look in quite detachedly, naturally, on the measures being taken for our event.

Even the minister preached on graduation the Sunday before. His subject was, "Let your light so shine that men will see your good works and praise your Father, Who is in Heaven." Although the sermon was purported to be addressed to us, he used the occasion to speak to backsliders, gamblers and general ne'er-do-wells. But since he had called our names at the beginning of the service we were mollified.

Among Negroes the tradition was to give presents to children going only from one grade to another. How much more important this was when the person was graduating at the top of the class. Uncle Willie and Momma had sent away for a Mickey Mouse watch like Bailey's. Louise gave me four embroidered handkerchiefs. (I gave her three crocheted doilies.) Mrs. Sneed, the minister's wife, made me an underskirt to wear for graduation, and nearly every customer gave me a nickel or maybe even a dime with the instruction "Keep on moving to higher ground," or some such encouragement.

Amazingly the great day finally dawned and I was out of bed before I knew it. I threw open the back door to see it more clearly, but Momma said, "Sister, come away from that door and put your robe on."

I hoped the memory of that morning would never leave me. Sunlight was itself still young, and the day had none of the insistence maturity would bring it in a few hours. In my robe and barefoot in the backyard, under cover of going to see about my new beans, I gave myself up to the gentle warmth and thanked God that no matter what evil I had done in my life He had allowed me to live to see this day. Somewhere in my fatalism I had expected to die, accidentally, and never have the chance to walk up the stairs in the auditorium and gracefully receive my hard-earned diploma. Out of God's merciful bosom I had won reprieve.

Bailey came out in his robe and gave me a box wrapped in Christmas paper. He said he had saved his money for months to pay for it. It felt like a box of chocolates, but I knew Bailey wouldn't save money to buy candy when we had all we could want under our noses.

He was as proud of the gift as I. It was a soft-leather-bound copy of a collection of poems by Edgar Allan Poe, or, as Bailey and I called him, "Eap." I turned to "Annabel Lee" and we walked up and down the garden rows, the cool dirt between our toes, reciting the beautifully sad lines.

Momma made a Sunday breakfast although it was only Friday. After we finished the blessing, I opened my eyes to find the watch on my plate. It was a dream of a day. Everything went smoothly and to my credit. I didn't have to be reminded or scolded for anything. Near evening I was too jittery to attend to chores, so Bailey volunteered to do all before his bath.

Days before, we had made a sign for the Store, and as we turned out the lights Momma hung the cardboard over the doorknob. It read clearly: CLOSED. GRADUATION.

My dress fitted perfectly and everyone said that I looked like a sunbeam in it. On the hill, going toward the school, Bailey walked behind with Uncle Willie, who muttered, "Go on, Ju." He wanted him to walk ahead with us because it embarrassed him to have to walk so slowly. Bailey said he'd let the ladies walk together, and the men would bring up the rear. We all laughed, nicely.

Little children dashed by out of the dark like fireflies. Their crepe-paper dresses and butterfly wings were not made for running and we heard more than one rip, dryly, and the regretful "uh uh" that followed.

The school blazed without gaiety. The windows seemed cold and unfriendly from the lower hill. A sense of ill-fated timing crept over me, and if Momma hadn't reached for my hand I would have drifted back to Bailey and Uncle Willie, and possibly beyond. She made a few slow jokes about my feet getting cold, and tugged me along to the now-strange building.

Around the front steps, assurance came back. There were my fellow "greats," the graduating class. Hair brushed back, legs oiled, new dresses and pressed pleats, fresh pocket handkerchiefs and little handbags, all home-sewn. Oh, we were up to snuff, all right. I joined my comrades and didn't even see my family go in to find seats in the crowded auditorium.

The school band struck up a march and all classes filed in as had been rehearsed. We stood in front of our seats, as assigned, and on a signal from the choir director, we sat. No sooner had this been accomplished than the band started to play the national anthem. We rose again and sang the song, after which we recited the pledge of allegiance. We remained standing for a brief minute before the choir director and the principal signaled to us, rather desperately I thought, to take our seats. The command was so unusual that our carefully rehearsed and smooth-running machine was thrown off. For a full minute we fumbled for our chairs and bumped into each other awkwardly. Habits change or solidify under pressure, so in our state of nervous tension we had been ready to follow our usual assembly pattern: the American national anthem, then the pledge of allegiance, then the song every Black person I knew called the Negro National Anthem. All done in the same key, with the same passion and most often standing on the same foot.

Finding my seat at last, I was overcome with a presentiment of worse things to come. Something unrehearsed, unplanned, was going to happen, and we were going to be made to look bad. I distinctly remember being explicit in the choice of pronoun. It was "we," the graduating class, the unit, that concerned me then.

The principal welcomed "parents and friends" and asked the Baptist minister to lead us in prayer. His invocation was brief and punchy, and for a second I thought we were getting back on the high road to right action. When the principal came back to the dais, however, his voice had changed. Sounds always affected me profoundly and the principal's voice was one of my favorites. During assembly it melted and lowed weakly into the audience. It had not been in my plan to listen to him, but my curiosity was piqued and I straightened up to give him my attention.

He was talking about Booker T. Washington, our "late great leader," who said we can be as close as the fingers on the hand, etc. . . . Then he said a few vague things about friendship and the friendship of kindly people to those less fortunate than themselves. With that his voice nearly faded, thin, away. Like a river diminishing to a stream and then to a trickle. But he cleared his throat and said, "Our speaker tonight, who is also our friend, came from Texarkana to deliver the commencement address, but due to the irregularity of the train schedule, he's going to, as they say, 'speak and run.' " He said that we understood and wanted the man to know that we were most grateful for the time he was able to give us and then something about how we were willing always to adjust to another's program, and without more ado— "I give you Mr. Edward Donleavy."

Not one but two white men came through the door offstage. The shorter one walked to the speaker's platform, and the tall one moved over to the center seat and sat down. But that was our principal's seat, and already occupied. The dislodged gentleman bounced around for a long breath or two before the Baptist minister gave him his chair, then with more dignity than the situation deserved, the minister walked off the stage.

Donleavy looked at the audience once (on reflection, I'm sure that he wanted only to reassure himself that we were really there), adjusted his glasses and began to read from a sheaf of papers.

He was glad "to be here and to see the work going on just as it was in the other schools."

At the first "Amen" from the audience I willed the offender to immediate death by choking on the word. But Amens and Yes, sir's began to fall around the room like rain through a ragged umbrella.

He told us of the wonderful changes we children in Stamps had in store. The Central School (naturally, the white school was Central) had already been granted improvements that would be in use in the fall. A well-known artist was coming from Little Rock to teach art to them. They were going to have the newest microscopes and chemistry equipment for their laboratory. Mr. Donleavy didn't leave us long in the dark over who made these improvements available to Central High. Nor were we to be ignored in the general betterment scheme he had in mind.

He said that he had pointed out to people at a very high level that one of the first-line football tacklers at Arkansas Agricultural and Mechanical College had graduated from good old Lafayette County Training School. Here fewer Amen's were heard. Those few that did break through lay dully in the air with the heaviness of habit.

He went on to praise us. He went on to say how he had bragged that "one of the best basketball players at Fisk sank his first ball right here at Lafayette County Training School."

The white kids were going to have a chance to become Galileos and Madame Curies and Edisons and Gauguins, and our boys (the girls weren't even in on it) would try to be Jesse Owenses and Joe Louises.

Owens and the Brown Bomber were great heroes in our world, but what school official in the white-goddom of Little Rock had the right to decide that those two men must be our only heroes? Who decided that for Henry

Reed to become a scientist he had to work like George Washington Carver, as a bootblack, to buy a lousy microscope? Bailey was obviously always going to be too small to be an athlete, so which concrete angel glued to what country seat had decided that if my brother wanted to become a lawyer he had to first pay penance for his skin by picking cotton and hoeing corn and studying correspondence books at night for twenty years?

The man's dead words fell like bricks around the auditorium and too many settled in my belly. Constrained by hard-learned manners I couldn't look behind me, but to my left and right the proud graduating class of 1940 had dropped their heads. Every girl in my row had found something new to do with her handkerchief. Some folded the tiny squares into love knots, some into triangles, but most were wadding them, then pressing them flat on their yellow laps.

On the dais, the ancient tragedy was being replayed. Professor Parsons sat, a sculptor's reject, rigid. His large, heavy body seemed devoid of will or willingness, and his eyes said he was no longer with us. The other teachers examined the flag (which was draped stage right) or their notes, or the windows which opened on our now-famous playing diamond.

Graduation, the hush-hush magic time of frills and gifts and congratulations and diplomas, was finished for me before my name was called. The accomplishment was nothing. The meticulous maps, drawn in three colors of ink, learning and spelling decasyllabic words, memorizing the whole of *The Rape of Lucrece*—it was for nothing. Donleavy had exposed us.

We were maids and farmers, handymen and washerwomen, and anything higher that we aspired to was farcical and presumptuous.

Then I wished that Gabriel Prosser and Nat Turner had killed all whitefolks in their beds and that Abraham Lincoln had been assassinated before the signing of the Emancipation Proclamation, and that Harriet Tubman had been killed by that blow on her head and Christopher Columbus had drowned in the *Santa María*.

It was awful to be Negro and have no control over my life. It was brutal to be young and already trained to sit quietly and listen to charges brought against my color with no chance of defense. We should all be dead. I thought I should like to see us all dead, one on top of the other. A pyramid of flesh with the whitefolks on the bottom, as the broad base, then the Indians with their silly tomahawks and teepees and wigwams and treaties, the Negroes with their mops and recipes and cotton sacks and spirituals sticking out of their mouths. The Dutch children should all stumble in their wooden shoes and break their necks. The French should choke to death on the Louisiana Purchase (1803) while silkworms ate all the Chinese with their stupid pigtails. As a species, we were an abomination. All of us.

Donleavy was running for election, and assured our parents that if he won we could count on having the only colored paved playing field in that part of Arkansas. Also—he never looked up to acknowledge the grunts of acceptance—also, we were bound to get some new equipment for the home economics building and the workshop.

He finished, and since there was no need to give any more than the most perfunctory thank-you's, he nodded to the men on the stage, and the tall white man who was never introduced joined him at the door. They left with the attitude that now they were off to something really important. (The graduation ceremonies at Lafayette County Training School had been a mere preliminary.)

The ugliness they left was palpable. An uninvited guest who wouldn't leave. The choir was summoned and sang a modern arrangement of "Onward, Christian Soldiers," with new words pertaining to graduates seeking their place in the world. But it didn't work. Elouise, the daughter of the Baptist minister, recited "Invictus," and I could have cried at the impertinence of "I am the master of my fate, I am the captain of my soul."

My name had lost its ring of familiarity and I had to be nudged to go and receive my diploma. All my preparations had fled. I neither marched up to the stage like a conquering Amazon, nor did I look in the audience for

Bailey's nod of approval. Marguerite Johnson, I heard
the name again, my honors were read, there were noises
in the audience of appreciation, and I took my place on
the stage as rehearsed.

I thought about colors I hated: ecru, puce, lavender,
beige and black.

There was shuffling and rustling around me, then
Henry Reed was giving his valedictory address, "To Be
or Not to Be." Hadn't he heard the whitefolks? We
couldn't *be*, so the question was a waste of time. Henry's
voice came out clear and strong. I feared to look at him.
Hadn't he got the message? There was no "nobler in the
mind" for Negroes because the world didn't think we
had minds, and they let us know it. "Outrageous for-
tune"? Now, that was a joke. When the ceremony was
over I had to tell Henry Reed some things. That is, if I
still cared. Not "rub," Henry, "erase." "Ah, there's the
erase." Us.

Henry had been a good student in elocution. His voice
rose on tides of promise and fell on waves of warnings.
The English teacher had helped him to create a sermon
winging through Hamlet's soliloquy. To be a man, a doer,
a builder, a leader, or to be a tool, an unfunny joke, a
crusher of funky toadstools. I marveled that Henry could
go through with the speech as if we had a choice.

I had been listening and silently rebutting each sentence with my eyes closed; then there was a hush, which
in an audience warns that something unplanned is happening. I looked up and saw Henry Reed, the conservative, the proper, the A student, turn his back to the
audience and turn to us (the proud graduating class of
1940) and sing, nearly speaking,

> "Lift ev'ry voice and sing
>   Till earth and heaven ring
>   Ring with the harmonies of Liberty . . ."

"Lift Ev'ry Voice and Sing"—words by James Weldon Johnson and
music by J. Rosamond Johnson. Copyright by Edward B. Marks
Music Corporation. Used by permission.

It was the poem written by James Weldon Johnson. It was the music composed by J. Rosamond Johnson. It was the Negro national anthem. Out of habit we were singing it.

Our mothers and fathers stood in the dark hall and joined the hymn of encouragement. A kindergarten teacher led the small children onto the stage and the buttercups and daisies and bunny rabbits marked time and tried to follow:

> "Stony the road we trod
> Bitter the chastening rod
> Felt in the days when hope, unborn, had died.
> Yet with a steady beat
> Have not our weary feet
> Come to the place for which our fathers sighed?"

Every child I knew had learned that song with his ABC's and along with "Jesus Loves Me This I Know." But I personally had never heard it before. Never heard the words, despite the thousands of times I had sung them. Never thought they had anything to do with me.

On the other hand, the words of Patrick Henry had made such an impression on me that I had been able to stretch myself tall and trembling and say, "I know not what course others may take, but as for me, give me liberty or give me death."

And now I heard, really for the first time:

> "We have come over a way that with tears
> has been watered,
> We have come, treading our path through
> the blood of the slaughtered."

While echoes of the song shivered in the air, Henry Reed bowed his head, said "Thank you," and returned to his place in the line. The tears that slipped down many faces were not wiped away in shame.

We were on top again. As always, again. We survived. The depths had been icy and dark, but now a bright sun spoke to our souls. I was no longer simply a member of the proud graduating class of 1940; I was a proud member of the wonderful, beautiful Negro race.

Oh, Black known and unknown poets, how often have your auctioned pains sustained us? Who will compute the lonely nights made less lonely by your songs, or by the empty pots made less tragic by your tales?

If we were a people much given to revealing secrets, we might raise monuments and sacrifice to the memories of our poets, but slavery cured us of that weakness. It may be enough, however, to have it said that we survive in exact relationship to the dedication of our poets (include preachers, musicians and blues singers).

Flannery O'Connor

Flannery O'Connor was born in 1925, in Savannah, Georgia, where she grew up and attended Catholic schools. She continued her education at Georgia College and the University of Iowa. At age 25 she was diagnosed as having lupus, the disease that had killed her father. She and her mother moved to a dairy farm outside Milledgeville, Georgia, where she spent the rest of her life. Flannery O'Connor wrote two novels, *Wise Blood* (1952) and *The Violent Bear It Away* (1960), but she is best known for her stories, for which she won three O. Henry prizes. They were collected in *The Complete Short Stories* (1971), a volume that won the National Book Award. Flannery O'Connor's works often deal with theological subjects, but whatever her subject, the fiction is set firmly in the South. Alice Walker was first drawn to her realistic characterizations, "these white folks without the magnolia . . . and these black folks without melons and superior racial patience, these are like the Southerners that I know." After O'Connor's death in 1964, Cecil Dawkins produced a two-act play, *The Displaced Person* (1966), based on five of her stories, Sally and Robert Fitzgerald edited her essays, *Mystery and Manners: Occasional Prose* (1969), and John Huston directed the movie version of *Wise Blood* (1980).

Everything That Rises Must Converge

Her doctor had told Julian's mother that she must lose twenty pounds on account of her blood pressure, so on Wednesday nights Julian had to take her downtown on the bus for a reducing class at the Y. The reducing class was designed for working girls over fifty, who weighed from 165 to 200 pounds. His mother was one of the slimmer ones, but she said ladies did not tell their age or weight. She would not ride the buses by herself at night since they had been integrated, and because the reducing class was one of her few pleasures, necessary for her health, and *free*, she said Julian could at least put himself out to take her, considering all she did for him. Julian did not like to consider all she did for him, but every Wednesday night he braced himself and took her.

She was almost ready to go, standing before the hall mirror, putting on her hat, while he, his hands behind him, appeared pinned to the door frame, waiting like Saint Sebastian for the arrows to begin piercing him. The hat was new and had cost her seven dollars and a half. She kept saying, "Maybe I shouldn't have paid that for it. No, I shouldn't have. I'll take it off and return it tomorrow. I shouldn't have bought it."

Julian raised his eyes to heaven. "Yes, you should have bought it," he said. "Put it on and let's go." It was a hideous hat. A purple velvet flap came down on one side of it and stood up on the other; the rest of it was green and looked like a cushion with the stuffing out. He decided it was less comical than jaunty and pathetic. Everything that gave her pleasure was small and depressed him.

She lifted the hat one more time and set it down slowly on top of her head. Two wings of gray hair protruded on either side of her florid face, but her eyes, sky-blue, were as innocent and untouched by experience as they must have been when she was ten. Were it not that she was a widow who had struggled fiercely to feed and clothe and put him through school and who was supporting him still, "until he got on his feet," she might have been a little girl that he had to take to town.

"It's all right, it's all right," he said. "Let's go." He opened the door himself and started down the walk to get her going. The sky was a dying violet and the houses stood out darkly against it, bulbous liver-colored monstrosities of a uniform ugliness though no two were alike. Since this had been a fashionable neighborhood forty years ago, his mother persisted in thinking they did well to have an apartment in it. Each house had a narrow collar of dirt around it in which sat, usually, a grubby child. Julian walked with his hands in his pockets, his head down and thrust forward and his eyes glazed with the determination to make himself completely numb during the time he would be sacrificed to her pleasure.

The door closed and he turned to find the dumpy figure, surmounted by the atrocious hat, coming toward him. "Well," she said, "You only live once and paying a little more for it, I at least won't meet myself coming and going."

"Some day I'll start making money," Julian said gloomily—he knew he never would—"and you can have one of those jokes whenever you take the fit." But first they would move. He visualized a place where the nearest neighbors would be three miles away on either side.

"I think you're doing fine," she said, drawing on her gloves. "You've only been out of school a year. Rome wasn't built in a day."

She was one of the few members of the Y reducing class who arrived in hat and gloves and who had a son who had been to college. "It takes time," she said, "and the world is in such a mess. This hat looked better on me than any of the others, though when she brought it out I said, 'Take that thing back. I wouldn't have it on my head,' and she said, 'Now wait till you see it on,' and when she put it on me, I said, 'We-ull,' and she said, 'If you ask me, that hat does something for you and you do something for the hat, and besides,' she said, 'with that hat, you won't meet yourself coming and going.' "

Julian thought he could have stood his lot better if she had been selfish, if she had been an old hag who drank and screamed at him. He walked along, saturated in depression, as if in the midst of his martyrdom he had lost his faith. Catching sight of his long, hopeless, irritated face, she stopped suddenly with a grief-stricken look, and pulled back on his arm. "Wait on me," she said. "I'm going back to the house and take this thing off and tomorrow I'm going to return it. I was out of my head. I can pay the gas bill with that seven-fifty."

He caught her arm in a vicious grip. "You are not going to take it back," he said. "I like it."

"Well," she said, "I don't think I ought . . ."

"Shut up and enjoy it," he muttered, more depressed than ever.

"With the world in the mess it's in," she said, "it's a wonder we can enjoy anything. I tell you, the bottom rail is on the top."

Julian sighed.

"Of course," she said, "if you know who you are, you can go anywhere." She said this every time he took her to the reducing class. "Most of them in it are not our kind of people," she said, "but I can be gracious to anybody. I know who I am."

"They don't give a damn for your graciousness," Julian said savagely. "Knowing who you are is good for one generation only. You haven't the foggiest idea where you stand now or who you are."

She stopped and allowed her eyes to flash at him. "I most certainly do know who I am," she said, "and if you don't know who you are, I'm ashamed of you."

"Oh hell," Julian said.

"Your great-grandfather was a former governor of this state," she said. "Your grandfather was a prosperous landowner. Your grandmother was a Godhigh."

"Will you look around you," he said tensely, "and see where you are now?" and he swept his arm jerkily out to indicate the neighborhood, which the growing darkness at least made less dingy.

"You remain what you are," she said. "Your great-grandfather had a plantation and two hundred slaves."

"There are no more slaves," he said irritably.

"They were better off when they were," she said. He groaned to see that she was off on that topic. She rolled onto it every few days like a train on an open track. He knew every stop, every junction, every swamp along the way, and knew the exact point at which her conclusion would roll majestically into the station: "It's ridiculous. It's simply not realistic. They should rise, yes, but on their own side of the fence."

"Let's skip it," Julian said.

"The ones I feel sorry for," she said, "are the ones that are half white. They're tragic."

"Will you skip it?"

"Suppose we were half white. We would certainly have mixed feelings."

"I have mixed feelings now," he groaned.

"Well let's talk about something pleasant," she said. "I remember going to Grandpa's when I was a little girl. Then the house had double stairways that went up to what was really the second floor—all the cooking was done on the first. I used to like to stay down in the kitchen on account of the way the walls smelled. I would sit with my nose pressed against the plaster and take deep breaths. Actually the place belonged to the Godhighs but your grandfather Chestny paid the mortgage and saved it for them. They were in reduced circumstances," she said, "but reduced or not, they never forgot who they were."

"Doubtless that decayed mansion reminded them," Julian muttered. He never spoke of it without contempt or thought of it without longing. He had seen it once when he was a child before it had been sold. The double stairways had rotted and been torn down. Negroes were living it it. But it remained in his mind as his mother had known it. It appeared in his dreams regularly. He would stand on the wide porch, listening to the rustle of oak leaves, then wander through the high-ceilinged hall into the parlor that opened onto it and gaze at the worn rugs and faded draperies. It occurred to him that it was he, not she, who could have appreciated it. He preferred its threadbare elegance to anything he could name and it was because of it that all the neighborhoods they had lived in had been a torment to him—whereas she had hardly known the difference. She called her insensitivity "being adjustable."

"And I remember the old darky who was my nurse, Caroline. There was no better person in the world. I've always had a great respect for my colored friends," she said. "I'd do anything in the world for them and they'd . . ."

"Will you for God's sake get off that subject?" Julian said. When he got on a bus by himself, he made it a point to sit down beside a Negro, in reparation as it were for his mother's sins.

"You're mighty touchy tonight," she said. "Do you feel all right?"

"Yes I feel all right," he said. "Now lay off."

She pursed her lips. "Well, you certainly are in a vile humor," she observed. "I just won't speak to you at all."

They had reached the bus stop. There was no bus in sight and Julian, his hands still jammed in his pockets and his head thrust forward, scowled down the empty street. The frustration of having to wait on the bus as well as ride on it began to creep up his neck like a hot hand. The presence of his mother was borne in upon him as she gave a pained sigh. He looked at her bleakly. She was holding herself very erect under the preposterous hat, wearing it like a banner of her imaginary dignity. There was in him an evil urge to break her spirit. He suddenly unloosened his tie and pulled it off and put it in his pocket.

She stiffened. "Why must you look like *that* when you

take me to town?" she said. "Why must you deliberately embarrass me?"

"If you'll never learn where you are," he said, "you can at least learn where I am."

"You look like a—thug," she said.

"Then I must be one," he murmured.

"I'll just go home," she said. "I will not bother you. If you can't do a little thing like that for me . . ."

Rolling his eyes upward, he put his tie back on. "Restored to my class," he muttered. He thrust his face toward her and hissed, "True culture is in the mind, the *mind*," he said, and tapped his head, "the mind."

"It's in the heart," she said, "and in how you do things and how you do things is because of who you *are*."

"Nobody in the damn bus cares who you are."

"I care who I am," she said icily.

The lighted bus appeared on top of the next hill and as it approached, they moved out into the street to meet it. He put his hand under her elbow and hoisted her up on the creaking step. She entered with a little smile, as if she were going into a drawing room where everyone had been waiting for her. While he put in the tokens, she sat down on one of the broad front seats for three which faced the aisle. A thin woman with protruding teeth and long yellow hair was sitting on the end of it. His mother moved up beside her and left room for Julian beside herself. He sat down and looked at the floor across the aisle where a pair of thin feet in red and white canvas sandals were planted.

His mother immediately began a general conversation meant to attract anyone who felt like talking. "Can it get any hotter?" she said and removed from her purse a folding fan, black with a Japanese scene on it, which she began to flutter before her.

"I reckon it might could," the woman with the protruding teeth said, "but I know for a fact my apartment couldn't get no hotter."

"It must get the afternoon sun," his mother said. She sat forward and looked up and down the bus. It was half filled. Everybody was white. "I see we have the bus to ourselves," she said. Julian cringed.

"For a change," said the woman across the aisle, the owner of the red and white canvas sandals. "I come on one the other day and they were thick as fleas—up front and all through."

"The world is in a mess everywhere," his mother said. "I don't know how we've let it get in this fix."

"What gets my goat is all those boys from good families stealing automobile tires," the woman with the protruding teeth said. "I told my boy, I said you may not be rich but you been raised right and if I ever catch you in any such mess, they can send you on to the reformatory. Be exactly where you belong."

"Training tells," his mother said. "Is your boy in high school?"

"Ninth grade," the woman said.

"My son just finished college last year. He wants to write but he's selling typewriters until he gets started," his mother said.

The woman leaned forward and peered at Julian. He threw her such a malevolent look that she subsided against the seat. On the floor across the aisle there was an abandoned newspaper. He got up and got it and opened it out in front of him. His mother discreetly continued the conversation in a lower tone but the woman across the aisle said in a loud voice, "Well that's nice. Selling typewriters is close to writing. He can go right from one to the other."

"I tell him," his mother said, "that Rome wasn't built in a day."

Behind the newspaper Julian was withdrawing into the inner compartment of his mind where he spent most of his time. This was a kind of mental bubble in which he established himself when he could not bear to be a part of what was going on around him. From it he could see out and judge but in it he was safe from any kind of penetration from without. It was the only place where he felt free of the general idiocy of his fellows. His mother had never entered it but from it he could see her with absolute clarity.

The old lady was clever enough and he thought that if she had started from any of the right premises, more might·have been expected of her. She lived according to the laws of her own fantasy world, outside of which he had never seen her set foot. The law of it was to sacrifice herself for him after she had first created the necessity to do so by making a mess of things. If he had permitted her sacrifices, it was only because her lack of foresight had made them necessary. All of her life had been a struggle to act like a Chestny without the Chestny goods, and to give him everything she thought a Chestny ought to have; but since, said she, it was fun to struggle, why complain? And when you had won, as she had won, what fun to look back on the hard times! He could not forgive her that she had enjoyed the struggle and that she thought *she* had won.

What she meant when she said she had won was that she had brought him up successfully and had sent him to college and that he had turned out so well—good looking (her teeth had gone unfilled so that his could be straightened), intelligent (he realized he was too intelligent to be a success), and with a future ahead of him (there was of course no future ahead of him). She excused his gloominess on the grounds that he was still growing up and his radical ideas on his lack of practical experience. She said he didn't yet know a thing about "life," that he hadn't even entered the real world—when already he was as disenchanted with it as a man of fifty.

The further irony of all this was that in spite of her, he had turned out so well. In spite of going to only a third-rate college, he had, on his own initiative, come out with a first-rate education; in spite of growing up dominated by a small mind, he had ended up with a large one; in spite of all her foolish views, he was free of prejudice and unafraid to face facts. Most miraculous of all, instead of being blinded by love for her as she was for him, he had cut himself emotionally free of her and could see her with complete objectivity. He was not dominated by his mother.

The bus stopped with a sudden jerk and shook him from his meditation. A woman from the back lurched forward with little steps and barely escaped falling in his newspaper as she righted herself. She got off and a large Negro got on. Julian kept his paper lowered to watch. It gave him a certain satisfaction to see injustice in daily operation. It confirmed his view that with a few exceptions there was no one worth knowing within a radius of three hundred miles. The Negro was well dressed and carried a briefcase. He looked around and then sat down on the other end of the seat where the woman with the red and white canvas sandals was sitting. He immediately unfolded a newspaper and obscured himself behind it. Julian's mother's elbow at once prodded insistently into his ribs. "Now you see why I won't ride on these buses by myself," she whispered.

The woman with the red and white canvas sandals had risen at the same time the Negro sat down and had gone further back in the bus and taken the seat of the woman who had got off. His mother leaned forward and cast her an approving look.

Julian rose, crossed the aisle, and sat down in the place of the woman with the canvas sandals. From this position, he looked serenely across at his mother. Her face had turned an angry red. He stared at her, making his eyes the eyes of a stranger. He felt his tension suddenly lift as if he had openly declared war on her.

He would have liked to get in conversation with the Negro and to talk with him about art or politics or any subject that would be above the comprehension of those around them, but the man remained entrenched behind his paper. He was either ignoring the change of seating or had never noticed it. There was no way for Julian to convey his sympathy.

His mother kept her eyes fixed reproachfully on his face. The woman with the protruding teeth was looking at him avidly as if he were a type of monster new to her.

"Do you have a light?" he asked the Negro.

Without looking away from his paper, the man reached in his pocket and handed him a packet of matches.

"Thanks," Julian said. For a moment he held the matches foolishly. A NO SMOKING sign looked down upon him from over the door. This alone would not have detered him; he had no cigarettes. He had quit smoking some months before because he could not afford it. "Sorry," he muttered and handed back the matches. The Negro lowered the paper and gave him an annoyed look. He took the matches and raised the paper again.

His mother continued to gaze at him but she did not take advantage of his momentary discomfort. Her eyes retained their battered look. Her face seemed to be unnaturally red, as if her blood pressure had risen. Julian allowed no glimmer of sympathy to show on his face. Having got the advantage, he wanted desperately to keep it and carry it through. He would have liked to teach her a lesson that would last her a while, but there seemed no way to continue the point. The Negro refused to come out from behind his paper.

Julian folded his arms and looked stolidly before him, facing her but as if he did not see her, as if he had ceased to recognize her existence. He visualized a scene in which, the bus having reached their stop, he would remain in his seat and when she said, "Aren't you going to get off?" he would look at her as at a stranger who had rashly addressed him. The corner they got off on was usually deserted, but it was well lighted and it would not hurt her to walk by herself the four blocks to the Y. He decided to wait until the time came and then decide whether or not he would let her get off by herself. He would have to be at the Y at ten to bring her back, but he could leave her wondering if he was going to show up. There was no reason for her to think she could always depend on him.

He retired again into the high-ceilinged room sparsely settled with large pieces of antique furniture. His soul expanded momentarily but then he became aware of his mother across from him and the vision shriveled. He studied her coldly. Her feet in little pumps dangled like a child's and did not quite reach the floor. She was train-ing on him an exaggerated look of reproach. He felt com-pletely detached from her. At that moment he could with pleasure have slapped her as he would have slapped a particularly obnoxious child in his charge.

He began to imagine various unlikely ways by which he could teach her a lesson. He might make friends with some distinguished Negro professor or lawyer and bring him home to spend the evening. He would be entirely justified but her blood pressure would rise to 300. He could not push her to the extent of making her have a stroke, and moreover, he had never been successful at making any Negro friends. He had tried to strike up an acquaintance on the bus with some of the better types, with ones that looked like professors or ministers or law-yers. One morning he had sat down next to a distin-guished-looking dark brown man who had answered his questions with a sonorous solemnity but who had turned out to be an undertaker. Another day he had sat down beside a cigar-smoking Negro with a diamond ring on his finger, but after a few stilted pleasantries, the Negro had rung the buzzer and risen, slipping two lottery tickets into Julian's hand as he climbed over him to leave.

He imagined his mother lying desperately ill and his being able to secure only a Negro doctor for her. He toyed with that idea for a few minutes and then dropped it for a momentary vision of himself participating as a sympathizer in a sit-in demonstration. This was possible but he did not linger with it. Instead, he approached the ultimate horror. He brought home a beautiful suspi-ciously Negroid woman. Prepare yourself, he said. There is nothing you can do about it. This is the woman I've chosen. She's intelligent, dignified, even good, and she's suffered and she hasn't thought it *fun*. Now persecute us, go ahead and persecute us. Drive her out of here, but remember, you're driving me too. His eyes were nar-rowed and through the indignation he had generated, he saw his mother across the aisle, purple-faced, shrunken to the dwarf-like proportions of her moral nature, sitting like a mummy beneath the ridiculous banner of her hat.

He was tilted out of his fantasy again as the bus stopped. The door opened with a sucking hiss and out of the dark a large, gaily dressed, sullen-looking colored woman got on with a little boy. The child, who might have been four, had on a short plaid suit and a Tyrolean hat with a blue feather in it. Julian hoped that he would sit down beside him and that the woman would push in beside his mother. He could think of no better arrangement.

As she waited for her tokens, the woman was surveying the seating possibilities—he hoped with the idea of sitting where she was least wanted. There was something familiar-looking about her but Julian could not place what it was. She was a giant of a woman. Her face was set not only to meet opposition but to seek it out. The downward tilt of her large lower lip was like a warning sign: DON'T TAMPER WITH ME. Her bulging figure was encased in a green crepe dress and her feet overflowed in red shoes. She had on a hideous hat. A purple velvet flap came down on one side of it and stood up on the other; the rest of it was green and looked like a cushion with the stuffing out. She carried a mammoth red pocketbook that bulged throughout as if it were stuffed with rocks.

To Julian's disappointment, the little boy climbed up on the empty seat beside his mother. His mother lumped all children, black and white, into the common category, "cute," and she thought little Negroes were on the whole cuter than little white children. She smiled at the little boy as he climbed on the seat.

Meanwhile the woman was bearing down upon the empty seat beside Julian. To his annoyance, she squeezed herself into it. He saw his mother's face change as the woman settled herself next to him and he realized with satisfaction that this was more objectionable to her than it was to him. Her face seemed almost gray and there was a look of dull recognition in her eyes, as if suddenly she had sickened at some awful confrontation. Julian saw that it was because she and the woman had, in a sense, swapped sons. Though his mother would not realize the symbolic significance of this, she would feel it. His amusement showed plainly on his face.

The woman next to him muttered something unintelligible to herself. He was conscious of a kind of bristling next to him, a muted growling like that of an angry cat. He could not see anything but the red pocketbook upright on the bulging green thighs. He visualized the woman as she had stood waiting for her tokens—the ponderous figure, rising from the red shoes upward over the solid hips, the mammoth bosom, the haughty face, to the green and purple hat.

His eyes widened.

The vision of the two hats, identical, broke upon him with the radiance of a brilliant sunrise. His face was suddenly lit with joy. He could not believe that Fate had thrust upon his mother such a lesson. He gave a loud chuckle so that she would look at him and see that he saw. She turned her eyes on him .slowly. The blue in them seemed to have turned a bruised purple. For a moment he had an uncomfortable sense of her innocence, but it lasted only a second before principle rescued him. Justice entitled him to laugh. His grin hardened until it said to her as plainly as if he were saying aloud: Your punishment exactly fits your pettiness. This should teach you a permanent lesson.

Her eyes shifted to the woman. She seemed unable to bear looking at him and to find the woman preferable. He became conscious again of the bristling presence at his side. The woman was rumbling like a volcano about to become active. His mother's mouth began to twitch slightly at one corner. With a sinking heart, he saw incipient signs of recovery on her face and realized that this was going to strike her suddenly as funny and was going to be no lesson at all. She kept her eyes on the woman and an amused smile came over her face as if the woman were a monkey that had stolen her hat. The little Negro was looking up at her with large fascinated eyes. He had been trying to attract her attention for some time.

"Carver!" the woman said suddenly. "Come heah!"

When he saw that the spotlight was on him at last,

Carver drew his feet up and turned himself toward Julian's mother and giggled.

"Carver!" the woman said. "You heah me? Come heah!"

Carver slid down from the seat but remained squatting with his back against the base of it, his head turned slyly around toward Julian's mother, who was smiling at him. The woman reached a hand across the aisle and snatched him to her. He righted himself and hung backwards on her knees, grinning at Julian's mother. "Isn't he cute?" Julian's mother said to the woman with the protruding teeth.

"I reckon he is," the woman said without conviction.

The Negress yanked him upright but he eased out of her grip and shot across the aisle and scrambled, giggling wildly, onto the seat beside his love.

"I think he likes me," Julian's mother said, and smiled at the woman. It was the smile she used when she was being particularly gracious to an inferior. Julian saw everything lost. The lesson had rolled off her like rain on a roof.

The woman stood up and yanked the little boy off the seat as if she were snatching him from contagion. Julian could feel the rage in her at having no weapon like his mother's smile. She gave the child a sharp slap across his leg. He howled once and then thrust his head into her stomach and kicked his feet against her shins. "Behave," she said vehemently.

The bus stopped and the Negro who had been reading the newspaper got off. The woman moved over and set the little boy down with a thump between herself and Julian. She held him firmly by the knee. In a moment he put his hands in front of his face and peeped at Julian's mother through his fingers.

"I see yoooooooo!" she said and put her hand in front of her face and peeped at him.

The woman slapped his hand down. "Quit yo' foolishness," she said, "before I knock the living Jesus out of you!"

Julian was thankful that the next stop was theirs. He

reached up and pulled the cord. The woman reached up and pulled it at the same time. Oh my God, he thought. He had the terrible intuition that when they got off the bus together, his mother would open her purse and give the little boy a nickel. The gesture would be as natural to her as breathing. The bus stopped and the woman got up and lunged to the front, dragging the child, who wished to stay on, after her. Julian and his mother got up and followed. As they neared the door, Julian tried to relieve her of her pocketbook.

"No," she murmured, "I want to give the little boy a nickel."

"No!" Julian hissed. "No!"

She smiled down at the child and opened her bag. The bus door opened and the woman picked him up by the arm and descended with him, hanging at her hip. Once in the street she set him down and shook him.

Julian's mother had to close her purse while she got down the bus step but as soon as her feet were on the ground, she opened it again and began to rummage inside. "I can't find but a penny," she whispered, "but it looks like a new one."

"Don't do it!" Julian said fiercely between his teeth. There was a streetlight on the corner and she hurried to get under it so that she could better see into her pocketbook. The woman was heading off rapidly down the street with the child still hanging backward on her hand.

"Oh little boy!" Julian's mother called and took a few quick steps and caught up with them just beyond the lamppost. "Here's a bright new penny for you," and she held out the coin, which shone bronze in the dim light.

The huge woman turned and for a moment stood, her shoulders lifted and her face frozen with frustrated rage, and stared at Julian's mother. Then all at once she seemed to explode like a piece of machinery that had been given one ounce of pressure too much. Julian saw the black fist swing out with the red pocketbook. He shut his eyes and cringed as he heard the woman shout, "He don't take nobody's pennies!" When he opened his eyes, the woman was disappearing down the street with the little boy staring wide-eyed over her shoulder. Julian's mother was sitting on the sidewalk.

"I told you not to do that," Julian said angrily. "I told you not to do that!"

He stood over her for a minute, gritting his teeth. Her legs were stretched out in front of her and her hat was on her lap. He squatted down and looked her in the face. It was totally expressionless. "You got exactly what you deserved," he said. "Now get up."

He picked up her pocketbook and put what had fallen out back in it. He picked the hat up off her lap. The penny caught his eye on the sidewalk and he picked that up and let it drop before her eyes into the purse. Then he stood up and leaned over and held his hands out to pull her up. She remained immobile. He sighed. Rising above them on either side were black apartment buildings, marked with irregular rectangles of light. At the end of the block a man came out of a door and walked off in the opposite direction. "All right," he said, "suppose somebody happens by and wants to know why you're sitting on the sidewalk?"

She took the hand and, breathing hard, pulled heavily up on it and then stood for a moment, swaying slightly as if the spots of light in the darkness were circling around her. Her eyes, shadowed and confused, finally settled on his face. He did not try to conceal his irritation. "I hope this teaches you a lesson," he said. She leaned forward and her eyes raked his face. She seemed trying to determine his identity. Then, as if she found nothing familiar about him, she started off with a headlong movement in the wrong direction.

"Aren't you going on to the Y?" he asked.

"Home," she muttered.

"Well, are we walking?"

For answer she kept going. Julian followed along, his hands behind him. He saw no reason to let the lesson she had had go without backing it up with an explanation of its meaning. She might as well be made to understand what had happened to her. "Don't think that was just an uppity Negro woman," he said. "That was the whole

colored race which will no longer take your condescend-
ing pennies. That was your black double. She can wear
the same hat as you, and to be sure," he added gratu-
itously (because he thought it was funny), "it looked better on her than it did on you. What all this means," he
said, "is that the old world is gone. The old manners are
obsolete and your graciousness is not worth a damn."
He thought bitterly of the house that had been lost for
him. "You aren't who you think you are," he said.

She continued to plow ahead, paying no attention to
him. Her hair had come undone on one side. She
dropped her pocketbook and took no notice. He stooped
and picked it up and handed it to her but she did not
take it.

"You needn't act as if the world had come to an end,"
he said, "because it hasn't. From now on you've got to
live in a new world and face a few realities for a change.
Buck up," he said, "it won't kill you."

She was breathing fast.

"Let's wait on the bus," he said.

"Home," she said thickly.

"I hate to see you behave like this," he said. "Just
like a child. I should be able to expect more of you."
He decided to stop where he was and make her stop and
wait for a bus. "I'm not going any farther," he said,
stopping. "We're going on the bus."

She continued to go on as if she had not heard him.
He took a few steps and caught her arm and stopped
her. He looked into her face and caught his breath. He
was looking into a face he had never seen before. "Tell
Grandpa to come get me," she said.

He stared, stricken.

"Tell Caroline to come get me," she said.

Stunned, he let her go and she lurched forward again,
walking as if one leg were shorter than the other. A
tide of darkness seemed to be sweeping her from him.
"Mother!" he cried. "Darling, sweetheart, wait!" Crum-
pling, she fell to the pavement. He dashed forward and
fell at her side, crying, "Mamma, Mamma!" He turned
her over. Her face was fiercely distorted. One eye, large

and staring, moved slightly to the left as if it had become unmoored. The other remained fixed on him, raked his face again, found nothing and closed.

"Wait here, wait here!" he cried and jumped up and began to run for help toward a cluster of lights he saw in the distance ahead of him. "Help, help!" he shouted, but his voice was thin, scarcely a thread of sound. The lights drifted farther away the faster he ran and his feet moved numbly as if they carried him nowhere. The tide of darkness seemed to sweep him back to her, postponing from moment to moment his entry into the world of guilt and sorrow.

Gail Godwin

Born in Birmingham, Alabama, in 1937, Gail Godwin grew up in Asheville, North Carolina. Her mother, a reporter and a writer of romantic fiction, was an early literary influence. After Godwin graduated from the University of North Carolina with a degree in English, she received an M.A. and a Ph.D. from the University of Iowa, where Kurt Vonnegut was her teacher. She went on to teach English and creative writing at a number of colleges and universities, including Vassar, Columbia, and the University of Illinois. She has written eight novels and two collections of stories, work for which she has received a number of awards and grants. Her novels *The Odd Woman* (1974), *Violet Clay* (1978), and *The Finishing School* (1985) concern the relationship between life and art, whereas the novels *A Mother and Two Daughters* (1982) and *A Southern Family* (1987) focus on small-town life in the South and intense family relationships. Literary critic Frances Taliaferro has called the character of Justin in *The Finishing School* "one of the most trustworthy protraits of an adolescent in current literature." Gail Godwin has defined her story collection, *Mr. Bedford and the Muses* (1983), from which the following story is taken, as "revisionist autobiography." Godwin, who has achieved both popular and critical acclaim, lives in Woodstock, New York.

The Angry Year

It was 1957, when the Big Bopper and Albert Camus still walked the earth and the Russians sent a dog into space. It was the year I was angry. The whole of my junior year, I went around angry. I had transferred at last from the modest junior college in my hometown to the big, prestigious university with the good program in English. My family was poor, they couldn't afford to send me, so I'd got there with a scholarship based on my freshman and sophomore grades. Yet, once I'd arrived where I'd slaved to get, I seethed from morning till night with a hot, unspecific anger. Everything infuriated me. I went through registration glaring at the coveys of girls with summer tans who welcomed one another back with shrill, delighted cries. I hated their skittish convertibles with the faded tops, bolting the orange traffic lights. I loathed the conformity of their Weejun loafers (though I wore them myself) and the little jeweled pins swinging saucily from their breasts. There was an enemy here who might destroy me unless I routed him out and destroyed him first, but I could not discover his identity.

I did a strange thing, under a sort of compulsion. I went out for sorority rush, although I knew perfectly well I could not afford to join one, even if asked. I dressed myself up and attended the Pan-Hellenic tea and signed the register as a rushee. I went to the first round of parties, hurrying from house to house under the autumn stars. My attitude was a queer blend of arrogance and obsequiousness. At the Chi Omega house I gulped my paper cup of cider and heard myself tell the most aston-

241

ishing lies. At the Tri Delt house I ate too many cookies
and insulted one of the sisters. I was calmer at the other
four houses and managed to participate in the established
ritual of chitchat without further incidents. Walking back
to my dorm afterward, I concluded that I had done no
worse than others, though—with the possible exception
of the first two houses—I had not made myself memorable. I went over the evening and decided that most of
the girls were shallow fools. I made out a budget in my
journal to see if I could squeeze sorority dues out of
the scholarship, even though there was a clause in the
scholarship saying the holder could not join a fraternity
or a sorority. I envisioned all six houses bidding for me,
and my polite rejection of them. I would remain inscruta-
bly independent. My roommate was a cheerful, sensible
girl, a Christian Scientist. She was lying hunched on the
floor of our room that evening, "working on" an injury
she'd received at basketball tryouts. She said her parents
had given her the choice of a sorority or a Volkswagen
and she'd taken the VW, of course.

Before rush began, I had met the president of the
Dekes, the big fraternity on campus, at a Get Acquainted
Dance at the Armory. I was offhand and rather rude to
him, and he kept asking me out. I had told him I might
go through rush "just for the experience." He seemed
pleased, but then Graham seemed pleased by most
things. He was a slow, courtly boy from Danville, Virginia. His family owned a textile mill. I never saw him
get excited about anything.

The second day of rush, he waited for me beneath a
shedding oak while I ran into the Union to check my
rushee mailbox. The first day, everyone got six white
invitations. The second day, the serious weeding-out
began. I came out of the Union enraged, my hands full
of tiny bits of white paper. With Graham as my witness,
I flung these into the wire trash basket beside the walk.
They floated down, like languid snow, upon crumpled
newsprint, paper cups, and apple cores.

"I've dropped out of rush," I said. "I've torn up all
my silly invitations. There was this poor girl in there.

She made me see what a cruel, stupid farce it is. There wasn't a single invitation in her box. She opened it and it was empty and there was this terrible look on her face. Sort of . . . stunned, like those newspaper pictures of people who have just been told their whole family has been wiped out. I refuse to be part of such a thing. You're looking at an Independent, Graham."

Agreeably, he hurried along the leaf-strewn path beside me. It was a splendid, crisp fall day, full of colors, the kind you breathe in exultantly if you're not preoccupied by anger. "Even though I'm a fraternity man myself," he said, "I admire you for taking a stand. Of course you must, feeling the way you do about that girl in there." He never knew how utterly alone his praise made me feel. For Graham really believed that girl existed. His world contained no necessity for inventing such lies, or for raiding a trash basket upstairs in order to have six invitations to tear up and throw away. He continued to take me out. His peaceful personality seemed to bask in the flames of my rebellion. I continued to be amazed that the president of the Dekes would want me as his girl. I never asked myself did I want him.

My second foray into the extracurricular was a visit to the student newspaper, which was published daily. I was curt and defiant. I said there were a lot of hypocrisies in the system I would love to expose. I asked for a personal column. The editor was a wild-eyed, brilliant Jewish boy from New York. He later became a well-known writer. "A mean Mary McCarthy type, that's what we need," he said. He agreed to give me a trial run: three eight-hundred-word columns a week. "And we'll run a half-column shot of you, with your hair flying, like it is now."

I worked very hard on the first three columns. They were titled, in order of appearance: "Worst of Bugs, Extracurricularalysis" (exhorting harassed freshmen not to load themselves down with band and basketball and chorus and student politics until they'd found their true and central interests); "Spit on Me or I on Thee" (a sermon, lifted in liberal chunks from Camus, in which I cautioned fellow students to judge not that they be not judged); and "The Mythical Booked-Up Maiden" (which put forth the proposition to campus males, who outnumbered the females ten to one, that dozens of beautiful coeds sat home on Saturday evenings because the boys assumed they were dated up for months in advance).

The first two columns were ignored. The third drew an amazing barrage of fan mail from the men's dorms. They offered various, sometimes unprintable, kinds of services to these stay-at-home maidens. The editor was pleased by the response and said I could keep my column. From then on I had my weapon: the powerful Fourth Estate. I titled my column "Without Restrictions," and set about avenging my private frustrations in vitriolic prose, beneath the photo of my flying hair.

Weekends I sat on the comfortable sofa at the Deke house and studied the enemy at close hand. I drank their Scotch and smiled my Mary McCarthy smile. I was surprised to discover that all the Dekes were a little scared of me. The house read "Without Restrictions" faithfully. Graham had told them about my stand that memorable fall day. To him, I was the girl who couldn't stop for fripperies when the world was smothering under a blanket of hypocrisy. The girls who came to the Deke house were another matter. Although they were friendly and polite to me, I couldn't decipher their true feelings. Most of them came from the three top sororities out of the five that hadn't asked me back. They sat draped over the arms of their boyfriends' chairs, or, with their Weejuns tucked chastely beneath their skirts, on the rug. Their faces were composed, above their jeweled pins, shutting out all disquiet. What was their secret? I asked myself. Had their wealth bought them their unshakable serenity, as it had bought their cashmere sweaters and their perfect even teeth? Was it that simple? Or was their poise due to some secret inner powers, such as the Rosicrucians advertised, powers denied me forever because of my innately angry heart? I watched these girls, fascinated; I looked forward to the weekends not because of Graham but because of them. I sat in the circle of Graham's arm and said witty, icy things, while my eyes darted back and forth, observing their languid, seamless gestures, the way they made a special art out of lighting a cigarette, their glossy, lacquered nails cupping the flame, the charms on their bracelets faintly jingling. Were they silently, en masse, smiling at me while condemning me as a fraud?

I was never sure, and my unsureness whetted my vituperation.

"Without Restrictions" dealt with second-semester rush under the subhead *John Paul Jones Had Better Be Your Friend*. The column ran a "tape recording" of a typical rush dialogue.

SISTER: And what is *youah* name?

RUSHEE: Mary Kathleen Jones.

SISTER: Jones! Are you by any chance related to John Paul?

RUSHEE: I don't believe so. There are lots of Joneses where I come from.

SISTER: And where is that?

RUSHEE: Bent Twig.

SISTER: Bent Twig! Why didn't you say so! Then you must be good friends with the Twigs who own the bank and the funeral parlor and the newspaper and the fish market.

RUSHEE: Well, I don't know them personally, but of course everybody's heard of the Twigs.

SISTER: Uh-huh. Well, Mary Catherine—oh, excuse me, Kath*leen*—it's been just grand talking to you. I'd like you to meet Attalee Hunt, our sister from Savannah. Attie, I think Mary Catherine might like a fresh glass of ice water. She seems to have eaten all her ice.

Not long after this, I received the following letter among my fan mail:

Dear Miss Lewis,

Your farce is ridiculous and futile. Why this endless stream of poison from a girl who professes to
keep late-night company with Kierkegaard and
Camus? Why waste your eye for the delicate and
obscure detail on such passing, boring trivia during
your short-term lease among the stars? Where is
the discrepancy? Your ambivalence haunts me. Do
you know who you are? If you did, I think you
would be less angry.

                                          Jack Krazowski
                                          211 Kerr Dorm

The letter upset me briefly. I put it out of my mind. I
sipped rum punch after the basketball game, in front of
a roaring fire at the Deke house. Suzanne Pinkerton,
the Chi O who, it was rumored, once loved Graham,
studied me curiously over the rim of her steaming mug
and asked softly, "Janie, why do you hate us so?" Graham squeezed my shoulder proudly. "Better watch out
for this one," he said. He was always saying about me,
"Look out, now," or, "Better watch out for this one."
That night, his lack of originality annoyed me.

At midterm, I got my first C. The sight of the letter-
grade gave me a shock. I remembered my former indus-
trious scholarship, the feeling I'd had for years that A's
were my birthright. Now my mental sharpness was
blurred by this constant association with people who
demanded little of my mind. All my energy went into
planning my next printed tirade against some small or
imagined slight. Graham took me to the Interfraternity
Ball. Before the dance, we were inconvenienced by a
new state liquor law that made it necessary for us to
drive twenty miles into the next county in order to purchase our bottles of J&B. Several days later, "Without
Restrictions" presented a scathing diatribe against red-
neck Baptist legislators who could not hold their liquor
and therefore assumed we students at the university
could not be trusted, either.

A second letter came from Kerr Dorm.

Dear Miss Lewis,
   Have you ever read Ben Franklin's story of the
tin whistle? You probably have—you seem to have
read everything—so I won't bore you by retelling
it. But your latest column put me in mind of little
Ben racing about the house in manic despair, blowing stubbornly on the useless whistle for which he
had given all his money.

Yours truly,
Jack Krazowski

I went to the library that evening for the first time in
weeks. It was a balmy evening, almost spring, and I
looked forward to browsing among shelves of books once
more. In a *Benjamin Franklin Reader*, I tracked down
the story of the tin whistle, how when Ben as a child had
been given a gift of money and sent off to a toy store he
had been "charmed" by the sound of another boy's whistle and given all his money for it at once.

I then came home and went whistling all over the
house, much pleased by my whistle, but disturbing
all the family. My brothers and sisters and cousins,
understanding the bargain I had made, told me I
had given four times as much for it as it was worth;
put me in mind what good things I might have
bought with the rest of my money; and laughed at
me so much for my folly, that I cried with vexation;
and the reflection gave me more chagrin than the
whistle gave me pleasure.

I left the library and walked slowly back to my dorm.
I passed students, some in groups, others solitary, whom
I did not know. I wondered who they were and whether
their private thoughts were poems or diatribes. Perhaps
the one I had just passed would become very famous
someday, and someone would say to me, "Oh did you
know —— at your university? You were there at the

same time." "No, I hung out mainly with the Dekes," I would answer.

I walked past Kerr Dorm nervously. It was the oldest men's dormitory, built of limestone and covered with ivy. It cost less to live there because there was no air conditioning. Which room on the second floor was 211? A pair of feet in white socks hung out of one of the lighted windows. From another came the sound of Brahms's Violin Concerto. I stood beneath the window, listening to the poignant solo of the violin. The stars were out and I was pleased I could recognize so many constellations. Then I heard footsteps and people coming along the walk laughing and I hurried away, not wanting to be discovered mooning outside Jack Krazowski's dorm.

WITHOUT RESTRICTIONS
"Night Sounds"

Last night, about nine, I walked home from the library. The air had that peculiar spring quality which clarifies a drowsy mind and conducts important sounds. As I passed my fellow students I seemed to hear the rhythms of their thoughts: some quick and angry, others slow and meditative. I heard voices out of the future speak to me and I heard my own voice, also in a future time, trying to explain, to justify, the way in which I'd used my short-term lease among the stars . . .

Dear Miss Janie Lewis,

Stick to your tirades, hon. "Night Sounds" are just not you at your best.

Your beer-drinking, frat-hating, establishment-stomping, ever-lovin' buddies from

Bingham Quad

It was Graham's twenty-first birthday. I gave up on men's stores. He had as many cuff links, sweaters, and pocket flasks as they stocked. Also, I had a limited amount to spend, and did not want to risk choosing the wrong brand, an inferior label. I went to the bookstore because here I knew I could trust my taste. Usually, for people I liked, I simply chose a book I wanted myself. Would Graham like a Kierkegaard anthology? The complete poetry of John Donne? I couldn't be sure. I went on to the hobby shelves and examined a glossy volume entitled *A Complete Guide to the World's Firearms*.

"Looking for new ammunition for your column, Miss Lewis?" asked an ironic male voice behind me. Somehow I knew who it was. I turned at last to see what Jack Krazowski looked like. He was tall, but otherwise a disappointment. Pale, hawklike face. Horn-rims, faded Levi's, and muddy combat boots. He was holding the Modern Library edition of *Thus Spake Zarasthustra*. His hands were surprisingly graceful and clean.

"I'm looking for a birthday present," I said. "A person I know is being given a surprise birthday party tonight."

"What sort of person?" he asked familiarly. His eyes were such a light blue, he looked as though he were perpetually squinting into the sun.

"One of those persons who have everything already." My sarcastic tone surprised me.

"Oh," he said, not very interested. He was looking at me, rather pleased about something. "You're a lot prettier than that bitchy picture of you they run," he said at last.

"I don't expect you to like my picture any better than you like my column."

"It's getting better. The one about the night sounds showed promise."

"I'm glad you think I have literary promise."

"Oh, that's never been in question. I wasn't referring to that kind of promise when I said you were getting better. Would you like a cup of coffee?"

"I can't. I have to go home and wash my hair for this party. And I haven't even bought a present."

"Let me help you. The purely impersonal shopper's guide. What is your friend like?"

"He's soft-spoken," I said, noting the flicker of disappointment at the masculine pronoun. "Well dressed," I added, looking down at his caked boots. I was being terrible, I couldn't help myself.

"Buy him this." He held up an ornate copy of the *Inferno*, with Doré engravings, on sale for $4.50. "It's a good book, if he wants to read it. And the pictures are nice if he doesn't. He'll be flattered to think that you think he'll read it, anyway."

I caught the implicit snub, but it did seem, somehow, the perfect choice. And the price was certainly right. I bought the book.

"If he likes it, you have to go to dinner with me sometime," said Jack, who then walked me back to the dorm. He had a loping long-distance walk; I had to run along awkwardly to keep up.

"Were you in the army?" I said. "You walk like you're on a long march."

"Nope. Marines."

"For how long?"

"Four years."

"Good grief, you must be ancient."

"A decrepit twenty-seven in June. I had to get somebody to pay for law school. My old man's a miner. I have nine brothers and sisters."

"Well, I'm an only child. But my father has this problem with his temper and keeps losing jobs. I had these war bonds, luckily, my aunt and uncle used to send me every Christmas, and I cashed them in so I could go to this measly little college in my hometown as a day student. The only reason I'm here is because I made straight A's for two years and did nothing but grind, grind, grind. Now I intend to have some fun." I was shocked at myself. I had not even told my Christian Scientist roommate the whole truth.

We were standing, by this time, at the entrance to my dorm. Jack suddenly gave me a paternal pat on top of my head. "That explains a lot," he said. "Yes. Well, after all my fan mail, I guess you know where I live now. Call me when you're ready to go out to dinner. Any night except Tuesday. That's my night to collect dorm laundry."

I hurried upstairs to wash my hair. I was annoyed at Jack for telling me to call him. Where were his manners? I was sorry I had talked to him about my family, but it had poured out before I could stop it. Under the shower I closed my eyes and luxuriated in thoughts of the evening to come. I felt in control of my life here at last. And Jack had said I was pretty. Maybe we could be friends. We could go off occasionally by ourselves and have quiet conversations. He was not exactly a show-piece, but I had my showpiece already. These were those pre-"Liberation" years, before girls felt guilty about treating men like objects because turnabout is fair play.

Graham liked his present. He said, "This is one classic I have always wanted to read. This is the kind of book you can keep for a lifetime." (And I am sure Graham still has the book.)

In the days that followed I became unusually depressed. All the anger had suddenly gone out of me. I read in the newspaper about a student from Texas who had jumped from the tower due to "pressures from overwork," and every time I thought of this I cried. In fact, I tried to think about it so I could cry. I wrote a column entitled "The Pressures That Bear Us Away," a disconnected, overwrought piece that, when it was published, prompted a call to the newspaper from the Director of Student Health, who pronounced it an irresponsible romanticizing of suicide. The editor called me into his office and more or less issued an ultimatum: Get funny again, or get out. I quickly redeemed myself by "crashing" the sororities' Spring Fashion Show. My next "Without Restrictions" was called "A Visitor from Mars Reports on Pan-Hellenic Couture," and put this shallow annual event in its cosmic place. Graham telephoned, sounding uncharacteristically sad. "I know these things don't seem important to you, Janie, but Suzanne Pinkerton devoted hours of work organizing that show, and she felt your column was unfair." He was as courteous and soft-spoken as ever, but I felt the censure in his words, and imagined his alliance with Suzanne against my clumsy fury.

That afternoon, I called Kerr Dorm, second floor. The phone rang for a long time. At last a boy answered. There was a great commotion in the background, shouts echoing and shower water running. "Who is it you want?" he kept repeating. "You'll have to speak up louder."

"I want Jack Krazowski!" I shouted.

"She wants Jack Krazowski!" he shouted. There was a lot of male laughter. I was getting ready to hang up in embarrassment.

"Hello," he said. "Don't mind them."

"This is Janie Lewis, from the bookstore," I said.

"I know that. When are we going to dinner? How about tonight?"

"That would be fine. Actually, I've been . . . it will be nice to talk to you."

"I'll be over in about an hour," he said. "I'll shave and put on a suit so you won't be ashamed of me."

"I look forward to it," I said, feeling better.

"I'm glad you finally got around to calling," he said. Was he laughing? I couldn't tell.

When I looked for him in the dorm parlor, I skipped right over him at first. I looked at the boys lounging self-consciously against armchairs and walls, huddling together in groups. One of these boys I recognized as a new Deke, who'd pledged in January. Jack, in a dark suit, turned from the window where he'd been standing. He'd been there all the time, but I had been looking for a boy, not a man.

"I didn't recognize you, all dressed up," I said, hurrying along beside his long-march strides into the early-spring evening. The new Deke looked after us. I supposed it would get back to Graham but I didn't care.

"It's only my charisma," said Jack. "You'll get used to it."

He took me to a steak house on the highway. None of the Greeks ever went there. Everything seemed strangely and pleasantly adult. Jack had borrowed a car, a pedestrian black Plymouth with the radio missing from the dashboard.

"What did you want to talk about?" he said.

"Oh nothing. Everything. I just feel I can be myself around you."

"Can't you be with your other friends? Your friend that had the birthday, for instance?"

"Oh God!" I laughed wildly. Then I amended, "It's just that . . . with a lot of people, I seem to be able to present only certain sides of myself. But with you, I can just let go."

"Knowing what I think I know," he said, "I'm not sure that's a compliment from you."

"What do you mean?"

"Oh, let's pass on that one. If you don't know, it's because you don't want to know yet. Besides, I'm glad you called." He reached over and tapped the back of my neck lightly with his finger, and a queer thing happened to my stomach.

The atmosphere of the steak house had a liberating effect on me. It seemed we were decades away from the college campus. Sitting across from each other in the dark little restaurant, eating our charcoaled steaks and drinking our beers, we might have been two highway travelers going anywhere. "I haven't felt so relaxed all year," I said. "If you only knew how much time I spend talking about nothing with people I don't even like."

"Why do you do it?" Jack asked, watching me closely. The way he had tapped my neck in the car: I hoped he would touch me again.

I said, "When I was growing up, all my friends belonged to a country club. Or, rather, their parents did. This club had the only swimming pool in town. There was another place, a sort of walled-in lake, but a girl had been molested there—a bunch of local hoodlums stood in a circle around her and made her let them feel under her bathing suit—and my mother wouldn't let me go. I was allowed into the country club pool, as a guest, twice a month. Once, a friend tried to sneak me in a third time

and the lifeguard caught us and made me leave. My
friend decided to stay on. I remember she gave me this
sort of pitying look through the fence and said, very cool
and sweet, 'We'll have better luck next time, Janie.' I
walked back home, over the golf course, and I felt so
ashamed."

"It was your so-called friend who should have felt
ashamed," said Jack. "Did that ever cross your mind?"

"No, I guess it didn't. Not until now. How funny that
it shouldn't have, until now."

"That's because you're in a rut," said Jack. "Do you
want to be accepted by people just because they remind
you of those rich kids in your hometown? Shouldn't you
ask yourself, first of all, whether you accept *them*?"

"I don't know," I said. "It's not that simple. These
people do have something. This kind of unshakable quality. I'm so . . . shakable. There's a mystery about these
people I need to decipher."

"Mystery!" scoffed Jack. He drummed his long fingers
on the checkered tablecloth.

"You have wonderful hands," I said, wanting an
excuse to touch him. "Have you ever taken piano?"

"Coal miners' sons aren't in the habit of taking piano
lessons," he replied, and I hated the smugness in his
voice.

"Why do you play up your proletarian role?" I said.

"I don't know. Do I play it up? Perhaps it's my Budapest defense. Do you know chess? No? I'll have to teach
you. It will develop your unshakable powers." He picked
up my hand.

"What is a Budapest defense?" I said rapturously.

"A gambit. A sort of counterattack. Get them before
they have a chance to get you. You of all people ought
to understand."

"I wish you would teach me," I said. "Chess, I mean.
No, I don't. I wish you could teach me everything." I
did not have to ask myself whether I accepted Jack.
There were other ways of knowing.

"Janie," he said. "Too bad we didn't meet earlier."

"But we've got now," I said recklessly. "We've got

two more months." I pushed it too quickly, promising more than I was sure I could give.

"We have, if you want it," he said, looking at me carefully.

As soon as we got back to the car, in the dark parking lot behind the steak house, we began kissing. Now and then, a car or a truck would hurtle down the highway, beaming its headlights momentarily on the tall yellow grasses growing wild. Then there was darkness and the stars scattered liberally across a black sky. Suddenly the world was so much bigger. Jack and I existed alone under that sky. We were members of the universe, and anything smaller was a bore.

But when we drove back again, into the lights of the town, and saw students coming out of the movies in pairs, and convertibles skimming around corners, my old paltry fear returned. Jack asked whether I would like to stop off at Harry's, a popular campus hangout, for a cup of coffee, but I said no. I was afraid for his charisma, under the fluorescent lights. It might dissolve, and I would be stuck in Harry's with a coal miner's son and his Budapest defense, and I was not ready yet. He seemed to understand, and drove me to the dorm.

At the front door, he took me by the shoulders and looked searchingly into my face. "Janie, there isn't unlimited time for all there is to do," he said. "Don't waste it. Don't be afraid of doing what you want."

"I enjoyed the dinner," I said, in a turmoil.

He sighed. "Well, you call me when you want another one," he said. "Only it probably won't be steak next time. I'm a poor man, remember."

The spring went quickly, like a 33 record somebody had turned up to 78. Graham became hyperattentive. He'd obviously been told of my stepping out by the new Deke trying to score a few Brownie points. Graham didn't pry. That was not his way. He asked me to accept his pin. I had hoped for this for a long time; it had seemed the answer to so many things. With a dry mouth, feeling a stranger to myself, I accepted the pin in an impressive candlelight ceremony. The brothers stood in a circle around us. Even Suzanne Pinkerton came up to me afterward and took my hand and said, as though she meant it, "I'm so happy for you, Janie."

I saw Jack only once more, at the bookstore. I had gone there to browse, hoping I might meet him.

"That's an elegant pin you've got on," he said, looking straight at my eyes and not at the pin. "Does it mean you're engaged?"

"Not exactly. Kind of engaged to be engaged."

"Hmm. What are those, rubies?"

"They're not tin," I said, without thinking, and could have bitten off my tongue.

"No, I can see that," he said quietly. A remote look came into his face. I remembered how we had kissed under the stars. It would be unthinkable, never to do it again. And yet his remoteness clearly proclaimed we wouldn't.

"Oh well," I said, "things happen. But they also unhappen. Will you be back in the fall?"

"I'm finishing up in June," he said. "I get my law degree in June. Then back to West Virginia, to study for the bar."

"Oh." There was nothing else I could think of to say, yet there was so much going on between us.

He broke the silence. "Well, take care, Janie." Then he went out of the bookstore, bouncing up and down on the balls of his feet, in his long-march style. I had an impulse to run after him. But what would I say when I caught up with him?

After finals, Graham gave a houseparty at his parents' summer cottage at the beach. There was much beer-drinking and water-skiing and necking, and I was so integral a part of the group that I found I could dispense altogether with my Mary McCarthy smile. I shared a bedroom with Suzanne Pinkerton and was able to penetrate her mystique at last. She worried terribly about her small breasts and had sent off secretly for a chest developer, which she used morning and night. She slept with a yellow rabbit, whose fur had come off in patches, which she'd been given as a child. She confided that she was not really in love with the boy who was her date for this houseparty. "There's someone . . . he's in Maine . . . in some ways he reminds me of you, Janie."

"Oh? In what ways?"

"Well, he's real smart, like you . . . and at first he seems, you know, kind of critical. But after you get to know him, he's a wonderful person."

We were lying on the beach one morning, doing our nails from the same bottle of polish. She said to me, "Marietta Porter is transferring to William and Mary in the fall. There'll be a vacancy at the Chi O house. I could speak to the others if you're interested, Janie."

I was lying on my stomach, listening to the dull, even plash of the sea at low tide, watching Suzanne's polish harden to a fine porcelain sheen on my fingernails. I pretended Jack Krazowski was within listening distance, hearing me utter the finale to that wasted year. But no one was listening as I thanked Suzanne and explained about the clause in my scholarship. No one at all, not even the Spirit of the Times, who had turned her back on us to scan the horizon. There were new things on the way for people to join or to be angry about. The sixties were coming.

Suzanne said, well, she hoped I'd come around to the house and have dinner sometime, she hoped we could get to know each other better. Then she started on her second coat of polish. I lay there beside her, staring at my own nails, getting angrier by the minute because I couldn't love them, even now that I'd made them love me.

Then the boys came back, carrying their surfboards, waving at us while they were still some distance away. Without my glasses I was not sure which of them, in their look-alike plaid bathing trunks, was Graham. The closer they came, the angrier I got, not with the deflected anger that went into the columns of "Without Restrictions," but with a deep, abiding, central anger at the real culprit, the crass conformist who'd been harboring inside the rebel all along. I dug my nails into the sand, ruining the careful polish job. What was the proper procedure for returning a fraternity pin without hurting anyone's feelings?

I don't remember the actual returning of Graham's pin. He must have been hurt, or baffled at the very least. What happened to him later I don't know.

The fall of my senior year I spent ministering to the almost constant anger of a new man, a young psychiatrist in the blackest depths of his training analysis. We spent most of our time together confusing me with his mother. In the spring I rallied and helped to found a new literary magazine on campus. It was called *Shock!!!* and had one triumphant issue before being quashed by the local postmaster. Then I graduated, with no *laudes*, and went out into the world, where I found new people to love and plenty of new things to be angry about.

But ever since the Angry-Year, I have reserved my most energetic fury for the Culprit. Though her powers have diminished as I've grown more sure of mine, she still keeps quarters for herself in some unreachable part of my psyche. She bores from inside at the braver scaffoldings erected by my imagination, and her favorite trick is posing as other people whom I hate until I realize I'm hating myself. She is forever trying to constrain me to the well-trodden paths of expression, even as I write this story. For every mental mile I succeed in traveling without her restrictions, she leadens my heart with her ceaseless plaint: *What are the others thinking? What will others think?*

Peter Taylor

Peter Taylor was born in Trenton, Tennessee, in 1917, and he often sets his fiction in the communities where he grew up: Trenton, Nashville, St. Louis, and Memphis. He studied with several famous southern writers and critics: Allen Tate, John Crowe Ransom, Robert Penn Warren, and Cleanth Brooks. Taylor left Vanderbilt to follow John Crowe Ransom to Kenyon College where Taylor received his B.A. He went on to lecture and to teach creative writing at a number of colleges and universities, and only recently retired from his professorship at the University of Virginia. Although he won a Pulitzer Prize for his novel, *A Summons to Memphis* (1986), and has written several plays, he is best known for his short stories, for which he won several O. Henry prizes. Many of his early stories were collected in one volume, *The Collected Stories of Peter Taylor* (1969). Since then, he has published *In the Miro District and Other Stories* (1977) and *The Old Forest and Other Stories* (1985), which won the PEN/Faulkner award. Reviewers have called Peter Taylor the most accomplished short-story writer of our time. He has been praised for his ear for dialogue and his eye for psychologically complex characterization. Like Eudora Welty, he thinks that growing up in a storytelling family inspired his writing. "My theory is that you listen to people talk when you're a child—a Southerner does especially—and they tell stories and stories and stories, and you feel those stories must mean something. So really, writing becomes an effort to find out what these stories mean in the beginning." A member of both the American Academy of Arts and Letters and the National Academy and Institute of Arts and Letters, Peter Taylor lives in Charlottesville, Virginia.

The Old Forest

Iwas already formally engaged, as we used to say, to the girl I was going to marry. But still I sometimes went out on the town with girls of a different sort. And during the very week before the date set for the wedding, in December, I was in an automobile accident at a time when one of those girls was with me. It was a calamitous thing to have happen—not the accident itself, which caused no serious injury to anyone, but the accident plus the presence of that girl.

As a matter of fact, it was not unusual in those days—forty years ago and a little more—for a well-brought-up young man like me to keep up his acquaintance, until the very eve of his wedding, with some member of what we facetiously and somewhat arrogantly referred to as the Memphis demimonde. (That was merely to say with a girl who was not in the Memphis debutante set.) I am not even sure how many of us knew what the word "demimonde" meant or implied. But once it had been applied to such girls, it was hard for us to give it up. We even learned to speak of them individually as demimondaines—and later corrupted that to demimondames. The girls were of course a considerably less sophisticated lot than any of this sounds, though they were bright girls certainly and some of them even highly intelligent. They read books, they looked at pictures, and they were apt to attend any concert or play that came to Memphis. When the old San Carlo Opera Company turned up in town, you could count on certain girls of the demimonde being present in their block of seats, and often with a

score of the opera in hand. From that you will understand that they certainly weren't the innocent, untutored
types that we generally took to dances at the Memphis
Country Club and whom we eventually looked forward
to marrying.

These girls I refer to would, in fact, very frequently
and very frankly say to us that the MCC (that's how we
always spoke of the Club) was the last place they wanted
to be taken. There was one girl in particular, not so
smart as some of the others perhaps and certainly less
restrained in the humor she sometimes poked at the
world we boys lived in, an outspoken girl, who was the
most vociferous of all in her disdain for the Country
Club. I remember one night, in one of those beer gardens
that became popular in Memphis in the late thirties,
when this girl suddenly announced to a group of us, "*I*
haven't lost anything at the MCC. That's something you
boys can bet your daddy's bottom dollar on." We were
gathered—four or five couples—about one of the big
wooden beer-garden tables with an umbrella in its center,
and when she said that, all the other girls in the party
went into a fit of laughter. It was a kind of giggling that
was unusual for them. The boys in the party laughed,
too, of course, but we were surprised by the way the
girls continued to giggle among themselves for such a
long time. We were out of college by then and thought
we knew the world pretty well; most of us had been
working for two or three years in our fathers' business
firms. But we didn't see why this joke was so very funny.
I suppose it was too broad for us in its reference. There
is no way of knowing, after all these years, if it was too
broad for our sheltered minds or if the rest of the girls
were laughing at the vulgar tone of the girl who had
spoken. She was, you see, a little bit coarser than the
rest, and I suspect they were laughing at the way she had
phrased what she said. For us boys, anyhow, it was pleasant that the demimondaines took the lighthearted view
they did about not going to the MCC, because it was the
last place most of us would have wished to take them.
Our *other* girls would have known too readily who they

were and would not willingly or gracefully have endured their presence. To have brought one of those girls to the Club would have required, at any rate, a boy who was a much bolder and freer spirit than I was at twenty-three.

To the liberated young people of today all this may seem a corrupting factor in our old way of life—not our snobbery so much as our continuing to see those demi-monde girls right up until the time of marriage. And yet I suspect that in the Memphis of today customs concerning serious courtship and customs concerning unacknowledged love affairs have not been entirely altered. Automobile accidents occur there still, for instance, the reports of which in the newspaper do not mention the name of the driver's "female companion," just as the report of my accident did not. If the driver is a "scion of a prominent local family" with his engagement to be married already announced at an MCC party, as well as in the Sunday newspaper, then the account of his automobile collision is likely to refer to the girl in the car with him only as his "female companion." Some newspaper readers might, I know, assume this to be a reference to the young man's fiancée. That is what is intended, I suppose—*for* the general reader. But it would almost certainly not have been the case—not in the Memphis, Tennessee, of 1937.

The girl with me in my accident was a girl whose origins nobody knew anything about. But she was a perfectly decent sort of girl, living independently in a respectable rooming house and working a respectable job. That was the sort of girl about whom the Memphis newspapers felt obliged to exercise the greatest care when making any reference to her in their columns. It was as though she were their special ward. Such a girl must be protected from any blaze of publicity. Such a girl must not suffer from the misconduct of any Memphis man or group of men—even newspaper publishers. That was fine for the girl, of course, and who could possibly resent it? It was splendid for her, but I, the driver of the car, had to suffer considerable anguish just because of such a girl's presence in the car and suffer still more because of her behavior afterward. Moreover, the response of certain older men in town to her subsequent behavior would cause me still further anguish and prolong my suffering by several days. Those men were the editors of the city's two newspapers, along with the lawyers called in by my father to represent me if I should be taken into court. There was also my father himself, and the father of my fiancée, *his* lawyer (for some reason or other), and, finally, no less a person than the mayor of Memphis, all of whom one would ordinarily have supposed to be indifferent to the caprices of such a girl. They were the civic leaders and merchant princes of the city. They had great matters on their minds. They were, to say the least, an imposing group in the eyes of a young man who had just the previous year entered his father's cotton-brokerage firm, a young man who was still learning how to operate under the pecking order of Memphis's male establishment.

The girl in question was named Lee Ann Deehart. She was a quite beautiful, fair-haired, hazel-eyed girl with a lively manner, and surely she was far from stupid. The thing she did which drew attention from the city fathers came very near, also, to changing the course of my entire life. I had known Lee Ann for perhaps two years at the time, and knew her to be more levelheaded and more reserved and self-possessed than most of her friends among the demimondaines. It would have been impossible for me to predict the behavior she was guilty of that winter afternoon. Immediately after the collision, she threw open the door on her side of the car, stepped out onto the roadside, and fled into the woods of Overton Park, which is where the accident took place. And from that time, and during the next four days, she was unheard from by people who wished to question her and protect her. During that endless-seeming period of four days no one could be certain of Lee Ann Deehart's whereabouts.

The circumstances of the accident were rather complicated. The collision occurred just after three o'clock on a very cold Saturday afternoon—the fourth of December.

Although at that time in my life I was already a member of my father's cotton firm, I was nevertheless—and strange as it may seem—enrolled in a Latin class out at Southwestern College, which is on the north side of Overton Park. (We were reading Horace's *Odes!*) The class was not held on Saturday afternoon, but I was on my way out to the college to study for a test that had been scheduled for Monday. My interest in Latin was regarded by my father and mother as one of my "anomalies"—a remnant of many "anomalies" I had annoyed them with when I was in my teens and was showing some signs of "not turning out well." It seemed now of course that I had "turned out well" after all, except that nobody in the family and nobody among my friends could understand why I went on showing this interest in Latin. I was not able to explain to them why. Any more than I was able to explain why to myself. It clearly had nothing to do with anything else in my life at that period. Furthermore, in the classroom and under the strict eye of our classics professor, a rotund, mustachioed little man hardly four feet in height (he had to sit on a large Latin dictionary in order to be comfortable at his desk), I didn't excel. I was often embarrassed by having to own up to Professor Bartlett's accusation that I had not so much as glanced at the assigned odes before coming to class. Sometimes other members of the class would be caught helping me with the translation, out in the hallway, when Professor Bartlett opened his classroom door to us. My real excuse for neglecting the assignments made by that earnest and admirable little scholar was that too many hours of my life were consumed by my job, by my courtship of the society girl I was going to marry, and by my old, bad habits of knocking about town with my boyhood cronies and keeping company with girls like Lee Ann Deehart.

Yet I had persisted with my Horace class throughout that fall (against the advice of nearly everyone, including Professor Bartlett). On that frigid December afternoon I had resolved to mend my ways as a student. I decided I would take my Horace and go out to Professor Bartlett's

Peter Taylor

classroom at the college and make use of his big dictionary in preparing for Monday's test. It was something we
had all been urged to do, with the promise that we would
always find the door unlocked. As it turned out, of
course, I was destined not to take the test on Monday
and never to enter Professor Bartlett's classroom again.

It happened that just before I was setting out from
home that afternoon I was filled suddenly with a dread
of the silence and the peculiar isolation of a college classroom building on a weekend afternoon. I telephoned my
fiancée and asked her to go along with me. At the other
end of the telephone line, Caroline Braxley broke into
laughter. She said that I clearly had no conception of all
the things she had to do within the next seven days
before we were to be married. I said I supposed I ought
to be helping in some way, though until now she had not
asked me so much as to help address invitations to the
wedding. "No indeed," said my bride-to-be, "I want to
do everything myself. I wouldn't have it any other way."

Caroline Braxley, this capable and handsome bride-to-
be of mine, was a very remarkable girl, just as today, as
my wife, she seems to me a very remarkable woman of
sixty. She and I have been married for forty-one years
now, and her good judgment in all matters relating to
our marriage has never failed her—or us. She had
already said to me before that Saturday afternoon that a
successful marriage depended in part on the two persons'
developing and maintaining a certain number of separate
interests in life. She was all for my keeping up my golf,
my hunting, my fishing. And, unlike my own family, she
saw no reason that I shouldn't keep up my peculiar interest in Latin, though she had to confess that she thought
it almost the funniest thing she had ever heard of a man
of my sort going in for.

Caroline liked any sort of individualism in men. But I
already knew her ways sufficiently well to understand
that there was no use trying to persuade her to come
along with me to the college. I wished she would come
with me, or maybe I wished even more she would try to
persuade me to come over to her house and help her

with something in preparation for the wedding. After I had put down the telephone, it even occurred to me that I might simply drive over to her house and present myself at her front door. But I knew what the expression on her face would be, and I could even imagine the sort of thing she would say: "No man is going to set foot in my house this afternoon, Nat Ramsey! *I'm* getting married next Saturday, in case the fact has slipped your mind. Besides, you're coming here for dinner tonight, aren't you? And there are parties every night next week!"

This Caroline Braxley of mine was a very tall girl. (Actually taller than she is nowadays. We have recently measured ourselves and found that each of us is an inch shorter than we used to be.) One often had the feeling that one was looking up at her, though of course she wasn't really so tall as that. Caroline's height and the splendid way she carried herself were one of her first attractions for me. It seems to me now that I was ever attracted to tall girls—that is, when there was the possibility of falling in love. And I think this was due in part to the fact that even as a boy I was half in love with my father's two spinster sisters, who were nearly six feet in height and were always more attentive to me than to the other children in the family.

Anyhow, only moments after I had put down the telephone that Saturday, when I still sat with my hand on the instrument and was thinking vaguely of rushing over to Caroline's house, the telephone underneath my hand began ringing. Perhaps, I thought, it was Caroline calling back to say that she had changed her mind. Instead, it was Lee Ann Deehart. As soon as she heard my voice, she began telling me that she was bored to death. Couldn't I think of something fun she and I could do on this dreary winter afternoon? I laughed aloud at her. "What a shameless wench you are, Lee Ann!" I said.

"Shameless? How so?" she said with pretended innocence.

"As if you weren't fully aware," I lectured her, "that I'm getting married a week from today!"

"What's that got to do with the price of eggs in Arkansas?" She laughed. "Do you think, old Nat, *I* want to marry you?"

"Well," I explained, "I happen to be going out to the college to cram for a Latin test on Monday."

I could hear her laughter at the other end. "Is your daddy going to let you off work long enough to take your Latin test?" she asked with heavy irony in her voice. It was the usual way those girls had of making fun of our dependence on our fathers.

"Ah, yes," I said tolerantly.

"And is he going to let you off next Saturday, too," she went on, "long enough to get married?"

"Listen," I said, "I've just had an idea. Why don't you ride out to the college with me, and fool around some while I do my Latin?" I suppose I didn't really imagine she would go, but suddenly I had thought again of the lonely isolation of Dr. Bartlett's classroom on a Saturday afternoon. I honestly wanted to go ahead out there. It was something I somehow felt I had to do. My preoccupation with the study of Latin poetry, ineffectual student though I was, may have represented a perverse wish to experience the isolation I was at the same time dreading or may have represented a taste for morbidity left over from my adolescence. I can allow myself to speculate on all that now, though it would not have occurred to me to do so at the time.

"Well," said Lee Ann Deehart presently, to my surprise and delight, "it couldn't be more boring out there than sitting here in my room is."

"I'll pick you up in fifteen minutes," I said quickly. And I hung up the telephone before she could possibly change her mind. Thirty minutes later, we were driving through Overton Park on our way to the college. We had passed the Art Gallery and were headed down the hill toward the low ground where the Park Pond is. Ahead of us, on the left, were the gates to the Zoo. And on beyond was the point where the road crossed the streetcar tracks and entered a densely wooded area which is actually the last surviving bit of the primeval forest that once grew right up to the bluffs above the Mississippi

River. Here are giant oak and yellow poplar trees older than the memory of the earliest white settler. Some of them surely may have been mature trees when Hernando de Soto passed this way, and were very old trees indeed when General Jackson, General Winchester, and Judge John Overton purchased this land and laid out the city of Memphis. Between the Art Gallery and the pond there used to be, in my day, a little spinney of woods which ran nearly all the way back to what was left of the old forest. It was just when I reached this spinney, with Lee Ann beside me, that I saw a truck approaching us on the wrong side of the icy road. There was a moderately deep snow on the ground, and the park roads had, to say the least, been imperfectly cleared. On the ice and the packed snow, the driver of the truck had clearly lost control of his vehicle. When he was within about seventy-five feet of us, Lee Ann said, "Pull off the road, Nat!"

Lee Ann Deehart's beauty was of the most feminine sort. She was a tiny, delicate-looking girl, and I had noticed, when I went to fetch her that day, in her fur-collared coat and knitted cap and gutta-percha boots she somehow seemed smaller than usual. And I was now struck by the tone of authority coming from this small person whose diminutive size and whose role in my life were such that it wouldn't have occurred to me to heed her advice about driving a car—or about anything else, I suppose. I remember feeling something like: This is an ordeal that I must, and that I want, to face in my own way. It was as though Professor Bartlett himself were in the approaching truck. It seemed my duty not to admit any weakness in my own position. At least I *thought* that was what I felt.

"Pull off the road, Nat!" Lee Ann urged again. And my incredible reply to her was "He's on *my* side of the road! Besides, trucks are not allowed in the park!" And in reply to this Lee Ann gave only a loud snicker.

I believe I did, in the last seconds, try to swing the car off onto the shoulder of the road. But the next thing I really remember is the fierce impact of the two vehicles' meeting.

It was a relatively minor sort of collision, or seemed so at the moment. Since the driver of the truck, which was actually a converted Oldsmobile sedan—and a rather ancient one at that—had the good sense not to put on his brakes and to turn off her motor, the crash was less severe than it might have been. Moreover, since I *had* pulled a little to the right it was not a head-on meeting. It is worth mentioning, though, that it was sufficiently bad to put permanently out of commission the car I was driving, which was not my own car (my car was in the shop, being refurbished for the honeymoon trip) but an aging Packard limousine of my mother's, which I knew she would actually be happy to see retired. I don't remember getting out of the car at all and I don't remember Lee Ann's getting out. The police were told by the driver of the truck, however, that within a second after the impact Lee Ann had thrown open her door, leaped out onto the snow-covered shoulder, jumped the ditch beyond, and run up the incline and into the spinney. The truck driver's account was corroborated by two ice skaters on the pond, who also saw her run through the leafless trees of the spinney and on across a narrow stretch of the public golf course which divides the spinney from the old forest. They agreed that, considering there was a deep snow on the ground and that she was wearing those gutta-percha boots, she traveled at a remarkable speed.

I didn't even know she was out of the car until I got around on the other side and saw the door there standing open and saw her tracks in the snow, going down the bank. I suppose I was too dazed even to follow the tracks with my eyes down the bank and up the other side of the ditch. I must have stood there for several seconds, looking down blankly at the tracks she had left just outside the car door. Presently I looked up at the truck driver, who was standing before me. I know now his eyes must have been following Lee Ann's progress. Finally he turned his eyes to me, and I could tell from his expression that I wasn't a pleasant sight. "Is your head hurt bad?" he asked. I put my hand up to my forehead and when I brought it down it was covered with blood. That was when I passed out. When I came to, they wouldn't let me get up. Besides the truck driver, there were two policemen and the two ice skaters standing over me. They told me that an ambulance was on the way.

At the hospital, the doctor took four stitches in my forehead; and that was it. I went home and lay down for a couple of hours, as I had been told to do. My parents and my two brothers and my little sister and even the servants were very much concerned about me. They hovered around in a way I had never before seen them do—not even when somebody was desperately sick. I suppose it was because a piece of violence like this accident was a very extraordinary thing in our quiet Memphis life in those years. They were disturbed, too, I soon realized, by my silence as I lay there on the daybed in the upstairs sitting room and particularly by my being reticent to talk about the collision. I had other things on my mind. Every so often I would remember Lee Ann's boot tracks in the snow. And I would begin to wonder where she was now. Since I had not found an opportunity to telephone her, I could only surmise that she had somehow managed to get back to the rooming house where she lived. I had not told anyone about her presence in the car with me. And as I lay there on the daybed, with the family and servants coming and going and making inquiries about how I felt, I would find myself wondering sometimes how and whether or not I could tell Caroline Braxley about Lee Ann's being with me that afternoon. It turned out the next day—or, rather, on Monday morning—that the truck driver had told the two policemen and then, later, repeated to someone who called from one of the newspapers that there had been a girl with me in the car. As a matter of fact, I learned that this was the case on the night of the accident, but as I lay there in the upstairs sitting room during the afternoon I didn't yet know it.

Shortly before five o'clock Caroline Braxley arrived at our house, making a proper sick call but also with the intention of taking me back to dinner with her parents and her two younger sisters. Immediately after she

entered the upstairs sitting room, and almost before she
and I had greeted each other, my mother's houseboy
and sometime chauffeur came in, bringing my volume of
Horace. Because Mother had thought it might raise my
spirits, she had sent him down to the service garage
where the wrecked car had been taken to fetch it for me.
Smiling sympathetically, he placed it on a table near the
daybed and left the room. Looking at the book, Caroline
said to me with a smile that expressed a mixture of sympathy and reproach, "I hope you see now what folly your
pursuit of Latin poetry is." And suddenly, then, the book
on the table appeared to me as an alien object. In retrospect it seems to me that I really knew then that I would
never open it again.

I went to dinner that night at Caroline's house, my
head still in bandages. The Braxley family treated me
with a tenderness equal to that I had received at home.
At table, the servingman offered to help my plate for
me, as though I were a sick child. I could have enjoyed
all this immensely, I think, since I have always been one
to relish loving, domestic care, if only I had not been
worrying and speculating all the while about Lee Ann.
As I talked genially with Caroline's family during the
meal and immediately afterward before the briskly burning fire at the end of the Braxleys' long living room, I
kept seeing Lee Ann's boot tracks in the snow. And then
I would see my own bloody hand as I took it down from
my face before I fainted. I remember still having the
distinct feeling, as I sat there in the bosom of the Braxley
family, that it had not been merely my bloody hand that
had made me faint but my bloody hand plus the tracks
in the deep snow. In a way, it is strange that I remember
all these impressions so vividly after forty years, because
it is not as though I have lived an uneventful life during
the years since. My Second World War experiences are
what I perhaps ought to remember best—those, along
with the deaths of my two younger brothers in the
Korean War. Even worse, really, were the deaths of my
two parents in a terrible fire that destroyed our house on
Central Avenue when they had got to be quite old, my

mother leaping from a second-story window, my father asphyxiated inside the house. And I can hardly mention without being overcome with emotion the accidental deaths that took two of my and Caroline's children when they were in their early teens. It would seem that with all these disasters to remember, along with the various business and professional crises I have had, I might hardly be able to recall that earlier episode. But I think that, besides its coming at that impressionable period of my life and the fact that one just does remember things better from one's youth, there is the undeniable fact that life *was* different in those times. What I mean to say is that all these later, terrible events took place in a world where acts of terror are, so to speak, all around us— everyday occurrences—and are brought home to us audibly and pictorially on radio and television almost every hour. I am not saying that some of these ugly acts of terror did not need to take place or were not brought on by what our world was like in those days. But I am saying that the context was different. Our tranquil, upper-middle-class world of 1937 did not have the rest of the world crowding in on it so much. And thus when something only a little ugly did crowd in or when we, often unconsciously, reached out for it, the contrasts seemed sharper. It was not just in the Braxley's household or in my own family's that everything seemed quiet and well ordered and unchanging. The households were in a context like themselves. Suffice it to say that though the Braxley's house in Memphis was situated on East Parkway and our house on Central Avenue, at least two miles across town from each other, I could in those days feel perfectly safe, and *was* relatively safe, in walking home many a night from Caroline's house to our house at two in the morning. It was when we young men in Memphis ventured out with the more adventurous girls of the demimonde that we touched on the unsafe zones of Memphis. And there were girls still more adventurous, of course, with whom some of my contemporaries found their way into the very most dangerous zones. But we did think of it that way, you see, thought of it in terms of the girls' being the adventurous ones, whom we followed or didn't follow.

Anyhow, while we were sitting there before the fire, with the portrait of Caroline's paternal grandfather peering down at us from above the mantel and with her father in his broad-lapelled, double-breasted suit standing on the marble hearth, occasionally poking at the logs with the brass poker or sometimes kicking a log with the toe of his wing-tipped shoes, suddenly I was called to the telephone by the Negro servingman who had wanted to help my plate for me. As he preceded me the length of the living room and then gently guided me across the hall to the telephone in the library, I believe he would have put his hand under my elbow to help me—as if a real invalid—if I had allowed him to. As we passed through the hall, I glanced through one of the broad, etched sidelights beside the front door and caught a glimpse of the snow on the ground outside. The weather had turned even colder. There had been no additional snowfall, but even at a glance you could tell how crisply frozen the old snow was on its surface. The servingman at my elbow was saying, "It's your daddy on the phone. I'd suppose he just wants to know how you'd be feeling by now."

But I knew in my heart it wasn't that. It was as if that glimpse of the crisp snow through the front-door sidelight had told me what it was. When I took up the telephone and heard my father's voice pronouncing my name, I knew almost exactly what he was going to say. He said that his friend the editor of the morning paper had called him and reported that there had been a girl in the car with me, and though they didn't of course plan to use her name, probably wouldn't even run the story until Monday, they would have to *know* her name. And would have to assure themselves she wasn't hurt in the crash. And that she was unharmed after leaving the scene. Without hesitation I gave my father Lee Ann Deehart's name, as well as her address and telephone number. But I made no further explanation to Father, and he asked me for none. The only other thing I said was that I'd be home in a little while. Father was silent a moment after that. Then he said, "Are you all right?"

I said, "I'm fine.'

And he said, "Good. I'll be waiting for you."

I hung up the telephone, and my first thought was that before I left Caroline tonight I'd have to tell her that Lee Ann had been in the car with me. Then, without thinking almost, I dialed Lee Ann's rooming-house number. It felt very strange to be doing this in the Braxleys' library. The woman who ran the rooming house said that Lee Ann had not been in since she left with me in the afternoon.

As I passed back across the wide hallway and caught another glimpse of the snow outside, the question arose in my mind for the first time: *Had* Lee Ann come to some harm in those woods? More than the density of the underbrush, more than its proximity to the Zoo, where certain unsavory characters often hung out, it was the great size and antiquity of the forest trees somehow and the old rumors that white settlers had once been ambushed there by Chickasaw Indians that made me feel that if anything had happened to the girl, it had happened there. And on the heels of such thoughts I found myself wondering for the first time if all this might actually lead to my beautiful, willowy Caroline Braxley's breaking off our engagement. I returned to the living room, and at the sight of Caroline's tall figure at the far end of the room, placed between that of her mother and that of her father, the conviction became firm in me that I would have to tell her about Lee Ann before she and I parted that night. And as I drew nearer to her, still wondering if something ghastly had happened to Lee Ann there in the old forest, I saw the perplexed and even suspicious expression on Caroline's face and presently observed similar expressions on the faces of her two parents. And from that moment began the gnawing wonder which would be with me for several days ahead: What precisely would Caroline consider sufficient provocation for breaking off our engagement to be married? I had no idea, really. Would it be sufficient that I had had one of those unnamed "female companions" in the car with me at the time of the accident? I knew of engagements like ours which had been broken with apparently less provocation. Or would it be the suspicious-seeming circumstances of Lee Ann's leaping out of the car and running off through the snow? Or might it be the final, worst possibility—that of delicate little Lee Ann Deehart's having actually met with foul play in that infrequently entered area of underbrush and towering forest trees?

Broken engagements were a subject of common and considerable interest to girls like Caroline Braxley. Whereas a generation earlier a broken engagement had been somewhat of a scandal—an engagement that had been formally announced at a party and in the newspaper, that is—it did not necessarily represent that in our day. Even in our day, you see, it meant something quite different from what it had once meant. There was, after all, no written contract and it was in no sense so unalterably binding as it had been in our parents' day. For us it was not considered absolutely dishonorable for either party to break off the plans merely because he or she had had a change of heart. Since the boy was no longer expected literally to ask the father for the girl's hand (though he would probably be expected to go through the form, as I had done with Mr. Braxley), it was no longer a breach of contract between families. There was certainly nothing like a dowry any longer—not in Memphis—and there was only rarely any kind of property settlement involved, except in cases where both families were extraordinarily rich. The thought pleased me—that is, the ease with which an engagement might be ended. I suppose in part I was simply preparing myself for such an eventuality. And there in the Braxleys' long living room in the very presence of Caroline and Mr. and Mrs. Braxley themselves, I found myself indulging in a perverse fantasy, a fantasy in which Caroline had broken off our engagement and I was standing up pretty well, was even seeking consolation in the arms, so to speak, of a safely returned Lee Ann Deehart.

But all at once I felt so guilty for my private indiscretion that actually for the first time in the presence of my prospective inlaws I put my arm about Caroline Braxley's waist. And I told her that I felt so fatigued by events of the afternoon that probably I ought now to go ahead home. She and her parents agreed at once. And they agreed among themselves that they each had just now been reflecting privately that I looked exhausted. Mrs. Braxley suggested that under the circumstances she ought to ask Robert to drive me home. I accepted. No other suggestion could have seemed so welcome. Robert was the same servingman who had offered to help my plate at dinner and who had so gently guided me to the telephone when my father called. Almost at once, after I got into the front seat of the car beside him—in his dark chauffeur's uniform and cap—I fell asleep. He had to wake me when we pulled up to the side door of my father's house. I remember how warmly I thanked him for bringing me home, even shaking his hand, which was a rather unusual thing to do in those days. I felt greatly refreshed and restored and personally grateful to Robert for it. There was not, in those days in Memphis, any time or occasion when one felt more secure and relaxed than when one had given oneself over completely to the care and protection of the black servants who surrounded us and who created and sustained for the most part the luxury which distinguished the lives we lived then from the lives we live now. They did so for us, whatever their motives and however degrading our demands and our acceptance of their attentions may have been to them.

At any rate, after my slumber in the front seat beside Robert I felt sufficiently restored to face my father (and his awareness of Lee Ann's having been in the car) with some degree of equanimity. And before leaving the Braxleys' house I had found a moment in the hallway to break the news to Caroline that I had not been alone in the car that afternoon. To my considerable surprise she revealed, after a moment's hesitation, that she already knew that had been the case. Her father, like my father, had learned it from one of the newspaper editors—only he had learned it several hours earlier than my father had. I was obliged to realize as we were saying good night to each other that she, along with her two parents, had known all evening that Lee Ann had been with me and had fled into the woods of Overton Park—that she, Caroline, had as a matter of fact known the full story when she came to my house to fetch me back to her house to dinner. "Where is Lee Ann now?" she asked me presently, holding my two hands in her own and looking me directly in the eye. "I don't know," I said. Knowing how much she knew, I decided I must tell her the rest of it, holding nothing back. I felt that I was seeing a new side to my fiancée and that unless I told her the whole truth there might be something of this other side of her that wouldn't be revealed to me. "I tried to telephone her after I answered my father's call tonight. But she was not in her room and had not been in since I picked her up at two o'clock." And I told Caroline about Lee Ann's telephoning me (after Caroline and I had talked in the early afternoon) and about my inviting her to go out to the college with me. Then I gave her my uncensored version of the accident, including the sight of Lee Ann's footprints in the snow.

"How did she sound on the telephone?" she asked.

"What do you mean by that?" I said impatiently. "I just told you she wasn't home when I called."

"I mean earlier—when she called you."

"But why do you want to know that? It doesn't matter, does it?"

"I mean, did she sound depressed? But it doesn't matter for the moment." She still held my hands in hers. "You do know, don't you," she went on after a moment, "that you are going to have to *find* Lee Ann? And you probably are going to need help."

Suddenly I had the feeling that Caroline Braxley was someone twenty years older than I; but, rather than sounding like my parents or her parents, she sounded like one or another of the college teachers I had had— even like Dr. Bartlett, who once had told me that I was going to need outside help if I was going to keep up with the class. To reassure myself, I suppose, I put my arm about Caroline's waist again and drew her to me. But in our good-night kiss there was a reticence on her part, or a quality that I could only define as conditional or possibly probational. Still, I knew now that she knew everything, and I suppose that was why I was able to catch such a good nap in the car on the way home.

Girls who had been brought up the way Caroline had, in the Memphis of forty years ago, knew not only what was going to be expected of them in making a marriage and bringing up a family there in Memphis—a marriage and a family of the kind their parents had had—they knew also from a fairly early time that they would have to contend with girls and women of certain sorts before and frequently after they were married: with girls, that is, who had no conception of what it was to have a certain type of performance expected of them, or girls of another kind (and more like themselves) who came visiting in Memphis from Mississippi or Arkansas—pretty little plantation girls, my mother called them—or from Nashville or from the old towns of West Tennessee. Oftentimes these other girls were their cousins, but that made them no less dangerous. Not being on their home ground—in their own country, so to speak—these Nashville or Mississippi or West Tennessee or Arkansas girls did not bother to abide by the usual rules of civilized warfare. They were marauders. But girls like Lee Ann Deehart were something else again. They were the Trojan horse, more or less, established in the very citadel. They were the fifth column, and were perhaps the most dangerous of all. At the end of a brilliant debutante season, sometimes the most eligible bachelor of all those on the list would still remain uncommitted, or even secretly committed to someone who had never seen the inside of the Memphis Country Club. This kind of thing, girls like Caroline Braxley understood, was not to be tolerated—not if the power of moral woman included the power to divine the nature of any man's commitment and the power to test the strength and nature of another kind of woman's power. Young people today may say that that old-fashioned behavior on the part of girls doesn't matter today, that girls don't have those problems anymore. But I suspect that in Memphis, if not everywhere, there must be something equivalent even nowadays in the struggle of women for power among themselves.

Perhaps, though, to the present generation these distinctions I am making won't seem significant, after all, or worth my bothering so much about—especially the present generation outside of Memphis and the Deep South. Even in Memphis the great majority of people might say, Why is this little band of spoiled rich girls who lived here forty years ago so important as to deserve our attention? In fact, during the very period I am writing about it is likely that the majority of people in Memphis felt that way. I think the significant point is that those girls took themselves seriously—girls like Caroline—and took seriously the forms of the life they lived. They imagined they knew quite well who they were and they imagined that that was important. They were what, at any rate, those girls like Lee Ann were not. Or they claimed to be what those girls like Lee Ann didn't claim to be and what very few people nowadays claim to be. They considered themselves the heirs to something, though most likely they could not have said what: something their forebears had brought to Memphis with them from somewhere else—from the country around Memphis and from other places, from the country towns of West Tennessee, from Middle Tennessee and East Tennessee, from the Valley of Virginia, from the Piedmont, even from the Tidewater. Girls like Caroline thought they were the heirs to something, and that's what the other girls didn't think about themselves, though probably they were, and probably the present generation, in and out of Memphis—even the sad generation of the sixties and seventies—is heir to more than it thinks it is, in the matter of manners, I mean to say, and of general behavior. And it is of course because these girls like Caroline are regarded as mere old-fashioned society girls that the present generation tends to dismiss them, whereas if it were their fathers we were writing about, the story would, shocking though it is to say, be taken more seriously by everyone. Everyone would recognize now that the fathers and grandfathers of these girls were the sons of the old plantation South come to town and converted or half-converted into modern Memphis businessmen, only with a certain something held over from the old order that made them both better and worse than businessmen elsewhere. They are the authors of much good and much bad in modern Memphis—and modern Nashville and modern Birmingham and modern Atlanta, too. The good they mostly brought with them from life in cities elsewhere in the nation, the thing they were imitating when they constructed the new life in Memphis. And why not judge their daughters and wives in much the same way? Isn't there a need to know what they were like, too? One thing those girls did know they were heirs to was the old, country manners and the insistence upon old, country connections. The first evidence of this that comes to mind is the fact that they often spoke of girls like Lee Ann as "city girls," by which they meant that such girls didn't usually have the old family connections back in the country on the cotton farms in West Tennessee, in Mississippi, in Arkansas, or back in Nashville or in Jonesboro or in Virginia.

When Robert had let me out at our side door that night and I came into the house, my father and mother both were downstairs. It was still early of course, but I had the sense of their having waited up for me to come in. They greeted me as though I were returning from some dangerous mission. Each of them asked me how the Braxleys "seemed." Finally Mother insisted upon examining the stitches underneath the bandage on my forehead. After that, I said that I thought I would hit the hay. They responded to that with the same enthusiasm that Mr. and Mrs. Braxley had evidenced when I told them I thought I should go ahead home. Nothing would do me more good than a good night's sleep, my parents agreed. It was a day everybody was glad to have come to an end.

After I got upstairs and in my room, it occurred to me

that my parents both suddenly looked very old. That seems laughable to me now almost, because my parents were then ten or fifteen years younger than I am today. I look back on them now as a youngish couple in their early middle age, whose first son was about to be married and about whose possible infidelity they were concerned. But indeed what an old-fashioned pair they seemed to me in the present day, waiting up for their children to come in. Because actually they stayed downstairs a long while after I went up to bed, waiting there for my younger brothers and my little sister to come in, all of whom were out on their separate dates. In my mind's eye I can see them there, waiting as parents had waited for hundreds of years for their grown-up children to come home at night. They would seem now to be violating the rights of young individuals and even interfering with the maturing process. But in those times it seemed only natural for parents to be watchful and concerned about their children's first flight away from the nest. I am referring mainly to my parents' waiting up for my brothers and my sister, who were in their middle teens, but also as I lay in my bed I felt, myself, more relaxed knowing that they were downstairs in the front room speculating upon what Lee Ann's disappearance meant and alert to whatever new development there might be. After a while, my father came up and opened the door to my room. I don't know how much later it was. I don't think I had been to sleep, but I could not tell for sure even at the time—my waking and sleeping thoughts were so much alike that night. At any rate, Father stepped inside the room and came over to my bed.

"I have just called down to the police station," he said, "and they say they have checked and that Lee Ann has still not come back to her rooming house. She seems to have gone into some sort of hiding." He said this with wonderment and with just the slightest trace of irritation in his voice. "Have you any notion, Nat, why she *might* want to go into hiding?"

*   *   *

The next day was Sunday, December 5. During the night it had turned bitterly cold, the snow had frozen into a crisp sheet that covered most of the ground. At about nine o'clock in the morning another snow began falling. I had breakfast with the family, still wearing the bandage on my forehead. I sat around in my bathrobe all morning, pretending to read the newspaper. I didn't see any report of my accident, and my father said it wouldn't appear till Monday. At ten o'clock, I dialed Lee Ann's telephone number. One of the other girls who roomed in the house answered. She said she thought Lee Ann hadn't come in last night and she giggled. I asked her if she would make sure about it. She left the phone and came back presently to say in a whisper that there was no doubt about it: Lee Ann had not slept in her bed. I knew she was whispering so that the landlady wouldn't hear. . . . And then I had a call from Caroline, who wanted to know how my head was this morning and whether or not there had been any word about Lee Ann. After I told her what I had just learned, we were both silent for a time. Finally she said she had intended to come over and see how I was feeling but her father had decreed that nobody should go out in such bad weather. It would just be inviting another automobile wreck, he said. She reported that her parents were not going to church, and I said that mine weren't either. We agreed to talk later and to see each other after lunch if the weather improved. Then I could hear her father's voice in the background, and she said that he wanted to use the telephone.

At noon the snow was still falling. My father stood at a front window in the living room, wearing his dark smoking jacket. He predicted that it might be the deepest snowfall we had ever had in Memphis. He said that people in other parts of the country didn't realize how much cold weather came all the way down the Mississippi Valley from Minneapolis to Memphis. I had never heard him pay so much attention to the weather and talk so much about it. I wondered if, like me, he was really thinking about the old forest out in Overton Park and wishing he

were free to go out there and make sure there was no
sign of Lee Ann Deehart's having come to grief in those
ancient woods. I wonder now if there weren't others
besides us who were thinking of the old forest all day
that day. I knew that my father, too, had been on the
telephone that morning—and he was on it again during
a good part of the afternoon. In retrospect, I am certain
that all day that day he was in touch with a whole circle
of friends and colleagues who were concerned about Lee
Ann's safety. It was not only the heavy snow that
checked his freedom—and mine, too, of course—to go
out and search those woods and put his mind at rest on
the possibility at least. It was more than just this snow,
which the radio reported as snarling up and halting all
traffic. What prevented him was his own unwillingness
to admit fully to himself and to others that this particular
danger was really there; what prevented him and perhaps
all the rest of us was the fear that the answer to the
gnawing question of Lee Ann's whereabouts might really
be out there within that immemorial grove of snow-laden
oaks and yellow poplars and hickory trees. It is a grove,
I believe, that men in Memphis have feared and wanted
to destroy for a long time and whose destruction they
are still working at even in this latter day. It has only
recently been saved by a very narrow margin from a great
highway that men wished to put through there—saved by
groups of women determined to save this last bit of the
old forest from the axes of modern men. Perhaps in old
pioneer days, before the plantation and the neoclassic
towns were made, the great forests seemed woman's last
refuge from the brute she lived alone with in the wilderness. Perhaps all men in Memphis who had any sense of
their past felt this, though they felt more keenly (or perhaps it amounts to the same feeling) that the forest was
woman's greatest danger. Men remembered mad pioneer
women, driven mad by their loneliness and isolation,
who ran off into the forest, never to be seen again, or
incautious women who allowed themselves to be cap-
tured by Indians and returned at last so mutilated that
they were unrecognizable to their husbands or who at

their own wish lived out their lives among their savage captors. I think that if I had said to my father (or to myself), "What is it that's so scary about the old forest?", he (or I) would have answered, "There's nothing at all scary about it. But we can't do anything today because of the snow. It's the worst snow in history!" I think that all day long my father—like me—was busily not letting himself believe that anything awful had happened to Lee Ann Deehart, or that if it had it certainly hadn't happened in those woods. Not just my father and me, though. Caroline's father, too, and all their friends— their peers. And the newspapermen and the police. If they waited long enough, it would come out all right and there would be no need to search the woods even. And it turned out, in the most literal sense, that they—we— were right. Yet what guilty feelings must not everyone have lived with—lived with in silence—all that snow-bound day.

At two o'clock, Caroline called again to say that because of the snow, her aunt was canceling the dinner party she had planned that night in honor of the bride and groom. I remember as well as anything else that terrible day how my father and mother looked at each other when they received this news. Surely they were wondering, as I had to also, if this was but the first gesture of withdrawal. There was no knowing what their behavior or the behavior of any of us that day meant. The day simply dragged on until the hour when we could decently go to bed. It was December, and we were near the shortest day of the year, but that day had seemed the longest day of my life.

On Monday morning, two uniformed policemen were at our house before I had finished my breakfast. When I learned they were waiting in the living room to see me, I got up from the table at once. I wouldn't let my father go in with me to see them. Mother tried to make me finish my eggs before going in, but I only laughed at her and kissed her on the top of the head as I left the break-fast room. The two policemen were sitting in the very chairs my parents had sat in the night before. This some-how made the interview easier from the outset. I felt initially that they were there to help me, not to harrass me in any way. They had already, at the break of dawn, been out to Overton Park. (The whole case—if case it was—had of course been allowed to rest on Sunday.) And along with four other policemen they had conducted a full-scale search of the old forest. There was no trace of Lee Ann Deehart there. They had also been to her rooming house on Tutwiler Avenue and questioned Mrs. Troxler, whose house it was, about all of Lee Ann's friends and acquaintances and about the habits of her daily life. They said that they were sure the girl would turn up but that the newspapers were putting pressure on them to explain her disappearance and—more particu-larly—to explain her precipitate flight from the scene of the accident.

I spent that day with the police, leaving them only for an hour at lunchtime, when they dropped me off at my father's office on Front Street, where I worked. There I made a small pretense of attending to some business for the firm while I consumed a club sandwich and milk shake that my father or one of my uncles in the firm had had sent up for me. At the end of the hour, I jogged down the two flights of steep wooden stairs and found the police car waiting for me at the curb, just outside the entrance. At some time during the morning, one of the policemen had suggested that they might have a bull-dozer or some other piece of machinery brought in to crack the ice on the Overton Park Pond and then drag the pond for Lee Ann's body. But I had pointed out that the two skaters had returned to the pond after the acci-dent and skated there until dark. There was no hole in the ice anywhere. Moreover, the skaters had reported that when the girl left the scene she did not go by way of the pond but went up the rise and into the wooded area. There was every indication that she had gone that way, and so the suggestion that the pond be dragged was dismissed. And we continued during the rest of the morning to make the rounds of the rooming houses and

apartments of Lee Ann's friends and acquaintances, as
well as the houses of the parents with whom some of
them lived. In the afternoon we planned to go to the
shops and offices in which some of the girls worked and
to interview them there concerning Lee Ann's whereabouts and where it was they last had seen her. It seemed
a futile procedure to me. But while I was eating my club
sandwich alone in our third-floor walkup office I received
a shocking telephone call.

Our offices, like most of the other cotton factors'
offices, were in one of the plain-faced, three- and four-
story buildings put up on Front Street during the middle
years of the last century, just before the Civil War. Cotton men were very fond of those offices, and the offices
did possess a certain rough beauty that anyone could see.
Apparently there had been few, if any, improvements or
alterations since the time they were built. All the electri-
cal wiring and all the plumbing, such as they were, were
"exposed." The wooden stairsteps and the floors were
rough and splintery and extremely worn down. The walls
were whitewashed and the ceilings were twelve or fourteen feet in height. But the chief charm of the rooms was
the tall windows across the front of the buildings—wide
sash windows with small windowlights, windows looking
down onto Front Street and from which you could catch
glimpses of the brown Mississippi River at the foot of
the bluff, and even of the Arkansas shoreline on the
other side. I was sitting on a cotton trough beside one
of those windows, eating my club sandwich, when I heard
the telephone ring back in the inner office. I remember
that when it rang my eyes were on a little stretch of the
Arkansas shoreline roughly delineated by its scrubby
trees and my thoughts were on the Arkansas roadhouses
where we often went with the demimonde girls on a Saturday night. At first I thought I wouldn't answer the
phone. I let it ring for a minute or two. It went on ringing—persistently. Suddenly I realized that a normal business call would have stopped ringing before now. I
jumped down from my perch by the window and ran
back between the cotton troughs to the office. When I

picked up the receiver, a girl's voice called my name
before I spoke.

"Yes," I said. The voice had sounded familiar, but I
knew it wasn't Caroline's. And it wasn't Lee Ann's. I
couldn't identify it exactly, though I did say to myself
right away that it was one of the city girls.

"Nat," the voice said, "Lee Ann wants you to stop
trying to trail her."

"Who is this?" I said. "Where is Lee Ann?"

"Never mind," the girl on the other end of the line
said. "We're not going to let you find her, and you're
making her very uncomfortable with your going around
with the police after her and all that."

"The police aren't 'after her,' " I said. "They just want
to be sure she's all right."

"She'll be all right," the voice said, "if you'll lay off
and stop chasing her. Don't you have any decency at all?
Don't you have a brain in your head? Don't you know
what this is like for Lee Ann? We all thought you were
her friend."

"I am," I said. "Just let me speak to Lee Ann."

But there was a click in the telephone, and no one was
there any longer.

I turned back into the room where the cotton troughs
were. When I saw my milk-shake carton and the sandwich paper up by the window, and remembered how the
girl had called my name as soon as I picked up the telephone, I felt sure that someone had been watching me
from down in the street or from a window across the
way. Without going back to my lunch, I turned quickly
and started down the stairs toward the street. But when
I looked at my watch, I realized it was time for the
policemen to pick me up again. And there they were, of
course, waiting at the entrance to our building. When I
got into the police car, I didn't tell them about my call.
And we began our rounds again, going to the addresses
where some of Lee Ann's friends worked.

Lee Ann Deehart and other girls like her that we went
about with, as I have indicated, were not literally ladies
of any Memphis demimonde. Possibly they got called

that first by the only member of our generation in Memphis who had read Marcel Proust, a literary boy who later became a college professor and who wanted to make his own life in Memphis—and ours—seem more interesting than it was. Actually, they were girls who had gone to the public high schools, and more often than not to some school other than Central High, which during those Depression years had a degree of acceptance in Memphis society. As anyone could have observed on that morning when I rode about town with the policemen, those girls came from a variety of backgrounds. We went to the houses of some of their parents, some of whom were day laborers who spoke in accents of the old Memphis Irish, descendants of the Irish who were imported to build the railroads to Texas. Today some of the girls would inevitably have been black. But they were the daughters also of bank clerks and salesmen and of professional men, too, because they made no distinction among themselves. The parents of some of them had moved to Memphis from cities in other sections of the country or even from Southern small towns. The girls were not interested in such distinctions of origin, were not conscious of them, had not been made aware of them by their parents. They would have been highly approved of by the present generation of young people. Like the present generation in general, these girls—Lee Ann included—tended to be bookish and artistic in a middlebrow sort of way, and some of them had real intellectual aspirations. They did not care who each other's families were or where they had gone to school. They met and got to know each other in roadhouses, on double dates, and in the offices and stores where they worked. As I have said, they tended to be bookish and artistic. If they had found themselves in Proust's Paris, instead of in our Memphis of the 1930s, possibly they would have played some role in the intellectual life of the place. But of course this is only my ignorant speculation. It is always impossible to know what changes might have been wrought in people under circumstances of the greatest or slightest degree of difference from the actual.

The girls we saw that afternoon at their places of work were generally more responsive to the policemen's questions than to my own. And I became aware that the two policemen—youngish men in their late thirties, for whom this special assignment was somehow distasteful—were more interested in protecting these girls from any embarrassment than in obtaining information about Lee Ann. With all but one of the half-dozen girls we sought out, the policemen sent me in to see the girl first, to ask her if she would rather be questioned by them in her place of business or in the police car. In each case the girl treated my question concerning this as an affront, but always she finally sent word back to the policemen to come inside. And in each case I found myself admiring the girl not only for her boldness in dealing with the situation (they seemed fearless in their talk with the police and refused absolutely to acknowledge close friendship with Lee Ann, insisting—all of them—that they saw her only occasionally at night spots, sometimes with me, sometimes with other young men, that they had no idea who her parents were or where she came to Memphis from) but also for a personal, feminine beauty that I had never before been fully aware of. Perhaps I saw or sensed it now for the first time because I had not before seen them threatened or in danger. It is true, I know, that the effect of all this questioning seemed somehow to put them in jeopardy. Perhaps I saw now how much more vulnerable they were than were the girls in the set my parents more or less intended me to travel in. There was a delicacy about them, a frailty even, that didn't seem to exist in other girls I knew and that contrasted strangely—and disturbingly—with the rough surroundings of the roadhouses they frequented at night and the harsh, businesslike atmosphere of the places where they worked. Within each of them, moreover, there seemed a contrast between the delicate beauty of their bodies, their prettily formed arms and legs, their breasts and hips, their small feet and hands, their soft natural hair—hair worn so becomingly, groomed, in each case, on their pretty little heads to direct one's eyes first of all

to the fair or olive complexion and the nicely propor-
tioned features of the face—a contrast, that is to say,
between this physical beauty and a bookishness and a
certain toughness of mind and a boldness of spirit which
were unmistakable in all of them.

The last girl we paid a call on that afternoon was one
Nancy Minnifee, who happened to be the girl who was
always frankest and crudest in making jokes about families like my own and who had made the crack that the
other girls had laughed at so irrepressibly in the beer
garden: "I haven't lost anything at the MCC." Or it may
not have been that she just happened to be the last we
called on. Perhaps out of dread of her jokes I guided the
police last of all to the farm-implement warehouse where
Nancy was a secretary. Or perhaps it wasn't so much
because of her personality as because I knew she was
Lee Ann's closest friend and I somehow dreaded facing
her for that reason. Anyway, at the warehouse she was
out on the loading platform with a clipboard and pencil
in her hands when we drove up.

"That's Nancy Minnifee up there," I said to the two
policemen in the front seat. I was sitting in the backseat
alone. I saw them shake their heads. I knew that it was
with a certain sadness and a personal admiration that
they did so. Nancy was a very pretty girl, and they hated
the thought of bothering this lovely creature with the
kind of questions they were going to ask. They hated it
without even knowing she was Lee Ann's closest friend.
Suddenly I began seeing all those girls through the policemen's eyes, just as next day, when I would make a similar expedition in the company of my father and the
newspaper editor, I'd see the girls through their eyes.
The worst of it, somehow, for the policemen, was that
the investigation wasn't really an official investigation but
was something the newspapers had forced upon the
police in case something had happened which they hadn't
reported. The girl hadn't been missing long enough for
anyone to declare her "officially" missing. Yet the
police, along with the mayor's office and the newspaper
editor, didn't want to risk something's having happened

to a girl like Lee Ann. They—all of them—thought of such girls, in a sense, as their special wards. It would be hard to say why they did. At any rate, before the police car had fully stopped I saw Nancy Minnifee up there on the platform. She was wearing a fur-collared overcoat but no hat or gloves. Immediately she began moving along the loading platform toward us, holding the clipboard up to shield her eyes from the late-afternoon winter sun. She came down the steps to the graveled area where we were stopped, and when the policeman at the wheel of the car ran down his window she bent forward and put her arm on his door. The casual way she did it seemed almost familiar—indeed, almost provocative. I found myself resenting her manner, because I was afraid she would give the wrong impression. The way she leaned on the door reminded me of the prostitutes down on Pontotoc Street when we, as teenage boys, used to stop in front of their houses and leave the motor running because we were afraid of them.

"I've been expecting you two gentlemen," Nancy said, smiling amiably at the two policemen and pointedly ignoring my presence in the backseat. The policemen broke into laughter.

"I suppose your friends have been calling ahead," the driver said. Then Nancy laughed as though he had said something very funny.

"I could draw you a map of the route you've taken this afternoon," she said. She was awfully polite in her tone, and the two policemen were awfully polite, too. But before they could really begin asking her their questions she began giving them her answers. She hadn't seen Lee Ann since several days before the accident. She didn't know anything about where she might be. She didn't know anything about her family. She had always understood that Lee Ann came from Texas.

"That's a big state," the policeman who wasn't driving said.

"Well, I've never been there," she said, "but I'm told it's a mighty big state."

The three of them burst into laughter again. Then the

driver said quite seriously, "But we understand you're her best friend."

"I don't know her any better than most of the other girls do," she said. "I can't imagine who told you that." Now for the first time she looked at me in the backseat. "Hello, Nat," she said. I nodded to her. I couldn't imagine why she was lying to them. But I didn't tell her, as I hadn't told the other girls or the police, about the call I had had in the cotton office. I knew that she must know all about it, but I said nothing.

When we had pulled away, the policeman who was driving the car said, "This Lee Ann must be all right or these girls wouldn't be closing ranks so. They've got too much sense for that. They're smart girls."

Presently the other policemen turned his head halfway around, though not looking directly at me, and asked, "She wouldn't be pregnant by any chance, would she?"

"Uh-uh," I said. It was all the answer it seemed to me he deserved. But then I couldn't resist echoing what he had said. "They've got too much sense for that. They're smart girls." He looked all the way around at me now and gave me what I am sure he thought was a straight look.

"Damn right they are," said the driver, glancing at his colleague with a frown on his forehead and speaking with a curled lip. "Get your mind out of the gutter, Fred. After all, they're just kids, all of them."

We rode on in silence after that. For the first time in several hours, I thought of Caroline Braxley, and I wondered again whether or not she would break our engagement.

When the policemen let me off at my office at five o'clock, I went to my car and drove straight to the apartment house at Crosstown where Nancy Minnifee lived. I was waiting for Nancy in the parking lot when she got home. She invited me inside, but without a smile.

"I want to know where Lee Ann is," I said as soon as she had closed the door.

"Do you imagine I'd tell you if I knew?" she said.

I sat myself down in an upholstered chair as if I were

going to stay there till she told me. "I want to know what the hell's going on," I said with what I thought was considerable force, "and why you told such lies to those policemen."

"If you don't know that now, Nat," she said, sitting down opposite me, "you probably won't ever know."

"She wouldn't be pregnant by any chance, would she?" I said, without really having known I was going to say it.

Nancy's mouth dropped open. Then she laughed aloud. Presently she said, "Well, one thing's certain, Nat. It wouldn't be any concern of yours if she were."

I pulled myself up out of the big chair and left without another word's passing between us.

Lee Ann Deehart and Nancy Minnifee and that whole band of girls that we liked to refer to as the girls of the Memphis demimonde were of course no more like the ladies of the demimonde as they appear in French literature than *they* were like some band of angels. And I hardly need say—though it does somehow occur to me to say—their manners and morals bore no resemblance whatsoever to those of the mercenary, filthy-mouthed whores on Pontotoc Street. I might even say that their manners were practically indistinguishable from those of the girls we knew who had attended Miss Hutchison's School and St. Mary's and Lausanne and were now members of the debutante set. The fact is that some of them—only a few perhaps—were from families that were related by blood, and rather closely related, to the families of the debutante set, but families that, for one reason or another, now found themselves economically in another class from their relatives. At any rate, they were all freed from old restraints put upon them by family and community, liberated in each case, so it seems to me, by sheer strength of character, liberated in many respects, but above all else—and I cannot say how it came about—liberated sexually. The most precise thing I can say about them is that they, in their little band, were like hordes of young girls today. It seems to me that in their attitude

toward sex they were at least forty years ahead of their
time. But I cannot say how it came about. Perhaps it
was an individual thing with each of them—or partly so.
Perhaps it was because they were the second or third
generation of women in Memphis who were working in
offices. They were not promiscuous—not most of them—
but they slept with the men they were in love with and
they did not conceal the fact. The men they were in
love with were usually older than we were. Generally
speaking, the girls merely amused themselves with us,
just as we amused ourselves with them. There was a wonderful freedom in our relations which I have never known
anything else quite like. And though I may not have had
the most realistic sense of what their lives were, I came
to know what I did know through my friendship with Lee
Ann Deehart.

She and I first met, I think, at one of those dives where
we all hung out. Or it may have been at some girl's
apartment. I suspect we both would have been hard put
to it to say where it was or exactly when. She was simply
one of the good-looking girls we ran around with. I
remember dancing with her on several occasions before
I had any idea what her name was. We drifted into our
special kind of friendship because, as a matter of fact,
she was the good friend of Nancy Minnifee, whom my
own close friend Bob Childress got very serious about
for a time. Bob and Nancy may even have been living
together for a while in Nancy's apartment. I think Bob,
who was one of six or eight boys of approximately my
background who used to go about with these girls, would
have married Nancy if she'd consented to have him. Possibly it was at Nancy's apartment that I met Lee Ann.
Anyway, we did a lot of double dating, the four of us,
and had some wonderful times going to the sort of rough
night spots that we all liked and found sufficiently exciting to return to again and again. We would be dancing
and drinking at one of those places until about two in
the morning, when most of them closed. At that hour
most of us would take our girls home, because we nearly

all of us had jobs—the girls and the boys, too—which we had to report to by eight or nine in the morning.

Between Lee Ann and me, as between most of the boys and their girls, I think, there was never a serious affair. That is, we never actually—as the young people today say—"had sex." But in the car on the way home or in the car parked outside her rooming house or even outside the night spot, as soon as we came out, we would regularly indulge in what used to be known as "heavy necking." Our stopping at that I must attribute first of all to Lee Ann's resistance, though also, in part, to a hesitation I felt about insisting with such a girl. You see, she was in all respects like the girls we called "nice girls," by which I suppose we really meant society girls. And most of us accepted the restriction that we were not to "go to bed" with society girls. They were the girls we were going to marry. These girls were not what those society girls would have termed shopgirls. They had much better taste in their clothes and in their general demeanor. And, as I have said, in the particular group I speak of there was at least an intellectual strain. Some of them had been to college for as much as a year or two, whereas others seemed hardly to have finished high school. Nearly all of them read magazines and books that most of us had never heard of. And they found my odd addiction to Latin poetry the most interesting thing about me. Most of them belonged to a national book club, from which they received a new book each month, and they nearly all bought records and listened to classical music. You would see them sometimes in groups at the Art Gallery. Or whenever there was an opera or a good play at the city auditorium they were all likely to be there in a group—almost never with dates. If you hadn't known who they were, you might easily have mistaken them for some committee from the Junior League or for an exceptionally pretty group of schoolteachers—from some fashionable girls' school probably.

But mostly, of course, one saw them with their dates at one of the roadhouses, over in Arkansas or down in Mississippi or out east on the Bristol Highway, or yet again at one of the places we called the "town joints." They preferred going to those roadhouses and town joints to going to the Peabody Hotel Roof or the Claridge—as I suppose nearly everyone else did, really, including society girls like Caroline. You would, as a matter of fact, frequently see girls like Caroline at such places. At her request, I had more than once taken Caroline to a town joint down on Adams Street called The Cellar and once to a roadhouse called The Jungle, over in Arkansas. She had met some of the city girls there and said she found them "dead attractive." And she once recognized them at a play I took her to see and afterward expressed interest in and asked me to tell her what they were like.

The fact may be that neither the roadhouses nor the town joints were quite as tough as they seemed. Or they weren't as tough as for the demimonde girls, anyway. Because the proprietors clearly had protective feelings about them. At The Jungle, for instance, the middle-aged couple who operated the place, an extremely obese couple who were forever grinning in our direction and who were usually barefoot (we called them Ma and Pa), would often come and stand by our table—one or the other of them—and sing the words to whatever was playing on the jukebox. Often as not, one of them would be standing there during the entire evening. Sometimes Ma would talk to us about her two little daughters, whom she kept in a private school in Memphis, and Pa, who was a practicing taxidermist, would talk to us about the dogs whose mounted heads adorned the walls on every side of the dimly lit room. All this afforded us great privacy and safety. No drunk or roughneck would come near our table while either Ma or Pa was close by. We had similar protection at other places. At The Cellar, for instance, old Mrs. Power was the sole proprietor. She had a huge goiter on her neck and was never known to smile. Not even in our direction. But it was easy to see that she watched our table like a hawk, and if any other patron lingered near us even momentarily she would begin moving slowly toward us. And whoever it was would catch one glimpse of her and move on. We went to these places quite regularly, though some of the girls had their favorites and dislikes among them. Lee Ann would never be taken to The Cellar. She would say only that the place depressed her. And Caroline, when I took her there, felt an instant dislike for The Jungle. She would shake her head afterward and say she would never go back and have those dogs' eyes staring down through the darkness at her.

On the day after I made the rounds with the policemen, I found myself following almost the same routine in the company of my father and the editor of the morning paper, and, as a matter of fact, the mayor of Memphis himself. The investigation or search was, you see, still entirely unofficial. And men like my father and the mayor and the editor wanted to keep it so. That's why after that routine and off-the-record series of questionings by the police they preferred to do a bit of investigation themselves rather than entrust the matter to someone else. As I have said, that generation of men in Memphis evidenced feelings of responsibility for such girls—for "working girls of a superior kind," as they phrased it—which I find somewhat difficult to explain. For it wasn't just the men I drove about town with that day. Or the dozen or so men who gathered for conference in our driveway before we set out—that is, Caroline's father, his lawyer, the driver of the other vehicle, his lawyer, my father's lawyer, ministers from three church denominations, the editor of the afternoon newspaper, and still others. That day, when I rode about town with my father and the two other men in our car, I came as near as I never had or ever would to receiving a satisfactory explanation of the phenomenon. They were a generation of American men who were perhaps the last to grow up in a world where women were absolutely subjected and under the absolute protection of men. While my father wheeled his big Cadillac through the side streets on which some of the girls lived and then along the wide boulevards of Memphis, they spoke of the changes they had seen. In referring to the character of the life girls like Lee Ann led—of which they showed a far greater awareness than I would have supposed they possessed—they agreed that this was the second or third generation there of women who had lived as independently, as freely as these girls did. I felt that what they said was in no sense as derogatory or critical as it would have been in the presence of their wives or daughters. They spoke almost affectionately and with a certain sadness of such girls. They spoke as if these were daughters of dead brothers of their own or of dead companions-in-arms during the First World War. And it seemed to me that they thought of these girls as the daughters of men who had abdicated their authority and responsibility as fathers, men who were not strangers or foreign to them, though they were perhaps of a different economic class. The family names of the girls were familiar to them. The fathers of these girls were Americans of the great hinterland like themselves, even Southerners like themselves. I felt that they were actually cousins of ours who had failed as fathers somehow, had been destined to fail, even required to do so in a changing world. And so these men of position and power had to act as surrogate fathers during a transitional period. It was a sort of communal fatherhood they were acting out. Eventually, they seemed to say, fathers might not be required. I actually heard my father saying, "That's what the whole world is going to be like someday." He meant like the life such girls as Lee Ann were making for themselves. I often think nowadays of Father's saying that whenever I see his prediction being fulfilled by the students in the university where I have been teaching for twenty years now, and I wonder if Father did really believe his prediction would come true.

Yet while he and the other two men talked their rather sanguine talk that day, I was thinking of a call I had had the night before after I came back from seeing Nancy Minnifee. One of the servants answered the telephone downstairs in the back part of the house, and she must have guessed it was something special. Because instead of buzzing the buzzer three times, which was the signal when a call was for me, the maid came up the backstairs and tapped gently on my door. "It's for you, Nat," she said softly. "Do you want to take it downstairs?"

There was nothing peculiar about her doing this, really. Since I didn't have an extension phone in my room, I had a tacit understanding with the servants that I preferred to take what I considered my private calls down in that quarter of the house. And so I followed the maid down the back stairway and shut myself in the little, servants' dining room that was behind the great white-tiled kitchen. I answered the call on the wall phone there.

A girl's voice, which wasn't the same voice I had heard on the office telephone at noon, said, "Lee Ann doesn't want another day like this one, Nat."

"Who is this?" I said, lowering my voice to be sure even the servants didn't hear me. "What the hell is going on?" I asked. "Where is Lee Ann?"

"She's been keeping just one apartment or one rooming house ahead of you all day."

"But why? Why is she hiding this way?"

"All I want to say is she's had about enough. You let up on pursuing her so."

"It's not me," I protested. "There's nothing I can do to stop them."

Over the phone there came a contemptuous laugh. "No. And you can't get married till they find her, can you?" Momentarily I thought I heard Lee Ann's voice in the background. "Anyhow," the same voice continued, "Lee Ann's had about as much as she can take of all this. She was depressed as it was when she called you in the first place. Why else do you think she would call you, Nat? She was desperate for some comic relief."

"Relief from what?"

"Relief from her depression, you idiot."

"But what's she depressed about?" I was listening carefully to the voice, thinking it was that of first one girl and then another.

"Nat, we don't always have to have something to be

depressed about. But Lee Ann will be all right, if you'll let her alone."

"But what is she depressed about?" I persisted. I had begun to think maybe it was Lee Ann herself on the phone, disguising her voice.

"About life in general, you bastard! Isn't that enough?" Then I knew it wasn't Lee Ann, after all.

"Listen," I said, "let me speak to Lee Ann. I want to speak to Lee Ann."

And then I heard whoever it was I was talking with break off the connection. I quietly replaced the receiver and went upstairs again.

In those days I didn't know what it was to be depressed—not, anyway, about "life in general." Later on, you see, I did know. Later on, after years of being married, and having three children, and going to grown-up Memphis dinner parties three or four times a week, and working in the cotton office six days a week, I got so depressed about life in general that I sold my interest in the cotton firm to a cousin of mine (my father and uncles were dead by then) and managed to make Caroline understand that what I needed was to go back to school for a while so that we could start our life all over. I took degrees at three universities, which made it possible for me to become a college professor. That may be an awful revelation about myself—I mean to say, awful that what decided me to become a teacher was that I was so depressed about life in general. But I reasoned that being an English professor—even if I was relegated to teaching composition and simpleminded survey courses—would be something useful and would throw us in with a different kind of people. (Caroline tried to persuade me to go into the sciences, but I told her she was just lucky that I didn't take up classics again.) Anyway, teaching has made me see a lot of young people over the years, in addition to my own children, and I think it is why, in retrospect, those Memphis girls I'm writing about still seem interesting to me after all these many years.

But the fact is I was still so uneasy about the significance of both those calls from Lee Ann's friends that I was unwilling to mention them to Caroline that night. At first I thought I would tell her, but as soon as I saw her tall and graceful figure in her white, pleated evening dress and wearing the white corsage I had sent, I began worrying again about whether or not she might still break off the engagement. Besides, we had plenty of other matters to discuss, including the rounds I had made with the two policemen that day and her various activities in preparation for the wedding. We went to a dinner that one of my aunts gave for us at the Memphis Country Club that night. We came home early and spent twenty minutes or so in her living room, telling each other how much we loved each other and how we would let nothing on earth interfere with our getting married. I felt reassured, or I tried to feel so. It seemed to me, though, that Caroline still had not really made up her mind. It worried me that she didn't have more to say about Lee Ann. After I got home, I kept waking all night and wondering what if that had not been Lee Ann's voice I had heard in the background and what if she never surfaced again. The circumstances of her disappearance would have to be made public, and that would certainly be too embarrassing for Caroline and her parents to ignore.

Next day, I didn't tell my father and his two friends, the editor and the mayor, about either of the two telephone calls. I don't know why I didn't, unless it was because I feared they might begin monitoring all my calls. I could not tolerate the thought of having them hear the things that girl said to me.

In preference to interviewing the girls whose addresses I could give them, those three middle-aged men seemed much more interested in talking to the girls' rooming-house landladies, or their apartment landlords, or their mothers. They did talk to some of the girls themselves, though, and I observed that the girls were so impressed by having these older men want to talk to them that they could hardly look at them directly. What I think is that the girls were *afraid* they would tell them the truth. They would reply to their questions respectfully, if evasively, but they were apt to keep their eyes on me. This was not the case, however, with the mothers and the land-lords and the landladies. There was an immediate rap-port between these persons and the three men. There hardly needed to be any explanation required of the unofficial nature of the investigation or of the concern of these particular men about such a girl as Lee Ann. One woman who told them that Lee Ann had roomed with her for a time described her as being always a moody sort of girl. "But lots of these girls living on their own are moody," she said.

"Where did Miss Deehart come from?" my father asked. "Who were her people?"

"She always claimed she came from Texas," the woman said. "But she could never make it clear to me where it was in Texas."

Later the mayor asked Lee Ann's current landlady, Mrs. Troxler, where she supposed Lee Ann might have gone. "Well," Mrs. Troxler said, "a girl, a decent girl, even among these modern girls, generally goes to her mother when there's trouble. Women turn to women," she said, "when there's real trouble."

The three men found no trace of Lee Ann, got no real clue to where she might have gone. When finally we were leaving the editor at his newspaper office on Union Avenue, he hesitated a moment before opening the car door. "Well," he began, but he sat for a moment beating his leg thoughtfully with a newspaper he had rolled up in his hand. "I don't know," he said. "It's going to be a matter for the police, after all, if we can't do any better than this." I still didn't say anything about my telephone calls. But the calls were worrying me a good deal, and that night I told Caroline.

And when I had told her about the calls and told her how the police and my father and his friends had failed to get any information from the girls, Caroline, who was then sitting beside me on the couch in her living room, suddenly took my hand in hers and, putting her face close to mine and looking me directly in the eye, said, "Nat, I don't want you to go to work at all tomorrow. Don't make any explanation to your father or to any-

body. Just get up early and come over here and get me.
I want you to take me to meet some of those girls."
Then she asked me which of the girls she might possibly
have met on the rare occasions when I had taken her
dancing at The Jungle or at The Cellar. And before I
left that night she got me to tell her all I knew about
"that whole tribe of city girls." I told her everything,
including an account of my innocent friendship with Lee
Ann Deehart, as well as an account of my earlier relations, which were not innocent, with a girl named Fern
Morris. When, next morning, I came to fetch Caroline
for our expedition, there were only three girls that she
wanted to be taken to see. One of the three was of course
Fern Morris.

There was something that had happened to me the day
before, when I was going about Memphis with my father
and his two friends, that I could not tell Caroline about.
You see, I had been imagining, each place we went, how
as we came in the front door Lee Ann was hurriedly,
quietly going out the back. This mental picture of her in
flight I found not merely appealing but strangely exciting.
And it seemed to me I was discovering what my true
feelings toward Lee Ann had been during the past two
years. I had never dared insist upon the occasional
advances I had naturally made to her, because she had
always seemed too delicate, too vulnerable, for me to
think of suggesting a casual sexual relationship with her.
She had seemed too clever and too intelligent for me to
deceive her about my intentions or my worth as a person.
And I imagined I relished the kind of restraint there was
between us because it was so altogether personal and not
one placed upon us by any element or segment of society,
or by any outside circumstances whatever. It kept coming
to my mind as we stood waiting for an answer to the
pressure on each doorbell that she was the girl I ought
and wanted to be marrying. I realized the absolute folly
of such thoughts and the utter impossibility of any such
conclusion to present events. But still such feelings and
thoughts had kept swimming in and out of my head all
that day. I kept seeing Lee Ann in my mind's eye and

hearing her soft, somewhat husky voice. I kept imagining how her figure would appear in the doorway before us. I saw her slender ankles, her small breasts, her head of ash-blond hair, which had a way of seeming to fall about her face when she talked but which with one shake of her head she could throw back into perfect place. But of course when the door opened there was the inevitable landlady or mother or friend. And when the next day came and I saw Caroline rolling up her sleeves, so to speak, to pitch in and settle this matter once and for all, then my thoughts and fantasies of the day before seemed literally like something out of a dream that I might have had.

The first two girls Caroline had wanted to see were the two that she very definitely remembered having met when I had taken her—"on a lark"—to my favorite night spots. She caught them both before they went to work that morning, and I was asked to wait in the car. I felt like an idiot waiting out there in the car, because I knew I'd been seen from some window as I gingerly hopped out and opened the door for Caroline when she got out— and opened it again when she returned. But there was no way around it. I waited out there, playing the car radio even at the risk of running down the battery.

When she came back from seeing the first girl, whose name was Lucy Phelan, Caroline was very angry. She reported that Lucy Phelan had pretended not to remember ever having met her. Moreover, Lucy had pretended that she knew Lee Ann Deehart only slightly and had no idea where she could be or what her disappearance meant. As Caroline fumed and I started up the car, I was picturing Lee Ann quietly tiptoeing out the backdoor of Lucy's rooming house just as Lucy was telling Caroline she scarcely knew the girl or while she was insisting that she didn't remember Caroline. As Caroline came back down the walk from the big Victorian house to the car, Lucy, who had stepped out onto the narrow porch that ran across the front of the house and around one corner of it, squatted down on her haunches at the top of the wooden porch steps and waved to me from behind Caro-

line's back. Though I knew it was no good, I pretended
not to see her there. As I put the car into second gear
and we sped away down the block, I took a quick glance
back at the house. Lucy was still standing on the porch
and waving to me the way one waves to a little child.
She knew I had seen her stooping and waving moments
before. And knew I would be stealing a glance now.

For a short time Caroline seemed undecided about
calling on the second girl. But she decided finally to press
on. Lucy Phelan she remembered meeting at The Cellar.
The next girl, Betsy Morehouse, she had met at The
Jungle and at a considerably more recent time. Caroline
was a dog fancier in those days and she recalled a conversation with Betsy about the mounted dogs' heads that
adorned the walls of The Jungle. They both had been
outraged. When she mentioned this to me there in the
car, I realized for the first time that by trying to make
these girls acknowledge an acquaintance with her she had
hoped to make them feel she was almost one of them
and that they would thus be more likely to confide in
her. But she failed with Betsy Morehouse, too. Betsy
lived in an apartment house—an old residence, that is,
converted into apartments—and when Caroline got inside
the entrance-hall door she met Betsy, who was just then
coming down the stairs. Betsy carried a purse and was
wearing a fur coat and overshoes. When Caroline got
back to the car and told me about it, I could not help
feeling that Betsy had had a call from Lucy Phelan and
even perhaps that Lee Ann was hiding in her apartment,
having just arrived there from Lucy's. Because Betsy
didn't offer to take Caroline back upstairs to her apartment for a talk. Instead, they sat down on two straight-
backed chairs in the entrance hall and exchanged their
few words there. Betsy at once denied the possibility of
Caroline's ever having met her before. She denied that
she had, herself, ever been to The Jungle. I knew this
to be a lie, of course, but I didn't insist upon it to Caroline. I said that perhaps both she and I were mistaken
about Betsy's being there on the night I had taken Caroline. As soon as Caroline saw she would learn nothing

from Betsy, she got up and began to make motions of leaving. Betsy followed her to the door. But upon seeing my car out at the curb—so Caroline believed—she turned back, saying that she had remembered a telephone call she had to make. Caroline suspected that the girl didn't want to have to face me with her lie. That possibly was true. But my thought was that Betsy just might, also, have a telephone call she wanted to make.

There was now no question about Caroline's wanting to proceed to the third girl's house. This was the girl I had told her about having had a real affair with—the one I had gone with before Lee Ann and I had become friends. Caroline knew that she and Fern Morris had never met, but she counted on a different psychology with Fern. Most probably she had hoped it wouldn't be necessary for her to go to see Fern. She had been sure that one of those two other girls would give her the lead she needed. But as a last resort she was fully prepared to call on Fern Morris and to take me into the house with her.

Fern was a girl who still lived at home with her mother. She was in no sense a mama's girl or even a home-loving girl, since she was unhappy unless she went out on a date every night of her life. Perhaps she was not so clever and not so intellectual as most of her friends—if reading books, that is, on psychology and on China and every new volume of Andre Maurois indicated intellectuality. And though she was not home-loving, I suppose you would have to say she was more domestic than the other girls were. She had never "held down" a job. Rather, she stayed at home in the daytime and kept house for her mother, who was said to "hold down" a high-powered job under Boss Crump down at City Hall. Mrs. Morris was a very sensible woman, who put no restrictions on her grown-up daughter and was glad to have her as a housekeeper. She used to tell me what a good cook and housekeeper Fern was and how well fixed she would leave her when she died. I really believe Mrs. Morris hoped our romance might end in matrimony, and, as a matter of fact, it was when I began to suspect that Fern,

too, was entertaining such notions that I stopped seeing
her and turned my attentions to Lee Ann Deehart.

Mrs. Morris still seemed glad to see me when I arrived
at their bungalow that morning with Caroline and when
I proceeded to introduce Caroline to her as my fiancée.
Fern herself greeted me warmly. In fact, when I told her
that Caroline and I were going to be married (though
she must certainly have already read about it in the newspaper) she threw her arms about my neck and kissed me.
"Oh, Natty," she said, "I'm so happy for you. Really I
am. But poor Lee Ann." And in later life, especially in
recent years, whenever Caroline has thought I was being
silly about some other woman, usually a woman she considers her mental and social inferior, she has delighted
in addressing me as "Natty." On more than one such
occasion I have even had her say to me, "I am so happy
for you, Natty. Really I am."

The fact is, Mrs. Morris was just leaving the house for
work when we arrived. And so there was no delay in
Caroline's interview with Fern. "I assume you know
about Lee Ann's disappearance?" Caroline began as
soon as we had seated ourselves in the little front parlor,
with which I was very familiar.

"Of course I do," said Fern, looking at me and laughing gleefully.

"You think it's a laughing matter, then?" Caroline
asked.

"I do indeed. It's all a big joke," Fern said at once.
It was as though she had her answers all prepared. "And
a very successful joke it is."

"Successful?" both Caroline and I asked. We looked
at each other in dismay.

"It's only my opinion, of course. But I think she only
wants to make you two suffer."

"Suffer?" I said. This time Caroline was silent.

Fern was now addressing me directly. "Everybody
knows Caroline is not going to marry you until Lee Ann
turns up safe."

"Everybody?" Both of us again.

"Everybody in the world practically," said Fern.

Caroline's face showed no expression. Neither, I believe, did mine.

"Fern, do you know where Lee Ann is?" Caroline asked gently.

Fern Morris, her eyes on me, shook her head, smiling.

"Do you know where her people are?" Caroline asked. "And whether she's with them or hiding with her friends?"

Fern shook her head again, but now she gazed directly at Caroline. "I'm not going to tell you anything!" she asserted. But after a moment she took a deep breath and said, still looking at Caroline, "You're a smart girl. I think you'll likely be going to Lee Ann's room in that place where she lives. If you do go there, and if you are a smart girl, you'll look in the left-hand drawer of Lee Ann's dressing table." Fern had an uneasy smile on her face after she had spoken, as if Caroline had got her to say something she hadn't really meant to say, as if she felt guilty for what she had just done.

Caroline had us out of there in only a minute or so and on our way to Lee Ann's rooming house.

It was a red-brick bungalow up in north Memphis. It looked very much like the one that Fern lived in but was used as a rooming house. When Mrs. Troxler opened the front door to us, Caroline said, "We're friends of Lee Ann's, and she wants us to pack a suitcase and bring it to her."

"You know where she is, then?" Mrs. Troxler asked. "Hello, Nat," she said, looking at me over Caroline's shoulder.

"Hello, Mrs. Troxler," I said. I was so stunned by what I had just heard Caroline say that I spoke in a whisper.

"She's with her mother—or with her family, at least," Caroline said. By now she had slipped into the hallway, and I had followed without Mrs. Troxler's really inviting us in.

"Where are her family?" Mrs. Troxler asked, giving way to Caroline's forward thrust. "She never volunteered to tell me anything about them. And I never think it's my business to ask."

Caroline nodded her head at me, indicating that I should lead the way to Lee Ann's room. I knew that her room was toward the back of the house and I headed in that direction.

"I'll have to unlock the room for you," said Mrs. Troxler. "There have been a number of people coming here and wanting to look about her room. And so I keep it locked."

"A number of people?" asked Caroline casually.

"Yes. Nat knows. There were the police. And then there were some other gentlemen. Nat knows about it, though he didn't come in. And there were two other girls. The girls just seemed idly curious, and so I've taken to locking the door. Where do her people live?"

"I don't know," said Caroline. "She's going to meet us downtown at the bus station and take a bus."

When Mrs. Troxler had unlocked the door she asked, "Is Lee Ann all right? Do you think she will be coming back here?"

"She's fine," Caroline said, "and I'm sure she'll be coming back. She just wants a few things."

"Yes, I've wondered how she's been getting along without a change of clothes. I'll fetch her suitcase. I keep my roomers' luggage in my storage closet down the hall." We waited till she came back with a piece of plaid luggage, and then we went into the room and closed the door. Caroline went to the oak dresser and began pulling things out and stuffing them in the bag. I stood by, watching, hardly able to believe what I saw Caroline doing. When she had closed the bag, she looked up at me as if to say, "What are you waiting for?" She had not gone near the little mahogany dressing table, and I had not realized that was going to be my part. I went over and opened the left-hand drawer. The only thing in the drawer was a small snapshot. I took it up and examined it carefully. I said nothing to Caroline, just handed her the picture. Finally I said, "Do you know who that is? And where the picture was taken?" She recognized the woman with the goiter who ran The Cellar. The picture had been taken with Mrs. Power standing in one of the flower beds against the side of the house. The big cut stones of the house were unmistakable. After bringing the snapshot up close to her face and peering into it for ten seconds or so, Caroline looked at me and said, "That's her family."

By the time we had stopped the car in front of The Cellar, I had told Caroline all that I knew about Lee Ann's schooling and about how it was that, though she had a "family" in Memphis, no one had known her when she was growing up. She had been to one boarding school in Shreveport, Louisiana, to one in East Texas, and to still another in St. Charles, Missouri. I had heard her make references to all of those schools. "They kept her away from home," Caroline speculated. "And so when she had finished school she wasn't prepared for the kind of 'family' she had. That's why she moved out on them and lived in a rooming house."

She reached that conclusion while I was parking the car at the curb, near the front entrance to the house. Meanwhile, I was preparing myself mentally to accompany Caroline to the door of the old woman's living quarters, which were on the main floor and above The Cellar. But Caroline rested her hand on the steering wheel beside mine and said, "This is something I have to do without you."

"But I'd like to see Lee Ann if she's here," I said.

"I know you would," said Caroline. "Of course you would."

"But, Caroline," I said, "I've made it clear that ours was an innocent—"

"I know," she said. "That's why I don't want you to see her again." Then she took Lee Ann's bag and went up to the front entrance of the house.

The main entrance to The Cellar was to the side of and underneath the high front stoop of the old house. Caroline had to climb a flight of ten or twelve stone steps to reach the door to the residence. From the car I saw a vague figure appear at one of the first-floor windows.

I was relatively certain that it was Lee Ann I saw. I could barely restrain myself from jumping from the car and running up that flight of steps and forcing myself past Caroline and into the house. During the hundred hours or so since she had fled into the woods of Overton Park, Lee Ann Deehart had come to represent feelings of mine that I didn't try to comprehend. The notion I had had yesterday that I was in love with her and wanted to marry her didn't really adequately express the emotions that her disappearance had stirred in me. I felt that I had never looked at her really or had any conception of what sort of person she was or what her experience in life was like. Now it seemed I would never know. I suddenly realized—at that early age—that there was experience to be had in life that I might never know anything about except through hearsay and through books. I felt that this was my last moment to reach out and understand something of the world that was other than my own narrow circumstances and my own narrow nature. When, nearly fifteen years later, I came into a comfortable amount of money—after my father's death—I made my extraordinary decision to go back to the university and prepare myself to become a teacher. But I knew then, at thirty-seven, that I was only going to try to comprehend intellectually the world about me and beyond me and that I had failed somehow at some time to reach out and grasp direct experience of a larger life which no amount of intellectualizing could compensate for. It may be that the moment of my great failure was when I continued to sit there in the car and did not force my way into the house where the old woman with the goiter lived and where it now seemed Lee Ann had been hiding for four days.

I was scarcely aware of the moment when the big front door opened and Caroline was admitted to the house. She was in there for nearly an hour. During that time I don't know what thoughts I had. It was as though I ceased to exist for the time that Lee Ann Deehart and Caroline Braxley were closeted together. When Caroline reappeared on the high stone stoop of the house, I was surprised to see she was still carrying Lee Ann's suitcase. But she would soon make it all clear. It *was* Lee Ann who received her at the door. No doubt she had seen that Caroline was carrying her own piece of luggage. And no doubt Caroline had counted on just that mystification and its efficacy, because Caroline is an extremely clever psychologist when she sets her mind to it. At any rate, in that relatively brief interview between them Caroline learned that all she had surmised about Lee Ann was true. Moreover, she learned that Lee Ann had fled the scene of the accident because she feared that the publicity would reveal to everyone who her grandmother was.

Lee Ann had crossed the little strip of snow-covered golf course and had entered the part of the woods where the old-forest trees were. And something had made her want to remain there for a while. She didn't know what it was. She had leaned against one of the trees, feeling quite content. It had seemed to her that she was not alone in the woods. And whatever the other presences were, instead of interfering with her reflections they seemed to wish to help her clear her thoughts. She stood there for a long time—perhaps for an hour or more. At any rate, she remained there until all at once she realized how cold she had grown and realized that she had no choice but to go back to the real world. Yet she wasn't going back to her room or to her pretty possessions there. That wasn't the kind of freedom she wanted any longer. She was going back to her grandmother. But still she hoped to avoid the publicity that the accident might bring. She decided to go, first of all, and stay with some of her friends, so that her grandmother would not suppose she was only turning to her because she was in trouble. And while making this important change in her life she felt she must be protected by her friends. She wanted to have an interval of time to herself and she wanted, above all, not to be bothered during that time by the silly society boy in whose car she had been riding.

During the first days she had gone from one girl's house to another. Finally she went to her grandmother. In the beginning she had, it was true, been mightily depressed. That was why she had telephoned me to start with, and had wanted someone to cheer her up. But during these four days she had much time for thinking and had overcome all her depression and had no other thought but to follow through with the decision to go and live openly with her old grandmother in her quarters above The Cellar.

Caroline also, in that single interview, learned other things about Lee Ann which had been unknown to me. She learned that Lee Ann's own mother had abandoned her in infancy to her grandmother but had always through the years sent money back for her education. She had had—the mother—an extremely successful career as a buyer for a women's clothing store in Lincoln, Nebraska. But she had never tried to see her daughter and had never expressed a wish to see her. The only word she ever sent was that children were not her dish, but that she didn't want it on her conscience that, because of her, some little girl in Memphis, Tennessee, had got no education and was therefore the domestic slave of some man. When Caroline told me all of this about the mother's not caring to see the daughter, it brought from her her first emotional outburst with regard to the whole business. But that was at a later time. The first thing she had told me when she returned to the car was that once Lee Ann realized that her place of hiding could no longer be concealed, she was quickly and easily persuaded to speak to the newspaper editor on the telephone and to tell him that she was safe and well. But she did this only after Caroline had first spoken to the editor herself, and obtained a promise from him that there would be no embarrassing publicity for Lee Ann's grandmother.

The reason Caroline had returned with Lee Ann's suitcase was that Lee Ann had emptied it there in her grandmother's front parlor and had asked that we return to her rooming house and bring all of her possessions to her at her grandmother's. We obliged her in this, making appropriate, truthless explanations to her landlady, whom Lee Ann had meanwhile telephoned and given whatever little authority Mrs. Troxler required in order to let us remove her things. It seemed to me that the poor woman scarcely listened to the explanations we gave. Another girl was already moving into the room before we had well got Lee Ann's things out. When we returned to the grandmother's house with these possessions in the car, Caroline insisted upon making an endless number of trips into the house, carrying everything herself. She was firm in her stipulation that Lee Ann and I not see each other again.

The incident was closed then. I could be certain that there would be no broken engagement—not on Caroline's initiative. But from that point—from that afternoon—my real effort and my real concern would be to try to understand why Caroline had not been so terribly enraged or so sorely wounded upon first discovering that there had been another girl with me in the car at the time of the accident, and by the realization that I had not immediately disclosed her presence, that she had not at least once threatened to end the engagement. What her mental processes had been during the past four days, knowing now as I did that she was the person with whom I was going to spend the rest of my life, became of paramount interest to me.

But at that age I was so unquestioning of human behavior in general and so accepting of events as they came, and so without perception or reflection regarding the binding and molding effect upon people of the circumstances in which they are born, that I actually might not have found Caroline's thoughts of such profound interest and so vitally important to be understood had not Caroline, as soon as we were riding down Adams Street and were out of sight of The Cellar and of Mrs. Power's great stone house above it, suddenly requested that I drive her out to the Bristol Highway, and once we were on the Bristol Highway asked me to drive as fast and as far out of town as I could or would, to drive and drive until she should beg me to turn around and take her home; and had she not, as soon as we were out of town and beyond city speed limits, where I could press down on the accelerator and send us flying along the three-lane strip of concrete which cut through the endless expanse of cotton fields and swamps on either side, had she not then at last, after talking quietly about Lee Ann's mother's sending back the money for her education, burst into weeping that began with a kind of wailing and grinding of teeth that one ordinarily associates more with a very old person in very great physical pain, a wailing that became mixed almost immediately with a sort of hollow laughter in which there was no mirth. I commenced slowing the car at once. I was searching for a place where I could pull off to the side of the road. But through her tears and her harsh, dry laughter she hissed at me, "Don't stop! Don't stop! Go on. Go on. Go as far and as fast as you can, so that I can forget this day and put it forever behind me!" I obeyed her and sped on, reaching out my right hand to hold her two hands that were resting in her lap and were making no effort to wipe away her tears. I was not looking at her—only thinking thoughts of a kind I had never before had. It was the first time I had ever witnessed a victim of genuine hysteria. Indeed, I wasn't to hear such noises again until six or seven years later, during the Second World War. I heard them from men during days after a battle, men who had stood with great bravery against the enemy—particularly, as I remember now, men who had been brought back from the first onslaught of the Normandy invasion, physically whole but shaken in their souls. I think that during the stress of the four previous days Caroline Braxley had shed not a tear of self-pity or of shame and had not allowed herself a moment of genuine grief for my possible faithlessness to her. She had been far too busy with thinking—with thinking her thoughts of how to cope with Lee Ann's unexplained disappearance, with, that is, its possible effect upon her own life. But now the time had come when her checked emotions could be checked no longer.

The Bristol Highway, along which we were speeding as she wept hysterically, was a very straight and a very wide roadway for those days. It went northeast from Memphis. As its name implied, it was the old road that shot more or less diagonally across the long hinterland that is the state of Tennessee. It was the road along which many of our ancestors had first made their way from Virginia and the Carolinas to Memphis, to settle in the forest wilderness along the bluffs above the Mississippi River. And it occurred to me now that when Caroline said go as fast and as far as you can she really meant to take us all the way back into our past and begin the journey all over again, not merely from a point of four days ago or from the days of our childhood but from a point in our identity that would require a much deeper delving and a more radical return.

When we had got scarcely beyond the outskirts of Memphis, the most obvious signs of her hysteria had abated. Instead, however, she began to speak with a rapidity and in tones I was not accustomed to in her speech. This began after I had seen her give one long look over her shoulder and out the rear window of the car. Sensing some significance in that look and sensing some connection between it and the monologue she had now launched upon, I myself gave one glance into the rearview mirror. What met my eye was the skyline of modern Memphis beyond the snow-covered suburban rooftops—the modern Memphis of 1937, with its two or three high-rise office buildings. It was not clear to me immediately what there was in that skyline to inspire all that followed. She was speaking to me openly about Lee Ann and about her own feelings of jealousy and resentment of the girl—of *that* girl and of all those other girls, too, whose names and personalities and way of life had occupied our thoughts and had seemed to threaten our future during the four-day crisis that had followed my accident in the park.

"It isn't only Lee Ann that disturbs me," she said. "It began with her, of course. It began not with what she might be to you but with her freedom to jump out of your car, her freedom *from* you, her freedom to run off into the woods—with her capacity, which her special way of living provided her, simply to vanish, to remove herself from the eyes of the world, literally to disappear

from the glaring light of day while the whole world, so
to speak, looked on."

"*You* would like to be able to do that?" I interrupted.
It seemed so unlike her role as I understood it.

"*Any*body would, wouldn't they?" she said, not looking at me but at the endless stretch of concrete that lay
straight ahead. "*Men* have always been able to do it,"
she said. "In my own family, for as many generations
back as our family stories go, there have been men who
seemed to disappear from the face of the earth just
because they wanted to. They used to write 'Gone to
Texas' on the front door and leave the house and the
farm to be sold for taxes. They walked out on dependent
old parents and on sweethearts or even on wives and
little children. And though they were considered black
sheep for doing so, they were something of heroes, too.
It seemed romantic to the rest of us that they had gone
Out West somewhere and got a new start or had begun
life over. But there was never a woman in our famiily
who did that! There was no way it could happen. Or
perhaps in some rare instance it did happen and the story
hasn't come down to us. Her name simply isn't recorded
in our family annals or reported in stories told around
the fire. The assumption of course is that she is a street-
walker in Chicago or she resides in a red-plush
whorehouse in Cheyenne. But with girls like Lee Ann
and Lucy and Betsy it's all different. They have made
their break with the past. Each of them had had the
strength and intelligence to make the break for herself.
But now they have formed a sort of league for their own
protection. How I do admire and envy them! And how
little you understand them, Nat. How little you understand Lee Ann's loneliness and depression and bravery.
She and all the others are wonderful—even Fern. They
occupy the real city of Memphis as none of the rest of
us do. They treat men just as they please. And not the
way men are treated in *our* circles. And men like them
better for it. Those girls have learned to enjoy life
together and to be mutually protective, but they enjoy a
protection also, I hope you have observed, a kind of

communal protection, from men who admire their very independence, from a league of men, mind you, not from individual men, from the police and from men like my father and your father, from men who would never say openly how much they admire them. Naturally we fear them. Those of us who are not like them in temperament—or in intelligence, because there is no use in denying it—we must fear them and find a means to give delaying action. And of course the only way we know is the age-old way!"

She became silent for a time now. But I knew I was going to hear what I had been waiting to hear. If I had been the least bit impatient with her explanation of Lee Ann and her friends, it was due in part to my impatience to see if she would explain *herself* to me. We were now speeding along the Bristol Highway at the very top speed the car would go. Except when we were passing through some crossroad or village I consciously kept the speed above ninety. In those days there was no speed limit in Tennessee. There were merely signs placed every so often along the roadside saying "Speed Limit: Please Drive Carefully." I felt somehow that, considering Caroline's emotional state and my own tension, it would be altogether unreasonable, it would constitute careless and unsafe driving, for me to reduce our speed to anything below the maximum capability of the car. And when we did of necessity slow down for some village or small town it was precisely as though we had arrived at some at once familiar and strange point in the past. And on each occasion I think we both experienced a sense of danger and disappointment. It was as though we expected to experience a satisfaction in having gone so far. But the satisfaction was not to be had. When we had passed that point, I felt only the need to press on at an even greater speed. And so we drove on and on, at first north and east through the wintry cotton land and cornland, past the old Orgill Plantation, the mansion house in plain view, its round brick columns on which the plaster was mostly gone, and now and then another white man's antebellum house, and always at the roadside or on the horizon, atop some distant ridge, a variety of black men's shacks and cabins, each with a little streamer of smoke rising from an improvised tin stovepipe or from an ill-made brick chimney bent away from the cabin at a precarious angle.

We went through the old villages of Arlington and Mason and the town of Brownsville—down streets of houses with columned porticoes and double galleries—and then we turned south to Bolivar, whose very name told you when it was built, and headed back to Memphis through Grand Junction and La Grange. (Mississippi towns really, though north of the Tennessee line.) I had slowed our speed after Bolivar, because that was where Caroline began her second monologue. The tone and pace of her speech were very different now. Her speech was slow and deliberate, her emotions more under control than usual, as she described what she had felt and thought in the time since the accident and explained how she came to reach the decision to take the action she had—that is, action toward searching out and finding Lee Ann Deehart. Though I had said nothing on the subject of what she had done about Lee Ann and not done about our engagement, expressed no request or demand for any explanation unless it was by my silence, when she spoke now it was almost as though Caroline were making a courtroom defense of accusations hurled at her by me. "I finally saw there was only one thing for me to do and saw why I had to do it. I saw that the only power in the world I had for saving myself lay in my saving you. And I saw that I could only save you by 'saving' Lee Ann Deehart. At first, of course, I thought I would have to break our engagement, or at least postpone the wedding for a year. That's what *every*body thought, of course—everybody in the family."

"Even your father and mother?" I could not help interjecting. It had seemed to me that Caroline's parents had—of all people—been most sympathetic to me.

"Yes, even my mother and father," she went on, rather serenely now. "They could not have been more sympathetic to you personally. Mother said that, after all, you were a mere man. Father said that, after all, you were only human. But circumstances were circumstances, and if some disaster had befallen Lee Ann, if she was murdered or if she was pregnant or if she was a suicide or whatever other horror you can conjure up, and it all came out, say, on our wedding day or came out afterward, for that matter—well, what then? *They* and *I* had to think of that. On the other hand, as I kept thinking, what if the wedding *was* called off? What then for me? The only power I had to save myself was to save you, and to save you by rescuing Lee Ann Deehart. It always came to that, and comes to that still. Don't you see, it was a question of how very much I had to lose and how little power I had to save myself. Because *I* had not set *my*self free the way those other girls have. One makes that choice at a much earlier age than this, I'm afraid. And so I knew already, Nat, and I know now what the only kind of power I can ever have must be."

She hesitated then. She was capable of phrasing what she said much more precisely. But it would have been indelicate, somehow, for her to have done so. And so I said it for her in my crude way: "You mean the power of a woman in a man's world."

She nodded and continued. "I had to protect *that*. Even if it had been *I* that broke our engagement, Nat, or even if you and I had been married before some second scandal broke, still I would have been a jilted, a rejected girl. And some part of my power to protect myself would be gone forever. Power, or strength, is what everybody must have some of if he—if she—is to survive in any kind of world. I have to protect and use whatever strength I have."

Caroline went on in that voice until we were back in Memphis and at her father's house on East Parkway. She kissed me before we got out of the car there, kissed me for my silence, I believe. I had said almost nothing during the whole of the long ride. And I think she has ever since been grateful to me for the silence I kept. Perhaps she mistook it for more understanding than I was capable of at the time. At any rate, I cannot help believing that it has much to do with the support and understanding—rather silent though it was—which she gave me when I made the great break in my life in my late thirties. Though it clearly meant that we must live on a somewhat more modest scale and live among people of a sort she was not used to, and even meant leaving Memphis forever behind us, the firmness with which she supported my decision, and the look in her eyes whenever I spoke of feeling I must make the change, seemed to say to me that she would dedicate her pride of power to the power of freedom I sought.

PART IV

Breaking
Southern Stereotypes

Anne Moody

Born in Mississippi in 1940, Anne Moody received a B.S. from Tougaloo College in 1964. She writes that she never really saw herself as a writer, "I was first and foremost an activist in the Civil Rights Movement in Mississippi." She was an organizer and fund-raiser for the Congress of Racial Equality (CORE) in Washington, D.C., and a civil rights project coordinator at Cornell University. She wrote about these experiences in her autobiography, *Coming of Age in Mississippi* (1969), from which the following excerpt is taken. A contributor to *Ms.* and *Mademoiselle*, she has published a collection of short stories, *Mr. Death* (1975), and worked as an artist-in-residence in Berlin. She makes her home in New York City.

from Coming of Age
in Mississippi

In mid-September I was back on campus. But didn't very much happen until February when the NAACP held its annual convention in Jackson. They were having a whole lot of interesting speakers: Jackie Robinson, Floyd Patterson, Curt Flood, Margaretta Belafonte, and many others. I wouldn't have missed it for anything. I was so excited that I sent one of the leaflets home to Mama and asked her to come.

Three days later I got a letter from Mama with dried-up tears on it, forbidding me to go to the convention. It went on for more than six pages. She said if I didn't stop that [expletive deleted] she would come to Tougaloo and kill me herself. She told me about the time I last visited her, on Thanksgiving, and she had picked me up at the bus station. She said she picked me up because she was scared some white in my hometown would try to do something to me. She said the sheriff had been by, telling her I was messing around with that NAACP group. She said he told her if I didn't stop it, I could not come back there any more. He said that they didn't need any of those NAACP people messing around in Centreville. She ended the letter by saying that she had burned the leaflet I sent her. "Please don't send any more of that stuff here. I don't want nothing to happen to us here," she said. "If you keep that up, you will never be able to come home again."

I was so damn mad after her letter, I felt like taking the NAACP convention to Centreville. I think I would have, if it had been in my power to do so. The remainder of the week I thought of nothing except going to the convention. I didn't know exactly what to do about it. I didn't want Mama or anyone at home to get hurt because of me.

I had felt something was wrong when I was home. During the four days I was there, Mama had tried to do everything she could to keep me in the house. When I said I was going to see some of my old classmates, she pretended she was sick and said I would have to cook. I knew she was acting strangely, but I hadn't known why. I thought Mama just wanted me to spend most of my time with her, since this was only the second time I had been home since I entered college as a freshman.

Things kept running through my mind after that letter from Mama. My mind was so active, I couldn't sleep at night. I remembered the one time I did leave the house to go to the post office. I had walked past a bunch of white men on the street on my way through town and one said, "Is that the gal goin' to Tougaloo?" He acted kind of mad or something, and I didn't know what was going on. I got a creepy feeling, so I hurried home. When I told Mama about it, she just said, "A lotta people don't like that school." I knew what she meant. Just before I went to Tougaloo, they had housed the Freedom Riders there. The school was being criticized by whites throughout the state.

The night before the convention started, I made up my mind to go, no matter what Mama said. I just wouldn't tell Mama or anyone from home. Then it occurred to me—how did the sheriff or anyone at home know I was working with the NAACP chapter on campus? Somehow they had found out. Now I knew I could never go to Centreville safely again. I kept telling myself that I didn't really care too much about going home, that it was more important to me to go to the convention.

I was there from the very beginning. Jackie Robinson was asked to serve as moderator. This was the first time I had seen him in person. I remembered how when Jackie became the first Negro to play Major League baseball, my uncles and most of the Negro boys in my hometown started organizing baseball leagues. It did something for them to see a Negro out there playing with all those white players. Jackie was a good moderator, I thought. He kept smiling and joking. People felt relaxed and proud. They appreciated knowing and meeting people of their own race who had done something worth talking about.

When Jackie introduced Floyd Patterson, heavyweight champion of the world, the people applauded for a long, long time. Floyd was kind of shy. He didn't say very much. He didn't have to, just his being there was enough to satisfy most of the Negroes who had only seen him on TV. Archie Moore was there too. He wasn't as smooth as Jackie, but he had his way with a crowd. He started telling how he was run out of Mississippi, and the people just cracked up.

I was enjoying the convention so much that I went back for the night session. Before the night was over, I had gotten autographs from every one of the Negro celebrities.

I had counted on graduating in the spring of 1963, but as it turned out, I couldn't because some of my credits still had to be cleared with Natchez College. A year before, this would have seemed like a terrible disaster, but now I hardly even felt disappointed. I had a good excuse to stay on campus for the summer and work with the Movement, and this was what I really wanted to do. I couldn't go home again anyway, and I couldn't go to New Orleans—I didn't have money enough for bus fare.

During my senior year at Tougaloo, my family hadn't sent me one penny. I had only the small amount of money I had earned at Maple Hill. I couldn't afford to eat at school or live in the dorms, so I had gotten permission to move off campus. I had to prove that I could finish school, even if I had to go hungry every day. I knew Raymond and Miss Pearl were just waiting to see me drop out. But something happened to me as I got more and more involved in the Movement. It no longer seemed important to prove anything. I had found something outside myself that gave meaning to my life.

I had become very friendly with my social science professor, John Salter, who was in charge of NAACP activities on campus. All during the year, while the NAACP conducted a boycott of the downtown stores in Jackson, I had been one of Salter's most faithful canvassers and church speakers. During the last week of school, he told me that sit-in demonstrations were about to start in Jackson and that he wanted me to be the spokesman for a team that would sit-in at Woolworth's lunch counter. The two other demonstrators would be classmates of mine, Memphis and Pearlena. Pearlena was a dedicated NAACP worker, but Memphis had not been very involved in the Movement on campus. It seemed that the organization had had a rough time finding students who were in a position to go to jail. I had nothing to lose one way or the other. Around ten o'clock the morning of the demonstrations, NAACP headquarters alerted the news services. As a result, the police department was also informed, but neither the policemen nor the newsmen knew exactly where or when the demonstrations would start. They stationed themselves along Capitol Street and waited.

To divert attention from the sit-in at Woolworth's, the picketing started at J. C. Penny's a good fifteen minutes before. The pickets were allowed to walk up and down in front of the store three or four times before they were arrested. At exactly 11 A.M., Pearlena, Memphis, and I entered Woolworth's from the rear entrance. We separated as soon as we stepped into the store, and made small purchases from various counters. Pearlena had given Memphis her watch. He was to let us know when it was 11:14. At 11:14 we were to join him near the lunch counter and at exactly 11:15 we were to take seats at it.

Seconds before 11:15 we were occupying three seats at the previously segregated Woolworth's lunch counter. In the beginning the waitresses seemed to ignore us, as if they really didn't know what was going on. Our waitress walked past us a couple of times before she noticed we had started to write our own orders down and realized we wanted service. She asked us what we wanted. We began to read to her from our order slips. She told us that we would be served at the back counter, which was for Negroes.

"We would like to be served here," I said.

The waitress started to repeat what she had said, then stopped in the middle of the sentence. She turned the lights out behind the counter, and she and the other waitressess almost ran to the back of the store, deserting all their white customers. I guess they thought that violence would start immediately after the whites at the counter realized what was going on. There were five or six other people at the counter. A couple of them just got up and walked away. A girl sitting next to me finished her banana split before leaving. A middle-aged white woman who had not yet been served rose from her seat and came over to us. "I'd like to stay here with you," she said, "but my husband is waiting."

The newsmen came in just as she was leaving. They must have discovered what was going on shortly after some of the people began to leave the store. One of the newsmen ran behind the woman who spoke to us and asked her to identify herself. She refused to give her name, but said she was a native of Vicksburg and a former resident of California. When asked why she had said what she had said to us, she replied, "I am in sympathy with the Negro movement." By this time a crowd of cameramen and reporters had gathered around us taking pictures and asking questions, such as Where were we from? Why did we sit-in? What organization sponsored it? Were we students? From what school? How were we classified?

I told them that we were all students at Tougaloo College, that we were represented by no particular organization, and that we planned to stay there even after the store closed. "All we want is service," was my reply to one of them. After they had finished probing for about twenty minutes, they were almost ready to leave.

At noon, students from a nearby white high school

started pouring in to Woolworth's. When they first saw us they were sort of surprised. They didn't know how to react. A few started to heckle and the newsmen became interested again. Then the white students started chanting all kinds of anti-Negro slogans. We were called a little bit of everything. The rest of the seats except the three we were occupying had been roped off to prevent others from sitting down. A couple of the boys took one end of the rope and made it into a hangman's noose. Several attempts were made to put it around our necks. The crowds grew as more students and adults came in for lunch.

We kept our eyes straight forward and did not look at the crowd except for occasional glances to see what was going on. All of a sudden I saw a face I remembered—the drunkard from the bus station sit-in. My eyes lingered on him just long enough for us to recognize each other. Today he was drunk too, so I don't think he remembered where he had seen me before. He took out a knife, opened it, put it in his pocket, and then began to pace the floor. At this point, I told Memphis and Pearlena what was going on. Memphis suggested that we pray. We bowed our heads, and all hell broke loose. A man rushed forward, threw Memphis from his seat, and slapped my face. Then another man who worked in the store threw me against an adjoining counter.

Down on my knees on the floor, I saw Memphis lying near the lunch counter with blood running out of the corners of his mouth. As he tried to protect his face, the man who'd thrown him down kept kicking him against the head. If he had worn hard-soled shoes instead of sneakers, the first kick probably would have killed Memphis. Finally a man dressed in plain clothes identified himself as a police officer and arrested Memphis and his attacker.

Pearlena had been thrown to the floor. She and I got back on our stools after Memphis was arrested. There were some white Tougaloo teachers in the crowd. They asked Pearlena and me if we wanted to leave. They said that things were getting too rough. We didn't know what to do. While we were trying to make up our minds, we were joined by Joan Trumpauer. Now there were three of us and we were integrated. The crowd began to chant, "Communists, Communists, Communists." Some old man in the crowd ordered the students to take us off the stools.

"Which one should I get first?" a big husky boy said.

"That white nigger," the old man said.

The boy lifted Joan from the counter by her waist and carried her out of the store. Simultaneously, I was snatched from my stool by two high school students. I was dragged about thirty feet toward the door by my hair when someone made them turn me loose. As I was getting up off the floor, I saw Joan coming back inside. We started back to the center of the counter to join Pearlena. Lois Chaffee, a white Tougaloo faculty member, was now sitting next to her. So Joan and I just climbed across the rope at the front end of the counter and sat down. There were now four of us, two whites and two Negroes, all women. The mob started smearing us with ketchup, mustard, sugar, pies, and everything on the counter. Soon Joan and I were joined by John Salter, but the moment he sat down he was hit on the jaw with what appeared to be brass knuckles. Blood gushed from his face and someone threw salt into the open wound. Ed King, Tougaloo's chaplain, rushed to him.

At the other end of the counter, Lois and Pearlena were joined by George Raymond, a CORE field worker and a student from Jackson State College. Then a Negro high school boy sat down next to me. The mob took spray paint from the counter and sprayed it on the new demonstrators. The high school student had on a white shirt; the word "nigger" was written on his back with red spray paint.

We sat there for three hours taking a beating when the manager decided to close the store because the mob had begun to go wild with stuff from other counters. He begged and begged everyone to leave. But even after fifteen minutes of begging, no one budged. They would not leave until we did. Then Dr. Beittel, the president of Tougaloo College, came running in. He said he had just heard what was happening.

About ninety policemen were standing outside the store; they had been watching the whole thing through the windows, but had not come in to stop the mob or do anything. President Beittel went outside and asked Captain Ray to come and escort us out. The captain refused, stating the manager had to invite him in before he could enter the premises, so Dr. Beittel himself brought us out. He had told the police that they had better protect us after we were outside the store. When we got outside, the policemen formed a single line that blocked the mob from us. However, they were allowed to throw at us everything they had collected. Within ten minutes, we were picked up by Reverend King in his station wagon and taken to the NAACP headquarters on Lynch Street.

After the sit-in, all I could think of was how sick Mississippi whites were. They believed so much in the segregated Southern way of life, they would kill to preserve it. I sat there in the NAACP office and thought of how many times they had killed when this way of life was threatened. I knew that the killing had just begun. "Many more will die before it is over with," I thought. Before the sit-in, I had always hated the whites in Mississippi. Now I knew it was impossible for me to hate sickness. The whites had a disease, an incurable disease in its final stage. What were our chances against such a disease? I thought of the students, the young Negroes who had just begun to protest, as young interns. When these young interns got older, I thought, they would be the best doctors in the world for social problems.

Before we were taken back to campus, I wanted to get my hair washed. It was stiff with dried mustard, ketchup and sugar. I stopped in at a beauty shop across the street from the NAACP office. I didn't have on any shoes because I had lost them when I was dragged across the floor at Woolworth's. My stockings were sticking to my legs from the mustard that had dried on them. The hairdresser took one look at me and said, "My land, you were in the sit-in, huh?"

"Yes," I answered. "Do you have time to wash my hair and style it?"

"Right away," she said, and she meant right away. There were three other ladies already waiting, but they seemed glad to let me go ahead of them. The hairdresser was real nice. She even took my stockings off and washed my legs while my hair was drying.

There was a mass rally that night at the Pearl Street Church in Jackson, and the place was packed. People were standing two abreast in the aisles. Before the speakers began, all the sit-inners walked out on the stage and were introduced by Medgar Evers. People stood and applauded for what seemed like thirty minutes or more. Medgar told the audience that this was just the beginning of such demonstrations. He asked them to pledge themselves to unite in a massive offensive against segregation in Jackson, and throughout the state. The rally ended with "We Shall Overcome" and sent home hundreds of determined people. It seemed as though Mississippi Negroes were about to get together at last.

Before I demonstrated, I had written Mama. She wrote me back a letter, begging me not to take part in the sit-in. She even sent ten dollars for bus fare to New Orleans. I didn't have one penny, so I kept the money. Mama's letter made me mad. I had to live my life as I saw fit. I had made that decision when I left home. But it hurt to have my family prove to me how scared they were. It hurt me more than anything else—I knew the whites had already started the threats and intimidations. I was the first Negro from my hometown who had openly demonstrated, worked with the NAACP, or anything. When Negroes threatened to do anything in Centreville, they were either shot like Samuel O'Quinn or run out of town, like Reverend Dupree.

I didn't answer Mama's letter. Even if I had written one, she wouldn't have received it before she saw the news on TV or heard it on the radio. I waited to hear from her again. And I waited to hear in the news that someone in Centreville had been murdered. If so, I knew it would be a member of the family.

On Wednesday, the day after the sit-in, demonstrations got off to a good start. Ten people picketed shortly after noon on Capitol Street, and were arrested. Another mass rally followed the demonstrations that night, where a six-man delegation of Negro ministers was chosen to meet Mayor Thompson the following Tuesday. They were to present to him a number of demands on behalf of Jackson Negroes. They were as follows:

1. Hiring of Negro policemen and school crossing guards

2. Removal of segregation signs from public facilities

3. Improvement of job opportunities for Negroes on city payrolls—Negro drivers of city garbage trucks, etc.

4. Encouraging public eating establishments to serve both whites and Negroes

5. Integration of public parks and libraries

6. The naming of a Negro to the City Parks and Recreation Committee.

7. Integration of public schools

8. Forcing service stations to integrate rest rooms

After this meeting, Reverend Haughton, the minister of Pearl Street Church, said that the Mayor was going to act on all the suggestions. But the following day, Thompson denied that he had made any promises. He said the Negro delegation "got carried away" following their discussion with him.

"It seems as though Mayor Thompson wants to play games with us," Reverend Haughton said at the next rally. "He is calling us liars and trying to make us sound like fools. I guess we have to show him that we mean business."

When Reverend Charles A. Jones, dean and chaplain at Campbell College, asked at the close of the meeting, "Where do we go from here?" the audience shouted, "To the streets." They were going to prove to Mayor Thompson and the white people of Jackson that they meant business.

Around ten the next morning, an entire day of demonstrations started. A little bit of everything was tried.

Some Negroes sat-in, some picketed, and some squatted in the streets and refused to move.

All of the five-and-ten stores (H. L. Green, Kress, and Woolworth) had closed their lunch counters as a result of the Woolworth sit-in. However, this did not stop the new sit-ins. Chain restaurants such as Primos Restaurant in downtown Jackson were now targets. Since police brutality was the last thing wanted in good, respectable Jackson, Mississippi, whenever arrested demonstrators refused to walk to a paddy wagon, garbage truck, or whatever was being used to take people to jail, Negro trusties from Jackson's city jail carted them away. Captain Ray and his men would just stand back with their hands folded, looking innocent as lambs for the benefit of the Northern reporters and photographers.

The Mayor still didn't seem to be impressed with the continuous small demonstrations and kept the streets hot. After eighty-eight demonstrators had been arrested, the Mayor held a news conference where he told a group of reporters, "We can handle 100,000 agitators." He also stated that the "good colored citizens are not rallying to the support of the outside agitators" (although there were only a few out-of-state people involved in the movement at the time) and offered to give Northern newsmen anything they wanted, including transportation, if they would "adequately" report the facts.

During the demonstrations, I helped conduct several workshops, where potential demonstrators, high school and college students mostly, were taught to protect themselves. If, for instance, you wanted to protect the neck to offset a karate blow, you clasped your hands behind the neck. To protect the genital organs you doubled up in a knot, drawing the knees up to the chest to protect your breasts if you were a girl.

The workshops were handled mostly by SNCC and CORE field secretaries and workers, almost all of whom were very young. The NAACP handled all the bail and legal services and public relations, but SNCC and CORE could draw teen-agers into the Movement as no other organization could. Whether they received credit for it or not, they helped make Jackson the center of attention throughout the nation.

During this period, civil rights workers who had become known to the Jackson police were often used to divert the cops' attention just before a demonstration. A few cops were always placed across the street from NAACP headquarters, since most of the demonstrations were organized there and would leave from that building. The "diverters" would get into cars and lead the cops off on a wild-goose chase. This would allow the real demonstrators to get downtown before they were noticed. One evening, a group of us took the cops for a tour of the park. After giving the demonstrators time enough to get to Capitol Street, we decided to go and watch the action. When we arrived there ourselves, we met Reverend King and a group of ministers. They told us they were going to stage a pray-in on the post office steps. "Come on, join us," Reverend King said. "I don't think we'll be arrested, because it's federal property."

By the time we got to the post office, the newsmen had already been informed, and a group of them were standing in front of the building blocking the front entrance. By now the group of whites that usually constituted the mob had gotten smart. They no longer looked for us, or for the demonstration. They just followed the newsmen and photographers. They were much smarter than the cops, who hadn't caught on yet.

We entered the post office through the side entrance and found that part of the mob was waiting inside the building. We didn't let this bother us. As soon as a few more ministers joined us, we were ready to go outside. There were fourteen of us, seven whites and seven Negroes. We walked out front and stood and bowed our heads as the ministers began to pray. We were immediately interrupted by the appearance of Captain Ray. "We are asking you people to disperse. If you don't, you are under arrest," he said.

Most of us were not prepared to go to jail. Doris Erskine, a student from Jackson State, and I had to take over a workshop the following day. Some of the ministers were in charge of the mass rally that night. But if we had dispersed, we would have been torn to bits by the mob. The whites standing out there had murder in their eyes. They were ready to do us in and all fourteen of us knew that. We had no other choice but to be arrested.

We had no plan of action. Reverend King and some of the ministers who were kneeling refused to move; they just kept on praying. Some of the others also attempted to kneel. The rest of us just walked to the paddy wagon. Captain Ray was using the Negro trusties. I felt so sorry for them. They were too small to be carrying all these heavy-ass demonstrators. I could tell just by looking at them that they didn't want to, either. I knew they were forced to do this.

After we got to jail we were mugged and fingerprinted, then taken to a cell. Most of the ministers were scared stiff. This was the first time some of them had seen the inside of a jail. Before we were mugged, we were all placed in a room together and allowed to make one call. Reverend King made the call to the NAACP headquarters to see if some of the ministers could be bailed out right away. I was so glad when they told him they didn't have money available at the moment. I just got my kicks out of sitting there looking at the ministers. Some of them looked so pitiful, I thought they would cry any minute, and here they were, supposed to be our leaders.

When Doris and I got to the cell where we would spend the next four days, we found a lot of our friends there. There were twelve girls altogether. The jail was segregated. I felt sorry for Jeanette King, Lois Chaffee, and Joan Trumpauer. Just because they were white they were missing out on all the fun we planned to have. Here we were going to school together, sleeping in the same dorm, worshipping together, playing together, even demonstrating together. It all ended in jail. They were rushed off by themselves to some cell designated for whites.

Our cell didn't even have a curtain over the shower. Every time the cops heard the water running, they came running to peep. After the first time, we fixed them. We took chewing gum and toilet tissue and covered the opening in the door. They were afraid to take it down. I guess they thought it might have come out in the newspaper. Their wives wouldn't have liked that at all. Peep through a hole to see a bunch of nigger girls naked? No! No! They certainly wouldn't have liked that. All of the girls in my cell were college students. We had a lot to talk about, so we didn't get too bored. We made cards out of toilet tissue and played Gin Rummy almost all day. Some of us even learned new dance steps from each other.

There were a couple of girls in with us from Jackson State College. They were scared they would be expelled from school. Jackson State, like most of the state-supported Negro schools, was an Uncle Tom school. The students could be expelled for almost anything. When I found this out, I really appreciated Tougaloo.

The day we were arrested one of the Negro trusties sneaked us a newspaper. We discovered that over four hundred high school students had also been arrested. We were so glad we sang freedom songs for an hour or so. The jailer threatened to put us in solitary if we didn't stop. At first we didn't think he meant it, so we kept singing. He came back with two other cops and asked us to follow them. They marched us down the hall and showed us one of the solitary chambers. "If you don't stop that damn singing, I'm gonna throw all of you in here together," said the jailer. After that we didn't sing any more. We went back and finished reading the paper.

We got out of jail on Sunday to discover that everyone was talking about the high school students. All four hundred who were arrested had been taken to the fairgrounds and placed in a large open compound without beds or anything. It was said that they were getting sick like flies. Mothers were begging to have their children released, but the NAACP didn't have enough money to bail them all out.

The same day we went to jail for the pray-in, the students at Lanier High School had started singing freedom songs on their lunch hour. They got so carried away they

ignored the bell when the break was over and just kept
on singing. The principal of the high school did not know
what to do, so he called the police and told them that
the students were about to start a riot.

When the cops came, they brought the dogs. The students refused to go back to their classrooms when asked,
so the cops turned the dogs loose on them. The students
fought them off for a while. In fact, I was told that mothers who lived near the school had joined the students in
fighting off the dogs. They had begun to throw bricks,
rocks, and bottles. The next day the papers stated that
ten or more cops suffered cuts or minor wounds. The
papers didn't say it, but a lot of students were hurt, too,
from dog bites and lumps on the head from billy clubs.
Finally, one hundred and fifty cops were rushed to the
scene and several students and adults were arrested.

The next day four hundred of the high school students
from Lanier, Jim Hill, and Brinkley High schools gathered in a church on Farish Street, ready to go to jail.
Willie Ludden, the NAACP youth leader, and some of
the SNCC and CORE workers met with them, gave a
brief workshop on nonviolent protective measures and
led them into the streets. After marching about two
blocks they were met by helmeted police officers and
ordered to disperse. When they refused, they were
arrested, herded into paddy wagons, canvas-covered
trucks, and garbage trucks. Those moving too slowly
were jabbed with rifle butts. Police dogs were there, but
were not used. From the way everyone was describing
the scene it sounded like Nazi Germany instead of Jackson, USA.

On Monday, I joined a group of high school students
and several other college students who were trying to get
arrested. Our intention was to be put in the fairgrounds
with the high school students already there. The cops
picked us up, but they didn't want to put us so-called
professional agitators in with the high school students.
We were weeded out, and taken back to the city jail.

I got out of jail two days later and found I had gotten
another letter from Mama. She had written it Wednesday

the twenty-ninth, after the Woolworth sit-in. The reason it had taken so long for me to get it was that it came by way of New Orleans. Mama sent it to Adline and had Adline mail it to me. In the letter she told me that the sheriff had stopped by and asked all kinds of questions about me the morning after the sit-in. She said she and Raymond told them that I had only been home once since I was in college, that I had practically cut off all my family connections when I ran away from home as a senior in high school. She said he said that he knew I had left home. "He should know," I thought, "because I had to get him to move my clothes for me when I left." She went on and on. She told me he said I must never come back there. If so he would not be responsible for what happened to me. "The whites are pretty upset about her doing these things," he told her. Mama told me not to write her again until she sent me word that it was O.K. She said that I would hear from her through Adline.

I also got a letter from Adline in the same envelope. She told me what Mama hadn't mentioned—that Junior had been cornered by a group of white boys and was about to be lynched, when one of his friends came along in a car and rescued him. Besides that, a group of white men had gone out and beaten up my old Uncle Buck. Adline said Mama told her they couldn't sleep, for fear of night riders. They were all scared to death. My sister ended the letter by cursing me out. She said I was trying to get every Negro in Centreville murdered.

I guess Mama didn't tell me these things because she was scared to. She probably thought I would have tried to do something crazy. Something like trying to get the organizations to move into Wilkinson County, or maybe coming home myself to see if they would kill me. She never did give me credit for having the least bit of sense. I knew there was nothing I could do. No organization was about to go to Wilkinson County. It was a little too tough for any of them. And I wasn't about to go there either. If they said they would kill me, I figured I'd better take their word for it.

Meantime, within four or five days Jackson became the hotbed of racial demonstrations in the South. It seemed as though most of the Negro college and high school students there were making preparations to participate. Those who did not go to jail were considered cowards by those who did. At this point, Mayor Allen Thompson finally made a decisive move. He announced that Jackson had made plans to house over 12,500 demonstrators at the local jails and at the state fairgrounds. And if this was not enough, he said, Parchman, the state penitentiary, 160 miles away, would be used. Governor Ross Barnett had held a news conference offering Parchman facilities to Jackson.

An injunction prohibiting demonstrations was issued by a local judge, naming NAACP, CORE, Tougaloo College, and various leaders. According to this injunction, the intent of the named organizations and individuals was to paralyze the economic nerve center of the city of Jackson. It used as proof the leaflets that had been distributed by the NAACP urging Negroes not to shop on Capitol Street. The next day the injunction was answered with another mass march.

The cops started arresting every Negro on the scene of a demonstration, whether or not he was participating. People were being carted off to jail every day of the week. On Saturday, Roy Wilkins, the National Director of NAACP, and Medgar Evers were arrested as they picketed in front of Woolworth's. Theldon Henderson, a Negro lawyer who worked for the Justice Department, and had been sent down from Washington to investigate a complaint by the NAACP about the fairgrounds facilities, was also arrested. It was said that when he showed his Justice Department credentials, the arresting officer started trembling. They let him go immediately.

Mass rallies had come to be an every night event, and at each one the NAACP had begun to build up Medgar Evers. Somehow I had the feeling that they wanted him to become for Mississippi what Martin Luther King had been in Alabama. They were well on the way to achieving that, too.

After the rally on Tuesday, June 11, I had to stay in Jackson. I had missed the ride back to campus. Dave Dennis, the CORE field secretary for Mississippi, and his wife put me up for the night. We were watching TV around twelve-thirty, when a special news bulletin interrupted the program. It said, "Jackson NAACP leader Medgar Evers has just been shot."

We didn't believe what we were hearing. We just sat there staring at the TV screen. It was unbelievable. Just an hour or so earlier we were all with him. The next bulletin announced that he had died in the hospital soon after the shooting. We didn't know what to say or do. All night we tried to figure out what had happened, who did it, who was next, and it still didn't seem real.

First thing the next morning we turned on the TV. It showed films taken shortly after Medgar was shot in his driveway. We saw the pool of blood where he had fallen. We saw his wife sobbing almost hysterically as she tried to tell what had happened. Without even having breakfast, we headed for the NAACP headquarters. When we got there, they were trying to organize a march to protest Medgar's death. Newsmen, investigators, and reporters flooded the office. College and high school students and a few adults sat in the auditorium waiting to march.

Dorie Ladner, a SNCC worker, and I decided to run up to Jackson State College and get some of the students there to participate in the march. I was sure we could convince some of them to protest Medgar's death. Since the march was to start shortly after lunch, we had a couple of hours to do some recruiting. When we got to Jackson State, class was in session. "That's a damn shame," I thought. "They should have dismissed school today, in honor of Medgar."

Dorie and I started going down each hall, taking opposite classrooms. We begged students to participate. They didn't respond in any way.

"It's a shame, it really is a shame. This morning Medgar Evers was murdered and here you sit in a damn classroom with books in front of your faces, pretending you don't even know he's been killed. Every Negro in

Jackson should be in the streets raising hell and protesting his death," I said in one class. I felt sick, I got so mad with them. How could Negroes be so pitiful? How could they just sit by and take all this [expletive deleted] without any emotions at all? I just didn't understand.

"It's hopeless, Moody, let's go," Dorie said.

As we were leaving the building, we began soliciting aloud in the hall. We walked right past the president's office, shouting even louder. President Reddix came rushing out. "You girls leave this campus immediately," he said. "You can't come on this campus and announce anything without my consent."

Dorie had been a student at Jackson State. Mr. Reddix looked at her. "You know better than this, Dorie," he said.

"But President Reddix, Medgar was just murdered. Don't you have any feelings about his death at all?" Dorie said.

"I am doing a job. I can't do this job and have feelings about everything happening in Jackson," he said. He was waving his arms and pointing his finger in our faces. "Now you two get off this campus before I have you arrested."

By this time a group of students had gathered in the hall. Dorie had fallen to her knees in disgust as Reddix was pointing at her, and some of the students thought he had hit her. I didn't say anything to him. If I had I would have been calling him every kind of [expletive deleted] Tom I could think of. I helped Dorie off the floor. I told her we'd better hurry, or we would miss the demonstration.

On our way back to the auditorium we picked up the Jackson *Daily News*. Headlines read JACKSON INTEGRATION LEADER EVERS SLAIN.

Negro NAACP leader Medgar Evers was shot to death when he stepped from his automobile here early today as he returned home from an integration strategy meeting.

Police said Evers, 37, was cut down by a high-powered bullet in the back of the driveway of his home.

I stopped reading. Medgar was usually followed home every night by two or three cops. Why didn't they follow him last night? Something was wrong. "They must have known," I thought. "Why didn't they follow him last night?" I kept asking myself. I had to get out of all this confusion. The only way I could do it was to go to jail. Jail was the only place I could think in.

When we got back to the auditorium, we were told that those who would take part in the first march had met at Pearl Street Church. Dorie and I walked over there. We noticed a couple of girls from Jackson State. They asked Dorie if President Reddix had hit her, and said it had gotten out on campus that he had. They told us a lot of students had planned to demonstrate because of what Reddix had done. "Good enough," Dorie said, "Reddix better watch himself, or we'll turn that school out."

I was called to the front of the church to help lead the marchers in a few freedom songs. We sang "Woke Up This Morning With My Mind on Freedom" and "Ain't Gonna Let Nobody Turn Me 'Round." After singing the last song we headed for the streets in a double line, carrying small American flags in our hands. The cops had heard that there were going to be Negroes in the streets all day protesting Medgar's death. They were ready for us.

On Rose Street we ran into a blockade of about two hundred policemen. We were called to a halt by Captain Ray, and asked to disperse. "Everybody ain't got a permit get out of this here parade," Captain Ray said into his bull horn. No one moved. He beckoned to the cops to advance on us.

The cops had rifles and wore steel helmets. They walked right up to us very fast and then sort of engulfed us. They started snatching the small American flags, throwing them to the ground, stepping on them, or stamping them. Students who refused to let go of the flags were jabbed with rifle butts. There was only one paddy wagon on the scene. The first twenty of us were thrown into it, although a paddy wagon is only large enough to seat about ten people. We were sitting and lying all over each other inside the wagon when garbage trucks arrived. We saw the cops stuff about fifty demonstrators in one truck as we looked out through the back glass. Then the driver of the paddy wagon sped away as fast as he could, often making sudden stops in the middle of the street so we would be thrown around.

We thought that they were going to take us to the city jail again because we were college students. We discovered we were headed for the fairgrounds. When we got there, the driver rolled up the windows, turned the heater on, got out, closed the door and left us. It was over a hundred degrees outside that day. There was no air coming in. Sweat began dripping off us. An hour went by. Our clothes were now soaked and sticking to us. Some of the girls looked as though they were about to faint. A policeman looked in to see how we were taking it. Some of the boys begged him to let us out. He only smiled and walked away.

Looking out of the back window again, we noticed they were now booking all the other demonstrators. We realized they had planned to do this to our group. A number of us in the paddy wagon were known to the cops. After the Woolworth sit-in, I had been known to every white in Jackson. I can remember walking down the street and being pointed out by whites as they drove or walked past me.

Suddenly one of the girls screamed. Scrambling to the window, we saw John Salter with blood gushing out of a large hole in the back of his head. He was just standing there dazed and no one was helping him. And we were in no position to help either.

After they let everyone else out of the garbage trucks, they decided to let us out of the paddy wagon. We had now been in there well over two hours. As we were getting out, one of the girls almost fell. A guy started to help her.

"Get ya hands off that gal. Whatta ya think, ya goin' to a prom or somethin'?" one of the cops said.

Water was running down my legs. My skin was soft and spongy. I had hidden a small transistor radio in my bra and some of the other girls had cards and other things in theirs. We had learned to sneak them in after we discovered they didn't search the women but now everything was showing through our wet clothes.

When we got into the compound, there were still some high school students there, since the NAACP bail money had been exhausted. There were altogether well over a hundred and fifty in the girls' section. The boys had been put into a compound directly opposite and parallel to us. Some of the girls who had been arrested after us shared their clothes with us until ours dried. They told us what had happened after we were taken off in the paddy wagon. They said the cops had stuffed so many in the garbage trucks that some were just hanging on. As one of the trucks pulled off, thirteen-year-old John Young fell out. When the driver stopped, the truck rolled back over the boy. He was rushed off to a hospital and they didn't know how badly he had been hurt. They said the cops had gone wild with their billy sticks. They had even arrested Negroes looking on from their porches. John Salter had been forced off some Negro's porch and hit on the head.

The fairgrounds were everything I had heard they were. The compounds they put us in were two large buildings used to auction off cattle during the annual state fair. They were about a block long, with large openings about twenty feet wide on both ends where the cattle were driven in. The openings had been closed up with wire. It reminded me of a concentration camp. It was hot and sticky and girls were walking around half dressed all the time. We were guarded by four policemen. They had rifles and kept an eye on us through the wired sides of the building. As I looked through the wire at them, I imagined myself in Nazi Germany, the policemen Nazi soldiers. They couldn't have been any rougher than these cops. Yet this was America, "the land of the free and the home of the brave."

About five-thirty we were told that dinner was ready. We were lined up single file and marched out of the compound. They had the cook from the city jail there. He was standing over a large garbage can stirring something in it with a stick. The sight of it nauseated me. No one was eating, girls or boys. In the next few days, many were taken from the fairgrounds sick from hunger.

When I got out of jail on Saturday, the day before Medgar's funeral, I had lost about fifteen pounds. They had prepared a special meal on campus for the Tougaloo students, but attempts to eat made me sicker. The food kept coming up. The next morning I pulled myself together enough to make the funeral services at the Masonic temple. I was glad I had gone in spite of my illness. This was the first time I had ever seen so many Negroes together. There were thousands and thousands of them there. Maybe Medgar's death had really brought them to the Movement, I thought. Maybe his death would strengthen the ties between Negroes and Negro organizations. If this resulted, then truly his death was not in vain.

Just before the funeral services were over, I went outside. There was a hill opposite the Masonic Temple. I went up there to watch the procession. I wanted to see every moment of it.

As the pallbearers brought the body out and placed it in a hearse, the tension in the city was as tight as a violin string. There were two or three thousand outside that could not get inside the temple, and as they watched, their expression was that of anger, bitterness, and dismay. They looked as though any moment they were going to start rioting. When Mrs. Evers and her two older children got into their black limousine, Negro women in the crowd began to cry and say things like "That's a shame," . . . "That's a young woman," . . .

"Such well-looking children," . . . "It's a shame, it really is a shame."

Negroes formed a seemingly endless line as they began the march to the funeral home. They got angrier and angrier; however, they went on quietly until they reached the downtown section where the boycott was. They tried to break through the barricades on Capitol Street, but the cops forced them back into line. When they reached the funeral home, the body was taken inside, and most of the procession dispersed. But one hard core of angry Negroes decided they didn't want to go home. With some encouragement from SNCC workers who were singing freedom songs outside the funeral home, these people began walking back toward Capitol Street.

Policemen had been placed along the route of the march, and they were still there. They allowed the crowd of Negroes to march seven blocks, but they formed a solid blockade just short of Capitol Street. This was where they made everyone stop. They had everything—shotguns, fire trucks, gas masks, dogs, fire hoses, and billy clubs. Along the sidewalks and on the fringes of the crowd, the cops knocked heads, set dogs on some marchers, and made about thirty arrests, but the main body of people in the middle of the street was just stopped.

They sang and shouted things like "Shoot, shoot" to the police, and then the police started to push them back slowly. After being pushed back about a block, they stopped. They wouldn't go any farther. So the cops brought the fire trucks up closer and got ready to use the fire hoses on the crowd. That really broke up the demonstration. People moved back faster and started to go home. But it also made them angrier. Bystanders began throwing stones and bottles at the cops and then the crowd started too; other Negroes were pitching stuff from second- and third-story windows. The crowd drew back another block, leaving the space between them and the fire trucks littered with rocks and broken glass. John Doar came out from behind the police barricade and walked toward the crowd of Negroes, with bottles flying all around him. He talked to some of the people at the front, telling them he was from the Justice Department and that this wasn't "the way." After he talked for a few minutes, things calmed down considerably, and Dave Dennis and a few others began taking bottles away from people and telling them they should go home. After that it was just a clean-up operation. One of the ministers borrowed Captain Ray's bull horn and ran up and down the street telling people to disperse, but by that time there were just a few stragglers.

After Medgar's death there was a period of confusion. Each Negro leader and organization in Jackson received threats. They were all told they were "next on the list." Things began to fall apart. The ministers, in particular, didn't want to be "next"; a number of them took that long-promised vacation to Africa or elsewhere. Meanwhile SNCC and CORE became more militant and began to press for more demonstrations. A lot of the young Negroes wanted to let the whites of Jackson know that even by killing off Medgar they hadn't touched the real core of the Movement. For the NAACP and the older, more conservative groups, however, voter registration had now become number one on the agenda. After the NAACP exerted its influence at a number of strategy meetings, the militants lost.

The Jackson *Daily News* seized the opportunity to cause more fragmentation. One day they ran a headline THERE IS A SPLIT IN THE ORGANIZATIONS, and sure enough, shortly afterward, certain organizations had completely severed their relations with each other. The whites had succeeded again. They had reached us through the papers by letting us know we were not together. "Too bad," I thought. "One day we'll learn. It's pretty tough, though, when you have everything against you, including the money, the newspapers, and the cops."

Within a week everything had changed. Even the rallies were not the same. The few ministers and leaders who did come were so scared—they thought assassins were going to follow them home. Soon there were rallies only twice a week instead of every night.

The Sunday following Medgar's funeral, Reverend Ed King organized an integrated church-visiting team of six of us from the college. Another team was organized by a group in Jackson. Five or six churches were hit that day, including Governor Ross Barnett's. At each one they had prepared for our visit with armed policemen, paddy wagons, and dogs—which would be used in case we refused to leave after "ushers" had read us the prepared resolutions. There were about eight of these ushers at each church, and they were never exactly the usherly type. They were more on the order of Al Capone. I think this must have been the first time any of these men had worn a flower in his lapel. When we were asked to leave, we did. We were never even allowed to get past the first step.

A group of us decided that we would go to church again the next Sunday. This time we were quite successful. These visits had not been publicized as the first ones were, and they were not really expecting us. We went first to a Church of Christ, where we were greeted by the regular ushers. After reading us the same resolution we had heard last week, they offered to give us cab fare to the Negro extension of the church. Just as we had refused and were walking away, an old lady stopped us. "We'll sit with you," she said.

We walked back to the ushers with her and her family. "Please let them in, Mr. Calloway. We'll sit with them," the old lady said.

"Mrs. Dixon, the church has decided what is to be done. A resolution has been passed, and we are to abide by it."

"Who are we to decide such a thing? This is a house of God, and God is to make all of the decisions. He is the judge of us all," the lady said.

The ushers got angrier then and threatened to call the police if we didn't leave. We decided to go.

"We appreciate very much what you've done," I said to the old lady.

As we walked away from the church, we noticed the

family leaving by a side entrance. The old lady was waving to us.

Two blocks from the church, we were picked up by Ed King's wife, Jeanette. She drove us to an Episcopal church. She had previously left the other two girls from our team there. She circled the block a couple of times, but we didn't see them anywhere. I suggested that we try the church. "Maybe they got in," I said. Mrs. King waited in the car for us. We walked up to the front of the church. There were no ushers to be seen. Apparently, services had already started. When we walked inside, we were greeted by two ushers who stood at the rear.

"May we help you?" one said.

"Yes," I said. "We would like to worship with you today."

"Will you sign the guest list, please, and we will show you to your seats," said the other.

I stood there for a good five minutes before I was able to compose myself. I had never prayed with white people in a white church before. We signed the guest list and were then escorted to two seats behind the other two girls in our team. We had all gotten in. The church service was completed without one incident. It was as normal as any church service. However, it was by no means normal to me. I was sitting there thinking any moment God would strike the life out of me. I recognized some of the whites, sitting around me in that church. If they were praying to the same God I was, then even God, I thought, was against me.

When the services were over the minister invited us to visit again. He said it as if he meant it, and I began to have a little hope.

Joan Williams

Joan Williams was born in 1928, in Memphis, Tennessee. After she graduated from Bard College in New York, she lived briefly in New Orleans and worked in a bookstore. She then moved to New York City, where she answered letters to the editor for *Look Magazine*. Her first novel, *The Morning and the Evening* (1961), won the John P. Marquand First Novel Award. She sets her fiction in the hill country of northwest Mississippi and focuses on characters who are isolated and alienated from their communities. Her novel, *The Wintering* (1972), based on her friendship with William Faulkner, portrays the relationship between an older man who is a famous author and a young woman who is an aspiring writer. She has written three other novels—*Old Powder Man* (1966), *County Woman* (1982), and *Pay the Piper* (1988)—as well as a collection of short stories, *Pariah and Other Stories* (1983). Her stories have appeared in *Atlantic Monthly*, *Saturday Evening Post*, and *Mademoiselle*. She lives in Westport, Connecticut.

Spring Is Now

Sandra heard first in Miss Loma's store about the Negroes. She was buying cornstarch for her mother when Mr. Mal Walker rushed in, leaving his car at the gas pump, without filling it, to tell the news. His hair plastered to his forehead, he was as breathless and hot as if he had been running. "The school bus was loaded and the driver passed up some niggers in De Soto," he said. "They threw rocks at the bus and a brick that broke the driver's arm." That was all he knew about that. "But," he said, pausing until everyone in the store was paying attention. "There's some registered for your high school in Indian Hill."

At that moment Sandra found the cornstarch. The thought of going to school with Negroes leapt at her as confusedly as the box's yellow-and-blue design. Coming slowly around the bread rack, she saw Mal Walker, rapidly swallowing a Dr. Pepper he had taken from the cold-drink case. She put the cornstarch on the counter. Miss Loma fitted a sack over the box and said, "Is that all?"

Sandra nodded and signed the credit pad Miss Loma shoved along the counter. In Miss Loma's pierced ears, small gold hoops shook as, turning back to Mal Walker, she said, "How many?"

"Three I heard." Almost smiling, he looked around and announced—as if the store were full of people, though there was only an apologetic-looking country woman, with a dime, waiting for the party line to clear— "If your kids haven't eat with niggers yet, they will have by Friday. I thank the Lord I live in Indian Hill. Mine will walk home to lunch. When it comes to eating with them, I draw the line."

"Sandra, you want something else?" Miss Loma said.

"No ma'am." Sandra went out and slowly up the hill toward her house opposite, thinking how many times she had eaten with Minnie, who worked for her mother, and how often her mother had eaten in the kitchen, while Minnie ironed. Even Grandmomma had said she would sit down with Minnie, Minnie was like one of the family, though Sandra could not remember that her grandmother ever had. For one reason, she was always in the living room looking at television. There now, she was shelling butter beans and Sandra passed behind her chair, saying nothing, because Grandmomma was hard of hearing. In the kitchen, Sandra put down the cornstarch and said, "Mother, Mister Mal Walker says there's Negroes coming to our high school."

"Are you sure?" Her mother, Flo, was frying chicken and stood suddenly motionless, a long-handled fork outstretched over the skillet full of popping meat and grease. She and Sandra had similar pale faces and placid gray-green eyes, which they widened now, in worry. "I guess we knew it was coming," Flo said.

"Three, he thinks."

In bifocals, Grandmomma's eyes looked enormous. She stood in the doorway saying, "Three what?" Having seen Flo motionless, she sensed something had happened and hearing what, she threw her hands to her throat and said, "Oh, you don't mean to tell me." With the fork, Flo stuck chicken pieces, lifting them onto paper toweling. "Now, Momma," she said, "we knew it was coming." Then Grandmomma, resigned to one more thing she had not expected to live to see, let her hands fall to her sides. "I sure do hate to hear it," she said. "Are they girls and boys?"

"I don't know," Sandra said.

"I just hope to goodness it's girls," Grandmomma said, looking at Flo, who said again, "Now, Momma."

At sundown, when her father came from the fields, Sandra was watching television with Grandmomma. The pickup stopped, a door slammed, but the motor continued to run. From the window she saw her father, a sturdy, graying man; he was talking to Willson, a field hand, who backed the truck from the drive as her father came inside. "Daddy," she said, "there's Negroes going to our school."

He stood a moment looking tired from more than work. Then he said, "I guess it had to happen." He frowned and his eyebrows drew together across his forehead. "The schools that don't take them don't get government money. I knew you'd be with them at the university. But I'm sorry you had to start a year earlier."

Grandmomma, looking up from her program, said, "I just hope they're girls."

"Oh, Grandmomma," Sandra said with irritation and followed her father across the hall. "Why'd Willson take the truck, Daddy?"

Having bent over the bathroom basin to wash, he lifted his head. "That boy of his sick in Memphis can come home tonight. I loaned him the truck to go get him," he said, and his splashed face seemed weighted by the drops of water falling away.

"The one that's had all that trouble with his leg swelling?" Flo said. She brought the platter of chicken to the table.

"He's on crutches but will be all right," the father said.

"I declare, that boy's had a time," Grandmomma said, joining them at the table. "When Willson brings the truck, give him some of my grape jelly to carry to the boy."

They bent their heads and Sandra's father said his usual long blessing. Afterward they looked at one another across the centerpiece of zinnias, as if words were left unsaid. But no one said anything and they began to eat. Then the father said, "Guess what happened? Willson and some of his friends asked if I'd run for road supervisor."

"Why, Tate," Flo said. "What'd you say?"

"I said, 'When would I find the time?' " he said.

"It shows the way they're thinking," Flo said.

"How?" Sandra said.

"They know they can't run one of them yet, but they want a man elected they choose," she said. "Still, Tate, it's a compliment."

"I guess it is," he said.

"The time's just going to come," Grandmomma said.

"Of course, it is," he said.

At six-fifteen the next morning, Sandra from her bed heard a repeated knock rattling the side door. There were the smells of coffee and sausage, and Flo, summoned, pushed her chair from the table to answer the door. Air-conditioning so early made the house too cold and Sandra, reaching for her thin blanket, kept her eyes closed.

"Morning, how're you?" It was Johnson, the Negro who cleaned the Methodist church. He had come to get his pay from Flo, the church's treasurer.

"Pretty good, Johnson, how're you?" Flo said.

"Good but not pretty." He and Flo laughed, then were quiet while she wrote the check. Sandra heard him walk off down the gravel drive and it seemed a long time before she fell back to sleep. Then Flo shook her, saying, "Louise wants to drive the car pool today. You have to be at school at ten to register. Hurry, it's after nine."

"Why'd Johnson come so early?" she said.

"Breakfast was the only time he knew he could catch me home," Flo said.

Drinking orange juice, Sandra stood by the refrigerator and Grandmomma called from the living room, "Are you going to school all winter with your hair streaming down your back like that? I wish you'd get it cut today."

"I don't want it cut," Sandra said.

"Well, I wish you'd wear it pretty like this girl on television then. Look, with it held back behind a band like that."

Sandra came into the living room to look. "Her hair's in a pageboy; it's shorter than mine," she said.

"At least comb it," her mother called from the kitchen.

"I combed it!" Sandra said.

"Well you need to comb it again," her mother said. "And eat something."

"I'm not hungry in the mornings," Sandra said and went out into the heat and down the steep driveway to wait for her friend Louise. There was no high school in their town and they went twenty miles away to a larger place. "Cold," Sandra said, getting in Louise's car.

"Turn that valve and the air conditioner won't blow straight on you," Louise said. She pushed back hair that fell, like a mane, over her glasses. "You heard?"

"About the Negroes?"

"Yes. I heard there were thirteen."

"Thirteen! I heard three."

Louise laughed. "Maybe there's none and everybody's excited about nothing."

There had been a drought all summer in northwest Mississippi. They rode looking out at cotton fields nowhere near bloom, corn limp and brown, and soybeans stunted, flat to the ground. Between the fields were stretches of crumbly dirt, enormous and empty, where crops failed from the drought had been plowed under. Nearby, a pickup raced along a gravel road and as far as they could see, dust trailed it, one cloud rising above the flatland. Once, workmen along the road turned to them faces yellowed by dust, with dark holes for eyes, and Sandra thought of the worry that had been on her father's face all summer, as farmers waited for rain. And all summer, wherever they went, her mother had said, "You don't remember what it was like before everybody had air-conditioned cars. All this dust blew in the windows. Whew! I don't know how we stood it."

And, not remembering she had said it before, Grandmomma would say, "You don't remember either what it was like trying to sleep. Sometimes we'd move our mattresses out into the yard and sleep under the trees. We'd wring out towels and put them on the bed wet to cool the sheets." That she had lived then, though she did not remember it, seemed strange to Sandra.

At school, she found out only that some Negroes had

already registered. None were there and the teachers would answer no other questions. Standing in long lines all morning, Sandra found she watched for the Negroes anyway. Other students said they had done the same. She thought the Negroes had been paid more attention by being absent than if they had been present. On the way home, Louise said, "If it weren't such a mystery, I don't think I'd think much about them. If there's a few, I just feel I'm not going to bother them and they're not going to bother me, if they're not smart-alecky."

"I know," Sandra said. "What's the difference, three or thirteen, with the rest of us white?" They stopped on the highway at the Mug'n Cone for hot dogs and root beer. Nearing home, Sandra began to dread questions she would be asked, particularly since she knew little more than when she left. At Miss Loma's, she got out to buy shampoo. The old men were gathered on the store porch playing dominoes, and she said only, "Afternoon," though her mother always said they would be glad for conversation. She thought of when her grandfather had been among them and entered the store.

Miss Loma had already heard the news from the Indian Hill school. She and a Memphis salesman were talking about a family nearby, in the Delta, who passed as white, though people steered clear of them, believing they had Negro blood. "I'll tell you how you can always tell a Negro," the salesman said. "By the blue moons on their nails. They can't hide those."

"I've heard," Miss Loma said, her earrings shaking, "they have black streaks at the ends of their spinal cords. Now, that's what men who've been with them in the army say. Of course, I don't know if it's true. I doubt it." She and the salesman could not decide whether she ought to stock up on straight-lined or dotted-lined primary tablets. With a practical finger, Miss Loma twirled the wire school-supply rack. The salesman pushed back a sporty straw hat with a fishing-fly ornament and said, "Wait till school starts and see what the teacher wants. One thing I hate to see is, somebody stuck with primary tablets they can't sell."

An amber container decided Sandra on a shampoo. She brought the bottle to the counter. "I've heard," she said, "they wear makeup on TV that'll make them look whiter."

"Of course they do," Miss Loma said.

Also, Sandra had heard that Negroes never kissed one another. They made love without preliminaries, like animals, or did nothing. But she was afraid to offer that information. Sometimes, even her mother and father did not seem to know she knew people made love.

Miss Loma said, "Honey, take that shampoo on home as a present. Happy birthday."

"How'd you know it was my birthday?"

"A bird told me."

"Grandmomma," Sandra said.

"You heard about the little nigger baby up in Memphis that's two parts animal?" the salesman said.

"No!" Miss Loma said.

"It's got a little dear face and bare feet," the salesman said, and when Sandra went out, he and Miss Loma were laughing.

In his dusty, green pickup, Sandra's father drew up to the gas pump. Willson's wife, along with another Negro woman, stepped from the truck's cab and went into a grocery across the road. "I see you got your nigger women with you today, Tate," said one of the old men playing dominoes.

Lifting the hose, Sandra's father stood putting in gas, laughing. "Yeah, I carried them with me today," he said. "Sandra, I got to go on back to the field. There's a dressed chicken on the front seat Ida sent. Take it on to your momma." Sandra opened the truck's door, thinking how many people made remarks about her father letting Negroes ride up front with him. He always answered that if somebody asked him for a ride, he gave it to them; why should they sit out in the open truck bed covered with dust and hit by gravel? She heard him call into the store, "Four-ninety for gas, Loma," and holding the chicken, Sandra waved as he drove off.

Ida's husband had been a field hand for Sandra's father

and now was too old to work. Sandra's father let the old couple stay on, rent free, in the cabin on his land. Ida raised chickens and brought one to Flo whenever she killed them. When Flo went to the bakery in Indian Hill, she brought Ida something sweet. Sandra came into the kitchen now and put the chicken on the sink. "That's a nice plump one," Flo said. "If we hadn't had chicken last night, I'd put it on to cook. I hope your daddy let Ida know how much we appreciate it."

"He says he always thanks her," Sandra said.

"But I don't know whether he thanks her enough," her mother said.

The kitchen smelled of cake baking and Sandra pretended not to notice. "Aren't you going to ask about the Negroes at school?" she said.

"Honey, I couldn't wait for you to come wandering in. I called around till I found out."

"I don't see why they got to register at a special time. Why couldn't they register when we did?" Sandra said.

"I don't understand it myself," Flo said.

"I don't understand why they have to be there at all," Grandmomma said, on her way to the bathroom during a commercial. "I declare, I don't."

"Oh Grandmomma," Sandra said.

"I guess they didn't want to take chances on trouble during registration," Flo said. "If the Negroes are just there when school starts, no one can say anything."

"There's plenty of things folks could say if they just would," Grandmomma called.

"I thought she was hard of hearing," Sandra said.

"Not all of the time," Flo said. When Grandmomma came back through the kitchen, Flo said, "We haven't had anything to say about what's happened so far. Everything else has just been shoved down our throats, Mother. I don't know why you think we'd have a chance to say anything now." Sandra, going out and down the hall, wondered why her mother bothered trying to explain to Grandmomma. "What are you going to do?" Flo called.

"Wash my hair," Sandra said.

"Well, for heaven's sake, roll it up as tight as you can and try to keep it curled."

"I wish you'd put it behind a band like that girl on television," Grandmomma called, and Sandra closed the bathroom door.

The candles flickered, then burned, as Flo hesitated in the doorway, smiling, before bringing the decorated cake in to supper. The family sang "Happy Birthday" to Sandra. Her father rolled in a portable television atop brass legs and she jumped up with a squeal. Her hair, waved and tied with a ribbon to please them, loosened and fell toward her shoulders. Now she could see programs without arguing with Grandmomma.

Flo's face was in wrinkles, anxious, as though she feared Ida had not been thanked enough for a chicken, and Sandra knew she was to like her grandmomma's present more than ordinarily. On pink tissue paper, in a tiny box, lay a heavy gold pin twisted like rope into a circle. "Why, Grandmomma!" Sandra said in surprise. Her exclamation was taken for admiration and everyone looked pleased. When she had gone into Grandmomma's room as a small child, to poke among her things, she had been shown the pin. Grandmomma's only heirloom, it had been her own mother's. "I've been afraid I wouldn't live till you were sixteen," Grandmomma said. "But I wanted to give you the pin when you were old enough to appreciate it."

"She never would give it even to me," Flo said.

"No, it was to be for my first grandchild," Grandmomma said. "I decided that when Momma died and left it to me. It was all in the world she had to leave and it's all I've got. But I want you to enjoy it now, instead of when I'm gone."

Had she made enough fuss over the pin? Sandra asked later. Flo said she had, but to thank her grandmother occasionally again. "Mother, it's not really the kind of pin anyone wears," Sandra said. The pin hung limply, lopsided, on her striped turtleneck jersey.

Flo said, "It is kind of heavy and antique. Maybe you'll like it when you're grown. Wear it a few times anyway."

The morning that school started, Sandra hung the pin on her coat lapel and forgot it. She walked into her class and there sat a Negro boy. His simply sitting there was disappointing; she felt like a child who had waited so long for Christmas that when it came, it had to be a letdown. He was to be the only Negro in school. The others had changed their minds, the students heard. But by then everyone had heard so many rumors, no one knew what to believe. The Negro was tall and light-skinned. Louise said the officials always tried to send light-skinned ones first. He was noticeably quiet and the girls, at lunch, found he had spoken in none of his classes. Everyone wondered if he was smart enough to be in the school. From her table Sandra saw him eating by a window with several other boys. Still, he seemed alone and she felt sorry for him.

In the car pool with her and Louise were two boys, Don and Mark. Don, the younger, was an athlete. Going home that afternoon, he said the Negro was not the type for football but was so tall, maybe he would be good at basketball. Sandra thought how little she knew about the Negro and how many questions she would be asked. He had worn a blue shirt, she remembered, and he was thin. Certainly, he was clean. Grandmomma would ask that. She did not even know the Negro's name until Don said, "He lives off this road."

"Who?" she said.

"The colored boy, Jack Lawrence," he said.

"We could ask him to be in the car pool," Louise said, laughing.

Mark, sandy-haired and serious, said, "You all better watch your talk. I had my interview at the university this summer and ate lunch in the cafeteria. There were lots of Negroes and all kinds of people. Indians. Not with feathers, from India. Exchange students."

Dust drifted like clouds over fields, and kudzu vine, taking over the countryside, filling ditches and climbing trees, was yellowed by it. Young pines, set out along the road banks, shone beneath a sun that was strong, even going down. Sandra looked out at tiny pink flowers just appearing on the cotton and tried to imagine going as far away, to a place as strange, as India. That Indians had come all the way to Mississippi to school made her think about people's lives in a way she never had. She entered the house saying, before Grandmomma could ask questions, "Grandmomma, you know they got Indians from India going to Ole Miss?"

Grandmomma looked up through the lower half of her glasses. "You don't mean to tell me," she said, and it took away some of her curiosity about the Negro too. At supper, Sandra gave all the information she could. The Negro boy was clean, looked nice, and his name was Jack Lawrence. All the information she could give in the next month was that he went his way and she went hers. Finally even Grandmomma stopped asking questions about him. He and Sandra had no reason to speak until one morning, she was working the combination to her locker when a voice, quite deep, said, "Sandra, you left this under your desk."

Her dark hair fell forward. In the moment that she pushed it back, something in the voice's deep tone made her think unaccountably how soft her own hair felt. Jack Lawrence held out the book she had forgotten, his face expressionless. It would have been much more natural for him to smile. She saw for the first time how carefully impersonal he was. Other students had mentioned that he never spoke, even to teachers, unless spoken to first. She smiled and said, "Lord, math. I'm bad enough without losing the book too. Thanks."

"Okay. I just happened to notice you left it." He started down the hall and Sandra joined him, as she would have anyone going the way she was. She held her books against her, as if hugging herself in anticipation, but of what, she did not know. She had a curiously excited feeling to be walking beside anyone so tall. No, she thought, not anyone, a boy. They talked about the afternoon's football game, then Jack Lawrence continued down the hall and Sandra turned into her class. There was certainly nothing to that, she thought. But Louise, leaning from her desk, whispered, "What were you talking *about*?"

"Football," Sandra said, shrugging. She thought of all the Negroes she had talked to in her life, of those she talked to every day, and wondered why it was strange to talk to Jack Lawrence. Her mother complained that at every meal, Sandra's father had to leave the table, answer the door, and talk to some Negro who worked for him. They would stand together a long time, like any two men, her father propping his foot on the truck's bumper, smoking and talking. Now she wondered what they talked about.

Jack Lawrence's eyes, when she looked into them, had been brown. Were the eyes of all Negroes? From now on, she would notice. On her way to the stadium that afternoon, she wondered if her gaiety was over the football game or the possibility of seeing—not the Negro, she thought, but Jack Lawrence? Louise went ahead of her up the steps and turned into the bleachers. "I have to sit higher," Sandra said, "or I can't see," adding, "Lon's up there." Louise was crazy about Lon, the basketball coach's son, and rising obediently, she followed Sandra to a seat below him. Lon was sitting with Jack Lawrence. Looking up, Sandra smiled but Jack Lawrence turned his eyes to the game and his lips made no movement at all. When she stood to cheer, to buy a Coke, popcorn, a hot dog, Sandra wondered if he watched her. After the game, he and Lon leapt from the bleachers and went out a back way. That night, she slept with a sense of disappointment.

At school, she always nodded and spoke to him and he spoke back: but they did not walk together again. Most often, he was alone. Even to football games, he did not bring a friend. There was a Thanksgiving dance in the gym, festooned with balloons and crepe paper, but he did not come. On Wednesday before the holiday, driving the car pool, Sandra had seen Jack Lawrence walking along a stretch of country road, hunched into his coat. The motor throbbed loudly in the cold country stillness as she stopped the car and said, "You want a ride?"

He stood, looking as if he did not want any favors, but with eyes almost sore-looking from the cold, then climbed into the back seat with Don and Mark. The countryside's stillness came again as Sandra stopped at the side road he mentioned. With coat collar turned up, untangling long legs, he got out. She was aware of the way her hair hung, of her grandmother's pin too old and heavy for her coat, of the skirt that did not cover her knees, which Grandmomma said was indecent. And she was aware of him, standing in the road against the melancholy winter sunset, looking down to say, "Thank you."

"You're welcome," she said, looking up.

That night she asked her father whether she should have given Jack Lawrence a ride. Her father said she was not to give a ride to Negroes when she was alone. "Not even to women?" she said.

"Oh well, to women," he said.

"Not even to Willson?" she said.

Her father seemed to look inward to himself a long time, then he answered, "No, not even to Willson."

Thanksgiving gave Sandra an excuse to start a conversation. She saw Jack Lawrence in the hall the first day afterward and said, "Did you have a nice holiday?"

"Yes," he said. "Did you?"

Sandra mentioned, briefly, things she had done. "Listen," she said. "We go your way every day, if you'd like a ride."

"Thanks," he said, "but most of the time I have one." He turned to his locker and put away his books and Sandra, going on down the hall, had the strangest feeling that he knew something she did not. She remained friendly, smiling when she saw him, though he made no attempt to talk. He only nodded and smiled when they met and she thought he seemed hesitant about doing that. She asked the boys in the car pool questions about him. Why hadn't he gone out for basketball, how were his grades, what did he talk about at lunch, did anybody know exactly where he lived, besides down that side road?—until one day, Louise said, "Sandra, you talk about that Negro so much, I think you like him."

"Yes, I like him. I mean, I don't dislike him, do you? What reason would we have?"

"No, I don't dislike him," Louise said. "He's not at all smart-alecky."

In winter when they came home from school, it was dark. Flo said, "If you didn't have those boys in your car pool, I'd drive you girls back and forth myself. I don't know what Don and Mark could do if anything happened, but I feel better they're there." Sandra's parents, everyone, lived in fear of something happening. South of them, in the Delta, there was demonstrating, and Negroes tried to integrate restaurants and movies in several larger towns. Friends of Sandra's mother began carrying tear gas and pistols in their pocketbooks. Repeatedly, at the dinner table, in Miss Loma's, Sandra heard grown-ups say, "It's going to get worse before it gets any better. We won't see the end of this in our lifetime." Grandmomma always added, "I just hate to think what Sandra and her children will live to see."

One day after Christmas vacation, those in the car pool again saw Jack Lawrence walking along the road. "Should we stop?" Louise said. She was driving, with Don beside her.

"Of course. Would you just drive past him?" Sandra said. She was sitting in the back seat with Mark, and when Jack Lawrence climbed into the car, she was sitting between them. They spoke of the cold, of the snow that had fallen after Christmas, the deepest they could ever remember, and of how you came across patches of it, still, in unexpected places. Side roads were full of frozen ruts. Jack Lawrence said he hated to think of the mud when a thaw came. There could be one at any time. That was the way their weather was. In the midst of winter, you could suddenly have a stretch of bright, warm, almost spring days. There was a silence and Jack Lawrence, looking down at Sandra, said, "Did you lose that pin you always wear?"

"Oh Lord," Sandra said, her hand going quickly, flat, against her lapel.

"Sandra, your grandmomma's pin!" Louise said, looking into the rearview mirror.

"Maybe it fell off in the car," Mark said. The three in back put their hands down the cracks around the seat. Sandra felt in her pockets, shook out her skirt. They held their feet up and looked under them. Don, turning, said, "Look up under the front seat."

Bending forward at the same instant, Sandra and Jack Lawrence knocked their heads together sharply. "Ow!" Mark cried out for them, while tears came to Sandra's eyes. They clutched their heads. Their faces were close, and though Sandra saw yellow, dancing dots, she thought, Of course Negroes kiss each other when they make love. She and Jack Lawrence fell back against the seat laughing, and seemed to laugh for miles, until she clutched her stomach in pain.

"Didn't it hurt? How can you laugh so?" Louise said.

"I got a hard head," Jack Lawrence said.

When he stood again in the road thanking them, his eyes, glancing into the car, held no message for Sandra. Tomorrow, he said silently, by ignoring her, they would smile and nod. That they had been for a time two people laughing together was enough. As they rode on, Sandra held tightly the pin he had found, remembering how she had looked at it one moment lying in his dark hand, with the lighter palm, and the next moment, she had touched the hand lightly, taking the pin. Opening her purse, she dropped the pin inside.

"Is the clasp broken?" Mark said.

"No, I guess I didn't have it fastened good," she said.

"Aren't you going to wear it anymore?" Louise said, looking back.

"No," she said.

"What will your grandmomma say?" Louise said.

"Nothing I can worry about," Sandra said.

William Faulkner

William Faulkner was born in 1897 in New Albany, Mississippi, and died in 1962. His great-grandfather, who bears some resemblance to Colonel Sartoris in the story that follows, built railroads, served in the Confederate Army, and wrote a novel called *The White Rose of Memphis* (1880). Faulkner himself worked a variety of jobs from postmaster to poet before he took writer Sherwood Anderson's advice and began to write fiction about the region where he grew up. Faulkner created a fictional county, Yoknapatawpha, with a county seat he called Jefferson, which was based on his hometown of Oxford, Mississippi. Returning to Oxford after a year in New Orleans, Faulkner began a period of incredible creativity, during which he wrote his most highly praised work: *Sartoris* (1929, an abridged version of *Flags in the Dust*, 1973), *The Sound and the Fury* (1929), *As I Lay Dying* (1930), *Sanctuary* (1931), *Light in August* (1932), *Absalom, Absalom!* (1936), *The Unvanquished* (1938), *The Hamlet* (1940), and *Go Down, Moses and Other Stories* (1942). More concerned with writing the way he wanted than with writing works that would sell, Faulkner often found himself short of cash. During these times he went to Hollywood to write screenplays for Metro-Goldwyn-Mayer and for Warner Brothers. Elected to the National Institute of Arts and Letters and the American Academy of Arts and Letters, Faulkner is the most honored writer in the United States. He won several O. Henry awards for his stories, two National Book Awards, the Pulitzer Prize, and the Nobel Prize for *A Fable* (1954). During the last years of his life, he was a writer-in-residence at the University of Virginia. The selection from *The Unvanquished* that follows points up several of his key themes: the problem of the past, the young boy's initiation into manhood, the clash between the individual and the community, and the sins of parents being visited on children. The selection also reveals his idiosyncratic style—convoluted sentences, repetition of words, minimal punctuation, and vague pronoun references. Helen Swink has suggested that his sentences, which often withhold meaning from readers, "intensify the emotional experience," and Michael Millgate has observed that they allow Faulkner "to hold a single moment in suspension while its full complexity is explored."

"An Odor of Verbena" is the last section in Faulkner's novel, *The Unvanquished* (1938). The narrator, Bayard Sartoris, is a law student at the University of Mississippi and a member of an old family in Jefferson, Mississippi. The Civil War has been over for seven years when his father, Colonel Sartoris, is killed by his business partner, B. J. Redmond. Bayard is under great pressure from the community, from his young stepmother Drusilla, from his servant Ringo, and from members of his father's Confederate troop to avenge his death. During the war, Bayard's grandmother was killed by a man named Grumby, and Bayard and Ringo found and killed him. But this killing and the brutality of war, so very different from his genteel upbringing, have had a traumatic effect on Bayard.

An Odor of Verbena

1

It was just after supper. I had just opened my *Coke* on the table beneath the lamp; I heard Professor Wilkins' feet in the hall and then the instant of silence as he put his hand to the door knob, and I should have known. People talk glibly of presentiment, but I had none. I heard his feet on the stairs and then in the hall approaching and there was nothing in the feet because although I had lived in his house for three college years now and although both he and Mrs. Wilkins called me Bayard in the house, he would no more have entered my room without knocking than I would have entered his—or hers. Then he flung the door violently inward against the doorstop with one of those gestures with or by which an almost painfully unflagging preceptory of youth ultimately aberrates, and stood there saying, "Bayard. Bayard, my son, my dear son."

I should have known; I should have been prepared. Or maybe I was prepared because I remember how I closed the book carefully, even marking the place, before I rose. He (Professor Wilkins) was doing something, bustling at something; it was my hat and cloak which he handed me and which I took although I would not need the cloak, unless even then I was thinking (although it was October, the equinox had not occurred) that the rains and the cool weather would arrive before I should see this room again and so I would need the cloak anyway to return to it if I returned, thinking 'God, if he had only done this last night, flung that door crashing and bouncing against the stop last night without knocking so I could have gotten there before it happened, been there when it did, beside him on whatever spot, wherever it was that he would have to fall and lie in the dust and dirt.'

"Your boy is downstairs in the kitchen," he said. It was not until years later that he told me (someone did; it must have been Judge Wilkins) how Ringo had apparently flung the cook aside and come on into the house and into the library where he and Mrs. Wilkins were sitting and said without preamble and already turning to withdraw: "They shot Colonel Sartoris this morning. Tell him I be waiting in the kitchen" and was gone before either of them could move. "He has ridden forty miles yet he refuses to eat anything." We were moving toward the door now—the door on my side of which I had lived for three years now with what I knew, what I knew now I must have believed and expected, yet beyond which I had heard the approaching feet yet heard nothing in the feet. "If there was just anything I could do."

"Yes, sir," I said. "A fresh horse for my boy. He will want to go back with me."

"By all means take mine—Mrs. Wilkins'," he cried. His tone was no different yet he did cry it and I suppose that at the same moment we both realised that was funny—a short-legged deep-barreled mare who looked exactly like a spinster music teacher, which Mrs. Wilkins drove to a basket phaeton—which was good for me, like being doused with a pail of cold water would have been good for me.

"Thank you, sir," I said. "We won't need it. I will get a fresh horse for him at the livery stable when I get my mare." Good for me, because even before I finished speaking I knew that would not be necessary either, that Ringo would have stopped at the livery stable before he came out to the college and attended to that and that the fresh horse for him and my mare both would be saddled and waiting now at the side fence and we would not have to go through Oxford at all. Loosh would not have thought of that if he had come for me, he would have come straight to the college, the Professor Wilkins', and told his news and then sat down and let me take charge from then on. But not Ringo.

He followed me from the room. From now until Ringo and I rode away into the hot thick dusty darkness quick and strained for the overdue equinox like a laboring delayed woman, he would be somewhere either just beside me or just behind me and I never to know exactly nor care which. He was trying to find the words with which to offer me his pistol too. I could almost hear him: "Ah, this unhappy land, not ten years recovered from the fever yet still men must kill one another, still we must pay Cain's price in his own coin." But he did not actually say it. He just followed me, somewhere beside or behind me as we descended the stairs toward where Mrs. Wilkins waited in the hall beneath the chandelier— a thin gray woman who reminded me of Granny, not that she looked like Granny probably but because she had known Granny—a lifted anxious still face which was thinking *Who lives by the sword shall die by it* just as Granny would have thought, toward which I walked, had to walk not because I was Granny's grandson and had lived in her house for three college years and was about the age of her son when he was killed in almost the last battle nine years ago, but because I was now The Sartoris. (The Sartoris: that had been one of the concomitant flashes, along with the *at last it has happened* when Professor Wilkins opened my door.) She didn't offer me a horse and pistol, not because she liked me any less than Professor Wilkins but because she was a woman and so wiser than any man, else the men would not have gone on with the War for two years after they knew they were whipped. She just put her hands (a small woman, no bigger than Granny had been) on my shoulders and said, "Give my love to Drusilla and your Aunt Jenny. And come back when you can."

"Only I don't know when that will be," I said. "I don't know how many things I will have to attend to." Yes, I lied even to her; it had not been but a minute yet since he had flung that door bouncing into the stop yet already

I was beginning to realise, to become aware of that which I still had no yardstick to measure save that one consisting of what, despite myself, despite my raising and background (or maybe because of them) I had for some time known I was becoming and had feared the test of it; I remember how I thought while her hands still rested on my shoulders: *At least this will be my chance to find out if I am what I think I am or if I just hope; if I am going to do what I have taught myself is right or if I am just going to wish I were.*

We went on to the kitchen, Professor Wilkins still somewhere beside or behind me and still offering me the pistol and horse in a dozen different ways. Ringo was waiting; I remember how I thought then that no matter what might happen to either of us, I would never be The Sartoris to him. He was twenty-four too, but in a way he had changed even less than I had since that day when we had nailed Grumby's body to the door of the old compress. Maybe it was because he had outgrown me, had changed so much that summer while he and Granny traded mules with the Yankees that since then I had had to do most of the changing just to catch up with him. He was sitting quietly in a chair beside the cold stove, spent-looking too who had ridden forty miles (at one time, either in Jefferson or when he was alone at last on the road somewhere, he had cried; dust was now caked and dried in the tear-channels on his face) and would ride forty more yet would not eat, looking up at me a little red-eyed with weariness (or maybe it was more than just weariness and so I would never catch up with him) then rising without a word and going on toward the door and I following and Professor Wilkins still offering the horse and the pistol without speaking the words and still thinking (I could feel that too) *Dies by the sword. Dies by the sword.*

Ringo had the two horses saddled at the side gate, as I had known he would—the fresh one for himself and my mare father had given me three years ago, that could do a mile under two minutes any day and a mile every eight minutes all day long. He was already mounted when I realised that what Professor Wilkins wanted was to shake my hand. We shook hands; I knew he believed he was touching flesh which might not be alive tomorrow night and I thought for a second how if I told him what I was going to do, since we had talked about it, about how if there was anything at all in the Book, anything of hope and peace for His blind and bewildered spawn which He had chosen above all others to offer immortality, *Thou shalt not kill* must be it, since maybe he even believed that he had taught it to me except that he had not, nobody had, not even myself since it went further than just having been learned. But I did not tell him. He was too old to be forced so, to condone even in principle such a decision; he was too old to have to stick to principle in the face of blood and raising and background, to be faced without warning and made to deliver like by a highwayman out of the dark: only the young could do that—one still young enough to have his youth supplied him gratis as a reason (not an excuse) for cowardice.

So I said nothing. I just shook his hand and mounted too, and Ringo and I rode on. We would not have to pass through Oxford now and so soon (there was a thin sickle of moon like the heel print of a boot in wet sand) the road to Jefferson lay before us, the road which I had travelled for the first time three years ago with Father and travelled twice at Christmas time and then in June and September and twice at Christmas time again and then June and September again each college term since alone on the mare, not even knowing that this was peace; and now this time and maybe last time who would not die (I knew that) but who maybe forever after could never again hold up his head. The horses took the gait which they would hold for forty miles. My mare knew the long road ahead and Ringo had a good beast too, had talked Hilliard at the livery stable out of a good horse too. Maybe it was the tears, the channels of dried mud across which his strain-reddened eyes had looked at me, but I rather think it was that same quality which used to enable him to replenish his and Granny's supply of United States Army letterheads during that time—

some outrageous assurance gained from too long and too close association with white people: the one whom he called Granny, the other with whom he had slept from the time we were born until Father rebuilt the house. We spoke one time, then no more:

"We could bushwhack him," he said. "Like we done Grumby that day. But I reckon that wouldn't suit that white skin you walks around in."

"No," I said. We rode on; it was October; there was plenty of time still for verbena although I would have to reach home before I would realise there was a need for it; plenty of time for verbena yet from the garden where Aunt Jenny puttered beside old Joby, in a pair of Father's old cavalry gauntlets, among the coaxed and ordered beds, the quaint and ordorous old names, for though it was October no rain had come yet and hence no frost to bring (or leave behind) the first half-warm half-chill nights of Indian Summer—the drowsing air cool and empty for geese yet languid still with the old hot dusty smell of fox grape and sassafras—the nights when before I became a man and went to college to learn law Ringo and I, with lantern and axe and crokersack and six dogs (one to follow the trail and five more just for the tonguing, the music) would hunt possum in the pasture where, hidden, we had seen our first Yankee that afternoon on the bright horse, where for the last year now you could hear the whistling of the trains which had no longer belonged to Mr. Redmond for a long while now and which at some instant, some second during the morning Father too had relinquished along with the pipe which Ringo said he was smoking, which slipped from his hand as he fell. We rode on, toward the house where he would be lying in the parlor now, in his regimentals (sabre too) and where Drusilla would be waiting for me beneath all the festive glitter of the chandeliers, in the yellow ball gown and the sprig of verbena in her hair, holding the two loaded pistols (I could see that too, who had had no presentiment; I could see her, in the formal brilliant room arranged formally for obsequy, not tall, not slender as a woman is but as a youth, a boy, is motionless, in yellow, the face calm, almost bemused, the head simple and severe, the balancing sprig of verbena above each ear, the two arms bent at the elbows, the two hands shoulder high, the two identical duelling pistols lying upon, not clutched in, one to each: the Greek amphora priestess of a succinct and formal violence).

2

Drusilla said that he had a dream. I was twenty then and she and I would walk in the garden in the summer twilight while we waited for Father to ride in from the railroad. I was just twenty then: that summer before I entered the University to take the law degree which Father decided I should have and four years after the one, the day, the evening when Father and Drusilla had kept old Cash Benbow from becoming United States Marshal and returned home still unmarried and Mrs. Habersham herded them into her carriage and drove them back to town and dug her husband out of his little dim hole in the new bank and made him sign Father's peace bond for killing the two carpet baggers, and took Father and Drusilla to the minister herself and saw that they were married. And Father had rebuilt the house too, on the same blackened spot, over the same cellar, where the other had burned, only larger, much larger: Drusilla said that the house was the aura of Father's dream just as a bride's trousseau and veil is the aura of hers. And Aunt Jenny had come to live with us now so we had the garden (Drusilla would no more have bothered with flowers than Father himself would have, who even now, even four years after it was over, still seemed to exist, breathe, in that last year of it while she had ridden in man's clothes and with her hair cut short like any other member of Father's troop, across Georgia and both Carolinas in front of Sherman's army) for her to gather sprigs of verbena from to wear in her hair because she said verbena was the only scent you could smell above the smell of horses and courage and so it was the only one that was worth the wearing. The railroad was hardly begun then and Father and Mr. Redmond were not only still partners, they were still friends, which as George Wyatt said was easily a record for Father, and he would leave the house at daybreak on Jupiter, riding up and down the unfinished line with two saddlebags of gold coins borrowed on Friday to pay the men on Saturday, keeping just two cross-ties ahead of the sheriff as Aunt Jenny said. So we walked in the dusk, slowly between Aunt Jenny's flower beds while Drusilla (in a dress now, who still would have worn pants all the time if Father had let her) leaned lightly on my arm and I smelled the verbena in her hair as I had smelled the rain in it and in Father's beard that night four years ago when he and Drusilla and Uncle Buck McCaslin found Grumby and then came home and found Ringo and me more than just asleep: escaped into that oblivion which God or Nature or whoever it was had supplied us with for the time being, who had had to perform more than should be required of children because there should be some limit to the age, the youth at least below which one should not have to kill. This was just after the Saturday night when he returned and I watched him clean the derringer and reload it and we learned that the dead man was almost a neighbor, a hill man who had been in the first infantry regiment when it voted Father out of command: and we never to know if the man actually intended to rob Father or not because Father had shot too quick, but only that he had a wife and several children in a dirt-floored cabin in the hills, to whom Father the next day sent some money and she (the wife) walked into the house two days later while we were sitting at the dinner table and flung the money at Father's face.

"But nobody could have more of a dream than Colonel Sutpen," I said. He had been Father's second-in-command in the first regiment and had been elected colonel when the regiment deposed Father after Second Manassas, and it was Sutpen and not the regiment whom Father never forgave. He was underbred, a cold ruthless man who had come into the country about thirty years before the War, nobody knew from where except Father said you could look at him and know he would not dare to tell. He had got some land and nobody knew how he did that either, and he got money from somewhere— Father said they all believed he robbed steamboats, either as a card sharper or as an out-and-out highway-man—and built a big house and married and set up as a gentleman. Then he lost everything in the War like everybody else, all hope of descendants too (his son killed his daughter's fiancé on the eve of the wedding and vanished) yet he came back home and set out sin-glehanded to rebuild his plantation. He had no friends to borrow from and he had nobody to leave it to and he was past sixty years old, yet he set out to rebuild his place like it used to be; they told how he was too busy to bother with politics or anything; how when Father and the other men organised the nightriders to keep the car-pet baggers from organising the Negroes into an insurrec-tion, he refused to have anything to do with it. Father stopped hating him long enough to ride out to see Sutpen himself and he (Sutpen) came to the door with a lamp and did not even invite them to come in and discuss it; Father said, "Are you with us or against us?" and he said, "I'm for my land. If every man of you would reha-bilitate his own land, the country will take care of itself" and Father challenged him to bring the lamp out and set it on a stump where they could both see to shoot and Sutpen would not. "Nobody could have more of a dream than that."

"Yes. But his dream is just Sutpen. John's is not. He is thinking of this whole country which he is trying to raise by its bootstraps, so that all the people in it, not just his kind nor his old regiment, but all the people, black and white, the women and children back in the hills who don't even own shoes—Don't you see?"

"But how can they get any good from what he wants to do for them if they are—after he has——"

"Killed some of them? I suppose you include those two carpet baggers he had to kill to hold that first elec-tion, don't you?"

"They were men. Human beings."

"They were Northerners, foreigners who had no business here. They were pirates." We walked on, her weight hardly discernible on my arm, her head just reaching my shoulder. I had always been a little taller than she, even on that night at Hawkhurst while we listened to the niggers passing in the road, and she had changed but little since—the same boy-hard body, the close implacable head with its savagely cropped hair which I had watched from the wagon above the tide of crazed singing niggers as we went down into the river—the body not slender as women are but as boys are slender. "A dream is not a very safe thing to be near, Bayard. I know; I had one once. It's like a loaded pistol with a hair trigger: if it stays alive long enough, somebody is going to be hurt. But if it's a good dream, it's worth it. There are not many dreams in the world, but there are a lot of human lives. And one human life or two dozen——"

"Are not worth anything?"

"No. Not anything.—Listen. I hear Jupiter. I'll beat you to the house." She was already running, the skirts she did not like to wear lifted almost to her knees, her legs beneath it running as boys run just as she rode like men ride.

I was twenty then. But the next time I was twenty-four; I had been three years at the University and in another two weeks I would ride back to Oxford for the final year and my degree. It was just last summer, last August, and Father had just beat Redmond for the State legislature. The railroad was finished now and the partnership between Father and Redmond had been dissolved so long ago that most people would have forgotten they were ever partners if it hadn't been for the enmity between them. There had been a third partner but nobody hardly remembered his name now; he and his name both had vanished in the fury of the conflict which set up between Father and Redmond almost before they began to lay the rails, between Father's violent and ruthless dictatorialness and will to dominate (the idea was his; he did think of the railroad first and then took Redmond in) and that quality in Redmond (as George Wyatt said, he was not a coward or Father would never have teamed with him) which permitted him to stand as much as he did from Father, to bear and bear and bear until something (not his will nor his courage) broke in him. During the War Redmond had not been a soldier, he had had something to do with cotton for the Government; he could have made money himself out of it but he had not and everybody knew he had not, Father knew it, yet Father would even taunt him with not having smelled powder. He was wrong; he knew he was when it was too late for him to stop just as a drunkard reaches a point where it is too late for him to stop, where he promises himself that he will and maybe believes he will or can but it is too late. Finally they reached the point (they had both put everything they could mortgage or borrow into it for Father to ride up and down the line, paying the workmen and the waybills on the rails at the last possible instant) where even Father realised that one of them would have to get out. So (they were not speaking then; it was arranged by Judge Benbow) they met and agreed to buy or sell, naming a price which, in reference to what they had put into it, was ridiculously low but which each believed the other could not raise—at least Father claimed that Redmond did not believe he could raise it. So Redmond accepted the price, and found out that Father had the money. And according to Father, that's what started it, although Uncle Buck McCaslin said Father could not have owned a half interest in even one hog, let alone a railroad, and not dissolve the business either sworn enemy or death-pledged friend to his recent partner. So they parted and Father finished the road. By that time, seeing that he was going to finish it, some Northern people sold him a locomotive on credit which he named for Aunt Jenny, with a silver oil can in the cab with her name engraved on it; and last summer the first train ran into Jefferson, the engine decorated with flowers and Father in the cab blowing blast after blast on the whistle when he passed Redmond's house; and there were speeches at the station, with more flowers and a Confederate flag and girls in white dresses and red sashes and a band, and Father stood on the pilot of the engine and made a direct and absolutely needless allusion to Mr. Redmond. That was it. He wouldn't let him alone. George Wyatt came to me right afterward and told me. "Right or wrong," he said, "us boys and most of the other folks in this county know John's right. But he ought to let Redmond alone. I know what's wrong: he's had to kill too many folks, and that's bad for a man. We all know Colonel's brave as a lion, but Redmond ain't no coward either and there ain't any use in making a brave man that made one mistake eat crow all the time. Can't you talk to him?"

"I don't know," I said. "I'll try." But I had no chance. That is, I could have talked to him and he would have listened, but he could not have heard me because he had stepped straight from the pilot of that engine into the race for the Legislature. Maybe he knew that Redmond would have to oppose him to save his face even though he (Redmond) must have known that, after that train ran into Jefferson, he had no chance against Father, or maybe Redmond had already announced his candidacy and Father entered the race just because of that, I don't remember. Anyway they ran, a bitter contest in which Father continued to badger Redmond without reason or need, since they both knew it would be a landslide for Father. And it was, and we thought he was satisfied. Maybe he thought so himself, as the drunkard believes that he is done with drink; and it was that afternoon and Drusilla and I walked in the garden in the twilight and I said something about what George Wyatt had told me and she released my arm and turned me to face her and said, "This from you? You? Have you forgotten Grumby?"

"No," I said. "I never will forget him."

"You never will. I wouldn't let you. There are worse things than killing men, Bayard. There are worse things than being killed. Sometimes I think the finest thing that can happen to a man is to love something, a woman preferably, well, hard hard hard, then to die young because he believed what he could not help but believe

and was what he could not (could not? would not) help
but be." Now she was looking at me in a way she never
had before. I did not know what it meant then and was
not to know until tonight since neither of us knew then
that two months later Father would be dead. I just
knew that she was looking at me as she never had before
and that the scent of the verbena in her hair seemed to
have increased a hundred times, to have got a hundred
times stronger, to be everywhere in the dusk in which
something was about to happen which I had never
dreamed of. Then she spoke. "Kiss me, Bayard."

"No. You are Father's wife."

"And eight years older than you are. And your fourth
cousin too. And I have black hair. Kiss me, Bayard."

"No."

"Kiss me, Bayard." So I leaned my face down to her.
But she didn't move, standing so, bent lightly back from
me from the waist, looking at me; now it was she who
said, "No." So I put my arms around her. Then she came
to me, melted as women will and can, the arms with
the wrist- and elbow-power to control horses about my
shoulders, using the wrists to hold my face to hers until
there was no longer need for the wrists; I thought then
of the woman of thirty, the symbol of the ancient and
eternal Snake and of the men who have written of her,
and I realised then the immitigable chasm between all
life and all print—that those who can, do, those who
cannot and suffer enough because they can't, write about
it. Then I was free, I could see her again, I saw her still
watching me with that dark inscrutable look, looking up
at me now across her down-slanted face; I watched her
arms rise with almost the exact gesture with which she
had put them around me as if she were repeating the
empty and formal gesture of all promise so that I should
never forget it, the elbows angling outward as she put
her hands to the sprig of verbena in her hair, I standing
straight and rigid facing the slightly bent head, the short
jagged hair, the rigid curiously formal angle of the bare
arms gleaming faintly in the last of light as she removed
the verbena sprig and put it into my lapel, and I thought

how the War had tried to stamp all the women of her
generation and class in the South into a type and how it
had failed—the suffering, the identical experience (hers
and Aunt Jenny's had been almost the same except that
Aunt Jenny had spent a few nights with her husband
before they brought him back home in an ammunition
wagon while Gavin Breckbridge was just Drusilla's
fiancé) was there in the eyes, yet beyond that was the
incorrigibly individual woman: not like so many men who
return from wars to live on Government reservations like
so many steers, emasculate and empty of all save an identical experience which they cannot forget and dare not,
else they would cease to live at that moment, almost
interchangeable save for the old habit of answering to a
given name.

"Now I must tell Father," I said.

"Yes," she said. "You must tell him. Kiss me." So
again it was like it had been before. No. Twice, a thousand times and never like—the eternal and symbolical
thirty to a young man, a youth, each time both cumula-
tive and retroactive, immitigably unrepetitive, each wherein
remembering excludes experience, each wherein experience antedates remembering; the skill without weariness,
the knowledge virginal to surfeit, the cunning secret mus-
cles to guide and control just as within the wrists and
elbows lay slumbering the mastery of horses: she stood
back, already turning, not looking at me when she spoke,
never having looked at me, already moving swiftly on in
the dusk: "Tell John. Tell him tonight."

I intended to. I went to the house and into the office
at once; I went to the center of the rug before the cold
hearth, I don't know why, and stood there rigid like soldiers stand, looking at eye level straight across the room
and above his head and said "Father" and then stopped.
Because he did not even hear me. He said, "Yes,
Bayard?" but he did not hear me although he was sitting
behind the desk doing nothing, immobile, as still as I
was rigid, one hand on the desk with a dead cigar in it,
a bottle of brandy and a filled and untasted glass beside
his hand, clothed quiet and bemused in whatever triumph

it was he felt since the last overwhelming return of votes had come in late in the afternoon. So I waited until after supper. We went to the dining room and stood side by side until Aunt Jenny entered and then Drusilla, in the yellow ball gown, who walked straight to me and gave me one fierce inscrutable look then went to her place and waited for me to draw her chair while Father drew Aunt Jenny's. He had roused by then, not to talk himself but rather to sit at the head of the table and reply to Drusilla as she talked with a sort of feverish and glittering volubility—to reply now and then to her with that courteous intolerant pride which had lately become a little forensic, as if merely being in a political contest filled with fierce and empty oratory had retroactively made a lawyer of him who was anything and everything except a lawyer. Then Drusilla and Aunt Jenny rose and left us and he said, "Wait" to me who had made no move to follow and directed Joby to bring one of the bottles of wine which he had fetched back from New Orleans when he went there last to borrow money to liquidate his first private railroad bonds. Then I stood again like soldiers stand, gazing at eye level above his head while he sat half-turned from the table, a little paunchy now though not much, a little grizzled too in the hair though his beard was as strong as ever, with that spurious forensic air of lawyers and the intolerant eyes which in the last two years had acquired that transparent film which the eyes of carnivorous animals have and from behind which they look at a world which no ruminant ever sees, perhaps dares to see, which I have seen before on the eyes of men who have killed too much, who have killed so much that never again as long as they live will they ever be alone. I said again, "Father," then I told him.

"Hah?" he said. "Sit down." I sat down, I looked at him, watched him fill both glasses and this time I knew it was worse with him than not hearing: it didn't even matter. "You are doing well in the law, Judge Wilkins tells me. I am pleased to hear that. I have not needed you in my affairs so far, but from now on I shall. I have now accomplished the active portion of my aims in which you could not have helped me; I acted as the land and the time demanded and you were too young for that, I wished to shield you. But now the land and the time too are changing; what will follow will be a matter of consolidation, of pettifogging and doubtless chicanery in which I would be a babe in arms but in which you, trained in the law, can hold your own—our own. Yes, I have accomplished my aim, and now I shall do a little moral house-cleaning. I am tired of killing men, no matter what the necessity nor the end. Tomorrow, when I go to town and meet Ben Redmond, I shall be unarmed."

3

We reached home just before midnight; we didn't have to pass through Jefferson either. Before we turned in the gates I could see the lights, the chandeliers—hall, parlor, and what Aunt Jenny (without any effort or perhaps even design on her part) had taught even Ringo to call the drawing room, the light falling outward across the portico, past the columns. Then I saw the horses, the faint shine of leather and buckle-glints on the black silhouettes and then the men too—Wyatt and others of Father's old troop—and I had forgot that they would be there. I had forgot that they would be there; I remember how I thought, since I was tired and spent with strain, *Now it will have to begin tonight. I won't even have until tomorrow in which to begin to resist.* They had a watchman, a picquet out, I suppose, because they seemed to know at once that we were in the drive. Wyatt met me, I halted the mare, I could look down at him and at the others gathered a few yards behind him with that curious vulture-like formality which Southern men assume in such situations.

"Well, boy," George said.

"Was it—" I said. "Was he——"

"It was all right. It was in front. Redmond ain't no coward. John had the derringer inside his cuff like always, but he never touched it, never made a move toward it." I have seen him do it, he showed me once:

the pistol (it was not four inches long) held flat inside
his left wrist by a clip he made himself of wire and an
old clock spring; he would raise both hands at the same
time, cross them, fire the pistol from beneath his left
hand almost as if he were hiding from his own vision
what he was doing; when he killed one of the men he
shot a hole through his own coat sleeve. "But you want
to get on to the house," Wyatt said. He began to stand
aside, then he spoke again: "We'll take this off your
hands, any of us. Me." I hadn't moved the mare yet and
I had made no move to speak, yet he continued quickly,
as if he had already rehearsed all this, his speech and
mine, and knew what I would say and only spoke himself
as he would have removed his hat on entering a house
or used 'sir' in conversing with a stranger: "You're
young, just a boy, you ain't had any experience in this
kind of thing. Besides, you got them two ladies in the
house to think about. He would understand, all right."

"I reckon I can attend to it," I said.

"Sure," he said; there was no surprise, nothing at all,
in his voice because he had already rehearsed this: "I
reckon we all knew that's what you would say." He
stepped back then; almost it was as though he and not I
bade the mare to move on. But they all followed, still
with that unctuous and voracious formality. Then I saw
Drusilla standing at the top of the front steps, in the light
from the open door and the windows like a theatre scene,
in the yellow ball gown and even from here I believed
that I could smell the verbena in her hair, standing there
motionless yet emanating something louder than the two
shots must have been—something voracious too and passionate. Then, although I had dismounted and someone
had taken the mare, I seemed to be still in the saddle
and to watch myself enter that scene which she had postulated like another actor while in the background for
chorus Wyatt and the others stood with the unctuous
formality which the Southern man shows in the presence
of death—that Roman holiday engendered by mist-born
Protestantism grafted onto this land of violent sun, of
violent alteration from snow to heat-stroke which has

produced a race impervious to both. I mounted the steps toward the figure straight and yellow and immobile as a candle which moved only to extend one hand; we stood together and looked down at them where they stood clumped, the horses too gathered in a tight group beyond them at the rim of light from the brilliant door and windows. One of them stamped and blew his breath and jangled his gear.

"Thank you, gentlemen," I said. "My aunt and my— Drusilla thank you. There's no need for you to stay. Goodnight." They murmured, turning. George Wyatt paused, looking back at me.

"Tomorrow?" he said.

"Tomorrow." Then they went on, carrying their hats and tiptoeing, even on the ground, the quiet and resilient earth, as though anyone in that house awake would try to sleep, anyone already asleep in it whom they could have wakened. Then they were gone and Drusilla and I turned and crossed the portico, her hand lying light on my wrist yet discharging into me with a shock like electricity that dark and passionate voracity, the face at my shoulder—the jagged hair with a verbena sprig above each ear, the eyes staring at me with that fierce exaltation. We entered the hall and crossed it, her hand guiding me without pressure, and entered the parlor. Then for the first time I realised it—the alteration which is death— not that he was now just clay but that he was lying down. But I didn't look at him yet because I knew that when I did I would begin to pant; I went to Aunt Jenny who had just risen from a chair behind which Louvinia stood. She was Father's sister, taller than Drusilla but no older, whose husband had been killed at the very beginning of the War, by a shell from a Federal frigate at Fort Moultrie, come to us from Carolina six years ago. Ringo and I went to Tennessee Junction in the wagon to meet her. It was January, cold and clear and with ice in the ruts; we returned just before dark with Aunt Jenny on the seat beside me holding a lace parasol and Ringo in the wagon bed nursing a hamper basket containing two bottles of old sherry and the two jasmine cuttings which were bushes in the garden now, and the panes of colored glass which she had salvaged from the Carolina house where she and Father and Uncle Bayard were born and which Father had set in a fanlight about one of the drawing room windows for her—who came up the drive and Father (home now from the railroad) went down the steps and lifted her from the wagon and said, "Well, Jenny," and she said, "Well, Johnny," and began to cry. She stood too, looking at me as I approached—the same hair, the same high nose, the same eyes as Father's except that they were intent and very wise instead of intolerant. She said nothing at all, she just kissed me, her hands light on my shoulders. Then Drusilla spoke, as if she had been waiting with a sort of dreadful patience for the empty ceremony to be done, in a voice like a bell: clear, unsentient, on a single pitch, silvery and triumphant: "Come, Bayard."

"Hadn't you better go to bed now?" Aunt Jenny said.

"Yes," Drusilla said in that silvery ecstatic voice, "Oh yes. There will be plenty of time for sleep." I followed her, her hand again guiding me without pressure; now I looked at him. It was just as I had imagined it—sabre, plumes, and all—but with that alteration, that irrevocable difference which I had known to expect yet had not realised, as you can put food into your stomach which for a while the stomach declines to assimilate—the illimitable grief and regret as I looked down at the face which I knew—the nose, the hair, the eyelids closed over the intolerance—the face which I realised I now saw in repose for the first time in my life; the empty hands still now beneath the invisible stain of what had been (once, surely) needless blood, the hands now appearing clumsy in their very inertness, too clumsy to have performed the fatal actions which forever afterward he must have waked and slept with and maybe was glad to lay down at last— those curious appendages clumsily conceived to begin with yet with which man has taught himself to do so much, so much more than they were intended to do or could be forgiven for doing, which had now surrendered that life to which his intolerant heart had fiercely held;

and then I knew that in a minute I would begin to pant. So Drusilla must have spoken twice before I heard her and turned and saw in the instant Aunt Jenny and Louvinia watching us, hearing Drusilla now, the unsentient bell quality gone now, her voice whispering into that quiet death-filled room with a passionate and dying fall: "Bayard." She faced me, she was quite near; again the scent of the verbena in her hair seemed to have increased a hundred times as she stood holding out to me, one in either hand, the two duelling pistols. "Take them, Bayard," she said, in the same tone in which she had said "Kiss me" last summer, already pressing them into my hands, watching me with that passionate and voracious exaltation, speaking in a voice fainting and passionate with promise: "Take them. I have kept them for you. I give them to you. Oh you will thank me, you will remember me who put into your hands what they say is an attribute only of God's, who took what belongs to heaven and gave it to you. Do you feel them? the long true barrels true as justice, the triggers (you have fired them) quick as retribution, the two of them slender and invincible and fatal as the physical shape of love?" Again I watched her arms angle out and upward as she removed the two verbena sprigs from her hair in two motions faster than the eye could follow, already putting one of them into my lapel and crushing the other in her other hand while she still spoke in that rapid passionate voice not much louder than a whisper: "There. One I give to you to wear tomorrow (it will not fade), the other I cast away, like this—" dropping the crushed bloom at her feet. "I abjure it. I abjure verbena forever more; I have smelled it above the odor of courage; that was all I wanted. Now let me look at you." She stood back, staring at me—the face tearless and exalted, the feverish eyes brilliant and voracious. "How beautiful you are: do you know it? How beautiful: young, to be permitted to kill, to be permitted vengeance, to take into your bare hands the fire of heaven that cast down Lucifer. No; I. I gave it to you; I put it into your hands; Oh you will thank me, you will remember me when I am dead and you are an old man saying to himself, 'I have tasted all things.'—It will be the right hand, won't it?" She moved; she had taken my right hand which still held one of the pistols before I knew what she was about to do; she had bent and kissed it before I comprehended why she took it. Then she stopped dead still, still stooping in that attitude of fierce exultant humility, her hot lips and her hot hands still touching my flesh, light on my flesh as dead leaves yet communicating to it that battery charge dark, passionate and damned forever of all peace. Because they are wise, women are—a touch, lips or fingers, and the knowledge, even clairvoyance, goes straight to the heart without bothering the laggard brain at all. She stood erect now, staring at me with intolerable and amazed incredulity which occupied her face alone for a whole minute while her eyes were completely empty; it seemed to me that I stood there for a full minute while Aunt Jenny and Louvinia watched us, waiting for her eyes to fill. There was no blood in her face at all, her mouth open a little and pale as one of those rubber rings women seal fruit jars with. Then her eyes filled with an expression of bitter and passionate betrayal. "Why, he's not—" she said. "He's not—And I kissed his hand," she said in an aghast whisper: "*I kissed his hand!*" beginning to laugh, the laughter, rising, becoming a scream yet still remaining laughter, screaming with laughter, trying herself to deaden the sound by putting her hand over her mouth, the laughter spilling between her fingers like vomit, the incredulous betrayed eyes still watching me across the hand.

"Louvinia!" Aunt Jenny said. They both came to her. Louvinia touched and held her and Drusilla turned her face to Louvinia.

"I kissed his hand, Louvinia!" she cried. "Did you see it? *I kissed his hand!*" the laughter rising again, becoming the scream again yet still remaining laughter, she still trying to hold it back with her hand like a small child who has filled its mouth too full.

"Take her upstairs," Aunt Jenny said. But they were already moving toward the door, Louvinia half-carrying

Drusilla, the laughter diminishing as they neared the door as though it waited for the larger space of the empty and brilliant hall to rise again. Then it was gone; Aunt Jenny and I stood there and I knew soon that I would begin to pant. I could feel it beginning like you feel regurgitation beginning, as though there were not enough air in the room, the house, not enough air anywhere under the heavy hot low sky where the equinox couldn't seem to accomplish, nothing in the air for breathing, for the lungs. Now it was Aunt Jenny who said "Bayard" twice before I heard her. "You are not going to try to kill him. All right."

"All right?" I said.

"Yes. All right. Don't let it be Drusilla, a poor hysterical young woman. And don't let it be him, Bayard, because he's dead now. And don't let it be George Wyatt and those others who will be waiting for you tomorrow morning. I know you are not afraid."

"But what good will that do?" I said. "What good will that do?" It almost began then; I stopped it just in time. "I must live with myself, you see."

"Then it's not just Drusilla? Not just him? Not just George Wyatt and Jefferson?"

"No," I said.

"Will you promise to let me see you before you go to town tomorrow?" I looked at her; we looked at one another for a moment. Then she put her hands on my shoulders and kissed me and released me, all in one motion. "Goodnight, son," she said. Then she was gone too and now it could begin. I knew that in a minute I would look at him and it would begin and I did look at him, feeling the long-held breath, the hiatus before it started, thinking how maybe I should have said, "Goodbye, Father" but did not. Instead I crossed to the piano and laid the pistols carefully on it, still keeping the panting from getting too loud too soon. Then I was outside on the porch and (I don't know how long it had been) I looked in the window and saw Simon squatting on a stool beside him. Simon had been his body servant during the War and when they came home Simon had a uniform

too—a Confederate private's coat with a Yankee briga-
dier's star on it and he had put it on now too, like they
had dressed Father, squatting on the stool beside him,
not crying, not weeping the facile tears which are the
white man's futile trait and which Negroes know nothing
about but just sitting there, motionless, his lower lip
slacked down a little; he raised his hand and touched the
coffin, the black hand rigid and fragile-looking as a clutch
of dead twigs, then dropped the hand; once he turned
his head and I saw his eyes roll red and unwinking in his
skull like those of a cornered fox. It had begun by that
time; I panted, standing there, and this was it—the regret
and grief, the despair out of which the tragic mute insen-
sitive bones stand up that can bear anything, anything.

4

After a while the whippoorwills stopped and I heard
the first day bird, a mockingbird. It had sung all night
too but now it was the day song, no longer the drowsy
moony fluting. Then they all began—the sparrows from
the stable, the thrush that lived in Aunt Jenny's garden,
and I heard a quail too from the pasture and now there
was light in the room. But I didn't move at once. I still
lay on the bed (I hadn't undressed) with my hands under
my head and the scent of Drusilla's verbena faint from
where my coat lay on a chair, watching the light grow,
watching it turn rosy with the sun. After a while I heard
Louvinia come up across the back yard and go into the
kitchen; I heard the door and then the long crash of her
armful of stovewood into the box. Soon they would begin
to arrive—the carriages and buggies in the drive—but not
for a while yet because they too would wait first to see
what I was going to do. So the house was quiet when I
went down to the diningroom, no sound in it except
Simon snoring in the parlor, probably still sitting on the
stool though I didn't look in to see. Instead I stood at the
diningroom window and drank the coffee which Louvinia
brought me, then I went to the stable; I saw Joby watching me from the kitchen door as I crossed the yard and

in the stable Loosh looked up at me across Betsy's head, a curry comb in his hand, though Ringo didn't look at me at all. We curried Jupiter then. I didn't know if we would be able to without trouble or not, since always Father would come in first and touch him and tell him to stand and he would stand like a marble horse (or pale bronze rather) while Loosh curried him. But he stood for me too, a little restive but he stood, then that was done and now it was almost nine o'clock and soon they would begin to arrive and I told Ringo to bring Betsy on to the house.

I went on to the house and into the hall. I had not had to pant in some time now but it was there, waiting, a part of the alteration, as though by being dead and no longer needing air he had taken all of it, all that he had compassed and claimed and postulated between the walls which he had built, along with him. Aunt Jenny must have been waiting; she came out of the diningroom at once, without a sound, dressed, the hair that was like Father's combed and smooth above the eyes that were different from Father's eyes because they were not intolerant but just intent and grave and (she was wise too) without pity. "Are you going now?" she said.

"Yes." I looked at her. Yes, thank God, without pity. "You see, I want to be thought well of."

"I do," she said. "Even if you spend the day hidden in the stable loft, I still do."

"Maybe if she knew that I was going. Was going to town anyway."

"No," she said. "No, Bayard." We looked at one another. Then she said quietly, "All right. She's awake." So I mounted the stairs. I mounted steadily, not fast because if I had gone fast the panting would have started again or I might have had to slow for a second at the turn or at the top and I would not have gone on. So I went slowly and steadily, across the hall to her door and knocked and opened it. She was sitting at the window, in something soft and loose for morning in her bedroom only she never did look like morning in a bedroom because here was no hair to fall about her shoulders. She looked up, she sat there looking at me with her feverish brilliant eyes and I remembered I still had the verbena sprig in my lapel and suddenly she began to laugh again. It seemed to come not from her mouth but to burst out all over her face like sweat does and with a dreadful and painful convulsion as when you have vomited until it hurts you yet still you must vomit again—burst out all over her face except her eyes, the brilliant incredulous eyes looking at me out of the laughter as if they belonged to somebody else, as if they were two inert fragments of tar or coal lying on the bottom of a receptacle filled with turmoil: "I kissed his hand! *I kissed his hand!*" Louvinia entered, Aunt Jenny must have sent her directly after me; again I walked slowly and steadily so it would not start yet, down the stairs where Aunt Jenny stood beneath the chandelier in the hall as Mrs. Wilkins had stood yesterday at the University. She had my hat in her hand. "Even if you hid all day in the stable, Bayard," she said. I took the hat; she said quietly, pleasantly, as if she were talking to a stranger, a guest: "I used to see a lot of blockade runners in Charleston. They were heroes in a way, you see—not heroes because they were helping to prolong the Confederacy but heroes in the sense that David Crockett or John Sevier would have been to small boys or fool young women. There was one of them, an Englishman. He had no business there; it was the money of course, as with all of them. But he was the Davy Crockett to us because by that time we had all forgot what money was, what you could do with it. He must have been a gentleman once or associated with gentlemen before he changed his name, and he had a vocabulary of seven words, though I must admit he got along quite well with them. The first four were, 'I'll have rum, thanks,' and then, when he had the rum, he would use the other three—across the champagne, to whatever ruffled bosom or low gown: 'No bloody moon.' No bloody moon, Bayard."

Ringo was waiting with Betsy at the front steps. Again he did not look at me, his face sullen, downcast even while he handed me the reins. But he said nothing, nor did I look back. And sure enough I was just in time; I passed the Compson carriage at the gates, General Compson lifted his hat as I did mine as we passed. It was four miles to town but I had not gone two of them when I heard the horse coming up behind me and I did not look back because I knew it was Ringo. I did not look back; he came up on one of the carriage horses, he rode up beside me and looked me full in the face for one moment, the sullen determined face, the eyes rolling at me defiant and momentary and red; we rode on. Now we were in town—the long shady street leading to the square, the new courthouse at the end of it; it was eleven o'clock now: long past breakfast and not yet noon so there were only women on the street, not to recognise me perhaps or at least not the walking stopped sudden and dead in midwalking as if the legs contained the sudden eyes, the caught breath, that not to begin until we reached the square and I thinking *If I could only be invisible until I reach the stairs to his office and begin to mount*. But I could not, I was not; we rode up to the Holston House and I saw the row of feet along the gallery rail come suddenly and quietly down and I did not look at them, I stopped Betsy and waited until Ringo was down then I dismounted and gave him the reins. "Wait for me here," I said.

"I'm going with you," he said, not loud; we stood there under the still circumspect eyes and spoke quietly to one another like two conspirators. Then I saw the pistol, the outline of it inside his shirt, probably the one we had taken from Grumby that day we killed him.

"No you ain't," I said.

"Yes I am."

"No you ain't." So I walked on, along the street in the hot sun. It was almost noon now and I could smell nothing except the verbena in my coat, as if it had gathered all the sun, all the suspended fierce heat in which the equinox could not seem to occur and were distilling it so that I moved in a cloud of verbena as I might have moved in a cloud of smoke from a cigar. Then George Wyatt was beside me (I don't know where he came from) and five or six others of Father's old troop a few yards behind, George's hand on my arm, drawing me into a doorway out of the avid eyes like caught breaths.

"Have you got that derringer?" George said.

"No," I said.

"Good," George said. "They are tricky things to fool with. Couldn't nobody but Colonel ever handle one right; I never could. So you take this. I tried it this morning and I know it's right. Here." He was already fumbling the pistol into my pocket, then the same thing seemed to happen to him that happened to Drusilla last night when she kissed my hand—something communicated by touch straight to the simple code by which he lived, without going through the brain at all: so that he too stood suddenly back, the pistol in his hand, staring at me with his pale outraged eyes and speaking in a whisper thin with fury: "Who are you? Is your name Sartoris? By God, if you don't kill him, I'm going to." Now it was not panting, it was a terrible desire to laugh, to laugh as Drusilla had, and say, "That's what Drusilla said." But I didn't. I said,

"I'm tending to this. You stay out of it. I don't need any help." Then his fierce eyes faded gradually, exactly as you turn a lamp down.

"Well," he said, putting the pistol back into his pocket. "You'll have to excuse me, son. I should have knowed you wouldn't do anything that would keep John from laying quiet. We'll follow you and wait at the foot of the steps. And remember: he's a brave man, but he's been sitting in that office by himself since yesterday morning waiting for you and his nerves are on edge."

"I'll remember," I said. "I don't need any help." I had started on when suddenly I said it without having any warning that I was going to: "No bloody moon."

"What?" he said. I didn't answer. I went on across the square itself now, in the hot sun, they following though not close so that I never saw them again until afterward, surrounded by the remote still eyes not following me yet either, just stopped where they were before the stores and about the door to the courthouse, waiting. I walked steadily on enclosed in the new fierce odor of the verbena sprig. Then shadow fell upon me; I did not pause, I looked once at the small faded sign nailed to the brick *B.J. Redmond. Atty at Law* and began to mount the stairs, the wooden steps scuffed by the heavy bewildered boots of countrymen approaching litigation and stained by tobacco spit, on down the dim corridor to the door which bore the name again, *B.J. Redmond* and knocked once and opened it. He sat behind the desk, not much taller than Father but thicker as a man gets who spends most of his time sitting and listening to people, freshly shaven and with fresh linen; a lawyer yet it was not a lawyer's face—a face much thinner than the body would indicate, strained (and yes, tragic; I know that now) and exhausted beneath the neat recent steady strokes of the razor, holding a pistol flat on the desk before him, loose beneath his hand and aimed at nothing. There was no smell of drink, not even of tobacco in the neat clean dingy room although I knew he smoked. I didn't pause. I walked steadily toward him. It was not twenty feet from door to desk yet I seemed to walk in a dreamlike state in which there was neither time nor distance, as though the mere act of walking was no more intended to encompass space than was his sitting. We didn't speak. It was as if we both knew what the passage of words would be and the futility of it; how he might have said, "Go out, Bayard. Go away, boy" and then, "Draw then. I will allow you to draw" and it would have been the same as if he had never said it. So we did not speak; I just walked steadily toward him as the pistol rose from the desk. I watched it, I could see the foreshortened slant of the barrel and I knew it would miss me though his hand did not tremble. I walked toward him, toward the pistol in the rocklike hand, I heard no bullet. Maybe I didn't even hear the explosion though I remember the sudden orange bloom and smoke as they appeared against his white shirt as they had appeared against Grumby's greasy Confederate coat; I still watched that foreshortened slant of barrel which I knew was not aimed at me and saw the second orange flash and smoke and heard no bullet that time either. Then I stopped; it was done then. I watched the pistol descend to the desk in short jerks; I saw him release it and sit back, both hands on the desk, I looked at his face and I knew too what it was to want air when there was nothing in the circumambience for the lungs. He rose, shoved the chair back with a convulsive motion and rose, with a queer ducking motion of his head; with his head still ducked aside and one arm extended as though he couldn't see and the other hand resting on the desk as if he couldn't stand alone, he turned and crossed to the wall and took his hat from the rack and with his head still ducked aside and one hand extended he blundered along the wall and passed me and reached the door and went through it. He was brave; no one denied that. He walked down those stairs and out onto the street where George Wyatt and the other six of Father's old troop waited and where the other men had begun to run now; he walked through the middle of them with his hat on and his head up (they told me how someone shouted at him: "Have you killed that boy too?"), saying no word, staring straight ahead and with his back to them, on to the station where the south-bound train was just in and got on it with no baggage, nothing, and went away from Jefferson and from Mississippi and never came back.

I heard their feet on the stairs then in the corridor then in the room, but for a while yet (it wasn't that long, of course) I still sat behind the desk as he had sat, the flat of the pistol still warm under my hand, my hand growing slowly numb between the pistol and my forehead. Then I raised my head; the little room was full of men. "My God!" George Wyatt cried. "You took the pistol away from him and then missed him, missed him *twice*?" Then he answered himself—that same rapport for violence which Drusilla had and which in George's case was actual character judgment: "No; wait. You walked in here without even a pocket knife and let him miss you twice. My God in heaven." He turned, shouting: "Get to hell out of here! You, White, ride out to Sartoris and tell his folks it's all over and he's all right.

Ride!" So they departed, went away; presently only
George was left, watching me with that pale bleak stare
which was speculative yet not at all ratiocinative. "Well
by God," he said. "—Do you want a drink?"

"No," I said. "I'm hungry. I didn't eat any breakfast."

"I reckon not, if you got up this morning aiming to do
what you did. Come on. We'll go to the Holston House."

"No," I said. "No. Not there."

"Why not? You ain't done anything to be ashamed of.
I wouldn't have done it that way, myself. I'd a shot at
him once, anyway. But that's your way or you wouldn't
have done it."

"Yes," I said. "I would do it again."

"Be damned if I would.—You want to come home
with me? We'll have time to eat and then ride out there
in time for the——" But I couldn't do that either.

"No," I said. "I'm not hungry after all. I think I'll go
home."

"Don't you want to wait and ride out with me?"

"No. I'll go on."

"You don't want to stay here, anyway." He looked
around the room again, where the smell of powder
smoke still lingered a little, still lay somewhere on the
hot dead air though invisible now, blinking a little with
his fierce pale unintroverted eyes. "Well by God," he
said again. "Maybe you're right, maybe there has been
enough killing in your family without—Come on." We
left the office. I waited at the foot of the stairs and soon
Ringo came up with the horses. We crossed the square
again. There were no feet on the Holston House railing
now (it was twelve o'clock) but a group of men stood
before the door who raised their hats and I raised mine
and Ringo and I rode on.

We did not go fast. Soon it was one, maybe after; the
carriages and buggies would begin to leave the square
soon, so I turned from the road at the end of the pasture
and I sat the mare, trying to open the gate without dis-
mounting, until Ringo dismounted and opened it. We
crossed the pasture in the hard fierce sun; I could have
seen the house now but I didn't look. Then we were in

the shade, the close thick airless shade of the creek bottom; the old rails still lay in the undergrowth where we had built the pen to hide the Yankee mules. Presently I heard the water, then I could see the sunny glints. We dismounted. I lay on my back, I thought *Now it can begin again if it wants to.* But it did not. I went to sleep. I went to sleep almost before I had stopped thinking. I slept for almost five hours and I didn't dream anything at all yet I waked myself up crying, crying too hard to stop it. Ringo was squatting beside me and the sun was gone though there was a bird of some sort still singing somewhere and the whistle of the north-bound evening train sounded and the short broken puffs of starting where it had evidently stopped at our flag station. After a while I began to stop and Ringo brought his hat full of water from the creek but instead I went down to the water myself and bathed my face.

There was still a good deal of light in the pasture, though the whippoorwills had begun, and when we reached the house there was a mockingbird singing in the magnolia, the night song now, the drowsy moony one, and again the moon like the rim print of a heel in wet sand. There was just one light in the hall now and so it was all over though I could still smell the flowers even above the verbena in my coat. I had not looked at him again. I had started to before I left the house but I did not, I did not see him again and all the pictures we had of him were bad ones because a picture could no more have held him dead than the house could have kept his body. But I didn't need to see him again because he was there, he would always be there; maybe what Drusilla meant by his dream was not something which he possessed but something which he had bequeathed us which we could never forget, which would even assume the corporeal shape of him whenever any of us, black or white, closed our eyes. I went into the house. There was no light in the drawing room except the last of the afterglow which came through the western window where Aunt Jenny's colored glass was; I was about to go on upstairs when I saw her sitting there beside the window. She

didn't call me and I didn't speak Drusilla's name, I just
went to the door and stood there. "She's gone," Aunt
Jenny said. "She took the evening train. She has gone
to Montgomery, to Dennison." Denny had been married
about a year now; he was living in Montgomery, reading
law.

"I see," I said. "Then she didn't——" But there wasn't
any use in that either; Jed White must have got there
before one o'clock and told them. And besides, Aunt
Jenny didn't answer. She could have lied to me but she
didn't, she said,

"Come here." I went to her chair. "Kneel down. I
can't see you."

"Don't you want the lamp?"

"No. Kneel down." So I knelt beside the chair. "So
you had a perfectly splendid Saturday afternoon, didn't
you? Tell me about it." Then she put her hands on my
shoulders. I watched them come up as though she were
trying to stop them; I felt them on my shoulders as if
they had a separate life of their own and were trying to
do something which for my sake she was trying to
restrain, prevent. Then she gave up or she was not strong
enough because they came up and took my face between
them, hard, and suddenly the tears sprang and streamed
down her face like Drusilla's laughing had. "Oh, damn
you Sartorises!" she said. "Damn you! Damn you!"

As I passed down the hall the light came up in the
diningroom and I could hear Louvinia laying the table
for supper. So the stairs were lighted quite well. But the
upper hall was dark. I saw her open door (that unmistakable way in which an open door stands open when
nobody lives in the room any more) and I realised I had
not believed that she was really gone. So I didn't look
into the room. I went on to mine and entered. And then
for a long moment I thought it was the verbena in my
lapel which I still smelled. I thought that until I had
crossed the room and looked down at the pillow on which
it lay—the single sprig of it (without looking she would
pinch off a half dozen of them and they would be all of

a size, almost all of a shape, as if a machine had stamped them out) filling the room, the dusk, the evening with that odor which she said you could smell alone above the smell of horses.

Ernest Gaines

Ernest Gaines writes about rural Louisiana, where he was born in 1933. He has created an imaginary plantation region called Bayonne, which a number of critics have compared to Faulkner's Yoknapatawpha. While Gaines acknowledges Faulkner's influence, he believes a greater influence on his work has been nineteenth-century Russian writers, like Gogol, Turgenev, and Chekhov: "The Russians were not talking about my people, but about a peasantry for which they seemed to show such feeling. Reading them, I could find a way to write about my own people." Gaines left Louisiana when he was 15 to go to high school and then college in California, first San Francisco State and than Stanford University for graduate study. Now he divides his time between California and the University of Southwestern Louisiana where he teaches. He has written five novels and a collection of short stories, *Bloodline* (1968). Two of his novels, *The Autobiography of Miss Jane Pittman* (1971) and *A Gathering of Old Men* (1983), were made into movies for television. The following excerpt from *A Gathering of Old Men* bears evidence of several themes of importance to Gaines: the rural black experience in the South, the changing relationship between blacks and whites, and the alienation between fathers and sons. The excerpt is also a good example of Gaines's first-person narrative style, which has been influenced by oral storytelling traditions. Like Eudora Welty and Peter Taylor, he says he spent a great deal of time listening to the people who visited his home when he was a boy. Jerry Bryant has called him "one of our most naturally gifted storytellers." Ernest

Gaines has won numerous awards and grants for his fiction.

A Gathering of Old Men (1983) takes place in the 1970s, primarily in the old slave quarters of the Marshall plantation in Louisiana where some of the slaves' descendants still reside. Beau Boutan, a Cajun man who rents the farmland, has been shot, allegedly by Mathu, one of the old black men who live on the plantation. Beau has a reputation for verbally and physically abusing the black men who work for him. Candy Marshall, a white woman whose family owns the plantation and who has been raised in part by Mathu, is determined to protect the blacks who live there from the vengeance of Beau's father Fix, who is a notorious bigot and vigilante. A number of old black men, who have all been the victims of racial discrimination, have gathered at the quarters to take their first stand against white injustice. Mapes, the local white sheriff, is trying not only to bring the murderer to justice, but to keep the people, both white and black, from taking matters into their own hands. In this section of the novel, Gil Boutan, a college student and football hero, has just learned of his brother Beau's death. This part of the story is narrated by a white college friend, Thomas Vincent Sullivan.

Thomas Vincent Sullivan

aka
Sully or T.V.

Gil and I had just come out of Sci-210 when Cal caught up with us and told Gil that coach wanted him in the office right away.

"I thought we had gone over all that," Gil said.

"I don't think it's football this time," Cal said.

Gil asked me if I would walk back to the gym with him, and since Cal wasn't doing anything that hour he walked back with us. Cal was Calvin "Pepper" Harrison, quite possibly the best halfback in the country that year, and already nominated for All-American. Gil was Gilbert "Salt" Boutan, definitely the best fullback in the Southeastern Conference, and many other conferences besides. Cal and Gil were known as Salt and Pepper at LSU. Gil being a Cajun, the publicity people had tried to think of a good Cajun nickname for him when he first came to the university, but after seeing how well he and Cal worked together, they finally settled on Salt and Pepper.

Gil was a football man all the way, and eventually he would go pro, but what he wanted most while attending LSU was to be All-American along with Cal. It would be the first time this had ever happened, black and white in the same backfield—and in the Deep South, besides. LSU was fully aware of this, the black and white communities in Baton Rouge were aware of this, and so was the rest of the country. Wherever you went, people spoke of Salt and Pepper of LSU. Both were good powerful runners, and excellent blockers. Gil blocked for Cal on sweeps around end, and Cal returned the favor when Gil went up the middle. It drove the defense crazy, because both Gil and Cal carried the ball about the same number of times in a game and the defensive team didn't know which to look out for. Besides that, you had "Sugar" Washington at quarterback, and he was no slouch, either.

Me? Well, I was no Sugar Washington. I was third-string quarterback. My name is Thomas Vincent Sullivan. My hair is red, my face is red, my eyes are green, and most people call me Sully. Others call me T.V.— especially the black guys on the team. Not for my initials necessarily, but for my avocation. I'm a television nut. A vidiot.

While Gil was in coach's office, Cal and I stood outside talking about the game coming up the next day, LSU and Ole Miss. It would be the game of the year. We knew if we dumped her, nobody else could stop us, and we would host the Sugar Bowl game on New Year's Day. Already the people had filled all the motels and hotels from Baton Rouge to New Orleans. The national press was covering the game. No matter where you went, that's all the people were talking about. If you were pro-LSU— and you were crazy if you were not—they said there was no possible way to stop Salt and Pepper. If you were anti-LSU, or pro-Ole Miss—and there were thousands of people from Mississippi who had come down for the game—they said that all Ole Miss had to do was stop one or the other, Salt or Pepper, and victory would be theirs to take back home. This kind of talk had been going on the past month, and now there was only a little more than twenty-four hours—thirty hours—before the whole thing would be settled. If you know anything about Louisiana weather, you know there's a lot of lightning and thundering before the big storm comes. Well, the big storm was going to be tomorrow night at eight o'clock, but the lightning and thundering had been going on for a month already, and nobody expected it to let up till the last moment.

After being in coach's office about ten minutes, Gil

came back out, and went right by Cal and me like we weren't even standing there. I thought he had forgotten where he had left us, and I called to him. But he kept on going. Cal and I looked at each other a second, and went after him. He was walking fast, and rubbing both his fists.

"Gil, wait up," I said to him. "Hey, Gil."

Cal was on one side, I was on the other.

"What's the matter, man?" Cal asked him.

He had stopped. He was breathing sharp and hard, the way you do in the huddle after you've been tackled. He was staring down at the ground, rubbing his fists, rubbing his knuckles hard, like he was trying to rub off the skin.

Cal put his hand on one shoulder, and I took the other arm.

"What's the matter, Gil?" I asked him.

He started shaking his head; he was still looking down at the ground.

"My brother, my brother. Killed."

"In a wreck?" Cal asked him.

Gil went on shaking his head like he might start crying. I held on to one of his arms, and Cal was patting him on the back to console him. Then suddenly he just turned against Cal. Out of the blue, he looked at Cal like he suddenly hated him. It surprised the hell out of both me and Cal.

"Gil, that's Cal," I said. "Gil."

He turned from Cal and looked at me. "Why today?" he said. He was crying now. "Why today?"

"Take it easy, Gil," I said. People had begun to crowd around us and ask questions. Cal or Gil couldn't sneeze but there wasn't a crowd around. "Take it easy," I said to him.

"I have to get home," he said. "Can I borrow your car? Mine's still in the shop."

"I'll drive you," I said. "I can skip that drama class."

"Why today, Sully?" he asked me. "Why?"

I didn't know how to answer him, and I looked at Cal. Cal was just standing there looking hurt. He didn't know why Gil had turned against him, and I didn't know either.

"Let's go," Gil said.

"That's Cal, Gil," I said.

"Come on, let's go," he said, and walked away.

I followed him, but it sure made me feel bad the way he treated Cal.

I had a '68 Karmann-Ghia parked on the other side of the gym. Driving across campus, I had to drive about one mile an hour because of all the loonies who recognized Gil and wanted to wish him well in the game the next day. These were not all students, either. Many of them were graduates who had already arrived for the game that wasn't for another thirty hours. Someone has said that Norman, Oklahoma, is the nuttiest town in this country over football, but if any place can get crazier than this one, I would like to see it—or maybe I would not, because it sure could be dangerous.

Gil kept his head down. He would not look out at the loonies. I was driving one mile an hour. About a dozen other cars driving one mile an hour behind me. Out on the Highland road, I could speed up some, driving about five miles an hour. Loonies all over the place. Tomorrow this time it would be twice as bad, three times as bad, four times as bad. If Gil ever made All-American, handsome as he was, he would own this town and all the women in it.

Gil was quiet all the time. I didn't know whether I should say anything, so I kept quiet, too. I was still thinking about Cal. It made me feel bad the way Gil had treated him. On the gridiron they depended on each other the way one hand must depend on the other swinging a baseball bat. I had never known Gil to be anything but a gentleman.

We had crossed the Mississippi River, and were on the main highway that would take us to his folks' place in St. Raphael Parish. I had left all the loonies, at least the ones walking around loose, so I could drive sixty now. But all the time, Gil just sat over there quiet, rubbing his fists and gazing out at the road. I stayed quiet, too,

not knowing what to say. I never know what to say to
people who lose someone in the family. Besides, I was
still thinking about Cal.

"God, I hope none of them had anything to do with
it," Gil said. He wasn't looking at me; he was still looking out at the road. "I hope for God's sake none of them
did it."

"Who are you talking about?"

"The black people there at Marshall. That's where he
was killed. I hope for God's sake none of them did it."

So that's why he went against Cal like that. Whether
he had anything to do with it or not, he was guilty
because of his color. Jesus Christ. Jesus Christ, man. The
two of you work on that field together as well as any two
people I've ever seen in my life work together, and
because of this—Jesus H. Christ. Come on, Gil, I
thought to myself, you're made of better stuff than that.

"You don't know my folks, Sully. So little you know
about me."

I know about you, I thought. I know a hell of a lot
about you. I didn't know this side of you, but I know a
hell of a lot about you, and about old Fix, too. I've heard
how he and his boys used to ride in the old days. I just
didn't know *you* were like that.

We could have stayed on this road to within a couple
of miles of his folks' place, but as we were coming up to
the junction that said St. Charles River, he told me to
take that turnoff. It was a good straight road for about
four miles, with the sugarcane fields on either side. Much
of the cane had been cut, and far across the field on the
right side of the road was that dark line of trees which
was the beginning of the swamps. Gil was looking across
the fields toward the swamps. He looked in that direction
until we made the turn that took us along the St. Charles
River. The river was grayish blue, and very calm. On the
other side of the river, probably three-quarters of a mile
away, I could see how small the cars looked moving on
the road.

After going about half a mile along the river, Gil nodded for me to pull off the highway. I didn't know before

then that his reason for not heading directly to his folks' place was that he first wanted to go to Marshall.

Just as we turned into Marshall Quarters, I noticed a patrolman's car parked beside the road. The patrolman, in his gray-blue uniform, got out of the car and raised his hand for us to stop. He came over to my car. He recognized Gil immediately.

"Gil," he said.

"Hilly," Gil said.

Hilly looked at me. He wasn't much older than we were. He had red hair and freckles. He didn't wear a cap or a tie. The two top buttons of his shirt were unfastened, and you could see the reddish hair below his neck. He looked back at Gil.

"Mapes told me to keep out trouble, but I guess you're okay."

"Mapes still down there?" Gil asked.

"Yes."

"Thanks," Gil said.

"Be pulling for you tomorrow night," Hilly said. But soon as he said it, you could see that he felt he had spoken badly.

"Thanks," Gil said, and we drove off.

Marshall Quarters was a narrow little country road, all white with dust, and weeds on both sides. The one or two old clapboard houses seemed deserted, causing the place to look like a Western ghost town. All you needed was a couple of tumbleweeds to come bouncing down the road. Halfway into the quarters I could make out a tractor and several cars. As we came closer, I recognized Lou Dimes's baby-blue Porsche with the white streak on the side. Lou Dimes had been a starting forward on LSU's basketball team about ten years ago, and he still came to most of the games. Sometimes he covered the games for the paper in Baton Rouge.

Gil nodded for me to park in front of the tractor. We hadn't been there half a minute when I saw a skinny little guy coming out of the weeds with a pistol dangling from his right hand. He was looking suspiciously at us until he recognized Gil; then you could see him smiling. He came over to the car to look inside at us.

"Didn't know it was you," he said. "Sorry what happened, Gil."

He looked at me and nodded, and I nodded back. I thought he looked too pale to be a policeman.

"You wanta speak to Mapes?" he asked Gil.

Gil and I got out of the car. Gil stopped to look at the tractor a moment; then we followed the deputy back toward the house.

But Gil and I stopped again. There in the yard and on the porch were all these old men with shotguns. Besides, there was the sheriff with a pump gun. Lou Dimes was with his woman, Candy. Three or four black women sat either on the porch or on the steps. Some little dirty-looking children sat on the steps with the women. Every last one of them was looking back at us. It was like looking into the *Twilight Zone*. Remember that old TV play *Twilight Zone*? You would be driving through this little out-of-the-way town, and suddenly you would come upon a scene that you knew shouldn't be there—it was something like that. Something like looking at a Brueghel painting. One of these real weird, weird Brueghels.

The sheriff lowered his pump gun when he recognized Gil. The rest of them did the same. You could see all those old shotguns being lowered an inch or two toward the ground.

Gil stepped across the little grassy ditch into the yard, and I was no more than a step behind him. The grass from his footsteps had not sprung back up before I was pressing it back down. And I intended to keep it that way until we got out of there.

"Gil." The sheriff spoke first. He was one of those great big guys, exactly what the people up North and in Hollywood thought a small-town Southern sheriff would look like.

Gil didn't answer him. I nodded to Dimes and Candy. Dimes spoke, but Candy didn't. She stood by the steps next to an old guy in a dirty tee shirt and green pants. She seemed lost in her own thoughts. She seemed no more interested in Gil and me than she did in anything else around her, except for that old guy, maybe. I had seen her at few of the games with Dimes, and she always seemed bored with everything. She acted like that now, bored. She also looked very tired.

"Where is my brother, Mapes?" I heard Gil asking.

"They took him into Bayonne," Mapes said.

Gil was looking at Mapes. He didn't think Mapes had told him enough. He wanted to hear more without asking for it. He didn't think, in a situation like this, it was necessary to ask.

"You're on your way home?" Mapes asked Gil. He was trying to show sympathy. But that was hard to do with a face and eyes like his.

Gil didn't answer this time either. He was doing everything he could to control himself. He wanted the sheriff to say more about his brother.

"I got Russell back there on the bayou," Mapes said. "I told him to keep your daddy back there. I don't want him here at Marshall, Gil. I don't want him in Bayonne till I send for him."

The sheriff said all of this gently, with as much sympathy as anybody could who looked like he did. His face was big, red, with heavy jowls; his eyes were the color of cement. Even when he was trying to be gentle, his eyes still remained hard and staring at you.

Gil stared back at him. He was waiting for the sheriff to tell him more about what had happened.

"I'll have it over with before sundown," Mapes said. "You can take my word."

"What over with, Mapes?" Gil asked. He was doing all he could to control himself. "What over with, Mapes?"

"The person who did it—I'll have him in jail before sundown, I guarantee that," Mapes said.

"Don't you know who did it?" Gil asked.

"I think I do," Mapes said. "I'm sure I do."

"Then why don't you arrest him?"

"They all say the same thing. They all claim they did it."

"But you know who did it?"

"Yes," Mapes said. "I know who did it. But the others threatened to come to town if I take him in. She says the same thing. I don't want this crowd in Bayonne. Not the way people are working themselves up for that game tomorrow. If you just come from Baton Rouge, you know what I'm talking about."

"What do you plan to do, Mapes?"

"I'll handle it my way."

"Your way?" Gil asked. "My brother been dead how long, four hours?"

"About four hours."

Gil looked at him the way you look at somebody who should be telling you much, much more. But instead of saying more, Mapes turned away. Gil started looking at the old men around him. His eyes finally settled on the one in the dirty tee shirt and green trousers, the one nearest Candy. He did not say anything to the old man for a while. The old man was looking out over the road.

"You, Mathu?"

"Yes," the old man said, without looking at Gil.

Gil's right hand slowly tightened into a fist. Not that he wanted to hurt the old man. His face didn't show hatred or anger—just disbelief in the dry, direct way that the old man had answered him. If the old man had dropped his head and muttered out the words, that might have made a difference. But no, dry and direct, without even looking at Gil: "Yes, I did it."

"Ask the others," Mapes said. "Ask Candy."

Gil was still looking at old Mathu. The old man was not trying to avoid Gil's stare; he was just looking, thoughtfully, away from him.

Mapes held the pump gun in one hand, and he laid his big arm around Gil's shoulders.

"Go home, Gil," he said gently. It was said as gently as someone with a face and eyes like his could say it. Not necessarily as gently as it could be said in a situation like this.

Gil was still looking at old Mathu. He showed no sign that he had even heard Mapes.

"Gil," Mapes said, shaking him a little. "Gil."

Gil looked at him. "What is going on here, Mapes?" he asked. He said it as if he had just come into the yard and didn't know a thing. "What is going on here?"

"What is going on?" Mapes asked himself.

He looked around at the old men with the guns. Maybe he knew the answers, maybe he didn't. But if he did, he didn't know how to explain it to Gil. Or maybe he didn't know how to put it so Gil could understand it. "Go home, Gil," he said.

Gil knocked Mapes's arm from his shoulders. Now he turned to Candy, who stood beside old Mathu. Up to now she hadn't shown any interest in our being there.

"What is going on here, Candy?" Gil asked her.

She raised her head slowly to look at him. She looked tired. But she showed no sympathy for him at all. She told him how Beau and somebody called Charlie had gotten into a fight back there in the fields. This Charlie fellow had run up to the front, and Beau had come after him with a gun. She was here talking to old Mathu. She told Beau not to come into the yard. She said she told him more than once not to come into the yard. He came in with the gun ready to shoot, and she stopped him. These other people heard about it and thought there would be trouble, and had come here to stand with her. She said she had already said all of that to Mapes.

"You're lying, Candy," Gil said. "Beau never would have come after Charlie with a gun. A stick, a stalk of cane, but never with a gun. Why are you saying all this? Why are you here in the first place? Why are all these old people here, Candy? To do what?"

She didn't answer him. She looked past him. She had made her point. She wasn't talking anymore.

Gil turned to Lou Dimes, who stood beside Candy.

"What's going on here, Lou?" Gil asked. "I know I can trust you. What's going on here?"

Lou was standing there beside Candy looking very uncomfortable. You could see he didn't like being here; he didn't like what was going on. He shook his head.

"I don't know, Gil," he said.

"Sure, you do," Gil said. I thought Gil was about to cry. "What's going on, Lou? Tell me what's going on."

"Gil, believe me," Lou said. "I don't know any more than what you see before you right now. Please believe me." He looked at me. "Why don't you take him home?"

"Come on, Gil," I said, and took him by the arm. But that was like pulling on a tree.

Gil turned back on Candy. "You never did like Beau," he said. "You never liked any of us. Looking at us as if we're a breed below you. But we're not, Candy. We're all made of the same bone, the same blood, the same skin. Your folks had a break, mine didn't, that's all."

She looked past him, like he wasn't even there. She looked tired, but other than that she showed no other expression.

"My God," Gil said. "My God, my God. Candy, if you only knew how sad, how pathetic you look."

She pretended not to even hear him. And maybe she didn't.

"Come on, Gil," I said, pulling on his arm again.

"Won't it ever stop?" he asked. He looked around at all of them. "Won't it ever stop? I do all I can to stop it. Every day of my life, I do all I can to stop it. Won't it ever stop?"

The people did not look at him. They were not looking down; they were just looking away.

"Come on," I told him. "Come on. Let's get out of here."

He looked around at all of them; then he turned quickly and walked away. And I followed him out of the yard.

———————

From Marshall to the Bayou Michel is about ten miles, five miles along the St. Charles River, and then you turn off the highway onto a blacktop road for another five miles. The Bayou Michel is then on your right, and houses on the left are facing the bayou. The road and bayou twist and turn like a snake. There's never more than a couple hundred yards of straight road before you have to go around another curve.

This was Cajun country. You had a few other whites, a few blacks, but mostly Cajuns, with names like Jarreau, Bonaventura, Mouton, Montemare, Boutan, Broussard, Guerin, Hebert, Boudreaux, Landreaux—all Cajun names. There were people back here with names like Smith and Kelly, and they claimed to be Cajuns, too, their fathers' having married Cajun women. The blacks on the bayou also spoke the Cajun French as well as English.

This was Gil's country. I had come back here with him a half-dozen times before, and it had always been pleasant. We would go hunting or fishing or just visit some of the people. Gil loved all the people back here, and they all loved him, white and black. He would shake a black man's hand as soon as he would a white man's, and the blacks would beam with pride when he did. But today I had not seen one black man, woman, or child since we left Marshall.

Gil, with his arm in the window, was looking out at the trees along the Bayou Michel. Most of the trees were weeping willows; their long, limp branches brushed against the ground and the surface of the water. Every now and then you would see a cypress, a sycamore, or some other kind of tree, but mostly willows, and lots of bushes. When there was a little space between the trees and bushes, you would see the dirty brown shallow water. No form of life was on the water itself. No animals, no birds, nothing green. Only twigs and dry leaves that had fallen from the trees along the bank. Gil was looking out of the window at the bayou, but never saying anything. He had not said a single word to me since we left Marshall.

We were coming up to his folks' place now, a great big white frame house with a screened-in porch, and screen over the doors and windows. There were quite a few cars and trucks parked in front of the place, so we had to go maybe a hundred yards before we could find room to park; then we got out and walked back. I saw a tall, sandy-haired fellow standing by a car watching us. He smiled as we came back.

"Gilly," he said.

"Russ," Gil said. Gil nodded toward me. "This is Sully."

Russ nodded. I nodded back. We shook hands.

Gil started looking around at all the trucks and cars parked before the house. A half-dozen men stood around one of the trucks in the yard.

"Waiting for you inside," Russ said to Gil.

"You coming in?" Gil asked him.

"I have to keep your daddy back here, Gil," Russ said.

"I'd like for you to come in, if you don't mind," Gil said.

"Sure, if you want me to," Russ said.

He reached into the car to get a necktie hanging over the stem of the rearview mirror. After he had made a good knot and drawn it tight, he stuffed his white shirt neatly into his gray pants, and reached back into the car to get his coat off the seat. The coat had been covering a revolver, a wooden-handled .38 special. He looked at the revolver a moment; then he put it inside the dash drawer and slammed the door shut. He passed his fingers through his long sandy hair, and we went into the yard.

The men in the yard spoke to Gil, but in a quiet, subdued way. You could see how much he was the hero among them, but there was no enthusiasm today. Gil nodded to most of them, and shook hands with a couple of them, but he did not stop to talk. The men didn't say anything to me or Russ. I stuck close behind Gil, and Russ was a step or two behind me. As we came up on the porch, I could hear people talking inside the house. Gil pulled the screen door and pushed open the wooden door, and we came into a room where there were at least three dozen people. Men, women, small children, all speaking either Cajun French or English.

"Bonjoure, Gi-bear," a little girl said to Gil.

Gil leaned over and kissed her. He shook hands with a couple more people; then he asked about his father. A

big man wearing khakis nodded toward a door to the
right. Russ and I followed Gil through the door and into
another room. This room was not as crowded—maybe a
dozen people. All men except two women and a little
boy. The two women sat on a four-poster brass bed
which had a mosquito net at the head of it. One of the
women had her head down and was crying, and the other
one had her arm around her. Fix Boutan was sitting in
a soft chair by the window, and the little boy was in his
lap. Fix was a short man with a big head, broad shoulders, thick chest, and big hands. He had practically no
neck at all, and his big head set on his shoulders the way
a volleyball sits on a bench. He must have just come
from the barbershop, because his gray hair was cut close
on the sides, brushed straight back on top, and I could
smell as well as see the oil in his hair. He probably had
gone to the barber to get himself all prettied up for the
big game the next day. He squinted up at Gil when we
came into the room, and you could see that he had been
crying.

"You got here," he said.

"Yes, Papa," Gil said, and kissed him on the side of
the face.

Gil passed his hand over the head of the little boy who
sat in Fix's lap; then he turned to the women on the bed.
One could have been in her late teens, the other one was
in her mid- or late twenties—she was the one crying. Gil
leaned over and kissed her. He said something to her
that I didn't understand; then after speaking to the
younger woman, he spoke and shook hands with two or
three of the other men in the room. The men shook
hands, nodded, and spoke quietly. Gil turned back to
Fix.

"Papa, I know this is a family matter, but Sully drove
me down from Baton Rouge, and I asked Russ to come
in, too."

Fix nodded to me. It was not the most enthusiastic nod
I had ever received, but I could understand after what
had happened today. He looked at Russ, but he didn't
speak or nod to him. He looked back at Gil.

"Why you so late getting here?"

"I went by Marshall, Papa."

"You see him?"

"They had already taken him to Bayonne."

The woman on the bed who was crying lowered her head more. The other woman held her close. Fix looked at the two women, and looked back at Gil. The little boy in Fix's lap, who was four or five, laid his head against Fix's chest.

Gil sat on the bed beside the woman and clasped his hands and looked down at the floor. Fix and the other men watched him.

"Well?" Fix said when Gil had not said anything for a while.

"He doesn't want you there, Papa," Gil said, looking up at Fix.

Fix squinted back at Gil. Several of the other men mumbled among themselves. Fix raised a big hand, not very high, and the men respected it.

"Don't want me where?" Fix asked Gil.

"Marshall, or Bayonne. Until he sends for you," Gil said.

"Mapes is crazy," one of them said.

"He's got to be crazy," someone else said.

"My boy laying dead in the morgue, shot down like a dog, and Mapes don't want me in Bayonne?" Fix asked Gil.

"He's crazy," one of the men said.

Fix looked at the man to shut him up. Fix had small dark pig eyes, and he didn't have to look at you very long or very hard to shut you up. He looked back at Gil.

"Mapes still at Marshall?"

"Yes, Papa," Gil said.

"What's he doing at Marshall?" Fix asked.

"Talking to the people," Gil said.

"Talking to the people about what? He don't know who did it?"

"He thinks Mathu did it."

"But why should Mathu kill my boy?"

"He claimed Beau came into his yard with a gun."

"What for?" Fix asked.

"He came after Charlie. He came with a gun."

"And Mathu killed him for that?" Fix asked.

"That's what Mapes believes."

"Ain't we wasting time, Fix?" a big, rough-looking guy standing in the back of the room asked Fix. He wore one of those Hawaiian shirts with all the red and blue and yellow flowers on it. The tail of the shirt was out of his pants. He stood next to another rough-looking guy, who wore a brown, short-sleeve shirt. Both wore khaki pants.

"Luke Will," Fix said. "You might have been a friend of Beau's. But you not a member of this family, and you don't speak."

"I was closer than a friend," Luke Will said. "I was a good friend. We had a beer last night."

"You still don't speak," Fix told him. "I speak. My sons speak. I tell you when to speak. That's clear, Luke Will?"

"I still say we're wasting valuable time," Luke Will said.

"You better go out, Luke Will, if you can't control your mouth," Fix told him.

Luke Will didn't move. Fix looked at him awhile; then he looked at the other big, rough-looking guy in the brown shirt, warning him, too. Fix turned back to Gil sitting on the bed.

"Well?" Fix said to him.

"Can I say something, Papa?" Gil said.

"I'm waiting," Fix said.

"Papa," Gil said, and leaned a little forward on the bed to look at him. "Papa," he said again. But he didn't say any more.

Fix looked at Gil, and patted the little boy on the leg. The little boy wore short blue pants and a white tee shirt. He didn't have on any shoes.

"Well?" Fix said to Gil.

"Papa," Gil said. "I went to Marshall."

"You said that," Fix said.

"I saw something over there, Papa—something you, I, none of us in this room has ever seen before. A bunch of old black men with shotguns, Papa. Old men, your age, Parrain's age, Monsieur Auguste's age, all with shotguns, Papa. Waiting for you."

"Niggers with shotguns waiting for me?" Fix asked. His dark piglike eyes opened just a little bit wider. He squeezed the little boy closer to his chest.

"Fifteen, and maybe even more," Gil said. "And Mapes there with a pump gun—all waiting for you."

"Then let's accommodate Mapes and his niggers," someone else said.

"Papa," Gil said, without ever looking around at the other person. "Old men, Papa. Cataracts. Hardly any teeth. Arthritic. Old men. Old black men, Papa. Who have been hurt. Who wait—not for you, Papa—what you're supposed to represent. Ask Sully. Tired old men trying hard to hold up their heads."

"What are you trying to say, Gi-bear?" Fix asked him.

Gil looked up at me to help out. "Sully, please tell him," he said.

"I'm not talking to your friend there, Gi-bear, I'm talking to you," Fix said.

"Papa," Gil said. He rubbed the knuckles of both fists, trying to figure out a way to say it. When it came to running that ball, he ran it as well as anybody I'd ever seen in my life, but trying to tell his father what he felt inside of him was the hardest thing for him to do. "Papa," Gil said. "All my life I have heard what my family have done to others. I hear it today—from the blacks, from the whites. I hear it from the opponents even when we play in another town. Don't tackle me too hard, because they would have to answer to the rest of the Boutans. It hurts me to hear that, Papa. It hurts me in here," he said, hitting his chest. "It hurts me because I know it's not true."

"What are you trying to say, Gi-bear?" Fix said. "Get to the point."

"Papa," Gil said, rubbing his knuckles again. "Papa, I want to be an All-American at LSU. I have a good chance—Cal and me. The first time ever, black and white, in the Deep South. I can't make it without Cal,

Papa. I depend on him. Every time I take that ball, I depend on his block, or his faking somebody out of my way. I depend on him, Papa, every moment I'm on that field."

Fix watched him. Gil looked down at the floor, biting his bottom lip. Fix waited. The rest of the people waited. If anybody was breathing, they were doing it quietly. The little boy in Fix's lap laid his head against Fix's chest and sucked his thumb. Everybody waited for Gil to go on. The woman on the bed who had been crying was quiet. The younger woman kept her arm around her. The people in the other room were not talking as much as before.

Gil looked up at Fix.

"I couldn't make All-American, Papa, if I was involved in something against the law," he said. "Even if our name was involved, the Yankee press would destroy me." Gil leaned closer toward his father. "Papa, I'm not putting things right. I'm not saying what I want to say. But do you understand what I'm trying to say? Do you understand, Papa?"

"What about your brother, Gi-bear?" Fix asked. Those little dark pig eyes looked deadly at Gil. "What about Beau?"

"I loved my brother, Papa. He was much older than me, but we were very close. He taught me everything I know about fishing and hunting. I loved my brother, Papa. But Beau is dead. Nothing we can do will bring him back. You understand what I'm trying to say, Papa?"

Fix's little dark pig eyes still looked deadly at Gil.

"You through, Gi-bear?" he asked him.

"Papa, I won't go along," Gil said, shaking his head. "You can beat me, but I won't go along."

"I ask if you through, Gi-bear? You through?"

Gil took in a deep breath and nodded his head. And he looked down at the floor.

"What do you think of our great All-American there, Alfonze?" Fix asked. "Hanh, A-goose?"

He was speaking to the two old men sitting over to his right, but he was still looking at Gil. Neither one of the old men answered him. One shrugged his shoulders, but the other one didn't even do that much.

"And you, Claude?" Fix looked up at the man standing near the foot of the bed.

Claude was Gil's older brother. He drove a truck for an oil company in Lafayette. He was a big guy, six two, six three, with jet-black curly hair. He wore khakis, and you could see the sweat marks in the back of the shirt and around the armpit. He was cleaning his fingernails with a small pearl-handled knife. Even after Fix had spoken to him, he went on cleaning his fingernails.

"Whatever you say, Papa," he answered, without looking at Fix.

Fix nodded his head. "Jean?"

Jean was another of Gil's brothers. He didn't look anything like Gil or Claude—or Fix either, for that matter. He was short like Fix, but too pale. He was probably in his mid-thirties. He wore a black-striped seersucker suit, a white shirt, and a little bow tie. He glanced around nervously at the people nearest him; then he moved close to Fix's chair. Fix was looking up at him, and patting the little boy on the leg.

"Papa, we ought to talk," Jean said.

"Then talk."

"What will we do when we go to Bayonne, Papa? Who will go to Bayonne?"

"You don't want to go to Bayonne?" Fix asked him.

"I live in Bayonne, Papa," Jean said. "My butcher shop is in Bayonne. But who else is going to Bayonne?" He looked around at the men in the room, then back to Fix again. "And for what reason, Papa?"

"I go to see my boy," Fix said. "And your brother."

"And the rest of these, Papa," Jean said, nodding toward the men in the back of the room. "Why are they going to Bayonne?"

"Your brother was brutally murdered today," Fix said. "You forget so easily, Jean?"

"No, Papa, I don't forget so easily," Jean said. "I won't ever forget this day, ever. But Gilly is right. We have law out there to do what many of these people would like to see us do. Some of these in the room with us right now."

"These people are your friends. My friends, Beau's friends."

"If they're friends of the family, show respect to the family. Stay out of Bayonne until Mapes has cleared this up."

"Mapes will never clear this up," Luke Will said, from the back of the room. "Beau's been dead for hours, shot down like a dirty dog, and Mapes hasn't done a thing about it."

"Don't y'all listen to Luke Will," Russ said. Russ had been standing next to me, and he had been quiet all the time.

"Don't listen to him. All he and that gang want is trouble."

"What gang's that, Russell?" Luke Will asked.

"You know what gang," Russ said, still looking at Fix.

"Scared to call their names?" Luke Will asked him. He grinned, a real mean grin, the kind of grin that comes from just the corner of the mouth.

"Everybody in here know who I'm talking about," Russ said. He never looked at Luke Will. "Don't listen to Luke Will, Fix. He's no friend."

"He's a friend," Fix said.

"Give the word, Fix," Luke Will said.

"What word is that, Luke Will?" Fix asked, looking back at him.

"We go to Marshall."

"That's my decision to make, Luke Will—and my sons'. Not yours."

Luke Will nodded. "All right, Fix. I'll wait your decision. Then I'll go to Marshall."

"Don't try it," Russ said, looking back at him for the first time.

Luke Will grinned at Russ. He was one of those big, hulking, beer-belly red-necks. He had long brown hair, and when he grinned from the side of his mouth, I could see that some of his teeth were missing. The guy standing next to him didn't look any better than Luke Will did, but at least he kept his mouth shut.

"I won't have none of that in my house," Fix said. "And you, Russell, I would be quiet if I were you."

"I'll do anything to keep you back here, Fix," Russ said. "And that goes for the rest of you," he said, looking around the room. He looked back at Fix. "I mean it, Fix," he said. "I have my orders."

"Russell," Fix said, pointing his finger at him. "You can't keep me back here. Only my sons can keep me back here. You remember that."

"Jean and Gilly are right," Russ said. "Luke Will is wrong. Luke Will wants trouble."

"In my house, I say what is right and what is wrong," Fix said, raising his voice now. He held the little boy with the left hand while he pointed the right hand at Russ. "I decide. Me, William Fix Boutan, I decide."

He stared at Russ to see if Russ had any more to say. Russ looked down at him, but remained quiet.

Fix turned to the old men sitting to his right. Both sat in their chairs erect as boards, listening, but staying quiet. The one nearest Fix wore a clean, ironed white shirt and khaki pants. His hat was on his knee. The other one wore a Hawaiian shirt with about six different colors in it. He wore white pants, and his hat hung on the back of his chair.

"What should I do, Alfonze?" Fix asked the one nearest him. His voice was calm again.

"I go along whatever you decide, Fix," the old man said.

"A-goose?" Fix asked the other one

"I'm an old man, Fix," Auguste said. "I don't know who is right and who is wrong anymore."

"I'm an old man, too," Fix said. "Twenty years ago I would not have asked questions. I would have been at Marshall by now."

"I would have been at Marshall with you twenty years ago, Fix."

"They're old as we are," Fix said. "They're waiting for me—according to this All-American here."

"Old men with guns waiting for old men with guns, Fix, but isn't that a farce?" Auguste said.

"And Beau on that cold slab in Bayoone, A-goose? Is that a farce also?"

"I christened him," Auguste said. "I'm his parrain. You must know how I feel."

"Ain't we wasting time, Fix?" Luke Will asked, from the back of the room again.

"Jean and Gi-bear say no, Luke Will. Even my good friend A-goose says no."

"A-goose is an old man, and don't have all his senses," Luke Will said. "Gilly and Jean want to keep their good names with the niggers. Gilly want to play football with niggers, mess around with them little stinky nigger gals. Beat Ole Miss tomorrow, that's what he wants. As for Mr. Jean there, he has to sell his hog guts and cracklings to the niggers. No decent white man would buy 'em."

"Is that so, Gi-bear?" Fix asked Gil. "Your brother's honor for the sake to play football side by side with the niggers—is that so?"

"Luke Will's days are over with, Papa," Gil said. "Luke Will's days are passed. Gone forever."

"And mine?" Fix asked him. "Mine, Gi-bear?"

"Those days are gone, Papa," Gil said. "Those days when you just take the law in your own hands—those days are gone. These are the '70s, soon to be the '80s. Not the '20s, the '30s, or the '40s. People died—people we knew—died to change those things. Those days are gone forever, I hope."

"What day is gone, Gi-bear?" Fix asked him. "The day when family responsibility is put aside for a football game? Is that the day you speak of, Gi-bear?"

"I'm not speaking of family responsibility, Papa," Gil said. "I'm speaking of the day of the vigilante. I'm speaking of Luke Will's idea of justice."

"So I'm a vigilante now, huh, Gi-bear?" Fix asked him.

"That's what Luke Will wants us to do," Gil said. "He and his gang still think the world needs them. The world has changed, Papa. Luke Will and his gang are a dying breed. They need a cause like this to pump blood back into their dying bodies."

"And Beau?" Luke Will asked Gil. He had to speak to Gil's back, because Gil would not give him the respect of looking round at him. "Beau," Luke Will said again. "He's more alive than I am at this moment?"

"Well, Gi-bear?" Fix asked.

"Beau is dead, and I'm sorry, Papa," Gil said. "But I would like people to know we're not what they think we are. They all expect us to ride tonight. They're all waiting for that. I say let them wait. Let them wait and wait and wait."

"And you there, Mr. Butcher of hog-gut fame?" Fix said, looking up at Jean.

"They want something to happen," Jean said, wiping his face with a handkerchief. He wiped the palms of his hands and put the handkerchief back. "I go along with Gilly."

Fix looked up at him, nodding his head; then he looked around at the rest of the people in the room.

"And the rest of you, how you feel?" he asked. "You feel that this, this butcher and this, this All-American got a point?"

"We're wasting time," Luke Will said.

No one else spoke out. They only mumbled among themselves. Neither Russ, Claude, nor I said anything. I was not about to open my mouth.

"Well, Gi-bear?" Fix asked.

"They'll listen to you, Papa," Gil said. "Make them see that it'll hurt the family. It'll hurt our name."

"But especially yours, huh, Mr. All-American?"

"It would hurt me, Papa. Yes."

Fix looked from Gil to the woman sitting on the bed with her head bowed. She had been quiet a long time, but never once raised her head to look at anyone. Fix looked at the little boy in his lap and patted him on the leg.

"You know this little boy I'm holding here?" he asked, looking back at Gil. "Tee Beau. No more papa." He looked at Gil awhile to let those words make an impression; then he nodded toward the woman on the bed. "You know that lady sitting there—Doucette? Huh? No more husband."

"I'm sorry, Papa," Gil said. "I'll do all I can for Tee Beau and Doucette."

"Sure, you will," Fix said. "We all will. But now her husband, his papa, your brother, lay dead on a cold slab in Bayonne, and we do nothing but sit here and talk. Well, Gi-bear?"

Gil lowered his head, and didn't answer.

"I wait, I wait. I wait for all my sons, but especially for you. The one we sent to LSU. The only one in the family to ever go to LSU. The only one to ever get a high education. The educated one, Alfonze, A-goose. We wait for Mr. Educated All-American. What does he say? He says don't move. He says sit, weep with the women. Because he wishes to be an All-American. The other one I can understand. He must sell his hog guts. He never was bright. An elementary education was his schooling. But this one—all the way to the university."

"We're doing nothing here but wasting time, Fix," Luke Will said again. "Mapes needs help."

"I won't go without my sons," Fix said. "All my sons. There will be no split in this family. This is family. Family. The majority, or none."

"And let those niggers stand there with guns, and we don't accommodate them? They want war, let's give them war," Luke Will said.

A couple of the other men agreed with him.

"I'm not interested in your war, Luke Will," Fix told him. "I'm interested only in my family. If the majority feels their brother is not worth it, then the family has spoken. I'm only interested in my family."

Gil raised his head to look at his father. He was crying.

"I'm sorry, Papa," he said.

"Sorry, Gi-bear? About what, Gi-bear."

"Everything."

"No. Explain, Gi-bear."

"For what happened, Papa. For Beau. For us all. That you think I've gone against you, I'm sorry. I'm sorry for those old men at Marshall. Yes, Papa, I'm sorry for them, too."

"A regular Christ," Fix said. He made the sign of the cross. "A regular Christ in our midst, Alfonze, A-goose. Feels sorry for the entire world."

The two old men, very thin, sat as erect as boards, and remained quiet.

Fix continued to look at Gil. Then his head began moving back and forth, back and forth, so slightly, though, that it was almost unnoticeable. The longer he looked at Gil, the more his head moved back and forth. His dark pig eyes narrowed to where they were almost closed. He was still looking at Gil, looking at him as though all trust and belief and hope had vanished. Now he jerked his head toward him.

"Leave, Gi-bear," he said. "Go on. That is your mon's bed you sit on. Where you were born, where Beau was born, where all you were born. Now you desecrate the bed with your body upon it. Go block. Go run the ball. Let it take the place of family. Let it bring flowers to that cemetery, La Toussaint. I don't wish to see you in this house, or at that cemetery. Go. Go run the ball."

Gil could not believe what he was hearing. None of us could. He stared at his father, wanting to say something, but he could not. Fix's small dark eyes in his broad, sunburnt face assured Gil that he meant every word he spoke.

"Fix." The old man nearest him leaned forward and touched him on the arm. "Fix," he said.

"I'm dead, Alfonze," Fix said. "The one we worked for, hoped for, sacrificed for. I may as well go lay beside Maltilde."

"You're not dead, Fix," the old man said.

"They say I am—the All-American and the butcher. They say my ideas are all past. They say to love family, to defend family honor, is all past. What is left? All my life, that is all I found worthwhile living for. My family. My family. No, there's only one place left to go now, to the cemetery there in Bayonne—Beau and me beside Maltilde."

"I'll go to Marshall with you, Fix," the old man said. His face did not show much emotion, and the long bony finger touching Fix's arm did not show too much life, either. "I'll take my gun and I'll go with you, if that is your wish," he said.

"Two old men, Alfonze? A-goose was right. That is a farce."

"Others will join us, I'm sure. Goudeau will join us— he has fire in him still. Montemare, Felix Richard—Anatole will get out of that chair."

"This is family, Alfonze," Fix told him. "I have no other cause to fight for. I'm too old for causes. Let Luke Will fight for causes. This is family. A member of the family has been insulted, and family, the family must seek justice. But these, they say no. They say it is past when man must live for his family. So what else is left but to go lay in that cemetery with Beau and Maltilde?" He looked at Gil sitting on the bed. "I told you to leave. Take your brother Mr. Hog Gut with you. I don't wish to see either one of you ever again. Go, change your name if that will help you be All-American. Get out of my house. Go tell your friend Mapes this old Cajun will come to Bayonne at the law's convenience. Now I have no more to say."

He took a big red print handkerchief from his back pocket and blew his nose. He put the handkerchief back and held the little boy close to his chest and looked down at the floor.

Gil stood up and turned to his brother Claude. Claude was scraping one of his thumbnails with the little pearl-handled knife.

"Claude?" Gil pleaded with him. "Claude?"

Claude went on scraping his thumbnail without answering Gil. He wouldn't even raise his head. Gil turned to one of the old men, old Alfonze. "Parrain," he said. "Haven't I been a good boy, Parrain? Haven't I always obeyed my father and obeyed you? When I come here to visit my father, don't I visit you and all the rest of the people on the bayou? Don't I go to mass with the family? Don't I get tickets so all of you can attend the games?

Don't I, Parrain?" The old man looked at Fix, not at
Gil. "Monsieur Auguste," Gil said to the other old man.
"Aren't I a good boy, Monsieur Auguste?" But the old
man only stared across the room. "Doucette?" Gil said
to the woman on the bed. "You don't like me anymore,
Doucette? You don't want Tee Beau to be like me anymore, Doucette? Hanh, Doucette?" The woman kept
her head down and did not answer him. Gil looked
around the room. The only people to look back at him
were Luke Will and the other rough-looking guy, and
they were not friendly looks, not by a long shot.

Gil turned back to Fix. Fix sat in the chair, head
bowed, slumped a little forward, like a stone bear.

"Beat me if you want to," Gil said. "I'll get the whip.
Beat me if you want to, but don't send me away from
this house. Don't send me away from home, Papa?"

Fix sat there like stone. He was not hearing anything
anymore.

Russ put his arm around Gil's shoulders and let him
out of the room, with me a step behind them. The people
in the other room had already heard what had happened,
and they were not looking at Gil the way they did when
he first came there. They gave him plenty of room to
pass this time, and I saw a woman holding back the same
little girl who had spoken to him before and wanted to
come to him again. The little girl struggled and struggled,
but the woman held her back, pressing the girl's head
against her thigh.

We pushed our way out onto the porch. Through the
screen, I could see the sun going down behind the trees
on the other side of the bayou. A thin purple cloud lay
across the sun, making the sky look like a nice, serene
painting.

"You had to do what you did," Russ said.

"I could have run the other way," Gil said.

"And that would have been better?" Russ asked him.

"It couldn't be any worse," Gil said.

While we stood out on the porch, Luke Will and that
other rough-looking guy came out there.

"If you think this is the end of it, you're crazy," Luke Will said to Gil.

"Get out of here, Luke Will," Russ said. "You don't speak for this family."

"Somebody better do it," Luke Will said.

"Nobody voted for you," Russ said.

"Maybe I'll just take it as my duty, on principle," Luke Will said.

"I don't want no trouble out of you, Luke Will," Russ said. "Stay away from Marshall, and stay out Bayonne. I'm warning you."

"You don't scare me, Russell," Luke Will said. "You or that fat belly of a boss you got there don't scare me the least."

"Just don't start any trouble," Russ said. "I'm warning you."

"The trouble already been started," Luke Will said. "When niggers start shooting down white men in broad daylight, the trouble was stared then."

"We don't need your kind to settle it."

"Somebody got to do it 'fore it gets out of hand," Luke Will said. "Next thing you know, they'll be raping the women."

"That's how it is," Russ said to me. "If they can't get you one way, they'll bring in the women every time."

"Maybe you don't mind if they rape your wife or your little daughter," Luke Will said. "Maybe something like that's been going on all the time, and you just don't care."

He grinned at Russ. He wanted Russ to take a swing at him. But Russ was too cool for that.

"You see the psychology behind it all?" he said to me.

But I kept my mouth shut. I wasn't going to say a word while those two were standing there. I wasn't going to even breathe out of my mouth.

"You and your kind, your time has passed, Luke Will," Russ said.

"It ain't my time you better worry about," Luke Will said. "I'll be around when you and your kind are long

gone. You might kill him off in there," he said to Gil.
"But I'm go'n be around. Let's go, Sharp."

They let the screen door slam behind them. They were
both big men, big country red-necks, the kind Bull Connor used as his deputies back there in the '60s. They
went across the road to a white pickup, which had a gun
rack in the cab and two guns on the rack. The truck also
had a CB radio, and Luke Will got on the radio and
began talking. The other guy, Sharp, started up the truck
and drove away. We watched it go down the road.

"What are you going to do?" Russ asked Gil.

"I don't know," Gil said.

"You want my opinion?" Russ said. "Go on back to
Baton Rouge, try to get yourself some rest, play football
tomorrow. Play the best game you ever played in your
life."

Gil looked at Russ as if he couldn't believe what he
had heard him say.

"What?" he said. "My brother is dead. Papa in there
hating me, Claude hating me, Doucette, Tee Beau hating
me—and you talk about a football game? Are you
crazy?"

"There isn't a thing you can do here tonight," Russ
said. "Tomorrow you can do something for yourself, and
for all the rest of us—play the best game you ever played.
Luke Will and his kind don't want to see you and Pepper
in that backfield tomorrow. He doesn't ever want to see
you and Pepper together."

"And what about my brother?" Gil asked. "Claude?
Papa? Doucette and Tee Beau? How would it look to
them?"

Russ shrugged his shoulders and shook his head. "A
lot wouldn't understand. Many would hate it. But that
game is going to be seen on TV by millions, and more
of them will be pulling for you and Pepper than pulling
against you."

"Damn the public," Gil said. "I'm talking about my
family. Not the damned public. My family."

"I'm thinking about your family, too," Russ said.
"Especially Tee Beau."

"And Papa?" Gil asked Russ.

"Tee Beau," Russ told him. "Tee Beau. Tee Beau's future. You want to do something for your dead brother? Do something for his son's future—play in that game tomorrow. Whether you win against Ole Miss or not, you'll beat Luke Will. Because if you don't, he'll win tomorrow, and if he does, he may just keep on winning. That's not much of a future for Tee Beau, is it?"

"What bout my papa?" Gil asked. "I've already killed him. Bury him tomorrow?"

Russ laid his hand on Gil's shoulder.

"Gilly," he said. "Sometimes you got to hurt something to help something. Sometimes you have to plow under one thing in order for something else to grow. You can help Tee Beau tomorrow. You can help this country tomorrow. You can help yourself."

Gil looked away from him.

"Well," Russ said. "No more speeches. I have to report to Mapes. I'll be out there in the car if you want to talk."

He left the porch, loosening his tie. Halfway to the road, he had already taken off the tie and the coat. He hung them on a hanger in the back seat of the car; then he got in front to speak on the radio.

"He is right, Gil," I said. "We ought to go back."

Gil didn't answer me. He was looking across the road toward the trees along the bayou. Then sun had sunk a little below the thin layer of purple cloud.

"What you say, Gil?"

"Leave me alone," he said. "I just want to think. Dammit, don't you see I just want to think?"

Richard Wright

Richard Wright was born in 1908, near Natchez, Mississippi, and was largely self-educated because his family's
frequent moves interrupted his formal schooling. After
working at odd jobs in Memphis and other cities and
clerking at a post office in Chicago, Wright was employed
by the Works Progress Administration Federal Writers'
Project in Chicago and New York. In 1938 he published
a collection of stories, *Uncle Tom's Children*, and won a
prize from *Story* magazine. These stories all deal with a
cycle of violence that involves white victimization of
blacks and black retaliation against whites. Wright's next
work was a novel, *Native Son* (1940), which Wright's
protégé James Baldwin called "the most powerful and
celebrated statement we have yet had of what it means
to be a Negro in America." Wright won the Spingarn
Medal from the National Association for the Advance-
ment of Colored People for *Native Son*, and the novel
was later made into a movie, for which Wright wrote
the screenplay. Many critics consider his autobiography,
Black Boy (1945), to be his most important work. Wright
moved to France in 1947 and lived in Paris until his death
in 1960. There he met existentialist writers Jean-Paul Sartre and Simone de Beauvoir, whose philosophy appealed
to his own feelings of rootlessness and alienation. During
this time, he began to write nonfiction about the national
independence movements in Africa, such works as *Black
Power* (1954), *The Color Curtain* (1956), and *White Man,
Listen!* (1957). Critics have called Wright one of the most
influential American writers of the twentieth century.

The Man Who Was
Almost a Man

Dave struck out across the fields, looking homeward through paling light. Whut's the use talkin wid em niggers in the field? Anyhow, his mother was putting supper on the table. Them niggers can't understan nothing. One of these days he was going to get a gun and practice shooting, then they couldn't talk to him as though he were a little boy. He slowed, looking at the ground. Shucks, Ah ain scareda them even ef they are biggern me! Aw, Ah know whut Ahma do. Ahm going by ol Joe's sto n git that Sears Roebuck catlog n look at them guns. Mebbe Ma will lemme buy one when she gits mah pay from ol man Hawkins. Ahma beg her t gimme some money. Ahm ol ernough to hava gun. Ahm seventeen. Almost a man. He strode, feeling his long loose-jointed limbs. Shucks, a man oughta hava little gun aftah he done worked hard all day.

He came in sight of Joe's store. A yellow lantern glowed on the front porch. He mounted steps and went through the screen door, hearing it bang behind him. There was a strong smell of coal oil and mackerel fish. He felt very confident until he saw fat Joe walk in through the rear door, then his courage began to ooze.

"Howdy, Dave! Whutcha want?"

"How yuh, Mistah Joe? Aw, Ah don wanna buy nothing. Ah just wanted t see ef yuhd lemme look at tha catlog erwhile."

"Sure! You wanna see it here?"

"Nawsuh. Ah wans t take it home wid me. Ah'll bring it back termorrow when Ah come in from the fiels."

"You plannin on buying something?"

"Yessuh."

"Your ma lettin you have your own money now?"

"Shucks. Mistah Joe, Ahm gittin t be a man like anybody else!"

Joe laughed and wiped his greasy white face with a red bandanna.

"Whut you plannin on buyin?"

Dave looked at the floor, scratched his head, scratched his thigh, and smiled. Then he looked up shyly.

"Ah'll tell yuh, Mistah Joe, ef yuh promise yuh won't tell."

"I promise."

"Waal, Ahma buy a gun."

"A gun? Whut you want with a gun?"

"Ah wanna keep it."

"You ain't nothing but a boy. You don't need a gun."

"Aw, lemme have the catlog, Mistah Joe. Ah'll bring it back."

Joe walked through the rear door. Dave was elated. He looked around at barrels of sugar and flour. He heard Joe coming back. He craned his neck to see if he were bringing the book. Yeah, he's got it. Gawddog, he's got it!

"Here, but be sure you bring it back. It's the only one I got."

"Sho, Mistah Joe."

"Say, if you wanna buy a gun, why don't you buy one from me? I gotta gun to sell."

"Will it shoot?"

"Sure it'll shoot."

"Whut kind is it?"

"Oh, it's kinda old . . . a left-hand Wheeler. A pistol. A big one."

"Is it got bullets in it?"

"It's loaded."

"Kin Ah see it?"

"Where's your money?"

"Whut yuh wan fer it?"

"I'll let you have it for two dollars."

"Just two dollahs? Shucks, Ah could buy tha when Ah git mah pay."

"I'll have it here when you want it."

"Awright, suh. Ah be in fer it."

He went through the door, hearing it slam again behind him. *Ahma git some money from Ma n buy me a gun! Only two dollahs!* He tucked the thick catalogue under his arm and hurried.

"Where yuh been, boy?" His mother held a steaming dish of black-eyed peas.

"Aw, Ma, Ah jus stopped down the road t talk wid the boys."

"Yuh know bettah t keep suppah waitin."

He sat down, resting the catalogue on the edge of the table.

"Yuh git up from there and git to the well n wash yosef! Ah ain feedin no hogs in mah house!"

She grabbed his shoulder and pushed him. He stumbled out of the room, then came back to get the catalogue.

"Whut this?"

"Aw, Ma, it's jusa catlog."

"Who yuh git it from?"

"From Joe, down at the sto."

"Waal, thas good. We kin use it in the outhouse."

"Naw, Ma." He grabbed for it. "Gimme ma catlog, Ma."

She held onto it and glared at him.

"Quit hollerin at me! Whut's wrong wid yuh? Yuh crazy?"

"But Ma, please. It ain mine! It's Joe's! He tol me t bring it back t im termorrow."

She gave up the book. He stumbled down the back steps, hugging the thick book under his arm. When he had splashed water on his face and hands, he groped back to the kitchen and fumbled in a corner for the towel. He bumped into a chair; it clattered to the floor. The catalogue sprawled at his feet. When he had dried his eyes he snatched up the book and held it again under his arm. His mother stood watching him.

"Now, ef yuh gonna act a fool over that ol book, Ah'll take it n burn it up."

"Naw, Ma, please."

"Waal, set down n be still!"

He sat down and drew the oil lamp close. He thumbed page after page, unaware of the food his mother set on the table. His father came in. Then his small brother.

"Whutcha got there, Dave?" his father asked.

"Jusa catlog," he answered, not looking up.

"Yeah, here they is!" His eyes glowed at blue-and-black revolvers. He glanced up, feeling sudden guilt. His father was watching him. He eased the book under the table and rested it on his knees. After the blessing was asked, he ate. He scooped up peas and swallowed fat meat without chewing. Buttermilk helped to wash it down. He did not want to mention money before his father. He would do much better by cornering his mother when she was alone. He looked at his father uneasily out of the edge of his eye.

"Boy, how come yuh don quit foolin wid tha book n eat yo suppah?"

"Yessuh."

"How you n ol man Hawkins gitten erlong?"

"Suh?"

"Can't yuh hear? Why don yuh lissen? Ah ast yu how wuz yuh n ol man Hawkins gittin erlong?"

"Oh, swell, Pa. Ah plows mo lan than anybody over there."

"Waal, yuh oughta keep yo mind on whut yuh doin."

"Yessuh."

He poured his plate full of molasses and sopped it up slowly with a chunk of cornbread. When his father and brother had left the kitchen, he still sat and looked again at the guns in the catalogue, longing to muster courage enough to present his case to his mother. Lawd, ef Ah only had tha pretty one! He could almost feel the slickness of the weapon with his fingers. If he had a gun like

that he would polish it and keep it shining so it would
never rust. N Ah'd keep it loaded, by Gawd!

"Ma?" His voice was hesitant.

"Hunh?"

"Ol man Hawkins give yuh mah money yit?"

"Yeah, but ain no usa yuh thinking bout throwin nona
it erway. Ahm keepin tha money sos yuh kin have cloes
t go to school this winter."

He rose and went to her side with the open catalogue
in his palms. She was washing dishes, her head bent low
over a pan. Shyly he raised the book. When he spoke,
his voice was husky, faint.

"Ma, Gawd knows Ah wans one of these."

"One of whut?" she asked, not raising her eyes.

"One of these," he said again, not daring even to
point. She glanced up at the page, then at him with wide
eyes.

"Nigger, is yuh gone plumb crazy?"

"Aw, Ma—"

"Git outta here! Don yuh talk t me bout no gun! Yuh
a fool!"

"Ma, Ah kin buy one fer two dollahs."

"Not ef Ah knows it, yuh ain!"

"But yuh promised me one—"

"Ah don care whut Ah promised! Yuh ain nothing but
a boy yit!"

"Ma, ef yuh lemme buy one Ah'll *never* ast yuh fer
nothing no mo."

"Ah tol yuh t git outta here! Yuh ain gonna toucha
penny of tha money fer no gun! Thas how come Ah has
Mistah Hawkins t pay yo wages t me, cause Ah knows
yuh ain got no sense."

"But, Ma, we needa gun. Pa ain got no gun. We needa
gun in the house. Yuh kin never tell whut might
happen."

"Now don yuh try to maka fool outta me, boy! Ef we
did hava gun, yuh wouldn't have it!"

He laid the catalogue down and slipped his arm around
her waist.

"Aw, Ma, Ah done worked hard alla summer n ain ast yuh fer nothin, is Ah, now?"

"Thas whut yuh spose t do!"

"But Ma, Ah wans a gun. Yuh kin lemme have two dollahs outta mah money. Please, Ma. I kin give it to Pa . . . Please, Ma! Ah loves yuh, Ma."

When she spoke her voice came soft and low.

"Whut yu wan wida gun, Dave? Yuh don need no gun. Yuh'll git in trouble. N ef yo pa jus thought Ah let yuh have money t buy a gun he'd hava fit."

"Ah'll hide it, Ma. It ain but two dollahs."

"Lawd, chil, whut's wrong wid yuh?"

"Ain nothin wrong, Ma. Ahm almos a man now. Ah wans a gun."

"Who gonna sell yuh a gun?"

"Ol Joe at the sto."

"N it don cos but two dollahs?"

"Thas all, Ma. Jus two dollahs. Please, Ma."

She was stacking the plates away; her hands moved slowly, reflectively. Dave kept an anxious silence. Finally, she turned to him.

"Ah'll let you git tha gun ef yuh promise me one thing."

"Whut's tha, Ma?"

"Yuh bring it straight back t me, yuh hear? It be fer Pa."

"Yessum! Lemme go now, Ma."

She stooped, turned slightly to one side, raised the hem of her dress, rolled down the top of her stocking, and came up with a slender wad of bills.

"Here," she said. "Lawd knows yuh don need no gun. But yer pa does. Yuh bring it right back t me, yuh hear? Ahma put it up. Now ef yuh don, Ahma have yuh pa lick yuh so hard yuh won fergit it."

"Yessum."

He took the money, ran down the steps, and across the yard.

"Dave! Yuuuuuh Daaaaave!"

He heard, but he was not going to stop now. "Naw, Lawd!"

*   *   *

The first movement he made the following morning was to reach under his pillow for the gun. In the gray light of dawn he held it loosely, feeling a sense of power. Could kill a man with a gun like this. Kill anybody, black or white. And if he were holding his gun in his hand, nobody could run over him; they would have to respect him. It was a big gun, with a long barrel and a heavy handle. He raised and lowered it in his hand, marveling at its weight.

He had not come straight home with it as his mother had asked; instead he had stayed out in the fields, holding the weapon in his hand, aiming it now and then at some imaginary foe. But he had not fired it; he had been afraid that his father might hear. Also he was not sure he knew how to fire it.

To avoid surrendering the pistol he had not come into the house until he knew that they were all asleep. When his mother had tiptoed to his bedside late that night and demanded the gun, he had first played possum; then he had told her that the gun was hidden outdoors, that he would bring it to her in the morning. Now he lay turning it slowly in his hands. He broke it, took out the cartridges, felt them, and then put them back.

He slid out of bed, got a long strip of old flannel from a trunk, wrapped the gun in it, and tied it to his naked thigh while it was still loaded. He did not go in to breakfast. Even though it was not yet daylight, he started for Jim Hawkins' plantation. Just as the sun was rising he reached the barns where the mules and plows were kept.

"Hey! That you, Dave?"

He turned. Jim Hawkins stood eying him suspiciously.

"What're yuh doing here so early?"

"Ah didn't know Ah wuz gittin up so early, Mistah Hawkins. Ah wuz fixin t hitch up ol Jenny n take her t the fiels."

"Good. Since you're so early, how about plowing that stretch down by the woods?"

"Suits me, Mistah Hawkins."

"O.K. Go to it!"

He hitched Jenny to a plow and started across the fields. Hot dog! This was just what he wanted. If he could get down by the woods, he could shoot his gun and nobody would hear. He walked behind the plow, hearing the traces creaking, feeling the gun tied tight to his thigh.

When he reached the woods, he plowed two whole rows before he decided to take out the gun. Finally, he stopped, looked in all directions, then untied the gun and held it in his hand. He turned to the mule and smiled.

"Know whut this is, Jenny? Naw, yuh wouldn know! Yuhs jusa ol mule! Anyhow, this is a gun, n it kin shoot, by Gawd!"

He held the gun at arm's length. Whut t hell, Ahma shoot this thing! He looked at Jenny again.

"Lissen here, Jenny! When Ah pull this ol trigger, Ah don wan yuh t run n acka fool now!"

Jenny stood with head down, her short ears pricked straight. Dave walked off about twenty feet, held the gun far out from him at arm's length, and turned his head. Hell, he told himself, Ah ain afraid. The gun felt loose in his fingers; he waved it wildly for a moment. Then he shut his eyes and tightened his forefinger. Bloom! A report half deafened him and he thought his right hand was torn from his arm. He heard Jenny whinnying and galloping over the field, and he found himself on his knees, squeezing his fingers hard between his legs. His hand was numb; he jammed it into his mouth, trying to warm it, trying to stop the pain. The gun lay at his feet. He did not quite know what had happened. He stood up and stared at the gun as though it were a living thing. He gritted his teeth and kicked the gun. Yuh almos broke mah arm! He turned to look for Jenny; she was far over the fields, tossing her head and kicking wildly.

"Hol on there, ol mule!"

When he caught up with her she stood trembling, walling her big white eyes at him. The plow was far away; the traces had broken. Then Dave stopped short, looking, not believing. Jenny was bleeding. Her left side was red and wet with blood. He went closer. Lawd, have

mercy! Wondah did Ah shoot this mule? He grabbed for
Jenny's mane. She flinched, snorted, whirled, tossing her
head.

"Hol on now! Hol on."

Then he saw the hole in Jenny's side, right between
the ribs. It was round, wet, red. A crimson stream
streaked down the front leg, flowing fast. Good Gawd!
Ah wuzn't shootin at tha mule. He felt panic. He knew
he had to stop that blood, or Jenny would bleed to death.
He had never seen so much blood in all his life. He
chased the mule for half a mile, trying to catch her.
Finally she stopped, breathing hard, stumpy tail half
arched. He caught her mane and led her back to where
the plow and gun lay. Then he stooped and grabbed
handfuls of damp black earth and tried to plug the bullet
hole. Jenny shuddered, whinnied, and broke from him.

"Hol on! Hol on now!"

He tried to plug it again, but blood came anyhow. His
fingers were hot and sticky. He rubbed dirt into his
palms, trying to dry them. Then again he attempted to
plug the bullet hole, but Jenny shied away, kicking her
heels high. He stood helpless. He had to do something.
He ran at Jenny; she dodged him. He watched a red
stream of blood flow down Jenny's leg and form a bright
pool at her feet.

"Jenny . . . Jenny," he called weakly.

His lips trembled. She's bleeding t death! He looked
in the direction of home, wanting to go back, wanting to
get help. But he saw the pistol lying in the damp black
clay. He had a queer feeling that if he only did something, this would not be; Jenny would not be there bleeding to death.

When he went to her this time, she did not move. She
stood with sleepy, dreamy eyes; and when he touched
her she gave a low-pitched whinny and knelt to the
ground, her front knees slopping in blood.

"Jenny . . . Jenny . . ." he whispered.

For a long time she held her neck erect; then her head
sank, slowly. Her ribs swelled with a mighty heave and
she went over.

Dave's stomach felt empty, very empty. He picked up the gun and held it gingerly between his thumb and fore-finger. He buried it at the foot of a tree. He took a stick and tried to cover the pool of blood with dirt—but what was the use? There was Jenny lying with her mouth open and her eyes walled and glassy. He could not tell Jim Hawkins he had shot his mule. But he had to tell something. Yeah, Ah'll tell em Jenny started gittin wil n fell on the joint of the plow. . . . But that would hardly happen to a mule. He walked across the field slowly, head down.

It was sunset. Two of Jim Hawkins' men were over near the edge of the woods digging a hole in which to bury Jenny. Dave was surrounded by a knot of people, all of whom were looking down at the dead mule.

"I don't see how in the world it happened," said Jim Hawkins for the tenth time.

The crowd parted and Dave's mother, father, and small brother pushed into the center.

"Where Dave?" his mother called.

"There he is," said Jim Hawkins.

His mother grabbed him.

"Whut happened, Dave? Whut yuh done?"

"Nothin."

"C mon, boy, talk," his father said.

Dave took a deep breath and told the story he knew nobody believed.

"Waal," he drawled. "Ah brung ol Jenny down here sos Ah could do mah plowin. Ah plowed bout two rows, just like yuh see." He stopped and pointed at the long rows of upturned earth. "Then somethin musta been wrong wid ol Jenny. She wouldn ack right a-tall. She started snortin n kickin her heels. Ah tried t hol her, but she pulled erway, rearin n goin in. Then when the point of the plow was stickin up in the air, she swung erroun n twisted herself back on it . . . She stuck herself n started t bleed. N fo Ah could do anything, she wuz dead."

"Did you ever hear of anything like that in all your life?" asked Jim Hawkins.

There were white and black standing in the crowd. They murmured. Dave's mother came close to him and looked hard into his face. "Tell the truth, Dave," she said.

"Looks like a bullet hole to me," said one man.

"Dave, whut yuh do wid the gun?" his mother asked.

The crowd surged in, looking at him. He jammed his hands into his pockets, shook his head slowly from left to right, and backed away. His eyes were wide and painful.

"Did he hava gun?" asked Jim Hawkins.

"By Gawd, Ah tol yuh tha wuz a gun wound," said a man, slapping his thigh.

His father caught his shoulders and shook him till his teeth rattled.

"Tell whut happened, yuh rascal! Tell whut . . ."

Dave looked at Jenny's still legs and began to cry.

"Whut yuh do wid tha gun?" his mother asked.

"Whut wuz he doin wida gun?" his father asked.

"Come on and tell the truth," said Hawkins. "Ain't nobody going to hurt you . . ."

His mother crowded close to him.

"Did yuh shoot tha mule, Dave?"

Dave cried, seeing blurred white and black faces.

"Ahh ddinn gggo tt sshooot hher . . . Ah ssswear ffo Gawd Ahh ddin. . . . Ah wuz a-tryin t sssee ef the old gggun would sshoot—"

"Where yuh git the gun from?" his father asked.

"Ah got it from Joe, at the sto."

"Where yuh git the money?"

"Ma give it t me."

"He kept worryin me, Bob. Ah had t. Ah tol im t bring the gun right back t me . . . It was fer yuh, the gun."

"But how yuh happen to shoot that mule?" asked Jim Hawkins.

"Ah wuzn shootin at the mule, Mistah Hawkins. The gun jumped when Ah pulled the trigger . . . N fo Ah knowed anythin Jenny was there a-bleedin."

Somebody in the crowd laughed. Jim Hawkins walked close to Dave and looked into his face.

"Well, looks like you have bought you a mule, Dave."

"Ah swear fo Gawd, Ah didn go t kill the mule, Mistah Hawkins!"

"But you killed her!"

All the crowd was laughing now. They stood on tiptoe and poked heads over one another's shoulders.

"Well, boy, looks like yuh done bought a dead mule! Hahaha!"

"Ain tha ershame."

"Hohohohoho."

Dave stood, head down, twisting his feet in the dirt.

"Well, you needn't worry about it, Bob," said Jim Hawkins to Dave's father. "Just let the boy keep on working and pay me two dollars a month."

"Whut yuh wan fer yo mule, Mistah Hawkins?"

Jim Hawkins screwed up his eyes.

"Fifty dollars."

"Whut yuh do wid tha gun?" Dave's father demanded.

Dave said nothing.

"Yuh wan me t take a tree n beat yuh till yuh talk!"

"Nawsuh!"

"Whut yuh do wid it?"

"Ah throwed it erway."

"Where?"

"Ah . . . Ah throwed it in the creek."

"Waal, c mon home. N firs thing in the mawnin git to tha creek n fin tha gun."

"Yessuh."

"Whut yuh pay fer it?"

"Two dollahs."

"Take tha gun n git yo money back n carry it t Mistah Hawkins, yuh hear? N don fergit Ahma lam you black bottom good fer this! Now march yosef on home, suh!"

Dave turned and walked slowly. He heard people laughing. Dave glared, his eyes welling with tears. Hot anger bubbled in him. Then he swallowed and stumbled on.

That night Dave did not sleep. He was glad that he

had gotten out of killing the mule so easily, but he was hurt. Something hot seemed to turn over inside him each time he remembered how they had laughed. He tossed on his bed, feeling his hard pillow. N Pa says he's gonna beat me . . . He remembered other beatings, and his back quivered. Naw, naw. Ah sho don wan im t beat me tha way no mo. Dam em all! Nobody ever gave him anything. All he did was work. They treat me like a mule, n then they beat me. He gritted his teeth. N Ma had t tell on me.

Well, if he had to, he would take old man Hawkins that two dollars. But that meant selling the gun. And he wanted to keep that gun. Fifty dollars for a dead mule.

He turned over, thinking how he had fired the gun. He had an itch to fire it again. Ef other men kin shoota gun, by Gawd, Ah kin! He was still, listening. Mebbe they all sleepin now. The house was still. He heard the soft breathing of his brother. Yes, now! He would go down and get that gun and see if he could fire it! He eased out of bed and slipped into overalls.

The moon was bright. He ran almost all the way to the edge of the woods. He stumbled over the ground, looking for the spot where he had buried the gun. Yeah, here it is. Like a hungry dog scratching for a bone, he pawed it up. He puffed his black cheeks and blew dirt from the trigger and barrel. He broke it and found four cartridges unshot. He looked around; the fields were filled with silence and moonlight. He clutched the gun stiff and hard in his fingers. But, as soon as he wanted to pull the trigger, he shut his eyes and turned his head. Naw, Ah can't shoot wid mah eyes closed n mah head turned. With effort he held his eyes open; then he squeezed. *Blooooom!* He was stiff, not breathing. The gun was still in his hands. Dammit, he'd done it! He fired again. *Bloooooom!* He smiled. *Blooooom! Bloooom! Click, click.* There! It was empty. If anybody could shoot a gun, he could. He put the gun into his hip pocket and started across the fields.

When he reached the top of a ridge he stood straight and proud in the moonlight, looking at Jim Hawkins' big white house, feeling the gun sagging in his pocket. Lawd, ef Ah had just one mo bullet Ah'd taka shot at tha house. Ah'd like t scare ol man Hawkins jusa little . . . Jusa enough t let im know Dave Saunders is a man.

To his left the road curved, running to the tracks of the Illinois Central. He jerked his head, listening. From far off came a faint *hoooof-hoooof; hoooof-hoooof; hoooof-hoooof.* . . . He stood rigid. Two dollahs a mont. Les see now . . . Tha means it'll take bout two years. Shucks! Ah'll be dam!

He started down the road, toward the tracks. Yeah, here she comes! He stood beside the track and held himself stiffly. Here she comes, erroun the ben . . . C mon, yuh slow poke! C mon! He had his hand on his gun; something quivered in his stomach. Then the train thundered past, the gray and brown box cars rumbling and clinking. He gripped the gun tightly; then he jerked his hand out of his pocket. Ah betcha Bill wouldn't do it! Ah betcha . . . The cars slid past, steel grinding upon steel. Ahm ridin yuh ternight, so hep me Gawd! He was hot all over. He hesitated just a moment; then he grabbed, pulled atop of a car, and lay flat. He felt his pocket; the gun was still there. Ahead the long rails were glinting in the moonlight, stretching away, away to somewhere, somewhere where he could be a man . . .

Mary Mebane

Mary Mebane was born in Durham, North Carolina, in 1933, the daughter of a farmer and a factory worker. She received a B.A. from North Carolina College and an M.A. and Ph.D. from the University of North Carolina. She has taught English at North Carolina College and at South Carolina State College, and currently she is teaching at the University of South Carolina. She is the author of a play, *Take a Sad Song* (1975), and two autobiographical works, *Mary* (1981) and *Mary Wayfarer* (1983). In the following excerpt from *Mary*, Mary and her mother, Nonnie, find themselves at odds about what a young black woman's aspirations should be.

from Mary

At first I didn't know any better; I thought that people all over the world washed clothes in the backyard, cooked their supper right out of the garden, churned milk and picked blackberries, got saved and were baptized, and went to church on Sunday. If the work was sheer drudgery, as undoubtedly it was, I didn't feel it as such and perhaps never would have.

But eventually I began to perceive that I was being prepared for my life's work. That's when the trouble really got bad—when I started resisting.

I am going to do great things in life, I secretly vowed.

No, you aren't, said the world around me. You're going to accept your lot just like the rest of us. Black women have always had it hard. Who are you to be so different?

Pick up your cross, said the Sunday school and the church. Everyone has a cross to bear.

Black women like me have scrubbed a hundred billion miles of tiled corridors and washed an equal number of dishes. I wasn't going to do that.

I am going to live my own life, I secretly said.

No, you aren't, said an adult. I am going to see to it that you don't. You might as well get those foolish notions out of your head, girl.

That adult was my mother.

Perhaps someday someone will discover the origin of the tension that sometimes develops between black mother and black daughter, especially when the daughter is ambitious. The spark that usually set off the conflict was my interest in things literary and cultural—worthless things for a girl like me, born black in the rural segregated American South. But that was only the tip of the iceberg. Unseen but hulking huge and more deadly was the feeling that there was some basic flaw in a personality that engaged in such pursuits.

Nonnie felt bitterly resentful and rejected when I refused to subscribe to her version of reality. She had managed to project her dislike of my interests so thoroughly into my consciousness that soon I, too, felt that there was something not quite right about valuing ideas. During intermittent periods I would self-consciously cast off the raiment of intellectuality and try on the garment of black folk culture, attempting to convince myself that it was sufficient, that to want more and—even more guilt-producing—to want better was an affectation on my part.

Nevertheless, I began to hope that music would be a way out, and I conceived the idea of becoming a concert pianist. I hadn't taken music lessons for a long time, having stopped when I could play for the Sunday school and the church choir. But I would take piano lessons and practice very hard and then one day I would be a great artist.

I had heard that Mrs. Shearin was the best teacher in town. I called and asked her how much the lessons were. She said one dollar each. I asked if I could work for her to pay for my lessons; she said that she was sure something could be arranged.

Soon I was making a weekly trip to Durham to Mrs. Shearin's studio. I was excited because it was an adventure for me. It was the first time I had been to the heart of the black community in Durham. My father's relatives lived in the northern and western sections of the city, but the center of the black population was in the southern part of the city. Located there were the homes of the "rich" blacks of Durham that I had heard about.

The first time I rode down the main street in the black section I was disappointed. There were a number of big two-story houses, but most of them needed painting, and

there were smaller, less-well-kept-up houses nearby and
in some cases right next to them. Interspersed among
them also were various small businesses, a taxi stand, an
ice-cream parlor, a hamburger stand, so that the community did not look like the well-off, prosperous communities in other sections of the city.

Right at the bus stop where I got off was North Carolina College, a state-supported black institution. It was
the best-kept piece of property in the neighborhood. It
had lustrous green grass kept cut very close, tall trimmed
hedges, and red-brick buildings. Saturday mornings I
would see students dressed in the latest college fashions
waiting for the bus on the other side of the street. I used
to look at the buildings and think how nice they were,
but I didn't really plan to go to NCC. I wanted desperately to go to one of those great centers of learning I
had read about in books and magazines. I wanted to go
to Radcliffe or Wellesley.

I liked my music lessons. Mrs. Shearin lived in a Span-
ish-style house, low and pink. It had nice things but nothing flashy. My tasks were not hard. I vacuumed the living
room, made up her son's bed, dusted, and fixed her a
large cup of tea for breakfast, which I took to her in the
studio, a large room at the back of the house. That over,
I waited for my turn.

I was stunned at my total ignorance about music, for
I had been playing hymns for a number of years. My
teacher in Wildwood had never taught me about the values of notes—that is, that a quarter note gets one beat,
a half note gets two beats, and a whole note gets four
beats. I had never even heard of an eighth note or a
sixteenth note, scales or keys. I was in despair. How was
I ever going to be a concert artist when I had never even
been taught the basics? I realized then why my teacher in
Wildwood practically started her pupils off with hymns,
concentrating on the top or melodic line. She knew the
familiar hymns by heart and was teaching her students
by rote.

Soon I began to understand the new terms, and the
joy of learning came back. Mrs. Shearin asked me to

subscribe to *Etude* magazine, which started coming to the house every month. I was working for my music, so Nonnie couldn't say much one way or the other. And each student had to buy a little book with the lives of the composers in it. When we played a piece by Mozart or some other composer, before we began we had to tell Mrs. Shearin some facts about his life. We had to be able to spell his name correctly, and she made sure that our pronunciation was correct. I loved it. Scales to me were fun—to be able to go over the whole keyboard, first with one hand, then with two, in key after key, major and minor, was a pleasure. I felt a sense of mastery. It was something new; that meant my world was opening up and I was happy.

Mrs. Shearin herself was very chic. I used to pay her close attention on the sly. She always wore fingernail polish; her hair and face were perfectly groomed and she wore attractive, colorful clothing. But more than what she wore, her manner was gracious and refined, always courteous, though she sometimes yelled at students about their mistakes. She was elegant. That's what I admired about her and my Aunt Jo; they both had style, class, and elegance. Mrs. Shearin had been born to wealth— her father was the best-known black businessman in the United States; Aunt Jo had not been born to wealth, but she had acquired style. They were the only black women that I ever really admired. I've always liked class, style, and elegance.

I was so enthusiastic about my studies in music that soon Esther, a girl in Wildwood, wanted to take piano and I had a partner for my adventures in Durham.

One day I was in my room lying on my bed on my stomach, turning the pages of a magazine on the floor. I liked to read this way. The room was cluttered—the bed was unmade and there were books and records and magazines everywhere.

Nonnie had had a long day at the factory, catching the bundles of tobacco as they came down the belt and cutting off the hard-tied part. (If one of the women on the line failed to turn the bundle of tobacco the right way, the knot end might go into the machine and America would have a bitter cigarette. Nonnie had a responsible job.)

"Mary!" Nonnie yelled.

At first I didn't hear her. I continued to read my book while Beethoven was playing on the record player.

"Mary!"

I put down my book and went to the kitchen.

"What is it, Mama?"

"What is the matter with you, girl?"

"What's wrong, Mama?"

"What's wrong? The okra's burned. That's what's wrong."

"I'm sorry," I said. "It's hard to fry it without burning. I cut it up like you said, but a whole lot of slime ran out; then I rolled it in flour, but I couldn't get it to brown right. I was cooking it longer, trying to make it brown, when it burned."

"You burned up the okra."

Both Nonnie and I knew that I occasionally burned up food. I often put on supper and then got a magazine and thumbed through it while the supper cooked, or started reading a book that I had gotten out of the school library or off the bookmobile that came into the county once a week. But, either way, the results were the same: scorched chicken and leatherlike fried potatoes—not often, but sometimes.

The quarrel was all the more frustrating because we both knew that it was not really about the scorched food. It was about something else, something I would neither stop doing nor apologize for. Something in me wouldn't let me. But the scene continued.

Nonnie stood there, her glasses glinting with the faint dust that all tobacco workers were covered with. Her blue uniform had dark-brown powder in the folds, and her apron, starched white in the morning, was now slightly beige from the tobacco. From her clothing came the faint smell of tobacco dust.

"The chicken's all right, isn't it, Mama?" I said.

"I'm not talking about the chicken."

"And I fixed the biscuits all right, too."

I desperately wanted my mother's approval. I wanted to do something that would make her smile at me and say, "That's good. I'm glad that you're my daughter."

"Listen when I'm talking to you, girl."

I knew that I didn't listen. I had learned the practical use of the "tune-out." When the stimuli from the outside world came in too strongly critical of what I was doing, of what I was interested in, I tuned out. The best substitute for listening was a smile. In that way my hearer didn't know that I had long ago ceased to listen. And I had a moment's peace. But Nonnie had me right where she wanted me—in the wrong, with no alibi, and she thoroughly enjoyed her position.

"And we have some nice Jell-O and I fixed some iced tea," I said. Please, just this one time say something nice, I silently prayed. Iced tea and Jello-O were my mother's favorites.

Nonnie was not to be deterred. "You somewhere with your head in a book and you let my okra burn."

"Mama, it never seems to come out right when I fry it."

"No. You don't watch it. You always got your head in a book or you listening to those old stories or you listening to that music all the time. Burned up my food."

"I'm sorry."

"I go and work hard and when I come home my food's burned."

That hurt, for I knew that my mother worked hard.

"But Mama, I got all A's on my report card this month."

Nonnie wasn't interested in extraneous issues. "And you don't wash the clothes right, either."

I was guilty. Washing and ironing, the measure of achievement for community girls, interested me not at all. For unspoken was the knowledge that these black girls were really being trained to work as domestics, not to keep house for themselves. But they and their mothers played a game that they were learning to be good housekeepers, and their mothers and the neighborhood ladies praised them for all evidence of homemaking skills.

I was later to observe that often cooks who planned, purchased, and prepared attractive menus on their job would at home serve ill-prepared, unbalanced meals. They were too tired to fix better, they said. And women who made their living cleaning and washing and ironing for other people frequently had unironed clothing piled to the ceiling at home and sat down in the midst of untidiness. They, too, were too tired.

But I hadn't trained properly. Instinct had taught me to see through that. It was a trap.

"And my teacher said that I could go far in life, Mama."

"Marguerita makes all of her own clothes." Nonnie neglected to mention that Marguerita's mother was a seamstress herself and that she took time and showed her daughter how to do things. No one took time to show me anything. Most of what I learned, I learned from books.

"And my teacher said that I was smart. You know I can't sew, Mama."

"And Miss Pearl says that Ida Mae does all of her washing and ironing."

"I'm going to play a piece at Mrs. Shearin's piano recital. She asked me to be on the program. She can't have her whole school on the program, just a few that she thinks are playing well. And she asked me to appear."

"You keep your head in a book all the time. What is the matter with you, girl?"

"Mama, I'm sorry that I can't do anything right. I'm sorry."

"No, if I ask you to cook, you hurry up. But if you get a book, you sit back in that room all day Saturday and all day Sunday, reading it. You don't go nowhere. Just sit in that room reading a book. Those old books and those old magazines. You going to end in Goldsboro, right with those other crazy people. You going to be just like Claudia's daughter. She read those books all the time and she went crazy and they sent her to Goldsboro."

"I'm sorry, Mama. I'm sorry, Mama. Sorry that I can't do anything right."

Aunt Jo had strange, big-city ways: she smoked cigarettes on the sly, used rouge, introduced strange cuisine in the household, and put unsuitable notions in my head. Getting rid of her was a long-drawn-out campaign, but Nonnie did it—Jo moved to town and shared rooms with two maiden sisters.

When she left, the light went out for me. I never knew again the warmth, feeling, and loving concern that Aunt Jo had shown for me during those years. There was no one to whisper to me about the marvelous things that I was going to accomplish or tell me that I was meant for really great things in life: dancer, pianist, college student. But the damage had been done. In her quiet, determined way, Aunt Jo had planted the seeds so deep that no one could ever uproot them.

Nevertheless, having maneuvered Jo out of the house, Nonnie set herself the task of eradicating those unsuitable notions from her daughter's head. They were nothing but foolishness and would lead Mary to nothing but trouble. She was sorry that Ruf had let Jo stay that long, bringing those Northern ideas and ways that she had learned from rich people into her home. Anything associated with Jo's notions—my being a pianist, an intellectual—she would attack; anything not done properly in the house she would severely condemn.

On my part, I was hardheaded and stubborn. And in spite of all the fussing, I would not change. I brought a book home every day and read it between the time I got home and the time I went to bed. The okra still burned, the chicken burned, and the bread burned. Not really bad, just spots here and there, and I became adept at scraping the burned places off and putting the food back into the frying pan to brown a little more. The flour for the gravy had to be attended to every minute or it would burn so bad I'd have to throw it out and start all over, and Nonnie could not tolerate whitish gravy. So, somewhere down the line I learned about paprika, and for a while produced the reddest, spiciest gravy you ever saw. But Nonnie got wise to that—I probably put in so much that she could taste it—and I learned to cook the flour a little, then use paprika a little, not so you'd notice, but enough to speed the browning time up a bit.

If my cooking was bad, my housekeeping was worse. It would take me half the night to wash the supper dishes, for if the book I was reading was a good one, I'd read a few pages, then go wash a dish or two, then go back and read a few more. The beds got "spreaded up," not made; I took the attitude, What's the difference? You're only going to sleep in them again, anyway. And as Nonnie's fussing became sharper and the negative things she said about me got worse, I hurried even more to finish the chores and get to what I really liked. Maybe I *would* go crazy and wind up in Goldsboro. Maybe I *was* an "odd" child. But I would read that book. I know now that subconsciously I was resisting her in the only way I knew how, not by saying anything but just by not doing what she valued and wanted me to value.

One Sunday morning I had just come in from Sunday school and was sitting in the kitchen, leaning back in a straight chair propped against the wall. It was a warm day; I was slightly sweaty from walking in the heat. I lost my balance and the chair I was sitting in tipped to the left. I fell in the same direction; my head and the knob on the back of the chair hit the window, cracking the pane.

"See what you done!" Nonnie said. "I told you and told you about leaning back in that chair." I was mortified. She had told me before, but what stunned me was the rage and triumph I heard in her voice.

"I'm going to make your daddy whip you. That's what you need. A good whipping! You're getting beside yourself!"

I was too stunned to answer. Aunt Jo was gone, and though my father was sick and irritable most of the time, he let me help him in the little store that he had set up near the house, and asked me to do little things for him— so I knew he liked me. Now she wanted him to turn against me, too.

I thought that there was a magical line that separated children from grown people, that when you reached a certain age you automatically stopped acting "childish"— no longer had such traits as jealousy, spitefulness, meanness—and began acting grown, which was the way the church taught. Those who didn't act that way were sinners. The church taught: "Children, obey your parents, for this is right" and "Honor thy father and mother that thy days may be long upon the land which the Lord thy God giveth thee"; and the minister preached of the Prodigal Son, who took his portion and went and wasted it, but when he came back his father welcomed him with a big feast. In the first grade, their mother loved Dick and Jane, and in the magazines that I read parents loved and cared for their children. So if my mother didn't like and didn't care for me and always spoke to me harshly, she must have a good reason.

I thought and thought as to what the matter was— maybe she knew what had happened to me that night in the rain when I was five years old. I didn't, for I could never clearly remember the part where I fell down. I could remember starting out in the rain and going to the barn and running back to bed, but the part where I was screaming and fell down was cloudy to me and I never could remember. Or maybe my mother knew about my secret longings and my erotic fantasies, though I kept them hidden and never showed any signs of interest in boys.

But today something snapped. Something inside said, No.

"Just wait until he comes to the house. I'm going to make him whip you," she said again.

I wanted to cry, I'm a woman now, I'm not supposed to get any more whippings. But I said nothing.

I wondered about the triumphant tone that I heard in my mother's voice and then realized that it was because at last she could confront my father with something damaging about me. He and Jesse had been bitter enemies for a long time, but my mother liked Jesse, for he had been her firstborn; so it must have been galling to her to have my father talk to him mean and try to whip him—and for Jesse to run away—while he never whipped me and seldom spoke harshly to me, let me go with him everywhere, stand right by him while he poured the steps for the back porch, and ride with him when he peddled vegetables.

I made up my mind then. I would leave and I wasn't ever coming back. Talking to me like that, trying to turn my father against me . . . She wouldn't ever see me anymore.

I went out to the store and asked my father for some money. The store was full of Sunday-school children buying cold drinks and peanuts. I looked at them all dressed up, feeling that if I could get away I'd never see them again. He gave me a quarter and I left the yard, walking with a bunch that was laughing and talking and drinking their cold drinks. One by one they dropped off, but I kept walking. I was on my way to the bus line. I had never ridden the bus, but I knew where it turned around; that was about two miles away. Aunt Jo lived in town now, and so did my father's cousins, and if I could get to them, they would help me; perhaps I could stay with them. I could finish school in town and I wouldn't have to come to Wildwood anymore.

Soon I was near the highway and alone. Everybody else was at home or at a friend's house, where they had asked permission to stop. The highway was different. There were fewer houses, but I had traveled this way hundreds of times on my father's wagon. There was one house close to Wildwood, tall and two-storied, many-windowed, with flapping shutters, that I was afraid of. People said that there was a ghost in it and the ghost made noises late at night. Farther ahead were two homes, one on either side of the highway. Both of the families were rich, but they were not friends, for one family had "old" money and one family had "new" money. Hazel and her family lived with the Richardses, the family with the "old" money, on a "farm" that was really an estate. Hazel was very proud of their house. It had running water and was well kept up, for it was practically in the Richardses' yard. The Ransoms lived in a tree-shaded park, one that occupied the full time of several yard men, practically across the street from the Richardses, but Hazel like to tell how the people her parents worked for would have nothing to do with them, for they had no "quality."

I walked on past the long hedge that separated the Ransoms' park from the highway, wondering how it must feel to live in a big house in a grove of trees, far away from the highway, never having to do anything, with a swarm of servants doing everything. Then I looked at the four-tiered white fence that surrounded the Richardses' "farm"; it took a long time to drive past it, and I knew that by the time I walked past it, I would be near the bus line.

Once when I was visiting Hazel, she proudly showed me the farm. There was a whole garage of nothing but old cars, all kinds, that used to belong to the family. Then she showed me the swimming pool and the barn where the cows were milked and the tennis courts. She was quite proud of the place; to her it was her "home."

Near the place where the Richardses' fence stopped, but across the highway, were little houses where other white people lived, those who didn't have the money that the Richardses had. Sometimes they sat on the porch and I wondered what they thought when they looked at all the Richardses had and compared it with what they had. From then on to the bus line, there were little houses, boxlike, with little lawns and hedges; the large estate and the farm were past.

When I got to the bus stop, there was no bus. I walked on, not really minding it, for the highway had become a street and now there was a sidewalk and I liked walking; so I continued, mile after mile, passing service stations, little box houses. I met a bus going to the end of the line when I was far down the street, and still I walked—

past more service stations and hot-dog stands and small
businesses and more houses. I felt so good that I thought
that I would walk all the way in to town, thus saving my
quarter.

Near the creek at the foot of Mangum Street hill a car
passed me. At first I didn't notice it, but when someone
yelled I looked up.

There were three or four white boys in the car. I wondered what they had said, but I didn't really pay attention, for I was getting closer and closer to town and I
was preoccupied with wondering how I was going to
make out. Was someone going to invite me to stay?
Would my mother let me stay? Would a new life start
for me? I hoped so. I knew that my father would come
and get me, and maybe then I could tell him how Nonnie
hurt me by talking so mean to me all the time and he
would make her stop. But then he was sick all the time
and dependent on her, and besides, who would feed me,
clothe me, give me money to go to school? There was
nobody who could but Aunt Jo, and Nonnie wouldn't, I
was sure, let me stay with her. I walked along on a bright
Sunday morning—it was near noon by then—hoping that
things would work out all right.

Then a black car passed me again and someone threw
ice on me. I was scared, for the same car had circled
around and come back up on me from behind. White
people—they were the evil, the danger, that existed in
the world. You avoided them like snakes. I didn't know
what to do. Would they harass me from then on, constantly circling and coming up from behind? I looked
back and saw the bus coming. It had gone to the end of
the line and waited and now was making a return trip;
it was Sunday and the buses weren't running frequently.
So, never having been on a bus, I stood at the foot of
the hill where there was a sign that said BUS, and when
it came I got on. A brief conversation with the driver
got me three tokens.

I was surprised to see Nancy on the bus; she taught
the little children in Sunday school. She was surprised to
see me, too. I told her that I was going to town to see

my folks. She soon discovered that I knew nothing about changing buses and getting a transfer, and told me how and where to change. I went to the front and got the little pink transfer and got off at Walgreen's at Main Street.

I got to West Durham all right. I was proud of myself for finding the way, the first time on my own. I went to see Aunt Jo, but I felt so sad, for she was living in a small dark room in a house with two unmarried sisters. She didn't like it; I had heard her tell my mother that once. She asked me about everybody and I said they were all right, but I knew that she knew that something was wrong, because I had come alone. I wanted to tell her so much and I started to several times—that I wanted to come to town to live, maybe even stay with her; but I felt so bad that I would be letting her down, for she held me up as a model to her nieces and nephews, and if they knew I was running away from home it would make her look bad for having so much faith in me. I couldn't make the words come out. So we sat and talked, awkwardly, for we hadn't been alone in a long time. She spoke again of education. I must get an education.

I didn't know it then, but she was already dying of cancer. Marva, my older cousin, who lived across the street from Aunt Jo, was surprised to see me, and her daughter Jerline barely spoke—though she had been to visit us in the country—and an older male cousin took the extra token that I had put in a dish on the coffee table. I saw him take it, but he was grown and I was scared to say "Don't."

In the late afternoon I started back home. I rode the bus downtown all right, but at Five Points I didn't know how to change buses and was too scared to ask; so I started walking right on Main Street, in the heart of Durham. I walked the eight miles home.

Near the bus line Jesse met me; he was on his way to town. "Mama's gonna whip you!" He laughed in that special way he had when something bad was going to happen to somebody. I said nothing, but walked on. It was soon deep night. Wildwood was dark and quiet when I got back, with a light here and there. I passed no one.

Nonnie was angry and I was defiant. She got her switches to whip me, but I started yelling that I was going to leave again and I wasn't coming back. She did a lot of fussing, but she hit me only a time or two. I knew that I had won, for I never got another whipping. I had learned the value of protest. And I, too, put my soul on ice. I had to, if I was to survive.

Katherine Anne Porter

Katherine Anne Porter was born in Indian Creek, Texas, in 1890, and educated at home and in girls' schools. She began her writing career as a reporter, then made several trips to Mexico to study Aztec and Mayan art. Mexico provided the basis for several stories in her first collection, *Flowering Judas* (1930), which was a Book-of-the-Month Club selection. Her collection of three novellas, *Pale Horse*, *Pale Rider* (1939), from which the following story was taken, won a gold medal from the Society of the Libraries of New York University. *The Collected Stories of Katherine Anne Porter* (1965) received both the Pulitzer Prize and the National Book Award. Her only novel, *Ship of Fools* (1962), was made into a movie by Columbia Pictures. A member of the National Institute of Arts and Letters and the American Academy of Arts and Letters, Katherine Anne Porter has been a writer-in-residence at a number of colleges and universities: Olivet, Stanford, Michigan, Virginia, Washington and Lee, and the University of California at Los Angeles and at Riverside. She spent the last twenty years of her life in Washington, D.C.; she died in 1980. She thought a great deal about gender roles and sexual identity, and expressed a broad range of attitudes about women. Porter's biographer Joan Givner suggests that "Porter was torn between wishing to be an accomplished, independent woman, speaking out authoritatively on literature and world events and wishing to be a charmingly capricious belle, sought after for her beauty and arousing chivalrous throught in every male breast." "Old Mortality" reflects her interest in gender stereotypes.

Old Mortality

She was a spirited-looking young woman, with dark curly hair cropped and parted on the side, a short oval face with straight eyebrows, and a large curved mouth. A round white collar rose from the neck of her tightly buttoned black basque, and round white cuffs set off lazy hands with dimples in them, lying at ease in the folds of her flounced skirt which gathered around to a bustle. She sat thus, forever in the pose of being photographed, a motionless image in her dark walnut frame with silver oak leaves in the corners, her smiling gray eyes following one about the room. It was a reckless indifferent smile, rather disturbing to her nieces Maria and Miranda. Quite often they wondered why every older person who looked at the picture said, "How lovely"; and why everyone who had known her thought her so beautiful and charming.

There was a kind of faded merriment in the background, with its vase of flowers and draped velvet curtains, the kind of vase and the kind of curtains no one would have any more. The clothes were not even romantic looking, but merely most terribly out of fashion, and the whole affair was associated, in the minds of the little girls, with dead things: the smell of Grandmother's medicated cigarettes and her furniture that smelled of beeswax, and her old-fashioned perfume, Orange Flower. The woman in the picture had been Aunt Amy, but she was only a ghost in a frame, and a sad, pretty story from old times. She had been beautiful, much loved, unhappy, and she had died young.

Maria and Miranda, aged twelve and eight years, knew they were young, though they felt they had lived a long time. They had lived not only their own years; but their memories, it seemed to them, began years before they were born, in the lives of the grown-ups around them, old people above forty, most of them, who had a way of insisting that they too had been young once. It was hard to believe.

Their father was Aunt Amy's brother Harry. She had been his favorite sister. He sometimes glanced at the photograph and said, "It's not very good. Her hair and her smile were her chief beauties, and they aren't shown at all. She was much slimmer than that, too. There were never any fat women in the family, thank God."

When they heard their father say things like that, Maria and Miranda simply wondered, without criticism, what he meant. Their grandmother was thin as a match; the pictures of their mother, long since dead, proved her to have been a candle-wick, almost. Dashing young ladies, who turned out to be, to Miranda's astonishment, merely more of Grandmother's grandchildren, like herself, came visiting from school for the holidays, boasting of their eighteen-inch waists. But how did their father account for great-aunt Eliza, who quite squeezed herself through doors, and who, when seated, was one solid pyramidal monument from floor to neck? What about great-aunt Keziah, in Kentucky? Her husband, great-uncle John Jacob, had refused to allow her to ride his good horses after she had achieved two hundred and twenty pounds. "No," said great-uncle John Jacob, "my sentiments of chivalry are not dead in my bosom; but neither is my common sense, to say nothing of charity to our faithful dumb friends. And the greatest of these is charity." It was suggested to great-uncle John Jacob that charity should forbid him to wound great-aunt Keziah's female vanity by such a comment on her figure. "Female vanity will recover," said great-uncle John Jacob, callously, "but what about my horses' backs? And if she had the proper female vanity in the first place, she would never have got into such shape." Well, great-aunt Keziah was famous for her heft, and wasn't she in the family? But something seemed to happen to their father's memory when he thought of the girls he had known in the family of his youth, and he declared steadfastly they had all been, in every generation without exception, as slim as reeds and graceful as sylphs.

This loyalty of their father's in the face of evidence contrary to his ideal had its springs in family feeling, and a love of legend that he shared with the others. They loved to tell stories, romantic and poetic, or comic with a romantic humor; they did not gild the outward circumstance, it was the feeling that mattered. Their hearts and imaginations were captivated by their past, a past in which worldly considerations had played a very minor role. Their stories were almost always love stories against a bright blank heavenly blue sky.

Photographs, portraits by inept painters who meant earnestly to flatter, and the festival garments folded away in dried herbs and camphor were disappointing when the little girls tried to fit them to the living beings created in their minds by the breathing words of their elders. Grandmother, twice a year compelled in her blood by the change of seasons, would sit nearly all of one day beside old trunks and boxes in the lumber room, unfolding layers of garments and small keepsakes; she spread them out on sheets on the floor around her, crying over certain things, nearly always the same things, looking again at pictures in velvet cases, unwrapping locks of hair and dried flowers, crying gently and easily as if tears were the only pleasure she had left.

If Maria and Miranda were very quiet, and touched nothing until it was offered, they might sit by her at these times, or come and go. There was a tacit understanding that her grief was strictly her own, and must not be noticed or mentioned. The little girls examined the objects, one by one, and did not find them, in themselves, impressive. Such dowdy little wreaths and necklaces, some of them made of pearly shells; such moth-eaten bunches of pink ostrich feathers for the hair; such clumsy big breast pins and bracelets of gold and colored enamel;

such silly-looking combs, standing up on tall teeth capped with seed pearls and French paste. Miranda, without knowing why, felt melancholy. It seemed such a pity that these faded things, these yellowed long gloves and mis-shapen satin slippers, these broad ribbons cracking where they were folded, should have been all those vanished girls had to decorate themselves with. And where were they now, those girls, and the boys in the odd-looking collars? The young men seemed even more unreal than the girls, with their high-buttoned coats, their puffy neck-ties, their waxed mustaches, their waving thick hair combed carefully over their foreheads. Who could have taken them seriously, looking like that?

No, Maria and Miranda found it impossible to sympa-thize with those young persons, sitting rather stiffly before the camera, hopelessly out of fashion; but they were drawn and held by the mysterious love of the living, who remembered and cherished these dead. The visible remains were nothing; they were dust, perishable as the flesh; the features stamped on paper and metal were nothing, but their living memory enchanted the little girls. They listened, all ears and eager minds, picking here and there among the floating ends of narrative, patching together as well as they could fragments of tales that were like bits of poetry or music, indeed were associ-ated with the poetry they had heard or read, with music, with the theater.

"Tell me again how Aunt Amy went away when she was married." "She ran into the gray cold and stepped into the carriage and turned and smiled with her face as pale as death, and called out 'Good-by, good-by,' and refused her cloak, and said, 'Give me a glass of wine.' And none of us saw her alive again." "Why wouldn't she wear her cloak, Cousin Cora?" "Because she was not in love, my dear." Ruin hath taught me thus to ruminate, that time will come and take my love away. "Was she really beautiful, Uncle Bill?" "As an angel, my child." There were golden-haired angels with long blue pleated skirts dancing around the throne of the Blessed Virgin. None of them resembled Aunt Amy in the least, nor the

kind of beauty they had been brought up to admire.
There were points of beauty by which one was judged
severely. First, a beauty must be tall; whatever color the
eyes, the hair must be dark, the darker the better; the
skin must be pale and smooth. Lightness and swiftness
of movement were important points. A beauty must be
a good dancer, superb on horseback, with a serene manner, an amiable gaiety tempered with dignity at all hours.
Beautiful teeth and hands, of course, and over and above
all this, some mysterious crown of enchantment that
attracted and held the heart. It was all very exciting and
discouraging.

Miranda persisted through her childhood in believing,
in spite of her smallness, thinness, her little snubby nose
saddled with freckles, her speckled gray eyes and habit-
ual tantrums, that by some miracle she would grow into
a tall, cream-colored brunette, like cousin Isabel; she
decided always to wear a trailing white satin gown.
Maria, born sensible, had no such illusions. "We are
going to take after Mamma's family," she said. "It's no
use, we are. We'll never be beautiful, we'll always have
freckles. And *you*," she told Miranda, "haven't even a
good disposition."

Miranda admitted both truth and justice in this
unkindness, but still secretly believed that she would one
day suddenly receive beauty, as by inheritance, riches
laid suddenly in her hands through no deserts of her own.
She believed for quite a while that she would one day
be like Aunt Amy, not as she appeared in the photograph, but as she was remembered by those who had
seen her.

When Cousin Isabel came out in her tight black riding
habit, surrounded by young men, and mounted gracefully, drawing her horse up and around so that he
pranced learnedly on one spot while the other riders
sprang to their saddles in the same sedate flurry, Miranda's heart would close with such a keen dart of admiration, envy, vicarious pride it was almost painful; but
there would always be an elder present to lay a cooling
hand upon her emotions. "She rides almost as well as

Amy, doesn't she? But Amy had the pure Spanish style, she could bring out paces in a horse no one else knew he had." Young namesake Amy, on her way to a dance, would swish through the hall in ruffled white taffeta, glimmering like a moth in the lamplight, carrying her elbows pointed backward stiffly as wings, sliding along as if she were on rollers, in the fashionable walk of her day. She was considered the best dancer at any party, and Maria, sniffing the wave of perfume that followed Amy, would clasp her hands and say, "Oh, I can't *wait* to be grown up." But the elders would agree that the first Amy had been lighter, more smooth and delicate in her waltzing; young Amy would never equal her. Cousin Molly Parrington, far past her youth, indeed she belonged to the generation before Aunt Amy, was a noted charmer. Men who had known her all her life still gathered about her; now that she was happily widowed for the second time there was no doubt that she would yet marry again. But Amy, said the elders, had the same high spirits and wit without boldness, and you really could not say that Molly had ever been discreet. She dyed her hair, and made jokes about it. She had a way of collecting the men around her in a corner, where she told them stories. She was an unnatural mother to her ugly daughter Eva, an old maid past forty while her mother was still the belle of the ball. "Born when I was fifteen, you remember," Molly would say shamelessly, looking an old beau straight in the eye, both of them remembering that he had been best man at her first wedding when she was past twenty-one. "Everyone said I was like a little girl with her doll."

Eva, shy and chinless, straining her upper lip over two enormous teeth, would sit in corners watching her mother. She looked hungry, her eyes were strained and tired. She wore her mother's old clothes, made over, and taught Latin in a Female Seminary. She believed in votes for women, and had traveled about, making speeches. When her mother was not present, Eva bloomed out a little, danced prettily, smiled, showing all her teeth, and was like a dry little plant set out in a gentle rain. Molly was merry about her ugly duckling. "It's lucky for me my daughter is an old maid. She's not so apt," said Molly naughtily, "to make a grandmother of me." Eva would blush as if she had been slapped.

Eva was a blot, no doubt about it, but the little girls felt she belonged to their everyday world of dull lessons to be learned, stiff shoes to be limbered up, scratchy flannels to be endured in cold weather, measles and disappointed expectations. Their Aunt Amy belonged to the world of poetry. The romance of Uncle Gabriel's long, unrewarded love for her, her early death, was such a story as one found in old books: unworldly books, but true, such as the Vita Nuova, the Sonnets of Shakespeare and the Wedding Song of Spenser; and poems by Edgar Allan Poe. "Her tantalized spirit now blandly reposes, Forgetting or never regretting its roses. . . ." Their father read that to them, and said, "He was our greatest poet," and they knew that "our" meant he was Southern. Aunt Amy was real as the pictures in the old Holbein and Dürer books were real. The little girls lay flat on their stomachs and peered into a world of wonder, turning the shabby leaves that fell apart easily, not surprised at the sight of the Mother of God sitting on a hollow log nursing her Child; not doubting either Death or the Devil riding at the stirrups of the grim knight; not questioning the propriety of the stiffly dressed ladies of Sir Thomas More's household, seated in dignity on the floor, or seeming to be. They missed all the dog and pony shows, and lantern-slide entertainments, but their father took them to see "Hamlet," and "The Taming of the Shrew," and "Richard the Third," and a long sad play with Mary, Queen of Scots, in it. Miranda thought the magnificent lady in black velvet was truly the Queen of Scots, and was pained to learn that the real Queen had died long ago, and not at all on the night she, Miranda, had been present.

The little girls loved the theater, the world of personages taller than human beings, who swept upon the scene and invested it with their presences, their more than human voices, their gestures of gods and goddesses ruling

a universe. But there was always a voice recalling other
and greater occasions. Grandmother in her youth had
heard Jenny Lind, and thought that Nellie Melba was
much overrated. Father had seen Bernhardt, and Madame Modjeska was no sort of rival. When Paderewski
played for the first time in their city, cousins came from
all over the state and went from the grandmother's house
to hear him. The little girls were left out of this great
occasion. They shared the excitement of the going away,
and shared the beautiful moment of return, when cousins
stood about in groups, with coffee cups and glasses in
their hands, talking in low voices, awed and happy. The
little girls, struck with the sense of a great event, hung
about in their nightgowns and listened, until someone
noticed and hustled them away from the sweet nimbus
of all that glory. One old gentleman, however, had heard
Rubinstein frequently. He could not but feel that Rubinstein had reached the final height of musical interpreta-
tion, and, for him, Paderewski had been something of
an anticlimax. The little girls heard him muttering on,
holding up one hand, patting the air as if he were calling
for silence. The others looked at him, and listened, without any disturbance of their grave tender mood. They
had never heard Rubinstein; they had, one hour since,
heard Paderewski, and why should anyone need to recall
the past? Miranda, dragged away, half understanding the
old gentleman, hated him. She felt that she too had heard
Paderewski.

There was then a life beyond a life in this world, as
well as in the next; such episodes confirmed for the little
girls the nobility of human feeling, the divinity of man's
vision of the unseen, the importance of life and death,
the depths of the human heart, the romantic value of
tragedy. Cousin Eva, on a certain visit, trying to interest
them in the study of Latin, told them the story of John
Wilkes Booth, who, handsomely garbed in a long cloak,
had leaped to the stage after assassinating President Lincoln. "Sic semper tyrannis," he had shouted superbly, in
spite of his broken leg. The little girls never doubted that
it had happened in just that way, and the moral seemed

to be that one should always have Latin, or at least a good classical poetry quotation, to depend upon in great or desperate moments. Cousin Eva reminded them that no one, not even a good Southerner, could possibly approve of John Wilkes Booth's deed. It was murder, after all. They were to remember that. But Miranda, used to tragedy in books and in family legends—two great-uncles had committed suicide and a remote ancestress had gone mad for love—decided that, without the murder, there would have been no point to dressing up and leaping to the stage shouting in Latin. So how could she disapprove of the deed? It was a fine story. She knew a distantly related old gentleman who had been devoted to the art of Booth, had seen him in a great many plays, but not, alas, at his greatest moment. Miranda regretted this; it would have been so pleasant to have the assassination of Lincoln in the family.

Uncle Gabriel, who had loved Aunt Amy so desperately, still lived somewhere, though Miranda and Maria had never seen him. He had gone away, far away, after her death. He still owned racehorses, and ran them at famous tracks all over the country, and Miranda believed there could not possibly be a more brilliant career. He had married again, quite soon, and had written to Grandmother, asking her to accept this new wife as a daughter in place of Amy. Grandmother had written coldly, accepting, inviting them for a visit, but Uncle Gabriel had somehow never brought his bride home. Harry had visited them in New Orleans, and reported that the second wife was a very good-looking well-bred blonde girl who would undoubtedly be a good wife for Gabriel. Still, Uncle Gabriel's heart was broken. Faithfully once a year he wrote a letter to someone of the family, sending money for a wreath for Amy's grave. He had written a poem for her gravestone, and had come home, leaving his second wife in Atlanta, to see that it was carved properly. He could never account for having written this poem; he had certainly never tried to write a single rhyme since leaving school. Yet one day when he had been thinking about Amy, the verse occurred to him, out of the air. Maria and Miranda had seen it, printed in gold on a mourning card. Uncle Gabriel had sent a great number of them to be handed around among the family.

> "She lives again who suffered life,
> Then suffered death, and now set free
> A singing angel, she forgets
> The griefs of old mortality."

"Did she really sing?" Maria asked her father.

"Now what has that to do with it?" he asked. "It's a poem."

"I think it's very pretty," said Miranda, impressed. Uncle Gabriel was second cousin to her father and Aunt Amy. It brought poetry very near.

"Not so bad for tombstone poetry," said their father, "but it should be better."

Uncle Gabriel had waited five years to marry Aunt Amy. She had been ill, her chest was weak; she was engaged twice to other young men and broke her engagements for no reason; and she laughed at the advice of older and kinder-hearted persons who thought it very capricious of her not to return the devotion of such a handsome and romantic young man as Gabriel, her second cousin, too; it was not as if she would be marrying a stranger. Her coldness was said to have driven Gabriel to a wild life and even to drinking. His grandfather was rich and Gabriel was his favorite; they had quarreled over the racehorses, and Gabriel had shouted, "By God, I must have *something*." As if he had not everything already: youth, health, good looks, the prospect of riches, and a devoted family circle. His grandfather pointed out to him that he was little better than an ingrate, and showed signs of being a wastrel as well. Gabriel said, "You had racehorses, and made a good thing of them." "I never depended upon them for a livelihood, sir," said his grandfather.

Gabriel wrote letters about this and many other things to Amy from Saratoga and from Kentucky and from New

Orleans, sending her presents, and flowers packed in ice, and telegrams. The presents were amusing, such as a huge cage full of small green lovebirds; or, as an ornament for her hair, a full-petaled enameled rose with paste dewdrops, with an enameled butterfly in brilliant colors suspended quivering on a gold wire above it; but the telegrams always frightened her mother, and the flowers, after a journey by train and then by stage into the country, were much the worse for wear. He would send roses when the rose garden at home was in full bloom. Amy could not help smiling over it, though her mother insisted it was touching and sweet of Gabriel. It must prove to Amy that she was always in his thoughts.

"That's no place for me," said Amy, but she had a way of speaking, a tone of voice, which made it impossible to discover what she meant by what she said. It was possible always that she might be serious. And she would not answer questions.

"Amy's wedding dress," said the grandmother, unfurling an immense cloak of dove-colored cut velvet, spreading beside it a silvery-gray watered-silk frock, and a small gray velvet toque with a dark red breast of feathers. Cousin Isabel, the beauty, sat with her. They talked to each other, and Miranda could listen if she chose.

"She would not wear white, nor a veil," said Grandmother. "I couldn't oppose her, for I had said my daughters should each have exactly the wedding dress they wanted. But Amy surprised me. 'Now what would I look like in white satin?' she asked. It's true she was pale, but she would have been angelic in it, and all of us told her so. 'I shall wear mourning if I like,' she said, 'it is *my* funeral, you know.' I reminded her that Lou and your mother had worn white with veils and it would please me to have my daughters all alike in that. Amy said, 'Lou and Isabel are not like me,' but I could not persuade her to explain what she meant. One day when she was ill she said, 'Mammy, I'm not long for this world,' but not as if she meant it. I told her, 'You might live as long as anyone, if only you will be sensible.' 'That's the whole trouble,' said Amy. 'I feel sorry for Gabriel,' she told me. He doesn't know what he's asking for.'

"I tried to tell her once more," said the grandmother, "that marriage and children would cure her of everything. 'All women of our family are delicate when they are young,' I said. 'Why, when I was your age no one expected me to live a year. It was called greensickness, and everybody knew there was only one cure.' 'If I live for a hundred years and turn green as grass,' said Amy, 'I still shan't want to marry Gabriel.' So I told her very seriously that if she truly felt that way she must never do it, and Gabriel must be told once for all, and sent away. He would get over it. 'I have told him, and I have sent him away,' said Amy. 'He just doesn't listen.' We both laughed at that, and I told her young girls found a hundred ways to deny they wished to be married, and a thousand more to test their power over men, but that she had more than enough of that, and now it was time for her to be entirely sincere and make her decision. As for me," said the grandmother, "I wished with all my heart to marry your grandfather, and if he had not asked me, I should have asked him most certainly. Amy insisted that she could not imagine wanting to marry anybody. She would be, she said, a nice old maid like Eva Parrington. For even then it was pretty plain that Eva was an old maid, born. Harry said, 'Oh, Eva—Eva has no chin, that's her trouble. If you had no chin, Amy, you'd be in the same fix as Eva, no doubt.' Your Uncle Bill would say, 'When women haven't anything else, they'll take a vote for consolation. A pretty thin bedfellow,' said your Uncle Bill. 'What I really need is a good dancing partner to guide me through life,' said Amy, 'that's the match I'm looking for.' It was no good trying to talk to her."

Her brothers remembered her tenderly as a sensible girl. After listening to their comments on her character and ways, Maria decided that they considered her sensible because she asked their advice about her appearance when she was going out to dance. If they found fault in any way, she would change her dress or her hair until

they were pleased, and say, "You are an angel not to let
your poor sister go out looking like a freak." But she
would not listen to her father, nor to Gabriel. If Gabriel
praised the frock she was wearing, she was apt to disappear and come back in another. He loved her long black
hair, and once, lifting it up from her pillow when she
was ill, said, "I love your hair, Amy, the most beautiful
hair in the world." When he returned on his next visit,
he found her with her hair cropped and curled close to
her head. He was horrified, as if she had willfully mutilated herself. She would not let it grow again, not even
to please her brothers. The photograph hanging on the
wall was one she had made at that time to send to
Gabriel, who sent it back without a word. This pleased
her, and she framed the photograph. There was a thin
inky scrawl low in one corner, "To dear brother Harry,
who likes my hair cut."

This was a mischievous reference to a very grave scandal. The little girls used to look at their father, and wonder what would have happened if he had really hit the
young man he shot at. The young man was believed to
have kissed Aunt Amy, when she was not in the least
engaged to him. Uncle Gabriel was supposed to have
had a duel with the young man, but Father had got there
first. He was a pleasant, everyday sort of father, who
held his daughters on his knee if they were prettily
dressed and well behaved, and pushed them away if they
had not freshly combed hair and nicely scrubbed fingernails. "Go away, you're disgusting," he would say, in a
matter-of-fact voice. He noticed if their stocking seams
were crooked. He caused them to brush their teeth with
a revolting mixture of prepared chalk, powdered charcoal
and salt. When they behaved stupidly he could not
endure the sight of them. They understood dimly that all
this was for their own future good; and when they were
snivelly with colds, he prescribed delicious hot toddy for
them, and saw that it was given them. He was always
hoping they might not grow up to be so silly as they
seemed to him at any given moment, and he had a dis-
concerting way of inquiring, "How do you *know*?" when

they forgot and made dogmatic statements in his presence. It always came out embarrassingly that they did not know at all, but were repeating something they had heard. This made conversation with him difficult, for he laid traps and they fell into them, but it became important to them that their father should not believe them to be fools. Well, this very father had gone to Mexico once and stayed there for nearly a year, because he had shot at a man with whom Aunt Amy had flirted at a dance. It had been very wrong of him, because he should have challenged the man to a duel, as Uncle Gabriel had done. Instead, he just took a shot at him, and this was the lowest sort of manners. It had caused great disturbance in the whole community and had almost broken up the affair between Aunt Amy and Uncle Gabriel for good. Uncle Gabriel insisted that the young man had kissed Aunt Amy, and Aunt Amy insisted that the young man had merely paid her a compliment on her hair.

During the Mardi Gras holidays there was to be a big gay fancy-dress ball. Harry was going as a bull-fighter because his sweetheart, Mariana, had a new black lace mantilla and high comb from Mexico. Maria and Miranda had seen a photograph of their mother in this dress, her lovely face without a trace of coquetry looking gravely out from under a tremendous fall of lace from the peak of the comb, a rose tucked firmly over her ear. Amy copied her costume from a small Dresden-china shepherdess which stood on the mantelpiece in the parlor; a careful copy with ribboned hat, gilded crook, very low-laced bodice, short basket skirts, green slippers and all. She wore it with a black half-mask, but it was no disguise. "You would have known it was Amy at any distance," said Father. Gabriel, six feet three in height as he was, had got himself up to match, and a spectacle he provided in pale blue satin knee breeches and a blond curled wig with a hair ribbon. "He felt a fool, and he looked like one," said Uncle Bill, "and he behaved like one before the evening was over."

Everything went beautifully until the party gathered downstairs to leave for the ball. Amy's father—he must have been born a grandfather, thought Miranda—gave one glance at his daughter, her white ankles shining, bosom deeply exposed, two round spots of paint on her cheeks, and fell into a frenzy of outraged propriety. "It's disgraceful," he pronounced, loudly. "No daughter of mine is going to show herself in such a rig-out. It's bawdy," he thundered. "Bawdy!"

Amy had taken off her mask to smile at him. "Why, Papa," she said very sweetly, "what's wrong with it? Look on the mantelpiece. She's been there all along, and you were never shocked before."

"There's all the difference in the world," said her father, "all the difference, young lady, and you know it. You go upstairs this minute and pin up that waist in front and let down those skirts to a decent length before you leave this house. *And wash your face!*"

"I see nothing wrong with it," said Amy's mother, firmly, "and you shouldn't use such language before innocent young girls." She and Amy sat down with several females of the household to help, and they made short work of the business. In ten minutes Amy returned, face clean, bodice filled in with lace, shepherdess skirt modestly sweeping the carpet behind her.

When Amy appeared from the dressing room for her first dance with Gabriel, the lace was gone from her bodice, her skirts were tucked up more daringly than before, and the spots on her cheeks were like pomegranates. "Now Gabriel, tell me truly, wouldn't it have been a pity to spoil my costume?" Gabriel, delighted that she had asked his opinion, declared it was perfect. They agreed with kindly tolerance that old people were often tiresome, but one need not upset them by open disobedience: their youth was gone, what had they to live for?

Harry, dancing with Mariana who swung a heavy train around her expertly at every turn of the waltz, began to be uneasy about his sister Amy. She was entirely too popular. He saw young men make beelines across the floor, eyes fixed on those white silk ankles. Some of the young men he did not know at all, others he knew too well and could not approve of for his sister Amy.

Gabriel, unhappy in his lyric satin and wig, stood about holding his ribboned crook as though it had sprouted thorns. He hardly danced at all with Amy, he did not enjoy dancing with anyone else, and he was having a thoroughly wretched time of it.

There appeared late, alone, got up as Jean Lafitte, a young Creole gentleman who had, two years before, been for a time engaged to Amy. He came straight to her, with the manner of a happy lover, and said, clearly enough for everyone near by to hear him, "I only came because I knew you were to be here. I only want to dance with you and I shall go again." Amy, with a face of delight, cried out, "Raymond!" as if to a lover. She had danced with him four times, and had then disappeared from the floor on his arm.

Harry and Mariana, in conventional disguise of romance, irreproachably betrothed, safe in their happiness, were waltzing slowly to their favorite song, the melancholy farewell of the Moorish King on leaving Granada. They sang in whispers to each other, in their uncertain Spanish, a song of love and parting and that sword's point of grief that makes the heart tender towards all other lost and disinherited creatures: Oh, mansion of love, my earthly paradise . . . that I shall see no more . . . whither flies the poor swallow, weary and homeless, seeking for shelter where no shelter is? I too am far from home without the power to fly. . . . Come to my heart, sweet bird, beloved pilgrim, build your nest near my bed, let me listen to your song, and weep for my lost land of joy. . . .

Into this bliss broke Gabriel. He had thrown away his shepherd's crook and he was carrying his wig. He wanted to speak to Harry at once, and before Mariana knew what was happening she was sitting beside her mother and the two excited young men were gone. Waiting, disturbed and displeased, she smiled at Amy who waltzed past with a young man in Devil costume, including illfitting scarlet cloven hoofs. Almost at once, Harry and Gabriel came back, with serious faces, and Harry darted on the dance floor, returning with Amy. The girls and the chaperones were asked to come at once, they must be taken home. It was all mysterious and sudden, and Harry said to Mariana, "I will tell you what is happening, but not now—"

The grandmother remembered of this disgraceful affair only that Gabriel brought Amy home alone and that Harry came in somewhat later. The other members of the party straggled in at various hours, and the story came out piecemeal. Amy was silent and, her mother discovered later, burning with fever. "I saw at once that something was very wrong. 'What has happened, Amy?' 'Oh, Harry goes about shooting at people at a party,' she said, sitting down as if she were exhausted. 'It was on your account, Amy,' said Gabriel. 'Oh, no, it was not,' said Amy. 'Don't believe him, Mammy.' So I said, 'Now enough of this. Tell me what happened, Amy.' And Amy said, 'Mammy, this is it. Raymond came in, and you know I like Raymond, and he is a good dancer. So we danced together, too much, maybe. We went on the gallery for a breath of air, and stood there. He said, "How well your hair looks. I like this new shingled style." ' She glanced at Gabriel. 'And then another young man came out and said, "I've been looking everywhere. This is our dance, isn't it?" And I went in to dance. And now it seems that Gabriel went out at once and challenged Raymond to a duel about something or other, but Harry doesn't wait for that. Raymond had already gone out to have his horse brought, I suppose one doesn't duel in fancy dress,' she said, looking at Gabriel, who fairly shriveled in his blue satin shepherd's costume, 'and Harry simply went out and shot at him. I don't think that was fair,' said Amy."

Her mother agreed that indeed it was not fair; it was not even decent, and she could not imagine what her son Harry thought he was doing. "It isn't much of a way to defend your sister's honor," she said to him afterward. "I didn't want Gabriel to go fighting duels," said Harry. "That wouldn't have helped much, either."

Gabriel had stood before Amy, leaning over, asking

once more the question he had apparently been asking her all the way home. "Did he kiss you, Amy?"

Amy took off her shepherdess hat and pushed her hair back. "Maybe he did," she answered, "and maybe I wished him to."

"Amy, you must not say such things," said her mother. "Answer Gabriel's question."

"He hasn't the right to ask it," said Amy, but without anger.

"Do you love him, Amy?" asked Gabriel, the sweat standing out on his forehead.

"It doesn't matter," answered Amy, leaning back in her chair.

"Oh, it does matter; it matters terribly," said Gabriel. "You must answer me now." He took both of her hands and tried to hold them. She drew her hands away firmly and steadily so that he had to let go.

"Let her alone, Gabriel," said Amy's mother. "You'd better go now. We are all tired. Let's talk about it tomorrow."

She helped Amy to undress, noticing the changed bodice and the shortened skirt. "You shouldn't have done that, Amy. That was not wise of you. It was better the other way."

Amy said, "Mammy, I'm sick of this world. I don't like anything in it. It's so _dull_," she said, and for a moment she looked as if she might weep. She had never been tearful, even as a child, and her mother was alarmed. It was then she discovered that Amy had fever.

"Gabriel is dull, Mother—he sulks," she said. "I could see him sulking every time I passed. It spoils things," she said. "Oh, I want to go to sleep."

Her mother sat looking at her and wondering how it had happened she had brought such a beautiful child into the world. "Her face," said her mother, "was angelic in sleep."

Some time during that fevered night, the projected duel between Gabriel and Raymond was halted by the offices of friends on both sides. There remained the open question of Harry's impulsive shot, which was not so easily settled. Raymond seemed vindictive about that, it was possible he might choose to make trouble. Harry, taking the advice of Gabriel, his brothers and friends, decided that the best way to avoid further scandal was for him to disappear for a while. This being decided upon, the young men returned about daybreak, saddled Harry's best horse and helped him pack a few things; accompanied by Gabriel and Bill, Harry set out for the border, feeling rather gay and adventurous.

Amy, being wakened by the stirring in the house, found out the plan. Five minutes after they were gone, she came down in her riding dress, had her own horse saddled, and struck out after them. She rode almost every morning; before her parents had time to be uneasy over her prolonged absence, they found her note.

What had threatened to be a tragedy became a rowdy lark. Amy rode to the border, kissed her brother Harry good-by, and rode back again with Bill and Gabriel. It was a three days' journey, and when they arrived Amy had to be lifted from the saddle. She was really ill by now, but in the gayest of humors. Her mother and father had been prepared to be severe with her, but, at sight of her, their feelings changed. They turned on Bill and Gabriel. "Why did you let her do this?" they asked.

"You know we could not stop her," said Gabriel helplessly, "and she did enjoy herself so much!"

Amy laughed. "Mammy, it was splendid, the most delightful trip I ever had. And if I am to be the heroine of this novel, why shouldn't I make the most of it?"

The scandal, Maria and Miranda gathered, had been pretty terrible. Amy simply took to bed and stayed there, and Harry had skipped out blithely to wait until the little affair blew over. The rest of the family had to receive visitors, write letters, go to church, return calls, and bear the whole brunt, as they expressed it. They sat in the twilight of scandal in their little world, holding themselves very rigidly, in a shared tension as if all their nerves began at a common center. This center had received a blow, and family nerves shuddered, even into the farthest reaches of Kentucky. From whence in due time great-great-aunt Sally Rhea addressed a letter to *Mifs Amy Rhea*. In deep brown ink like dried blood, in a spidery hand adept at archaic symbols and abbreviations, great-great-aunt Sally informed Amy that she was fairly convinced that this calamity was only the forerunner of a series shortly to be visited by the Almighty God upon a race already condemned through its own wickedness, a warning that man's time was short, and that they must all prepare for the end of the world. For herself, she had long expected it, she was entirely resigned to the prospect of meeting her Maker; and Amy, no less than her wicked brother Harry, must likewise place herself in God's hands and prepare for the worst. *"Oh, my dear unfortunate young relative,"* twittered great-great-aunt Sally, *"we must in our Extremty join hands and appr before ye Dread Throne of Jdgmnt a United Fmly, if One is Mssg from ye Flock, what will Jesus say?"*

Great-great-aunt Sally's religious career had become comic legend. She had forsaken her Catholic rearing for a young man whose family were Cumberland Presbyterians. Unable to accept their opinions, however, she was converted to the Hard-Shell Baptists, a sect as loathsome to her husband's family as the Catholic could possibly be. She had spent a life of vicious self-indulgent martyrdom to her faith; as Harry commented: "Religion put claws on Aunt Sally and gave her a post to whet them on." She had out-argued, out-fought, and out-lived her entire generation, but she did not miss them. She bedeviled the second generation without ceasing, and was beginning hungrily on the third.

Amy, reading this letter, broke into her gay full laugh that always caused everyone around her to laugh too, even before they knew why, and her small green lovebirds in their cage turned and eyed her solemnly. "Imagine drawing a pew in heaven beside Aunt Sally," she said. "What a prospect."

"Don't laugh too soon," said her father. "Heaven was made to order for Aunt Sally. She'll be on her own territory there."

"For my sins," said Amy, "I must go to heaven with Aunt Sally."

During the uncomfortable time of Harry's absence, Amy went on refusing to marry Gabriel. Her mother could hear the voices going on in their endless colloquy, during many long days. One afternoon Gabriel came out, looking very sober and discouraged. He stood looking down at Amy's mother as she sat sewing, and said, "I think it is all over, I believe now that Amy will never have me." The grandmother always said afterward, "Never have I pitied anyone as I did poor Gabriel at that moment. But I told him, very firmly, 'Let her alone, then, she is ill.' " So Gabriel left, and Amy had no word from him for more than a month.

The day after Gabriel was gone, Amy rose looking extremely well, went hunting with her brothers Bill and Stephen, bought a velvet wrap, had her hair shingled and curled again, and wrote long letters to Harry, who was having a most enjoyable exile in Mexico City.

After dancing all night three times in one week, she woke one morning in a hemorrhage. She seemed frightened and asked for the doctor, promising to do whatever he advised. She was quiet for a few days, reading. She asked for Gabriel. No one knew where he was. "You should write him a letter; his mother will send it on." "Oh, no," she said. "I miss him coming in with his sour face. Letters are no good."

Gabriel did come in, only a few days later, with a very sour face and unpleasant news. His grandfather had died, after a day's illness. On his death bed, in the name of God, being of a sound and disposing mind, he had cut off his favorite grandchild Gabriel with one dollar. "In the name of God, Amy," said Gabriel, "the old devil has ruined me in one sentence."

It was the conduct of his immediate family in the matter that had embittered him, he said. They could hardly conceal their satisfaction. They had known and envied Gabriel's quite just, well-founded expectations. Not one of them offered to make any private settlement. No one even thought of repairing this last-minute act of senile vengeance. Privately they blessed their luck. "I have been cut off with a dollar," said Gabriel, "and they are all glad of it. I think they feel somehow that this justifies every criticism they ever made against me. They were right about me all along. I am a worthless poor relation," said Gabriel. "My God, I wish you could see them."

Amy said, "I wonder how you will ever support a wife, now."

Gabriel said, "Oh, it isn't so bad as that. If you would, Amy—"

Amy said, "Gabriel, if we get married now there'll be just time to be in New Orleans for Mardi Gras. If we wait until after Lent, it may be too late."

"Why, Amy," said Gabriel, "how could it ever be too late?"

"You might change your mind," said Amy. "You know how fickle you are."

There were two letters in the grandmother's many packets of letters that Maria and Miranda read after they were grown. One of them was from Amy. It was dated ten days after her marriage.

"Dear Mammy, New Orleans hasn't changed as much as I have since we saw each other last. I am now a staid old married woman, and Gabriel is very devoted and kind. Footlights won a race for us yesterday, she was the favorite, and it was wonderful. I go to the races every day, and our horses are doing splendidly; I had my choice of Erin Go Bragh or Miss Lucy, and I chose Miss Lucy. She is mine now, she runs like a streak. Gabriel says I made a mistake, Erin Go Bragh will stay better. I think Miss Lucy will stay my time.

"We are having a lovely visit. I'm going to put on a domino and take to the streets with Gabriel sometime during Mardi Gras. I'm tired of watching the show from a balcony. Gabriel says it isn't safe. He says he'll take me if I insist, but I doubt it. Mammy, he's very nice. Don't worry about me. I

have a beautiful black-and-rose-colored velvet
gown for the Proteus Ball. Madame, my new mother-in-law, wanted to know if it wasn't a little dashing. I told her I hoped so or I had been cheated.
It is fitted perfectly smooth in the bodice, very low
in the shoulders—Papa would not approve—and
the skirt is looped with wide silver ribbons between
the waist and knees in front, and then it surges
around and is looped enormously in the back, with
a train just one yard long. I now have an eighteen-
inch waist, thanks to Madame Duré. I expect to be
so dashing that my mother-in-law will have an
attack. She has them quite often. Gabriel sends
love. Please take good care of Graylie and Fiddler.
I want to ride them again when I come home.
We're going to Saratoga, I don't know just when.
Give everybody my dear love. It rains all the time
here, of course. . . .

"P.S. Mammy, as soon as I get a minute to
myself, I'm going to be terribly homesick. Good-
by, my darling Mammy."

The other was from Amy's nurse, dated six weeks after
Amy's marriage.

"I cut off the lock of hair because I was sure you
would like to have it. And I do not want you to
think I was careless, leaving her medicine where
she could get it, the doctor has written and explained. It would not have done her any harm
except that her heart was weak. She did not know
how much she was taking, often she said to me,
one more of those little capsules wouldn't do any
harm, and so I told her to be careful and not take
anything except what I gave her. She begged me
for them sometimes but I would not give her more
than the doctor said. I slept during the night
because she did not seem to be so sick as all that
and the doctor did not order me to sit up with her.
Please accept my regrets for your great loss and

please do not think that anybody was careless with
your dear daughter. She suffered a great deal and
now she is at rest. She could not get well but she
might have lived longer. Yours respectfully. . . ."

The letters and all the strange keepsakes were packed
away and forgotten for a great many years. They seemed
to have no place in the world.

Part II: 1904

During vacation on their grandmother's farm, Maria and
Miranda, who read as naturally and constantly as ponies
crop grass, and with much the same kind of pleasure,
had by some happy chance laid hold of some forbidden
reading matter, brought in and left there with missionary
intent, no doubt, by some Protestant cousin. It fell into
the right hands if enjoyment had been its end. The reading matter was printed in poor type on spongy paper, and
was ornamented with smudgy illustrations all the more
exciting to the little girls because they could not make
head or tail of them. The stories were about beautiful
but unlucky maidens, who for mysterious reasons had
been trapped by nuns and priests in dire collusion; they
were then "immured" in convents, where they were
forced to take the veil—an appalling rite during which
the victims shrieked dreadfully—and condemned forever
after to most uncomfortable and disorderly existences.
They seemed to divide their time between lying chained
in dark cells and assisting other nuns to bury throttled
infants under stones in moldering rat-infested dungeons.
Immured! It was the word Maria and Miranda had
been needing all along to describe their condition at the
Convent of the Child Jesus, in New Orleans, where they
spent the long winters trying to avoid an education.
There were no dungeons at the Child Jesus, and this
was only one of numerous marked differences between
convent life as Maria and Miranda knew it and the thrilling paperbacked version. It was no good at all trying to

fit the stories to life, and they did not even try. They
had long since learned to draw the lines between life,
which was real and earnest, and the grave was not its
goal; poetry, which was true but not real; and stories, or
forbidden reading matter, in which things happened as
nowhere else, with the most sublime irrelevance and
unlikelihood, and one need not turn a hair, because there
was not a word of truth in them.

It was true the little girls were hedged and confined,
but in a large garden with trees and a grotto; they were
locked at night into a long cold dormitory, with all the
windows open, and a sister sleeping at either end. Their
beds were curtained with muslin, and small night-lamps
were so arranged that the sisters could see through the
curtains, but the children could not see the sisters.
Miranda wondered if they ever slept, or did they sit there
all night quietly watching the sleepers through the muslin? She tried to work up a little sinister thrill about this,
but she found it impossible to care much what either of
the sisters did. They were very dull good-natured women
who managed to make the whole dormitory seem dull.
All days and all things in the Convent of the Child Jesus
were dull, in fact, and Maria and Miranda lived for
Saturdays.

No one had even hinted that they should become nuns.
On the contrary Miranda felt that the discouraging attitude of Sister Claude and Sister Austin and Sister Ursula
towards her expressed ambition to be a nun barely veiled
a deeply critical knowledge of her spiritual deficiencies.
Still Maria and Miranda had got a fine new word out of
their summer reading, and they referred to themselves
as "immured." It gave a romantic glint to what was otherwise a very dull life for them, except for blessed Saturday afternoons during the racing season.

If the nuns were able to assure the family that the
deportment and scholastic achievements of Maria and
Miranda were at least passable, some cousin or other
always showed up smiling, in holiday mood, to take them
to the races, where they were given a dollar each to bet
on any horse they chose. There were black Saturdays

now and then, when Maria and Miranda sat ready, hats
in hand, curly hair plastered down and slicked behind
their ears, their stiffly pleated navy-blue skirts spread out
around them, waiting with their hearts going down slowly
into their high-topped laced-up black shoes. They never
put on their hats until the last minute, for somehow it
would have been too horrible to have their hats on,
when, after all, Cousin Henry and Cousin Isabel, or
Uncle George and Aunt Polly, were not coming to take
them to the races. When no one appeared, and Saturday
came and went a sickening waste, they were then given
to understand that it was a punishment for bad marks
during the week. They never knew until it was too late
to avoid the disappointment. It was very wearing.

One Saturday they were sent down to wait in the visitors' parlor, and there was their father. He had come all
the way from Texas to see them. They leaped at sight of
him, and then stopped short, suspiciously. Was he going
to take them to the races? If so, they were happy to see
him.

"Hello," said Father, kissing their cheeks. "Have you
been good girls? Your Uncle Gabriel is running a mare
at the Crescent City today, so we'll all go and bet on
her. Would you like that?"

Maria put on her hat without a word, but Miranda
stood and addressed her father sternly. She had suffered
many doubts about this day. "*Why* didn't you send word
yesterday? I could have been looking forward all this
time."

"We didn't know," said Father, in his easiest paternal
manner, "that you were going to deserve it. Remember
Saturday before last?"

Miranda hung her head and put on her hat, with the
round elastic under the chin. She remembered too well.
She had, in midweek, given way to despair over her
arithmetic and had fallen flat on her face on the classroom floor, refusing to rise until she was carried out.
The rest of the week had been a series of novel depriva-
tions, and Saturday a day of mourning; secret mourning,

for if one mourned too noisily, it simply meant another bad mark against deportment.

"Never mind," said Father, as if it were the smallest possible matter, "today you're going. Come along now. We've barely time."

These expeditions were all joy, every time, from the moment they stepped into a closed one-horse cab, a treat in itself with its dark, thick upholstery, soaked with strange perfumes and tobacco smoke, until the thrilling moment when they walked into a restaurant under big lights and were given dinner with things to eat they never had at home, much less at the convent. They felt worldly and grown up, each with her glass of water colored pink with claret.

The great crowd was always exciting as if they had never seen it before, with the beautiful, incredibly dressed ladies, all plumes and flowers and paint, and the elegant gentlemen with yellow gloves. The bands played in turn with thundering drums and brasses, and now and then a wild beautiful horse would career around the track with a tiny, monkey-shaped boy on his back, limbering up for his race.

Miranda had a secret personal interest in all this which she knew better than to confide to anyone, even Maria. Least of all to Maria. In ten minutes the whole family would have known. She had lately decided to be a jockey when she grew up. Her father had said one day that she was going to be a little thing all her life, she would never be tall; and this meant, of course, that she would never be a beauty like Aunt Amy, or Cousin Isabel. Her hope of being a beauty died hard, until the notion of being a jockey came suddenly and filled all her thoughts. Quietly, blissfully, at night before she slept, and too often in the daytime when she should have been studying, she planned her career as a jockey. It was dim in detail, but brilliant at the right distance. It seemed too silly to be worried about arithmetic at all, when what she needed for her future was to ride better—much better. "You ought to be ashamed of yourself," said father, after watching her gallop full tilt down the lane at the farm, on Trixie, the mustang mare. "I can see the sun, moon and stars between you and the saddle every jump." Spanish style meant that one sat close to the saddle, and did all kinds of things with the knees and reins. Jockeys bounced lightly, their knees almost level with the horse's back, rising and falling like a rubber ball. Miranda felt she could do that easily. Yes, she would be a jockey, like Tod Sloan, winning every other race at least. Meantime, while she was training, she would keep it a secret, and one day she would ride out, bouncing lightly, with the other jockeys, and win a great race, and surprise everybody, her family most of all.

On that particular Saturday, her idol, the great Tod Sloan, was riding, and he won two races. Miranda longed to bet her dollar on Tod Sloan, but father said, "Not now, honey. Today you must bet on Uncle Gabriel's horse. Save your dollar for the fourth race, and put it on Miss Lucy. You've got a hundred to one shot. Think if she wins."

Miranda knew well enough that a hundred to one shot was no bet at all. She sulked, the crumpled dollar in her hand grew damp and warm. She could have won three dollars already on Tod Sloan. Maria said virtuously, "It wouldn't be nice not to bet on Uncle Gabriel. That way, we keep the money in the family." Miranda put out her under lip at her sister. Maria was too prissy for words. She wrinkled her nose back at Miranda.

They had just turned their dollar over to the bookmaker for the fourth race when a vast bulging man with a red face and immense tan ragged mustaches fading into gray hailed them from a lower level of the grandstand, over the heads of the crowd, "Hey, there, Harry?" Father said, "Bless my soul, there's Gabriel." He motioned to the man, who came pushing his way heavily up the shallow steps. Maria and Miranda stared, first at him, then at each other. "Can that be our Uncle Gabriel?" their eyes asked. "Is that Aunt Amy's handsome romantic beau? Is that the man who wrote the poem about our Aunt Amy?" Oh, what did grown-up people *mean* when they talked, anyway?

He was a shabby fat man with bloodshot blue eyes, sad beaten eyes, and a big melancholy laugh, like a groan. He towered over them shouting to their father, "Well, for God's sake, Harry, it's been a coon's age. You ought to come out and look 'em over. You look just like yourself, Harry, how are you?"

The band struck up "Over the River" and Uncle Gabriel shouted louder. "Come on, let's get out of this. What are you doing up here with the pikers?"

"Can't," shouted Father. "Brought my little girls. Here they are."

Uncle Gabriel's bleared eyes beamed blindly upon them. "Fine looking set, Harry," he bellowed, "pretty as pictures, how old are they?"

"Ten and fourteen now," said Father; "awkward ages. Nest of vipers," he boasted, "perfect batch of serpent's teeth. Can't do a thing with 'em." He fluffed up Miranda's hair, pretending to tousle it.

"Pretty as pictures," bawled Uncle Gabriel, "but rolled into one they don't come up to Amy, do they?"

"No, they don't," admitted their father at the top of his voice, "but they're only half-baked." *Over the river, over the river,* moaned the band, *my sweetheart's waiting for me.*

"I've got to get back now," yelled Uncle Gabriel. The little girls felt quite deaf and confused. "Got the God-damnedest jockey in the world, Harry, just my luck. Ought to tie him on. Fell off Fiddler yesterday, just plain fell off on his tail— Remember Amy's mare, Miss Lucy? Well, this is her namesake, Miss Lucy IV. None of 'em ever came up to the first one, though. Stay right where you are, I'll be back."

Maria spoke up boldly. "Uncle Gabriel, tell Miss Lucy we're betting on her." Uncle Gabriel bent down and it looked as if there were tears in his swollen eyes. "God bless your sweet heart," he bellowed, "I'll tell her." He plunged down through the crowd again, his fat back bowed slightly in his loose clothes, his thick neck rolling over his collar.

Miranda and Maria, disheartened by the odds, by their

first sight of their romantic Uncle Gabriel, whose language was so coarse, sat listlessly without watching, their chances missed, their dollars gone, their hearts sore. They didn't even move until their father leaned over and hauled them up. "Watch your horse," he said, in a quick warning voice, "watch Miss Lucy come home."

They stood up, scrambled to their feet on the bench, every vein in them suddenly beating so violently they could hardly focus their eyes, and saw a thin little mahogany-colored streak flash by the judges' stand, only a neck ahead, but their Miss Lucy, oh, their darling, their lovely—oh, Miss Lucy, their Uncle Gabriel's Miss Lucy, had won, had won. They leaped up and down screaming and clapping their hands, their hats falling back on their shoulders, their hair flying wild. *Whoa, you heifer,* squalled the band with snorting brasses, and the crowd broke into a long roar like the falling of the walls of Jericho.

The little girls sat down, feeling quite dizzy, while their father tried to pull their hats straight, and taking out his handkerchief held it to Miranda's face, saying very gently, "Here, blow your nose," and he dried her eyes while he was about it. He stood up then and shook them out of their daze. He was smiling with deep laughing wrinkles around his eyes, and spoke to them as if they were grown young ladies he was squiring around.

"Let's go out and pay our respects to Miss Lucy," he said. "She's the star of the day."

The horses were coming in, looking as if their hides had been drenched and rubbed with soap, their ribs heaving, their nostrils flaring and closing. The jockeys sat bowed and relaxed, their faces calm, moving a little at the waist with the movement of their horses. Miranda noted this for future use; that was the way you came in from a race, easy and quiet, whether you had won or lost. Miss Lucy came last, and a little handful of winners applauded her and cheered the jockey. He smiled and lifted his whip, his eyes and shriveled brown face perfectly serene. Miss Lucy was bleeding at the nose, two thick red rivulets were stiffening her tender mouth and chin, the round velvet chin that Miranda thought the nicest kind of chin in the world. Her eyes were wild and her knees were trembling, and she snored when she drew her breath.

Miranda stood staring. That was winning, too. Her heart clinched tight; that was winning, for Miss Lucy. So instantly and completely did her heart reject that victory, she did not know when it happened, but she hated it, and was ashamed that she had screamed and shed tears for joy when Miss Lucy, with her bloodied nose and bursting heart had gone past the judges' stand a neck ahead. She felt empty and sick and held to her father's hand so hard that he shook her off a little impatiently and said, "What is the matter with you? Don't be so fidgety."

Uncle Gabriel was standing there waiting, and he was completely drunk. He watched the mare go in, then leaned against the fence with its white-washed posts and sobbed openly. "She's got the nosebleed, Harry," he said. "Had it since yesterday. We thought we had her all fixed up. But she did it, all right. She's got a heart like a lion. I'm going to breed her, Harry. Her heart's worth a million dollars, by itself, God bless her." Tears ran over his brick-colored face and into his straggling mustaches. "If anything happens to her now I'll blow my brains out. She's my last hope. She saved my life. I've had a run," he said, groaning into a large handkerchief and mopping his face all over, "I've had a run of luck that would break a brass billy goat. God, Harry, let's go somewhere and have a drink."

"I must get the children back to school first, Gabriel," said their father, taking each by a hand.

"No, no, don't go yet," said Uncle Gabriel desperately. "Wait here a minute, I want to see the vet and take a look at Miss Lucy, and I'll be right back. Don't go, Harry, for God's sake. I want to talk to you a few minutes."

Maria and Miranda, watching Uncle Gabriel's lumbering, unsteady back, were thinking that this was the first time they had ever seen a man that they knew to be drunk. They had seen pictures and read descriptions, and had heard descriptions, so they recognized the symptoms at once. Miranda felt it was an important moment in a great many ways.

"Uncle Gabriel's a drunkard, isn't he?" she asked her father, rather proudly.

"Hush, don't say such things," said Father, with a heavy frown, "or I'll never bring you here again." He looked worried and unhappy, and, above all, undecided. The little girls stood stiff with resentment against such obvious injustice. They loosed their hands from his and moved away coldly, standing together in silence. Their father did not notice, watching the place where Uncle Gabriel had disappeared. In a few minutes he came back, still wiping his face, as if there were cobwebs on it, carrying his big black hat. He waved at them from a short distance, calling out in a cheerful way, "She's going to be all right, Harry. It's stopped now. Lord, this will be good news for Miss Honey. Come on, Harry, let's all go home and tell Miss Honey. She deserves some good news."

Father said, "I'd better take the children back to school first, then we'll go."

"No, no," said Uncle Gabriel, fondly. "I want her to see the girls. She'll be tickled pink to see them, Harry. Bring 'em along."

"Is it another racehorse we're going to see?" whispered Miranda in her sister's ear.

"Don't be silly," said Maria. "It's Uncle Gabriel's second wife."

"Let's find a cab, Harry," said Uncle Gabriel, "and take your little girls out to cheer up Miss Honey. Both of 'em rolled into one look a lot like Amy, I swear they do. I want Miss Honey to see them. She's always liked our family, Harry, though of course she's not what you'd call an expansive kind of woman."

Maria and Miranda sat facing the driver, and Uncle Gabriel squeezed himself in facing them beside their father. The air became at once bitter and sour with his breathing. He looked sad and poor. His necktie was on crooked and his shirt was rumpled. Father said, "You're going to see Uncle Gabriel's second wife, children," exactly if they had not heard everything; and to Gabriel, "How *is* your wife nowadays? It must be twenty years since I saw her last."

"She's pretty gloomy, and that's a fact," said Uncle Gabriel. "She's been pretty gloomy for years now, and nothing seems to shake her out of it. She never did care for horses, Harry, if you remember; she hasn't been near the track three times since we were married. When I think how Amy wouldn't have missed a race for anything . . . She's very different from Amy, Harry, a very different kind of woman. As fine a woman as ever lived in her own way, but she hates change and moving around, and she just lives in the boy."

"Where is Gabe now?" asked Father.

"Finishing college," said Uncle Gabriel; "a smart boy, but awfully like his mother. Awfully like," he said, in a melancholy way. "She hates being away from him. Just wants to sit down in the same town and wait for him to get through with his education. Well, I'm sorry it can't be done if that's what she wants, but God Almighty— And this last run of luck has about got her down. I hope you'll be able to cheer her up a little, Harry, she needs it."

The little girls sat watching the streets grow duller and dingier and narrower, and at last the shabbier and shabbier white people gave way to dressed-up Negroes, and then to shabby Negroes, and after a long way the cab stopped before a desolate-looking little hotel in Elysian Fields. Their father helped Maria and Miranda out, told the cabman to wait, and they followed Uncle Gabriel through a dirty damp-smelling patio, down a long gas-lighted hall full of a terrible smell, Miranda couldn't decide what it was made of but it had a bitter taste even, and up a long staircase with a ragged carpet. Uncle Gabriel pushed open a door without warning, saying, "Come in, here we are."

A tall pale-faced woman with faded straw-colored hair and pink-rimmed eyelids rose suddenly from a squeaking rocking chair. She wore a stiff blue-and-white-striped shirtwaist and a stiff black skirt of some hard shiny material. Her large knuckled hands rose to her round, neat pompadour at sight of her visitors.

"Honey," said Uncle Gabriel, with large false heartiness, "you'll never guess who's come to see you." He gave her a clumsy hug. Her face did not change and her eyes rested steadily on the three strangers. "Amy's brother Harry, Honey, you remember, don't you?"

"Of course," said Miss Honey, putting out her hand straight as a paddle, "of course I remember you, Harry." She did not smile.

"And Amy's two little nieces," went on Uncle Gabriel, bringing them forward. They put out their hands limply, and Miss Honey gave each one a slight flip and dropped it. "And we've got good news for you," went on Uncle Gabriel, trying to bolster up the painful situation. "Miss Lucy stepped out and showed 'em today, Honey. We're rich again, old girl, cheer up."

Miss Honey turned her long, despairing face towards her visitors. "Sit down," she said with a heavy sigh, seating herself and motioning towards various rickety chairs. There was a big lumpy bed, with a grayish-white counterpane on it, a marble-topped washstand, grayish coarse lace curtains on strings at the two small windows, a small closed fireplace with a hole in it for a stovepipe, and two trunks, standing at odds as if somebody were just moving in, or just moving out. Everything was dingy and soiled and neat and bare; not a pin out of place.

"We'll move to the St. Charles tomorrow," said Uncle Gabriel, as much to Harry as to his wife. "Get your best dresses together, Honey, the long dry spell is over."

Miss Honey's nostrils pinched together and she rocked slightly, with her arms folded. "I've lived in the St. Charles before, and I've lived here before," she said, in a tight deliberate voice, "and this time I'll just stay where I am, thank you. I prefer it to moving back here in three months. I'm settled now, I feel at home here," she told him, glancing at Harry, her pale eyes kindling with blue fire, a stiff white line around her mouth.

The little girls sat trying not to stare, miserably ill at ease. Their grandmother had pronounced Harry's children to be the most unteachable she had ever seen in her long experience with the young; but they had learned by indirection one thing well—nice people did not carry on quarrels before outsiders. Family quarrels were sacred, to be waged privately in fierce hissing whispers, low choked mutters and growls. If they did yell and stamp, it must be behind closed doors and windows. Uncle Gabriel's second wife was hopping mad and she looked ready to fly out at Uncle Gabriel any second, with him sitting there like a hound when someone shakes a whip at him.

"She loathes and despises everybody in this room," thought Miranda, coolly, "and she's afraid we won't know it. She needn't worry, we knew it when we came in." With all her heart she wanted to go, but her father, though his face was a study, made no move. He seemed to be trying to think of something pleasant to say. Maria, feeling guilty, though she couldn't think why, was calculating rapidly, "Why, she's only Uncle Gabriel's second wife, and Uncle Gabriel was only married before to Aunt Amy, why, she's no kin at all, and I'm glad of it." Sitting back easily, she let her hands fall open in her lap; they would be going in a few minutes, undoubtedly, and they need never come back.

Then Father said, "We mustn't be keeping you, we just dropped in for a few minutes. We wanted to see how you are."

Miss Honey said nothing, but she made a little gesture with her hands, from the wrist, as if to say, "Well, you see how I am, and now what next?"

"I must take these young ones back to school," said Father, and Uncle Gabriel said stupidly, "Look, Honey, don't you think they resemble Amy a little? Especially around the eyes, especially Maria, don't you think, Harry?"

Their father glanced at them in turn. "I really couldn't say," he decided, and the little girls saw he was more monstrously embarrassed than ever. He turned to Miss

Honey, "I hadn't seen Gabriel for so many years," he said, "we thought of getting out for a talk about old times together. You know how it is."

"Yes, I know," said Miss Honey, rocking a little, and all that she knew gleamed forth in a pallid, unquenchable hatred and bitterness that seemed enough to bring her long body straight up out of the chair in a fury, "I know," and she sat staring at the floor. Her mouth shook and straightened. There was a terrible silence, which was broken when the little girls saw their father rise. They got up, too, and it was all they could do to keep from making a dash for the door.

"I must get the young ones back," said their father. "They've had enough excitement for one day. They each won a hundred dollars on Miss Lucy. It was a good race," he said, in complete wretchedness, as if he simply could not extricate himself from the situation. "Wasn't it, Gabriel?"

"It was a grand race," said Gabriel, brokenly, "a grand race."

Miss Honey stood up and moved a step towards the door. "Do you take them to the races, actually?" she asked, and her lids flickered towards them as if they were loathsome insects, Maria felt.

"If I feel they deserve a little treat, yes," said their father, in an easy tone but with wrinkled brow.

"I had rather, much rather," said Miss Honey clearly, "see my son dead at my feet than hanging around a race track."

The next few moments were rather a blank, but at last they were out of it, going down the stairs, across the patio, with Uncle Gabriel seeing them back into the cab. His face was sagging, the features had fallen as if the flesh had slipped from the bones, and his eyelids were puffed and blue. "Goody-by, Harry," he said soberly. "How long you expect to be here?"

"Starting back tomorrow," said Harry. "Just dropped in on a little business and to see how the girls were getting along."

"Well," said Uncle Gabriel, "I may be dropping into

your part of the country one of these days. Good-by, children," he said, taking their hands one after the other in his big warm paws. "They're nice children, Harry. I'm glad you won on Miss Lucy," he said to the little girls, tenderly. "Don't spend your money foolishly, now. Well, so long, Harry." As the cab jolted away he stood there fat and sagging, holding up his arm and wagging his hand at them.

"Goodness," said Maria, in her most grown-up manner, taking her hat off and hanging it over her knee, "I'm glad that's over."

"What I want to know is," said Miranda, "*is* Uncle Gabriel a real drunkard?"

"Oh, hush," said their father, sharply, "I've got the heartburn."

There was a respectful pause, as before a public monument. When their father had the heartburn it was time to lay low. The cab rumbled on, back to clean gay streets, with the lights coming on in the early February darkness, past shimmering shop windows, smooth pavements, on and on, past beautiful old houses set in deep gardens, on, on back to the dark walls with the heavy-topped trees hanging over them. Miranda sat thinking so hard she forgot and spoke out in her thoughtless way: "I've decided I'm not going to be a jockey, after all." She could as usual have bitten her tongue, but as usual it was too late.

Father cheered up and twinkled at her knowingly, as if that didn't surprise him in the least. "Well, well," said he, "so you aren't going to be a jockey! That's very sensible of you. I think she ought to be a lion-tamer, don't you, Maria? That's a nice, womanly profession."

Miranda, seeing Maria from the height of her fourteen years suddenly joining with their father to laugh at her, made an instant decision and laughed with them at herself. That was better. Everybody laughed and it was such a relief.

"Where's my hundred dollars?" asked Maria, anxiously.

"It's going in the bank," said their father, "and yours too," he told Miranda. "That is your nest-egg."

"Just so they don't buy my stockings with it," said Miranda, who had long resented the use of her Christmas money by their grandmother. "I've got enough stockings to last me a year."

"I'd like to buy a racehorse," said Maria, "but I know it's not enough." The limitations of wealth oppressed her. "*What* could you buy with a hundred dollars?" she asked fretfully.

"Nothing, nothing at all," said their father, "a hundred dollars is just something you put in the bank."

Maria and Miranda lost interest. They had won a hundred dollars on a horse race once. It was already in the far past. They began to chatter about something else.

The lay sister opened the door on a long cord, from behind the grille; Maria and Miranda walked in silently to their familiar world of shining bare floors and insipid wholesome food and cold-water washing and regular prayers; their world of poverty, chastity and obedience, of early to bed and early to rise, of sharp little rules and tittle-tattle. Resignation was in their childish faces as they held them up to be kissed.

"Be good girls," said their father, in the strange serious, rather helpless way he always had when he told them good-by. "Write to your daddy, now, nice long letters," he said, holding their arms firmly for a moment before letting go for good. Then he disappeared, and the sister swung the door closed after him.

Maria and Miranda went upstairs to the dormitory to wash their faces and hands and slick down their hair again before supper.

Miranda was hungry. "We didn't have a thing to eat, after all," she grumbled. "Not even a chocolate nut bar. I think that's mean. We didn't even get a quarter to spend," she said.

"Not a living bite," said Maria. "Not a nickel." She poured out cold water into the bowl and rolled up her sleeves.

Another girl about her own age came in and went to a washbowl near another bed. "Where have you been?" she asked. "Did you have a good time?"

"We went to the races, with our father," said Maria, soaping her hands.

"Our uncle's horse won," said Miranda.

"My goodness," said the other girl, vaguely, "that must have been grand."

Maria looked at Miranda, who was rolling up her own sleeves. She tried to feel martyred, but it wouldn't go. "Immured for another week," she said, her eyes sparkling over the edge of her towel.

Part III: 1912

Miranda followed the porter down the stuffy aisle of the sleeping-car, where the berths were nearly all made down and the dusty green curtains buttoned, to a seat at the further end. "Now yo' berth's ready any time, Miss," said the porter.

"But I want to sit up a while," said Miranda. A very thin old lady raised choleric black eyes and fixed upon her a regard of unmixed disapproval. She had two immense front teeth and a receding chin, but she did not lack character. She had piled her luggage around her like a barricade, and she glared at the porter when he picked some of it up to make room for his new passenger. Miranda sat, saying mechanically, "May I?"

"You may, indeed," said the old lady, for she seemed old in spite of a certain brisk, rustling energy. Her taffeta petticoats creaked like hinges every time she stirred. With ferocious sarcasm, after a half second's pause, she added, "You may be so good as to get off my hat!"

Miranda rose instantly in horror, and handed to the old lady a wilted contrivance of black horsehair braid and shattered white poppies. "I'm dreadfully sorry," she stammered, for she had been brought up to treat ferocious old ladies respectfully, and this one seemed capable of spanking her, then and there. "I didn't dream it was your hat."

"And whose hat did you dream it might be?" inquired

the old lady, baring her teeth and twirling the hat on a forefinger to restore it.

"I didn't think it was a hat at all," said Miranda with a touch of hysteria.

"Oh, you didn't think it was a hat? Where on earth are your eyes, child?" and she proved the nature and function of the object by placing it on her head at a somewhat tipsy angle, though still it did not much resemble a hat. "Now can you see what it is?"

"Yes, oh, yes," said Miranda, with a meekness she hoped was disarming. She ventured to sit again after a careful inspection of the narrow space she was to occupy.

"Well, well," said the old lady, "let's have the porter remove some of these encumbrances," and she stabbed the bell with a lean sharp forefinger. There followed a flurry of rearrangements, during which they both stood in the aisle, the old lady giving a series of impossible directions to the Negro which he bore philosophically while he disposed of the luggage exactly as he had meant to do. Seated again, the old lady asked in a kindly, authoritative tone, "And what might your name be, child?"

At Miranda's answer, she blinked somewhat, unfolded her spectacles, straddled them across her high nose competently, and took a good long look at the face beside her.

"If I'd had my spectacles on," she said, in an astonishingly changed voice, "I might have known. I'm Cousin Eva Parrington," she said, "Cousin Molly Parrington's daughter, remember? I knew you when you were a little girl. You were a lively little girl," she added as if to console her, "and very opinionated. The last thing I heard about you, you were planning to be a tight-rope walker. You were going to play the violin and walk the tight rope at the same time."

"I must have seen it at the vaudeville show," said Miranda. "I couldn't have invented it. Now I'd like to be an air pilot!"

"I used to go to dances with your father," said Cousin Eva, busy with her own thoughts, "and to big holiday parties at your grandmother's house, long before you were born. Oh, indeed, yes, a long time before."

Miranda remembered several things at once. Aunt Amy had threatened to be an old maid like Eva. Oh, Eva, the trouble with her is she has no chin. Eva has given up, and is teaching Latin in a Female Seminary. Eva's gone out for votes for women, God help her. The nice thing about an ugly daughter is, she's not apt to make me a grandmother. . . . "They didn't do you much good, those parties, dear Cousin Eva," thought Miranda.

"They didn't do me much good, those parties," said Cousin Eva aloud as if she were a mind-reader, and Miranda's head swam for a moment with fear that she had herself spoken aloud. "Or at least, they didn't serve their purpose, for I never got married; but I enjoyed them, just the same. I had a good time at those parties, even if I wasn't a belle. And so you are Harry's child, and here I was quarreling with you. You do remember me, don't you?"

"Yes," said Miranda, and thinking that even if Cousin Eva had been really an old maid ten years before, still she couldn't be much past fifty now, and she looked so withered and tired, so famished and sunken in the cheeks, so *old*, somehow. Across the abyss separating Cousin Eva from her own youth, Miranda looked with painful premonition. "Oh, must I ever be like that?" She said aloud, "Yes, you used to read Latin to me, and tell me not to bother about the sense, to get the sound in my mind, and it would come easier later."

"Ah, so I did," said Cousin Eva, delighted. "So I did. You don't happen to remember that I once had a beautiful sapphire velvet dress with a train on it?"

"No, I don't remember that dress," said Miranda.

"It was an old dress of my mother's made over and cut down to fit," said Eva, "and it wasn't in the least becoming to me, but it was the only really good dress I ever had, and I remember it as if it were yesterday. Blue was never my color." She sighed with a humorous bitterness. The humor seemed momentary, but the bitterness was a constant state of mind.

Miranda, trying to offer the sympathy of fellow suffering, said, "I know. I've had Maria's dresses made over for me, and they were never right. It was dreadful."

"Well," said Cousin Eva, in the tone of one who did not wish to share her unique disappointments. "How is your father? I always liked him. He was one of the finest-looking young men I ever saw. Vain, too, like all his family. He wouldn't ride any but the best horses he could buy, and I used to say he made them prance and then watched his own shadow. I used to tell this on him at dinner parties, and he hated me for it. I feel pretty certain he hated me." An overtone of complacency in Cousin Eva's voice explained better than words that she had her own method of commanding attention and arousing emotion. "How is your father, I asked you my dear?"

"I haven't seen him for nearly a year," answered Miranda, quickly, before Cousin Eva could get ahead again. "I'm going home now to Uncle Gabriel's funeral; you know, Uncle Gabriel died in Lexington and they have brought him back to be buried beside Aunt Amy."

"So that's how we meet," said Cousin Eva. "Yes, Gabriel drank himself to death at last. I'm going to the funeral, too. I haven't been home since I went to Mother's funeral, it must be, let's see, yes, it will be nine years next July. I'm going to Gabriel's funeral, though. I wouldn't miss that. Poor fellow, what a life he had. Pretty soon, they'll all be gone."

Miranda said, "We're left, Cousin Eva," meaning those of her own generation, the young, and Cousin Eva said, "Pshaw, you'll live forever, and you won't bother to come to our funerals." She didn't seem to think this was a misfortune, but flung the remark from her like a woman accustomed to saying what she thought.

Miranda sat thinking, "Still, I suppose it would be pleasant if I could say something to make her believe that she and all of them would be lamented, but—but—" With a smile which she hoped would be her denial of Cousin Eva's cynicism about the younger generation, she said, "You were right about the Latin, Cousin Eva, your

reading did help when I began with it. I still study," she
said. "Latin, too."

"And why shouldn't you?" asked Cousin Eva, sharply,
adding at once mildly, "I'm glad you are going to use
your mind a little child. Don't let yourself rust away.
Your mind outwears all sorts of things you may set your
heart upon; you can enjoy it when all other things are
taken away." Miranda was chilled by her melancholy.
Cousin Eva went on: "In our part of the country, in my
time, we were so provincial—a woman didn't dare to
think or act for herself. The whole world was a little that
way," she said, "but we were the worst, I believe. I
suppose you must know how I fought for votes for
women when it almost made a pariah of me—I was
turned out of my chair at the Seminary, but I'm glad I
did it and I would do it again. You young things don't
realize. You'll live in a better world because we worked
for it."

Miranda knew something of Cousin Eva's career. She
said sincerely, "I think it was brave of you, and I'm glad
you did it, too. I loved your courage."

"It wasn't just showing off, mind you," said Cousin
Eva, rejecting praise, fretfully. "Any fool can be brave.
We were working for something we knew was right, and
it turned out that we needed a lot of courage for it. That
was all. I didn't expect to got to jail, but I went three
times, and I'd go three times three more if it were necessary. We aren't voting yet," she said, "but we will be."

Miranda did not venture any answer, but she felt convinced that indeed women would be voting soon if nothing fatal happened to Cousin Eva. There was something
in her manner which said such things could be left safely
to her. Miranda was dimly fired for the cause herself; it
seemed heroic and worth suffering for, but discouraging,
too, to those who came after: Cousin Eva so plainly had
swept the field clear of opportunity.

They were silent for a few minutes, while Cousin Eva
rummaged in her handbag, bringing up odds and ends:
peppermint drops, eye drops, a packet of needles, three
handkerchiefs, a little bottle of violet perfume, a book

of addresses, two buttons, one black, one white, and, finally, a packet of headache powders.

"Bring me a glass of water, will you, my dear?" she asked Miranda. She poured the headache powder on her tongue, swallowed the water, and put two peppermints in her mouth.

"So now they're going to bury Gabriel near Amy," she said after a while, as if her eased headache had started her on a new train of thought. "Miss Honey would like that, poor dear, if she could know. After listening to stories about Amy for twenty-five years, she must lie alone in her grave in Lexington while Gabriel sneaks off to Texas to make his bed with Amy again. It was a kind of lifelong infidelity, Miranda, and now an eternal infidelity on top of that. He ought to be ashamed of himself."

"It was Aunt Amy he loved," said Miranda, wondering what Miss Honey could have been like before her long troubles with Uncle Gabriel. "First, anyway."

"Oh, that Amy," said Cousin Eva, her eyes glittering. "Your Aunt Amy was a devil and a mischief-maker, but I loved her dearly. I used to stand up for Amy when her reputation wasn't worth that." Her fingers snapped like castanets. "She used to say to me, in that gay soft way she had, 'Now, Eva, don't go talking votes for women when the lads ask you to dance. Don't recite Latin poems to 'em,' she would say, 'they got sick of that in school. Dance and say nothing, Eva,' she would say, her eyes perfectly devilish, 'and hold your chin up, Eva.' My chin was my weak point, you see. 'You'll never catch a husband if you don't look out,' she would say. Then she would laugh and fly away, and where did she fly to?" demanded Cousin Eva, her sharp eyes pinning Miranda down to the bitter facts of the case. "To scandal and to death, nowhere else."

"She was joking, Cousin Eva," said Miranda, innocently, "and everybody loved her."

"Not everybody, by a long shot," said Cousin Eva in triumph. "She had enemies. If she knew, she pretended she didn't. If she cared, she never said. You couldn't make her quarrel. She was sweet as a honeycomb to everybody. *Everybody*," she added, "that was the trouble. She went through life like a spoiled darling, doing as she pleased and letting other people suffer for it, and pick up the pieces after her. I never believed for one moment," said Cousin Eva, putting her mouth close to Miranda's ear and breathing peppermint hotly into it, "that Amy was an impure woman. Never! But let me tell you, there were plenty who did believe it. There were plenty to pity poor Gabriel for being so completely blinded by her. A great many persons were not surprised when they heard that Gabriel was perfectly miserable all the time, on their honeymoon, in New Orleans. Jealousy. And why not? But I used to say to such persons that, no matter what the appearances were, I had faith in Amy's virtue. Wild, I said, indiscreet, I said, heartless, I said, but *virtuous*, I feel certain. But you could hardly blame anyone for being mystified. The way she rose up suddenly from death's door to marry Gabriel Breaux, after refusing him and treating him like a dog for years, looked odd, to say the least. To say the very least," she added, after a moment, "odd is a mild word for it. And there was something very mysterious about her death, only six weeks after marriage."

Miranda roused herself. She felt she knew this part of the story and could set Cousin Eva right about one thing. "She died of a hemorrhage from the lungs," said Miranda. "She had been ill for five years, don't you remember?"

Cousin Eva was ready for that. "Ha, that was the story, indeed. The official account, you might say. Oh, yes, I heard that often enough. But did you ever hear about that fellow Raymond somebody-or-other from Calcasieu Parish, almost a stranger, who persuaded Amy to elope with him from a dance one night, and she just ran out into the darkness without even stopping for her cloak, and your poor dear nice father Harry—you weren't even thought of then—had to run him down to earth and shoot him?"

Miranda leaned back from the advancing flood of

speech. "Cousin Eva, my father shot *at* him, don't you remember? He didn't hit him. . . ."

"Well, that's a pity."

". . . and they had only gone out for a breath of air between dances. It was Uncle Gabriel's jealousy. And my father shot at the man because he thought that was better than letting Uncle Gabriel fight a duel about Aunt Amy. There was *nothing* in the whole affair except Uncle Gabriel's jealousy."

"You poor baby," said Cousin Eva, and pity gave a light like daggers to her eyes, "you dear innocent, you— do you believe that? How old are you, anyway?"

"Just past eighteen," said Miranda.

"If you don't understand what I tell you," said Cousin Eva portentously, "you will later. Knowledge can't hurt you. You mustn't live in a romantic haze about life. You'll understand when you're married, at any rate."

"I'm married now, Cousin Eva," said Miranda, feeling for almost the first time that it might be an advantage, "nearly a year. I eloped from school." It seemed very unreal even as she said it, and seemed to have nothing at all to do with the future; still, it was important, it must be declared, it was a situation in life which people seemed to be most exacting about, and the only feeling she could rouse in herself about it was an immense weariness as if it were an illness that she might one day hope to recover from.

"Shameful, shameful," cried Cousin Eva, genuinely repelled. "If you had been my child I should have brought you home and spanked you."

Miranda laughed out. Cousin Eva seemed to believe things could be arranged like that. She was so solemn and fierce, so comic and baffled.

"And you must know I should have just gone straight out again, through the nearest window," she taunted her. "If I went the first time, why not the second?"

"Yes, I suppose so," said Cousin Eva. "I hope you married rich."

"Not so very," said Miranda. "Enough." As if anyone could have stopped to think of such a thing!

Cousin Eva adjusted her spectacles and sized up Miranda's dress, her luggage, examined her engagement ring and wedding ring, with her nostrils fairly quivering as if she might smell out wealth on her.

"Well, that's better than nothing," said Cousin Eva. "I thank God every day of my life that I have a small income. It's a Rock of Ages. What would have become of me if I hadn't a cent of my own? Well, you'll be able now to do something for your family."

Miranda remembered what she had always heard about the Parringtons. They were money-hungry, they loved money and nothing else, and when they had got some they kept it. Blood was thinner than water between the Parringtons where money was concerned.

"We're pretty poor," said Miranda, stubbornly allying herself with her father's family instead of her husband's, "but a rich marriage is no way out," she said, with the snobbishness of poverty. She was thinking, "You don't know my branch of the family, dear Cousin Eva, if you think it is."

"Your branch of the family," said Cousin Eva, with that terrifying habit she had of lifting phrases out of one's mind, "has no more practical sense than so many children. Everything for love," she said, with a face of positive nausea, "that was it. Gabriel would have been rich if his grandfather had not disinherited him, but would Amy be sensible and marry him and make him settle down so the old man would have been pleased with him? No. And what could Gabriel do without money? I wish you could have seen the life he led Miss Honey, one day buying her Paris gowns and the next day pawning her earrings. It just depended on how the horses ran, and they ran worse and worse, and Gabriel drank more and more."

Miranda did not say, "I saw a little of it." She was trying to imagine Miss Honey in a Paris gown. She said, "But Uncle Gabriel was so mad about Aunt Amy, there was no question of her not marrying him at last, money or no money."

Cousin Eva strained her lips tightly over her teeth, let them fly again and leaned over, gripping Miranda's arm.

"What I ask myself, what I ask myself over and over again," she whispered, "is, what connection did this man Raymond from Calcasieu have with Amy's sudden marriage to Gabriel, and *what* did Amy do to make away with herself so soon afterward? For mark my words, child, Amy wasn't so ill as all that. She'd been flying around for years after the doctors said her lungs were weak. Amy did away with herself to escape some disgrace, some exposure that she faced."

The beady black eyes glinted; Cousin Eva's face was quite frightening, so near and so intent. Miranda wanted to say, "Stop. Let her rest. What harm did she ever do you?" but she was timid and unnerved, and deep in her was a horrid fascination with the terrors and the darkness Cousin Eva had conjured up. What was the end of this story?

"She was a bad, wild girl, but I was fond of her to the last," said Cousin Eva. "She got into trouble somehow, and she couldn't get out again, and I have every reason to believe she killed herself with the drug they gave her to keep her quiet after a hemorrhage. If she didn't, what happened, what happened?"

"I don't know," said Miranda. "How should I know? She was very beautiful," she said, as if this explained everything. "Everybody said she was very beautiful."

"Not everybody," said Cousin Eva, firmly, shaking her head. "I for one never thought so. They made entirely too much fuss over her. She was good-looking enough, but why did they think she was beautiful? I cannot understand it. She was too thin when she was young, and later I always thought she was too fat, and again in her last year she was altogether too thin. She always got herself up to be looked at, and so people looked, of course. She rode too hard, and she danced too freely, and she talked too much, and you'd have to be blind, deaf and dumb not to notice her. I don't mean she was loud or vulgar, she wasn't, but she was *too free*," said Cousin Eva. She stopped for breath and put a peppermint in her mouth. Miranda could see Cousin Eva on the platform, making her speeches, stopping to take a peppermint. But why did she hate Aunt Amy so, when Aunt Amy was dead and she alive? Wasn't being alive enough?

"And her illness wasn't romantic either," said Cousin Eva, "though to hear them tell it she faded like a lily. Well, she coughed blood, if that's romantic. If they had made her take proper care of herself, if she had been nursed sensibly, she might have been alive today. But no, nothing of the kind. She lay wrapped in beautiful shawls on a sofa with flowers around her, eating as she liked or not eating, getting up after a hemorrhage and going out to ride or dance, sleeping with the windows closed; with crowds coming in and out laughing and talking at all hours, and Amy sitting up so her hair wouldn't get out of curl. And why wouldn't that sort of thing kill a well person in time? I have almost died twice in my life," said Cousin Eva, "and both times I was sent to a hospital where I belonged and left there until I came out. And I came out," she said, her voice deepening to a bugle note, "and I went to work again."

"Beauty goes, character stays," said the small voice of axiomatic morality in Miranda's ear. It was a dreary prospect; why was a strong character so deforming? Miranda felt she truly wanted to be strong, but how could she face it, seeing what it did to one?

"She had a lovely complexion," said Cousin Eva, "perfectly transparent with a flush on each cheekbone. But it was tuberculosis, and is disease beautiful? And she brought it on herself by drinking lemon and salt to stop her periods when she wanted to go to dances. There was a superstition among young girls about that. They fancied that young men could tell what ailed them by touching their hands, or even by looking at them. As if it mattered? But they were terribly self-conscious and they had immense respect for man's worldly wisdom in those days. My own notion is that a man couldn't—but anyway, the whole thing was stupid."

"I should have thought they'd have stayed at home if they couldn't manage better than that," said Miranda, feeling very knowledgeable and modern.

"They didn't dare. Those parties and dances were their

market, a girl couldn't afford to miss out, there were always rivals waiting to cut the ground from under her. The rivalry—" said Cousin Eva, and her head lifted, she arched like a calvary horse getting a whiff of the battle-field—"you can't imagine what the rivalry was like. The way those girls treated each other—nothing was too mean, nothing too false—"

Cousin Eva wrung her hands. "It was just sex," she said in despair; "their minds dwelt on nothing else. They didn't call it that, it was all smothered under pretty names, but that's all it was, sex." She looked out of the window into the darkness, her sunken cheek near Miranda flushed deeply. She turned back. "I took to the soap box and the platform when I was called upon," she said proudly, "and I went to jail when it was necessary, and my condition didn't make any difference. I was booed and jeered and shoved around just as if I had been in perfect health. But it was part of our philosophy not to let our physical handicaps make any difference to our work. You know what I mean," she said, as if until now it was all mystery. "Well, Amy carried herself with more spirit than the others, and she didn't seem to be making any sort of fight, but she was simply sex-ridden, like the rest. She behaved as if she hadn't a rival on earth, and she pretended not to know what marriage was about, but I know better. None of them had, and they didn't want to have, anything else to think about, and they didn't really know anything about that, so they simply festered inside—they festered—"

Miranda found herself deliberately watching a long procession of living corpses, festering women stepping gaily towards the charnel house, their corruption concealed under laces and flowers, their dead faces lifted smiling, and thought quite coldly, "Of course it was not like that. This is no more true than what I was told before, it's every bit as romantic," and she realized that she was tired of her intense Cousin Eva, she wanted to go to sleep, she wanted to be at home, she wished it were tomorrow and she could see her father and her sister, who were so alive and solid; who would mention her freckles and ask her if she wanted something to eat.

"My mother was not like that," she said, childishly. "My mother was a perfectly natural woman who liked to cook. I have seen some of her sewing," she said. "I have read her diary."

"Your mother was a saint," said Cousin Eva, automatically.

Miranda sat silent, outraged. "My mother was nothing of the sort," she wanted to fling in Cousin Eva's big front teeth. But Cousin Eva had been gathering bitterness until more speech came of it.

" 'Hold your chin up, Eva,' Amy used to tell me," she began, doubling up both her fists and shaking them a little. "All my life the whole family bedeviled me about my chin. My entire girlhood was spoiled by it. Can you imagine," she asked, with a ferocity that seemed much too deep for this one cause, "people who call themselves civilized spoiling life for a young girl because she had one unlucky feature? Of course, you understand perfectly it was all in the very best humor, everybody was very amusing about it, no harm meant—oh, no, no harm at all. That is the hellish thing about it. It is that I can't forgive," she cried out, and she twisted her hands together as if they were rags. "Ah, the family," she said, releasing her breath and sitting back quietly, "the whole hideous institution should be wiped from the face of the earth. It is the root of all human wrongs," she ended, and relaxed, and her face became calm. She was trembling. Miranda reached out and took Cousin Eva's hand and held it. The hand fluttered and lay still, and Cousin Eva said, "You've not the faintest idea what some of us went through, but I wanted you to hear the other side of the story. And I'm keeping you up when you need your beauty sleep," she said grimly, stirring herself with an immense rustle of petticoats.

Miranda pulled herself together, feeling limp, and stood up. Cousin Eva put out her hand again, and drew Miranda down to her. "Good night, you dear child," she said, "to think you're grown up." Miranda hesitated, then quite suddenly kissed her Cousin Eva on the cheek. The black eyes shone brightly through water for an instant, and Cousin Eva said with a warm note in her sharp clear orator's voice, "Tomorrow we'll be at home again. I'm looking forward to it, aren't you? Good night."

Miranda fell asleep while she was getting off her clothes. Instantly it was morning again. She was still trying to close her suitcase when the train pulled into the small station, and there on the platform she saw her father, looking tired and anxious, his hat pulled over his eyes. She rapped on the window to catch his attention, then ran out and threw herself upon him. He said, "Well, here's my big girl," as if she were still seven, but his hands on her arms held her off, the tone was forced. There was no welcome for her, and there had not been since she had run away. She could not persuade herself to remember how it would be; between one home-coming and the next her mind refused to accept its own knowledge. Her father looked over her head and said, without surprise, "Why, hello, Eva, I'm glad somebody sent you a telegram." Miranda, rebuffed again, let her arms fall away again, with the same painful dull jerk of the heart.

"No one in my family," said Eva, her face framed in the thin black veil she reserved, evidently, for family funerals, "ever sent me a telegram in my life. I had the news from young Keziah who had it from young Gabriel. I suppose Gabe is here?"

"Everybody seems to be here," said Father. "The house is getting full."

"I'll go to the hotel if you like," said Cousin Eva.

"Damnation, no," said Father. "I didn't mean that. You'll come with us where you belong."

Skid, the handy man, grabbed the suitcases and started down the rocky village street. "We've got the car," said Father. He took Miranda by the hand, then dropped it again, and reached for Cousin Eva's elbow.

"I'm perfectly able, thank you," said Cousin Eva, shying away.

"If you're so independent now," said Father, "God help us when you get that vote."

Cousin Eva pushed back her veil. She was smiling merrily. She liked Harry, she always had liked him, he could tease as much as he liked. She slipped her arm through his. "So it's all over with poor Gabriel, isn't it?"

"Oh, yes," said Father, "it's all over, all right. They're pegging out pretty regularly now. It will be our turn next, Eva?"

"I don't know, and I don't care," said Eva, recklessly. "It's good to be back now and then, Harry, even if it is only for funerals. I feel sinfully cheerful."

"Oh, Gabriel wouldn't mind, he'd like seeing you cheerful. Gabriel was the cheerfullest cuss I ever saw, when we were young. Life for Gabriel," said Father, "was just one perpetual picnic."

"Poor fellow," said Cousin Eva.

"Poor old Gabriel," said Father, heavily.

Miranda walked along beside her father, feeling homeless, but not sorry for it. He had not forgiven her, she knew that. When would he? She could not guess, but she felt it would come of itself, without words and without acknowledgment on either side, for by the time it arrived neither of them would need to remember what had caused their division, nor why it had seemed so important. Surely old people cannot hold their grudges forever because the young want to live, too, she thought, in her arrogance, her pride. I will make my own mistakes, not yours; I cannot depend upon you beyond a certain point, why depend at all? There was something more beyond, but this was a first step to take, and she took it, walking in silence beside her elders who were no longer Cousin Eva and Father, since they had forgotten her presence, but had become Eva and Harry, who knew each other well, who were comfortable with each other, being contemporaries on equal terms, who occupied by right their place in this world, at the time of life to which they had arrived by paths familiar to them both. They need not play their roles of daughter, of son, to aged persons who did not understand them; nor of father and elderly female cousin to young persons whom they did not understand. They were precisely themselves; their eyes cleared, their voices relaxed into perfect naturalness, they need not weigh their words or calculate the effect of their manner. "It is I who have no place," thought Miranda. "Where are my own people and my own time?" She resented, slowly and deeply and in profound silence, the presence of these aliens who lectured and admonished her, who loved her with bitterness and denied her the right to look at the world with her own eyes, who demanded that she accept their version of life and yet could not tell her the truth, not in the smallest thing. "I hate them both," her most inner and secret mind said plainly, *"I will be free of them, I shall not even remember them."*

She sat in the front seat with Skid, the Negro boy. "Come back with us, Miranda," said Cousin Eva, the sharp little note of elderly command, "there is plenty of room."

"No, thank you," said Miranda, in a firm cold voice. "I'm quite comfortable. Don't disturb yourself."

Neither of them noticed her voice or her manner. They sat back and went on talking steadily in their friendly voices, talking about their dead, their living, their affairs, their prospects, their common memories, interrupting each other, catching each other up on small points of dispute, with a gaiety and freshness which Miranda had not known they were capable of, going over old memories and finding new points of interest in them.

Miranda could not hear the stories above the noisy motor, but she felt she knew them well, or stories like them. She knew too many stories like them, she wanted something new of her own. The language was familiar to them, but not to her, not any more. The house, her father had said, was full. It would be full of cousins, many of them strangers. Would there be any young cousins there, to whom she could talk about things they both knew? She felt a vague distaste for seeing cousins. There were too many of them and her blood rebelled against the ties of blood. She was sick to death of cousins. She did not want any more ties with this house, she was going to leave it, and she was not going back to her husband's family either. She would have no more bonds that smothered her in love and hatred. She knew now why she had run away to marriage, and she knew that she was going to run away from marriage, and she was not going to stay in any place, with anyone, that threatened to forbid her making her own discoveries, that said "No" to her. She hoped no one had taken her old room, she would like to sleep there once more, she would say good-by there where she had loved sleeping once, sleeping and waking and waiting to be grown, to begin to live. Oh, what is life, she asked herself in desperate seriousness, in those childish unanswerable words, and what shall I do with it? It is something of my own, she thought in a fury of jealous possessiveness, what shall I make of it? She did not know that she asked herself this because all her earliest training had argued that life was a substance, a material to be used, it took shape and direction and meaning only as the possessor guided and worked it; living was a progress of continuous and varied acts of the will directed towards a definite end. She had been assured that there were good and evil ends, one must make a choice. But what was good, and what was evil? I hate love, she thought, as if this were the answer, I hate loving and being loved, I hate it. And her disturbed and seething mind received a shock of comfort from this sudden collapse of an old painful structure of distorted images and misconceptions. "You don't know anything about it," said Miranda to herself, with extraordinary clearness as if she were an elder admonishing some younger misguided creature. "You have to find out about it." But nothing in her prompted her to decide, "I will now do this, I will be that, I will go yonder, I will take a certain road to a certain end." There are questions to be asked first, she thought, but who will answer them? No one, or there will be too many answers, none of them right. What is the truth, she asked herself as intently as if the question had never been asked, the truth, even about the smallest, the least important of all the things

I must find out? and where shall I begin to look for it? Her mind closed stubbornly against remembering, not the past but the legend of the past, other people's memory of the past, at which she had spent her life peering in wonder like a child at a magic-lantern show. Ah, but there is my own life to come yet, she thought, my own life now and beyond. I don't want any promises, I won't have false hopes, I won't be romantic about myself. I can't live in their world any longer, she told herself, listening to the voices back of her. Let them tell their stories to each other. Let them go on explaining how things happened. I don't care. At least I can know the truth about what happens to me, she assured herself silently, making a promise to herself, in her hopefulness, her ignorance.